PRESENTING TERRA SF

For many years DAW Books and its publisher have brought SF readers annual selections of the best short stories and novelettes, as available in the English language. Despite the use of the long-established identity phrase "World's Best", these selections have of necessity been limited to works published in the United States and the British Commonwealth lands. Now, in an effort to rectify this and to make available more of the full spectrum of the world's best SF, we present the first of a series devoted to translating and publishing for the English-speaking audience the best of recent years from the countries of Western Europe. This is TERRA SF. Its editor is a dedicated French science-fictionist who has been aided in his task by similar devotees in other countries.

In TERRA SF you will discover new worlds of science fiction by the "name" writers of other lands.

Anthologies from DAW

THE 1976 ANNUAL WORLD'S BEST SF
THE 1977 ANNUAL WORLD'S BEST SF
THE 1978 ANNUAL WORLD'S BEST SF
THE 1979 ANNUAL WORLD'S BEST SF
THE 1980 ANNUAL WORLD'S BEST SF

WOLLHEIM'S WORLD'S BEST SF: Vol. 1
WOLLHEIM'S WORLD'S BEST SF: Vol. 2
WOLLHEIM'S WORLD'S BEST SF: Vol. 3
WOLLHEIM'S WORLD'S BEST SF: Vol. 4

THE YEAR'S BEST FANTASY STORIES: 1
THE YEAR'S BEST FANTASY STORIES: 2
THE YEAR'S BEST FANTASY STORIES: 3
THE YEAR'S BEST FANTASY STORIES: 4
THE YEAR'S BEST FANTASY STORIES: 5

THE BEST FROM THE REST OF THE WORLD

AMAZONS!

HEROIC FANTASY

ASIMOV PRESENTS THE GREAT SF STORIES: 1
ASIMOV PRESENTS THE GREAT SF STORIES: 2
ASIMOV PRESENTS THE GREAT SF STORIES: 3
ASIMOV PRESENTS THE GREAT SF STORIES: 4

TERRA SF

The Year's Best European SF

Selected and Edited by
RICHARD D. NOLANE

DAW BOOKS, INC.
DONALD A. WOLLHEIM, PUBLISHER

1633 Broadway, New York, NY 10019

FIRST PRINTING, FEBRUARY 1981

1 2 3 4 5 6 7 8 9

 DAW TRADEMARK REGISTERED
U.S. PAT. OFF. MARCA
REGISTRADA. HECHO EN U.S.A.

PRINTED IN U.S.A.

ACKNOWLEDGMENTS

THIS BOOK IS DEDICATED TO

MY PARENTS AND MY SISTER STEPHANIE

AND TO

CHARLES MOREAU

JOE F. RANDOLPH

and   DONALD A. WOLLHEIM

WITHOUT WHOM NOTHING WOULD
HAVE BEEN POSSIBLE . . .

ACKNOWLEDGMENTS

Among all those who have contributed to the realization of this anthology and whose advice has been invaluable to me, I must specifically thank Jean-Pierre Moumon, Sam J. Lundwall, Ronald M. Hahn, Gianni Montanari as well as Marianne and Claude Avice (Pierre Barbet), who introduced me to Donald Wollheim in Dublin in 1978.

Richard D. Nolane

CONTENTS

IN SEARCH OF
EUROPEAN SCIENCE FICTION

Actually, I should say *"New* European Science Fiction." Only now have independent European science fiction authors come to the fore after a quarter of a century of the domination of English-language authors—ever since the Second World War blew out the flickering flame of the first great era of science fiction in Europe. There had been a flourishing European science fiction movement before the onset of World Wars—and this was not, as some think, limited to Jules Verne. During the nineteenth and beginning of the twentieth century science fiction was on the verge of becoming a full-fledged literary movement, especially in France. But the First World War put an end to that. Return was difficult in the 1920s. Then, in 1939, just when the genre seemed to be recovering its own, the Second World War paralyzed European science fiction—and that paralysis was to last well after the British and Americans had taken over the scene.

In the USA after the First World War leadership in the field was claimed by the Munsey chain's all-action pulps, and then those of the *Amazing Stories* type. Those were the days of the greats, like Bob Davis, Hugo Gernsback and John W. Campbell. Davis felt that the public wanted "different stories" and other "scientific romances" and he spent his time promoting them. Gernsback created the specialized market, and Campbell made it into a serious adult literature.

Meanwhile in Europe, few big-name writers ventured into the genre, while science fiction specialists often were shunted to the juvenile market. For the rest, an ossification set in—a certain lack of imagination. With the exception of some uncommonly gifted people like J.H. Rosny, none of them knew how to get out of the Earth's gravitational pull or to venture beyond simple forecasting. So, while E.E. "Doc" Smith and Edmond Hamilton were sending their interstellar patrols out to smash through the boundaries of the universe, while Stanley Weinbaum was speculating about extraterrestrial intelligence, and while the future giants of the forties, fifties, and sixties were sharpening their imaginative tools, European authors were stuck with Earthbound stories. Too often intensive introspection by the characters got in the way of the action.

As a result, by the beginning of the fifties, a veritable tidal wave of English-language science fiction washed into the countries of Western Europe. To get published, native authors either had to write like the Americans or use English-sounding pen names (like Clark Darlton, whose real name is Walter Ernsting). It was not until the seventies that a truly authentic European science fiction began to reappear. Even then, it followed the trends of English-language models, asserting itself as a political literature, examining the world in all its aspects, especially those aspects that showed signs of trouble.

But European science fiction took this new political assertiveness and made of it a literature all its own. Of course, this politicalization still gives rise to the worst excesses, but it became the force by which the literature could express a wide range of nuances according to country, the sharpest features developing in those countries where social upheavals were the most important—Italy, West Germany, and France. In these three countries true schools of literature emerged, while in other places only brilliant individuals came to the fore (you will find some of them in this volume). Prime among them has been Sam J. Lundwall, who has been so active in the genre that he must be known world-wide.

Now, science fiction in Europe is finally in the process of becoming accepted. It is starting to appear on TV and to be taught in universities, and this tends to encourage its development and bring it out of the realm of specialized literature, where it has been confined for more than half a century.

I should note that there is only one woman writer represented in this anthology. This is an indication of how far Europeans have yet to go: they still have to get over the idea that science fiction is a masculine endeavor. But that view is being undermined by the incursion of the great English-language women writers such as Ann McCaffrey, Vonda McIntyre, Leigh Brackett, Carolyn Cherryh, Ursula Le Guin, and others, who have been published in translation in most Western European countries.

I would like to end by saying that I have tried to bring together in *Terra SF* a collection of wide-ranging stories in order to convey some idea of the breadth of possibilities in current European science fiction. I hope I've been successful. Now, let me wish you a pleasant journey through the essential ideas and sensibilities of the old World. . . .

RICHARD D. NOLANE

TEST FLESH
(Carne di Stato)

GIANNI MONTANARI

Translated from the Italian
by Joe F. Randolph

There was another storm brewing. Duke was suddenly
awakened by that odd, annoying throbbing in his temples
without knowing if it was day or night. Only after a few moments did he realize where he was and what time it was according to the colony's arbitrary chronometer; then he ran to
warn Irene.

He found her sleeping by her baby, in the strong smell of
worms that still lingered in the shelter after the evening meal.
Irene listened to him without saying a word; she bent over to
pick up the kid, wrapping it up in a blanket, and followed
him outside. Duke immediately headed toward the doctor's
dome to have him warn the whole colony of the now-impend-
ing storm. Antonji, the old doctor on board, always had the
seismograph in operation that was salvaged from the shipwreck, but he knew he would do better by relying on Duke's
premonitions. The doctor knew how to maintain the electronic seismograph and knew as well that those storms were
heralded by slight ground tremors imperceptible to human
beings. The cadmium needle could record those tremors on
the graph, but as a rule it happened a few minutes after
Duke had given the alarm; that is why his warnings served as
a valuable indicator.

Irene did not have to cover a long distance; her dome was

13

the closest one to the cave entrance. She was also farthest
away from the center of the encampment where the radio
was kept on constantly but with no results. Irene did not
mind being that far away. She did not get many visitors, and
she had been quite shrewd at the beginning to discourage any
familiarity with the rest of the survivors. She preferred being
by herself, the quiet, and solitude. She had the kid and that
was enough for her. She also had Duke later on, and he was
more than adequate to help her. Alone in the past, she knew
how to go about getting needed food.

When Duke reached Irene, the colony was already assembling in the caverns. Duke was the only one able to warn of
the approach of a storm without instruments, but what alerted the other survivors was a system of bells, installed in all
the domes, that was activated by the doctor. All Antonji had
to do was push a button, and all the colonists would rush to
the caverns. By that time the danger was well known, since
the first storms had swept away two-thirds of the colony.

In the whole ship, the control room was perhaps the least
lighted area. Every operator's screen stood out pale and phos-
phorescent in the half-light, like old-fashioned clocks out of
focus, in the brightness from the huge main panel. Here, on a
transparent magnetic wall standing in the middle of the room
any changes in the subjects were recorded. The technicians
assigned to the screens could not abandon their posts for an
instant; the main board was only for the use of the coordinator and diagnosticians. No technician could take his eyes off
his own screen for any reason. The keyboards beneath their
fingers relayed any variation in the behavior of the subjects,
but monitoring had to be continuous along with tests for mal-
functions. The long rest periods for the technicians were ex-
pressly intended to reduce errors and every type of fatigue.

Fatigue that Belaes was now experiencing as he sat in his
coordinator seat. His seat, located slightly off to the side at
the entrance to the control room, overlooked a long line of
screens and a big enlarger to observe the main board close
up.

Belaes rubbed his eyes hard. He had not been trained as a
control technician, and the half-light often bothered him.
When he opened his eyes, they burned worse than before and
every movement they made caused sharp pains in his temples.

He checked the chronograph and did some quick figuring; within a few minutes he would be able to leave. All he had to do was look over the screens one more time. The storm was approaching and it was almost certain that Duke had already warned the rest of the colony.

The screens confirmed that the subjects were on the move. By that time Belaes was just about through checking the screens when he noticed a draft from the pneumatic tunnel behind him. Someone was coming up. Without turning around, he knew from the panting it was Vulture. Only his relief found the trip between his own cabin and the control room tiring. Vulture was too fat, and Belaes did not like that. Maybe it was because Belaes harbored strange suspicions about his relief.

"Any change, commander?"

Belaes finished his monitoring before answering.

"Not at the present. There's a storm approaching, but the subjects are already heading toward the caverns. Shortly they will all be safe."

Vulture came up alongside the chair.

"The diagnosticians have examined the latest samples," he began in an indifferent tone of voice.

Belaes's jaws tightened and his hand suddenly shot up. "I know," he said, knowing how to lie; he had forgotten all about it. "I would've asked for details later, but now you can fill me in."

Vulture nodded understandingly without taking his eyes off the room below. Belaes still wondered if by some chance he was a censor . . . he knew of their existence in a vague way, but he knew too that the censors had the job of checking up on the behavior of new coordinators.

"The corpses have been autopsied and hardly anything new has turned up," his relief mumbled. "They keep on eating worms and nothing happens. A slight alteration in the percentage of amino acids has come to light as well as touches of anasarca, but it seems that swelling of the tissue may be due to the planet's atmosphere. The only verified fact, according to the diagnosticians, is that none of the bodies shows any traces of the primary diseases. Death is due to accidental causes."

Belaes rubbed his eyes again.

"Still nothing. So," he whispered, "it's all yours."

His relief did not move. Belaes thought that Vulture had not heard him and was on the verge of repeating what he had said, but he noticed Vulture concentrating on the control room too much.

"The main board, commander," was Vulture's soft reply. "The worms are coming to the surface. But there's something odd going on."

Irene held onto the baby in her arms with unaccustomed force, almost afraid she would let it slip out of her grasp because of a bump or too-quick movement.

The smooth walls of the caverns usually had some shelves with a few things the refugees could use and a few benches had been arranged on the floor, but the side tunnel where Irene had taken shelter was completely bare. Duke located her and the kid at the end of the shaft. He made sure that the lamp was securely placed in a niche, and only then did he lean against the wall the long quartz staff he had chiseled during the first months after the shipwreck. The staff looked more like a javelin, long and heavy, with one end pointed and honed like a blade. Duke had made it his talisman, his weapon, his fetish against whatever danger might threaten him or Irene. Or the baby.

In the colony everybody knew of Duke's skill in hunting the big worms which, after every storm, crawled out of the reddish soil. Many depended on this ability after the first unwary people ventured to the entrance while the storm was still raging. Duke was the only one who could tell when a storm was over and who could then safely rush up to ground level to kill the big worms that were lingering to lay eggs. Those worms would feed a good part of the colony after Duke cut off just what was necessary to feed Irene and the little one; but in rare instances he remembered his own needs and cut off some pieces for himself. On the other hand, since Duke was well-known, the colony made sure to guarantee his survival until the next storm.

Nevertheless, no one joined Duke and Irene during the storms. The caverns branched out into the rock for a score of meters from the only entrance, forking off into two different shafts. The first one, almost level, led to a large grotto that could house the whole colony, while the second one, deeper and sloping slightly, wound up at the pits. That is what the holes in the rock near the end of the second shaft were called. Nobody took shelter there anymore since three crew members who had tried to explore it during the first days disappeared. That waste of human life was enough. The pits must be avoided. But Duke and Irene seemed to ignore that prohibition.

Duke helped Irene sit down; the kid seemed to be sleeping peacefully. The woman did not show the slightest concern about the fact that they were so close to where the holes were. If dread for Duke was a sensation reserved for cases impossible to solve with staff or with his sensitivity, for Irene it seemed to be quite an unnecessary feeling.

The colony had been struck by a succession of terrible epidemics some months previously. Irene had never set foot out of her dome. While the others were moving to the slopes of Brown Hill, she stayed in her refuge and Duke visited her frequently. The multiple plagues had never touched her. Duke, in contrast, got sick once. His skin broke out in pustules just two days before the doctor announced the outbreak was over and led the survivors back to their domes. The disease made its appearance during an afternoon Duke was spending with Irene and the little one; the pustules swelled up slowly yet were always visible to the naked eye on cheeks and neck, then on hands and wrists. When Duke made a move to leave, Irene said nothing; she just held him back by an arm pointing him to a bunk. Toward evening the pustules had burst to spill their yellowish pus, and Duke complained repeatedly about a burning thirst.

Irene gave him worm juice she still had and sat up with him until morning. When the greenish dawn broke, Duke had partially regained his strength; and he went to look for other food. Neither one of them had spoken to the others about his sick spell.

Duke cured himself with Irene's help.

Or vice versa?

Duke merely thought he had been fortunate.

Then he thought that the entire colony had been fortunate. The deaths caused by the epidemic and the preceding ones had been very few in number. Was it really an epidemic? The doctor had determined it was after examining the symptoms, but he was taken aback by the extremely low rate of mortality.

Better that way had been Duke's quick conclusion.

Belaes held his breath. Something strange was *indeed* happening, and maybe it was something that they had been expecting for a year.

"Alert the diagnostic section and holographs," he tersely ordered Vulture.

"I've already taken care of that, commander. They're on the way."

Belaes was on the verge of protesting, but due to some vague fear he held his tongue one more time. Calling those people into the control room was a right reserved for the coordinator, but if Vulture was really a censor. . . . Otherwise, the thing would be pointed out along with other complaints in his final report.

"OK. Activate the screens. Direct observation and analysis of every photogram. I want the complete holographic documentation."

"The first satellite holograms are coming in. Should I put security on alert?"

Those words gave Belaes the exact status of the situation. The worms were coming to the surface, but it was not a simple emergence during a storm; they were not coming just to lay eggs. It was a true mass exodus. Under such conditions any member of the colony could be driven to extreme action. Security had to prevent any act detrimental to the mission goal; and they were the only ones on board able to activate the sacs of pyretic fuels implanted into the bodies of all the members of Expedition Nordcall. *Maybe we all have one of those sacs,* Belaes thought for an instant; but he had an immediate reaction—he blocked out the thought and pushed the button.

"Done," he mumbled.

Then he verbally relayed the order to turn the recorder on because it came from the computer. So far that order had cost three subjects, those who in the first days had unwittingly gone down against the worms. The thermal detectors on the ship could not penetrate below thirty meters of rock, and any individual who ventured beyond that range would escape control. A quick blaze in that case would solve the problem. The electronic code, known only to members of security, would set off the pyretic sacs, and within seconds any deserter or transgressor would be destroyed.

The box beneath Belaes's chair emitted a weak glow; a screen started humming.

"Diagnosticians, report."

The short list of names that followed confirmed that all the specialists were present. Vulture was now standing behind the coordinator because Belaes was giving all the orders.

The ship was ready to begin the operation.

Here we go, Belaes said slowly in his own mind. *The worms are coming up and out. Something's been unleashed in them. They're coming en masse and we're ready to meet them. Now we'll find out if they can really cure us.*

Duke sat down next to Irene and took out of a pocket on his long pale-skin coat (from a big worm that probably had been close to death from old age; it had let itself be killed without offering any resistance) a small metal flask. He handed it to Irene, who accepted it without a word. The flask was dented and dirty; the opening under the plastic top was black from the slightly acidic juice from the herbs Duke distilled every so often together with worm juice. Irene downed only one swig of the dark-looking liquid before returning the flask to Duke. He gulped down a couple of drinks and put the flask back in his side pocket.

Then he closed his eyes and noticed a sense of physical discomfort.

"They're coming," he muttered with difficulty.

Irene watched him hesitantly under the yellow lamplight; for a long time Duke did not speak. The kid moved around in its sleep, letting out a weak cry. Irene started to rock it. She too now noticed an odd restlessness. The air was getting colder and sultrier. Duke put a hand up to his right temple; the throbbing that at times tormented him was starting up again, similar to the dull pounding of a hammer on an anvil. The storm was bearing down on the encampment.

Irene looked down at the kid. She saw a small and perhaps pretty face, unusual in that light. The baby also opened its eyes and stared at its mother.

Duke rubbed his temple. It was not only because of the storm; that smarting was a pounding, a continuous throbbing and his mind was seething. He had never experienced anything like it before.

Irene smiled at the baby and slowly turned to look at Duke.

"For our son?" she whispered.

Nothing was happening.

Belaes bit his lips and again looked over the main board. The thermal outlines of the people on the planet stood out in undeniable red; there were fifty-one of them. In a softer color leaning more toward a straw-colored yellow the myriad dots indicating the big worms located a few meters below the surface showed up. Belaes had already used the computer to count them. There were more than two thousand. *They're determined,* he repeated to himself. *But why aren't they moving anymore?*

The yellow dots seemed to have stopped at a depth of ten meters almost as if waiting for something.

Why don't they come to the surface? Why aren't they going into the caves?

Two red dots were isolated from the others; they were subjects 23 and 49 in a branch of the caves that the rest of the colony usually avoided.

"Duke and Irene seem to be getting along well together," mumbled a voice behind Belaes. "I wonder if an error's been made."

The muscles in Belaes's neck stiffened.

"Vulture, could you explain yourself more clearly?"

Belaes did not expect that an opportunity to be able to get back at his relief would only come for disciplinary reasons. Direct censure of a coordinator's conduct would be enough.

"Their son," Vulture went on, undisturbed. "He was born on the planet and is not equipped with a pyretic sac. He's a risk. I've recommended the operation for him."

Belaes knew that the conversation was being recorded by the on-board computer. He could permit himself the luxury of playing the game for a few minutes more.

"I don't understand. What harm could a baby do us?"

"A baby could prove dangerous. I certainly don't have to tell you that, commander."

Belaes ignored the unmoving worms on the main board to look at his subordinate out of the corner of his eye.

"What do you mean? This is a medical and scientific mission, not a repressive military operation. Our guinea pigs aren't a bunch of rebels."

"But they could turn into rebels."

"We're here to observe and study those alien parasites that seem to have unexplained miracle properties and not for a police action."

"You're mistaken, commander."

Belaes was almost surprised speechless.

"You're in no condition to conduct this operation as I have already pointed out to Earth command. A whole year here without results is the best proof!"

Belaes looked at his relief incredulously. One thought and only one thought raced through his mind. *Now that success is so close. . . .*

"Commander, if you're thinking of bringing charges against me for what I've just said, I'll give you some time to think over your accusations in the brig." Vulture's smile seemed more like a sneer there in the half-light. "I'm relieving you of command, coordinator."

Belaes's relief took a tiny device out of his pocket and pressed a button. Four security officers threw open the door behind the chair.

"Go with them, commander. Don't try to make the charge of incompetency already hanging over your head any worse."

A few seconds later Vulture was in the coordinator's chair.

Duke was trembling. Many had died during the first months of their stay on the planet. At first there were the storms, then the strange accidents and epidemics. At times he thought their situation was rather odd. Antonji stated that at least two of the epidemics had to do with already-known diseases as yet clinically incurable. How could they have gotten on the planet? Was there an unaffected carrier among them? However, there had been few deaths in proportion to the seriousness of the diseases. Was it their food, the flesh from the big worms?

Duke had nothing against the worms. They were the rightful owners of the planet, he knew, but killing them meant survival.

The pounding in his brain was getting stronger. Duke reached out an arm to grasp his quartz staff, and the throb-

bing seemed to decrease in severity. Irene moved. Duke knew
she had spoken a few words to him, but he could not remember them.

He grabbed his staff, squeezing its irregular edges against
the palm of his hand. In that same instant the reverberations
started. The cave walls were vibrating imperceptibly, sympa-
thetically with the tremors caused by the storm beating down
on the surface of the planet. Then came the rustling noises,
similar to wind gusts that could not exist, and almost at once
the regular hum of audible sound waves.

Let's talk, Duke thought. *You and I, we who are living for
our people. I don't know what they've done to me, but think
of who among us will be able to replace me tomorrow. Think
of my son.*

Duke let go of the staff, which fell beside the wall.

Irene pressed the baby close to her.

"I want an immediate answer!" Vulture roared into the microphone, and his yelling carried across the control room like
an explosion, sending echoes back from the farthest corners.

"I want to know your people's opinion right now," the new
coordinator insisted in a lowered voice, "and no more excuses. We have more than two thousand worms down there,
and I want to know if it's worth the trouble to go down and
round 'em up! I want to know if you've finally isolated their
mysterious essence, and if it still retains its effectiveness when
taken off the planet. That's what I want to know!"

A very short and excited flood of chatter issued from the
diagnostic section. Then someone broke the connection.

Vulture suddenly slumped against the back of his chair,
furious. The main board flashing with lights was under his
scrutiny. This could be his big chance. Success in that mission
would get rid of any doubts about the propriety of his actions
and the need to get rid of Belaes. All he had to do was get a
report from the diagnosticians, official support that would
help in his effort to land the ship.

An old diagnostician, maybe Roven, coughed into the microphone.

"Well?" Vulture exclaimed.

"We can't say," the old man stammered. "The data we
have are still insufficient. We're familiar with some of the
characteristics displayed by the native life on this planet, but

it is impossible for us to determine them on a medical level. We don't know *what* produces them or how they can be applied. We therefore cannot presume they will remain unchanged in different environments."

"But that's impossible! The computer can give you all the information on the first expedition and what was discovered during the first explorations. You have the results from a year of uninterrupted observations, and the reports sent from Earth. We're absolutely certain that something in those worms may cure many maladies besetting humanity. Why can't you come to some decision?"

"I'm sorry, commander," the diagnostician mumbled. "The data are scanty. We know that something our medicine cannot explain exists in the organism of the native life, but our knowledge stops there. Nor do we know how our guinea pigs got through the epidemics we loosed on the colony. Autopsies of victims have revealed nothing useful." There was another bout of coughing. "Besides, I must remind you, commander, that the first explorers on the planet, members of a military expedition, returned to base cured of diverse genetic defects, but that happened several months before anybody noticed it."

Vulture did deep-breathing exercises trying to keep calm. He could still wait a little more.

"You're right," he said into the microphone. "We'll wait. But when the worms come to the surface, I'll make the decision."

Irene moved; Duke felt his coat rub up against the wall for a few moments, and he turned to look at her. The first thing he saw was the baby with its eyes open.

But it was not crying.

Irene got to her feet. Wordlessly, Duke followed and went with her down to where the pits began. The descent would not be hard; the shafts sloped obliquely, and the walls offered footholds.

Duke looked Irene straight in the eye.

Then they started down.

The two separate red lights began changing color and turning increasingly oranger. Vulture did not immediately realize what was happening.

"Subjects 23 and 49! What does this increase in depth mean?"

Relevant information appeared on two of the screens facing him; there were the usual biological and psychological readouts, and in the lower righthand corner, below the digital clock, the depth the two subjects were at was displayed. Seven meters.

Vulture forced himself to remember the maximum depth of the shaft leading to the pits; he knew it was the deepest one, but it could not exceed four meters. What was going on?

"Control! Storm status!"

"Eighteen minutes twenty seconds into the storm, estimated twenty-five minutes until termination with rather strong aftershocks."

"When can the subjects come back out into the open by using the emergency command?"

"To be on the safe side, not before the next twenty minutes."

Vulture felt stimulated. And the feeling got stronger when his gaze again fell on the main board. The yellow dots, the thousands of worms which had started to surface, had by that time all turned pale and weak except for one spot, the pit area.

His big chance was slipping away. The miracle worms were going back to the bowels of their world, and two of his guinea pigs were following them. By now, the colored dots of the two human beings who had been deprived of their memories and forced to crash-land on the planet with their fellow crew members were getting increasingly weaker.

Vulture was having a fit.

"Security! Prepare to activate the pyretic devices on subjects 23 and 49. Communications! Prepare to send a report to home base."

The operation was stopped again. Contact, almost within a hand's reach, vanished at the last moment. Vulture would have to wait patiently, and get ready to make some new moves.

But there was still one detail to take care of.

"Security! Activate PS on subjects 23 and 49!"

Maybe the worms were a little disappointed; they found only two burned smoking masses and a small being scorched but alive and kicking waiting for them. They took the little creature with them while some young ones stayed behind to sniff at and taste the remains of Duke and Irene who were joined together by a long gleaming staff.

PARALLEL WORLDS

PAUL VAN HERCK

Translated from the Dutch (Belgium)
by Joe F. Randolph

He was to pick his wife Betty up at the airport as they had agreed. She was on the courteous Friendship Fokker, that he sensed before the bird had landed. He even thought he saw her wave from a window, but that was impossible, of course.

He took one last, long swig out of the umpteenth pint he had downed in the airport bar and hurried off to the arrival gate.

Outside, the aircraft engines roared, but it had not gotten to its parking place yet.

He lit up another cigarette. The full impact of what she—or he—both of them perhaps—had done had still not hit him with full force, he was so used to it. Tomorrow, the day after tomorrow, maybe even later the delayed shock would come, he knew.

Abortion.

God, what a word. A chic word, probably coined especially to cover up the ugly deed just as some dolt in the seventeenth century was named Mans and then renamed Mansion. As if the fancy ending made it all right.

But he knew better.

The aircraft was now parked. The engines let out a howl and stank. A Fokker stinks to high heaven.

Whatever the word ended in, it was nevertheless abortion, which hardly made it any better.

Interruption of a pregnancy or, as a bunch of bishops wanted to put it, murder, murder of an unborn child, but in any case still murder.

No, the progressives screamed in unison, no. And they hid behind the misfortune of the unwanted child and the family that could afford to have only so many children.

Abortion was modern, the in thing.

The short staircase was rolled up, and the door swung open. It was all quiet on the short runway but it still stank. Will knew that he could not shut up after making excuses, and deep inside he knew that it was indeed murder to him.

They could have more children; they had enough money, otherwise he would not have been able to cheerfully plunk down the thirty thousand smackers that the whole two-day venture in London had cost. They also had enough time left.

Strangely enough his wife played no part in his guilt feelings. She came down in a strange, free-moving motion he could not explain. Was it masochism? Did he want to heap all the guilt on himself?

He knew that there was guilt.

She was the next to the last one out of the plane. She seemed to be beaming, saw him, and waved.

It would still be a few minutes before she reclaimed her luggage, got through customs, and so forth.

Will knew that it was dumb for him to hide behind the extreme philosophical views which he brought up as he discussed the subject with the few friends and family members whom he trusted with his secret. The secret that he was one of the few who realized that the Earth was overpopulated, no fooling, really overcrowded with people, and that it was criminal to bring children into the world when the future looked so bleak. Children who would have to contend for a sad, stinking existence. It therefore was an act of civic courage to have no children, and one of a still greater courage for one person to stave off what was to come.

He tried to smile away the deep frown creasing his forehead, but it took a lot of effort.

Betty looked to be a little lighter. When he kissed her, she was just like another person. It was as if a black cloud had been lifted from their life, and that was the way it used to be. She seemed to be livelier and dapper, much younger too.

"How'd it go?" He picked up her overnight bag, and together they walked toward the exit, where their car was waiting.

"It wasn't bad at all," she said. "I didn't even know what was happening. A chic, pay-first clinic. They do it while you're asleep, you wake up, and they tell you it's all over with."

"Good!" he said. He put her bag into the trunk, gallantly gave her his arm to get into the car, something he had never done since they were married. He felt a bit like an idiot because she did not seem to be sick or weak at all.

"Huh hum," she sighed with relief as they drove the twenty kilometers to their house through the heavy evening traffic. "That's all over and done with."

"That's that," he echoed, hardly original.

"I even have some money left over," she said a little proudly. "But in any case, you still deserve my thanks for what you've done for me, dear. I know how set you were on buying a new car and now we have to put it off for almost a year."

"Mmm," he grumbled. He really found it rather indelicate to argue about the car, that is, to play off a new car against a child. That was where the sore point was, whether someone was going to give in or not. There was no truth to the horrible pictures of the future that had been painted when it came to light that she was pregnant. Cross off the evening parties. Say good-bye to the many carefree trips in their brand-new though cramped little sports car.

Gone for now, just snatched away.

He wished she would be less talkative. The pints of beer he had drunk were making him lightheaded. He felt terribly depressed and unhappy now, with an alcoholic blood content that was probably too high for the men with Breathalyzers, which was what they could do without right now.

But she talked on, an endless stream, about how everything had gone so unbelievably well. Over and over she said what she thought of him and was so thankful that she would never forget it.

That soaked in a little. She would never forget it, but neither would he. Oh no.

"Was it a boy or girl?" he asked, and he could have bitten his tongue for saying that. It was a question he had also been banging around all month long. He had not meant to ask her, but it just blurted out.

She was not offended by it.

"They won't tell you," she said. "They think you must be going to blame yourself. . . ."

He nodded gloomily. "Exactly. They're right, of course." But he could not put the question out of his mind.

At home, in a strange atmosphere, he had champagne to order. On the table it stood cold, but you cannot do everything right, and for an amateur it was a very well-prepared meal.

She was moved and brightened the whole affair up. They drank champagne and smiled at each other.

They did not broach the subject again.

Nor have they since as if it had been a bad dream which had never really happened. That was the beginning.

It certainly was not the end of things. It got to Will in a severe way. The worst thing was that he took it very badly.

He railed at himself for being oversensitive and silly, but there was nothing to straighten out, and he had nobody he could talk to about his troubles. Such things helped. He read about it all once before in paperback novels. His wife certainly had not. For her the episode was closed, she plunged as never before, with him in tow, into the fickle and expensive night life of the big city, and he went downhill.

He forced himself to follow the oh-so-long-lasting debate about abortion, first in the scandal sheets, then in the opinion polls, next in the establishment press, in parliament, in endless TV interviews with people on the street who knew how to explain it all in great detail, but damn it, he knew that if they were in the same boat he was, they would be talking out of the other side of their mouth. Or most likely not saying anything whatsoever. . . .

The worst thing was that, as the years passed by, he found himself unconsciously beginning to ponder what his son—because it had been a son, that he knew for sure—would look like, he would take after his father—and what kind of mischief he would get into.

It seemed to be nagging at him from all sides. The neighbors multiplied like rabbits and they raced by.

Will caught himself beginning to think about college when his son would have turned six and how he fought and acted. He could not help it. Worse, his job—advertising—brought him into contact with children more than he wanted. The advertising business is heavily oriented toward children because you can get at mother's purse through them.

It happened that he saw a curly-headed boy about six years old, and then Will tousled his hair. It amused him to find such a fine boy, and then it hit him immediately like a hard, ruthless, aching fear . . . Why?

"There is a way," the psychiatrist whom he had finally gotten used to said.

"Oh," Will said.

"Yes." The psychiatrist had turned rather sour-toned. He was not all that young a guy, a guy who was unfamiliar with the problems outside his own experience, Will knew, and that took away a whole lot of rapport.

"You're still young," the psychiatrist said. "And your guilt feelings will get you down if you don't try to overcome them."

"How?" Will spoke up impatiently. He was crabby the last time, much too crabby.

"A child," the psychiatrist said. "Take a stab at it."

"My wife," he said. "She'll never agree to it."

The psychiatrist smiled. "The deepest instinct in any woman," he said in a pompous manner, "is to become a mother. You can't change that at all. Neither can she. Whether she admits it or not. And if you told me that she doesn't blame herself, my good man, my response to that would be nonsense, she can keep it to herself better, and she can get through it better than you." The man folded his hands and assumed a sweet-as-honey expression.

"Are you going to talk to her?"

Will hesitated.

"Or do you want me to?"

Will looked into his lackluster, fatherly, and professional eyes and shuddered.

"I'll talk it over with her," he said.

And he did talk it over with her that very evening after he had drunk his courage out of half a bottle of bourbon. After that, such things went better. At first he was not in a good mood, he beat around the bush a bit, disgusted with himself, finished off the rest of the bourbon, and then got right in the mood with the unequaled honesty that overindulgence in alcohol brings out.

He admitted that he felt rotten every year.

He admitted that every now and then his thoughts turned to that unborn boy.

He admitted that he suspected himself of murder.

And that, at wit's end, he had finally gone to a psychiatrist.

And that the psychiatrist had told him that she must have a child to care for.

She cried for a little while. Oh, why had he never opened up to her about anything before? . . . The bourbon hit and Will wailed a sour tune, too.

More than half-drunk, he performed in bed.

Nothing resulted, and the following year again nothing.

Will accused Betty of taking the pill even though she had so faithfully assured him that she would put her all into the effort to get pregnant. But nothing happened.

The unborn child would have been in his second year of school by now, he would have been able to read pretty well. In the evenings along about bedtime he would have come to sit in daddy's lap and asked surprising questions about the headlines in the paper.

He tried a couple of other psychiatrists. It cost him a good deal of money and three times it got him nowhere.

Then he came to me.

"Do you know," I said after I had listened to him for a full hour, "anything about the existence of parallel worlds?"

That made him sit up and take notice. "Parallel worlds?" he said dumbly. "You mean the foolishness about . . . wait a minute . . . where other possibilities come into being on request? About . . . where I can be married to somebody else . . . or not exactly married . . . or even not existing . . . or . . ."

"Yep, that's what I mean."

"And what good was all that to me before?" Will asked. He had lit up one of my expensive cigars and puffed on it nervously.

"But you don't understand, buddy," I flared up. "On one, or perhaps several, of the parallel worlds your son exists. Right now he's sitting next to you, and you're helping him with his homework. Well?"

Will did not have a quick and ready answer for that one. He was clearly perplexed. I plainly saw that he did not believe me completely, but he still had doubts.

"You really believe in parallel worlds?" he asked.

I nodded convincingly. Of course I did—I believe more now than I ever did before—I believed wholeheartedly in parallel worlds since I myself have just recently chanced upon one and . . . but that's neither here nor there.

He left, obviously deep in thought and not completely untroubled.

Two weeks later I heard from him. He called me, and his voice sounded shaky, on the verge of terror. "To get to your parallel worlds," he said, "do you think that you . . . you could cross over under the right conditions?"

"If you only could," I said. "It's not entirely possible. You draw a pentagram and you mumble—"

"Spare me the details," he said rather abruptly. "The point is can someone from a . . . parallel world cross over to here?"

"Yes, someone can," I said.

"Then let me tell you," he said, audibly swallowing, "that I have seen my son. It can't be anybody else but him. Don't ask me how I know . . . but I do."

I thought quickly and appropriately about something that had struck me from time to time. Will had a problem, of course, but something did not quite fit.

"Look," I said. "Just look at the problem from all angles, will you? On one of the parallel worlds it is more than likely that a would-be father of your . . . your last abortion. Right?"

"So what."

"But would you consider dedicating your life to looking for this boy? To say nothing of the difficulties of arriving on a lousy parallel world . . ."

"You have something there," he said. He was following my logic. His voice sounded a bit on the relieved side, but still . . . Will had a problem on his hands.

"So you think . . . that it's quite likely that my son . . . is after me?"

I chuckled. "That's practically out of the question, my good man. Put that out of your mind. Try to remember. Do you have a new kid on the way?"

"Nope," he said, "no such luck."

A week later Will was dead.

It was a strange business.

Even Betty swore it was suicide. Overwork, guilt feelings. A few small details I learned after making some discreet inquiries still worry me.

Will was hit by a projectile from a weapon the experts have yet to identify—if it can be.

There were no fingerprints.

It was established that the shot came from below.

As if a little kid had shot up at . . . someone much bigger.

I have mulled that over for a long, long time.

And I don't like it.

THE FIFTH TIME OUT
(Den Femte Resan)

BERTIL MÅRTENSSON

Translated from the Swedish
by Joe F. Randolph

He had been standing there watching her out of the corner of his eye for a long time. She was leaning against the gym wall just a few meters from him, with her hands folded in front of her, and she was wearing a pastel-blue dress which contrasted with her light suntan and her blond hair. She was the most beautiful girl he had ever laid eyes on, the girl he had always dreamed of meeting, and he stood there nervously wondering if he had the courage to go over and ask her to dance. Only a few meters separated them, but it might as well have been a kilometer, and he was convinced that if he just took a step toward her, the worn boards in the floor would dissolve and give way under his feet so that he would fall down into an immense, bottomless abyss. Intermission finally ended. The other people streamed back in, and the band struck up the first bars of a dance tune. Now he had to. . . .

He silently counted to ten and hesitantly took a step. And another. And to his great surprise he found that nothing happened. The floor did not give way. But while he was stealthily approaching her, he kept telling himself that it was just to lull him into a false sense of security. He quietly slipped across the floor, so quietly that she did not hear him until he was standing in front of her, and when she turned her head, there

34

was a surprised and almost startled look in her eyes.

I'm gonna stutter, he thought in despair while he drew in his breath and opened his mouth. *I'm gonna stutter and not get out one word, and she's gonna smile indulgently and a bit contemptuously, and somebody else will come up and ask her for a dance right in front of me. . . .*

"May I . . . ?"

But he did not stutter at all as he stood there. And nobody else came up and took her from him, and when their looks met, he was suddenly nervous no more. She smiled and nodded. But just as he was going to put his arm around her, just as the band started playing—he heard way off in the distance, way down inside of him, a bell start to ring, an alarm clock, a warning, and everything around him blurred, and she slipped out of his arms like thin air. . . .

Waking up was always like that. It was emptiness and grief and the whole time the unbearable ringing which cut through everything like a cold, sharp knife.

He was lying stretched out on a soft bed staring up at a ceiling colored a shade he could not identify.

He was lying stretched out on a bed and just a moment ago he had been busy asking the most beautiful girl he had ever seen to dance.

He was thirty years old and had just been seventeen.

A stream of memories surged through him, a cold shower which washed away whatever remained of his drowsy stupor, and he groaned and turned over in despair. . . .

He was in a spaceship among the stars, but just a moment ago he had been at a school dance in Springfield, Illinois—thirteen years before.

He was awake, and he had been dreaming. He had been awakened. The bells had awakened him.

The bells. He got numb thinking about them.

Something was wrong, but he could not put his finger on it. But it had something to do with the bells that were ringing. They should not have been ringing. The bells should ring only when. . . .

Something was out of whack. Something was screwy.

The machines had roused him. There was something they could not handle. And when the machines could not cope with an element of danger, it became his job.

His hands started working automatically, routinely, by rote.

They pulled down small levers, and the massage machine moved aside with a faint hum. At the same time the bells stopped ringing as if the response to their signal had now finally been received and understood and they had completed their task. He turned a knob, and needles withdrew from his body causing an unpleasant prickling sensation.

In a single, swift, hypnotically induced movement he got up out of his bed, equipped with an acceleration pad, and in the same motion he slipped into the pressure suit, pulled down the helmet, and adjusted the pressure. He cast a quick glance at the acceleration pad and checked to see that the dream machine lights were out. The wake-up signal was supposed to turn off the dream machine, but during a crisis period he could not take anything for granted. Everything had to be checked. It was deeply impressed on his mind, and that was the way it had to be.

He looked at the pressure gauge and watched the pressure normalize as he waited.

All done automatically without wasting a thought on it. All according to hypnotically suggested routine instructions. All exactly as he had done it countless times before usually to find it was a false alarm.

But this time it was somehow different. His hands were trembling while he made his way to the control room as slowly as he always had to move in order for the magnets in the suit to get a good grip. But not from fear. There was really nothing to be afraid of. He was protected by an intricate mechanism, the development of nearly a millennium of space travel, a mechanism which was designed for any and all eventualities known up to that time, and presumably a great deal more that would never happen other than in a space engineer's nightmare. . . .

Except anger.

He had asked a girl to dance for the first time, and she had said yes, but he had never gotten the chance to dance with her.

Anger at being awakened.

Furious, he let his gaze scan the panels and at first noticed nothing out of the ordinary. Had he been roused without good cause? . . .

But a light feverishly blinking red caught his attention.

And he stared at it. It should not have been blinking at all. It should have been out.

The light indicated that a defense mechanism had been activated in the ship. He got closer and looked over what it showed, and then did a double take, so amazed that he had forgotten all about his anger for the moment. Section five in the ship, the midsection, the heart of the ship, had been isolated. And that could only mean one thing, a severe drop in pressure, a meteor hit.

He straightened up, unable to believe what he was seeing. A meteor hit. Impossible. Even in a star system a meteor big enough to puncture a ship's hull was a rarity unless you got caught up in one of the meteor storms, something that could of course prove fatal.

But not out here. He had never heard of that happening before.

He shook his head and scanned the other instruments. Most of them seemed to be completely within normal range, one section showed nothing at all. One section of lights burned bright red, yellow, and green. One section had gone out, and one was blinking red urgently.

Anger. A meteor. He had finally asked her to dance and she had said yes, but they had never gotten a chance to dance.

He stared at the red light as if he could make it go out by merely looking at it.

If the midsection was leaking, that meant he had to go out himself and patch the leak. He could not enter the midsection before the difference in pressure was once again equalized. He stooped down and opened a hatch on the floor. With an impatient gesture he took out a new welding unit. He straightened up and studied it. It was a new model, of course. He had not used it before on this trip, but according to the instructions it was in principle no different from the one he had used on the previous trip—and it was also just like the last one, only more effective, better, and a little smaller, more sensitive and more useful.

Once again he adjusted his suit pressure and clumsily moved into the small air lock. He stepped in, pushed a red button, and turned a little wheel.

The door closed behind him, and a faint whistling marked the air rapidly being pumped out. Automatically, when the pressure in the air lock approached a vacuum, the outside door opened, and as soon as he had secured his lifeline, he carefully climbed out.

He stood on a small section of finished metal suspended in the void. Surrounding him was limitless space and an infinity of specks of light. But he was oblivious of them. A regular three-D movie was much more imaginative than space to a spaceman's eye.

His helmet filters muted all contrasts and transformed reality into a flat cloth, a black-velvet surface sprinkled with myriads of small white pinpoints. He felt as if he could reach out his hand and touch them.

He got his bearings and crept toward the midsection, accompanied by the resounding clicking of the magnets that traveled up through his suit. It took him almost fifteen minutes to locate the leak, but he finally found it, a tiny hole a centimeter in diameter with a rounded border melted inward.

He stood awhile looking at it and wondering how he was ever going to patch it. A plug of some sort would do if he reinforced it on the inside. He went back toward the nose of the ship and carefully climbed down into the air lock.

Just a pebble.

He had finally asked her to dance and she had said yes.

But that pebble had come between them. That was wrong. It should not have turned out that way. But it always did. . . .

Somehow.

It was only a rumor, of course. A rumor which was always ignored and avoided at the highest levels, but which had never directly been denied.

Every so often a starship never returned.

Every so often it happened that a starfarer got tired of having his dream interrupted for exercise or to do routine checks—something that was completely logical, and something that was expected because the dream machine was strictly licensed on all planets, and its use was restricted to certain incurables and to the minority that had enough money to bribe the governing planet, for all intents and purposes forbidden.

The dream machine was enticing and you never wanted to wake up from your dream.

Because in the dream you always got what you wanted. And in the dream you did not know whether it was a dream until you were awakened and were confronted with reality, maybe awakened by a terrible ringing to remind you that you had a job to do.

And it got worse each time. Afterward the dreams settled down. If they would only not turn into hair-raising episodes that always ended happily. They flowed together and got consistent and came to life, an ideal life, tailored to every imaginable individual need, a life which was reality itself as long as the dream lasted—and whoever was living the ideal life would be awakened at regular intervals and find that it was just a dream, a semblance of life. . . .

With a faint hiss the air flowed back into the lock and the door opened. He went in and gathered up the materials he needed. Then he went back outside.

He patched it up in a few minutes. When he was through, he stood up and stayed there for a long while looking out into space. Somewhere out there they were waiting for him, for him and his ship and his cargo.

They could very well perish if they did not get what he was carrying.

Sweaty and tired because he was in poor shape and it required a great deal of strength to break the magnetic grip at every step, he went back inside the ship. When he entered the control room, the light on the panel had gone out. The automatic controls had equalized the pressure and reunited the midsection with the rest of the ship. He paused briefly and then continued down the small corridor to the midsection to inspect the damage done there and to reinforce the temporary path from the inside. It took him over half an hour to reinforce it and repair the damage; a few cables that ran along the opposite wall had been broken. He could find no other signs of damage, but for safety's sake he took another twenty minutes to check things out.

When he got back to the control room, the right lights were on and glowing steadily, and all instruments registered normal values.

He was finished. His job was done. He could get back to the dream machine.

But he kept standing in front of the panel motionless. Finally, he reached out and turned a dial in front of him. A large gray screen flashed on and in a few seconds the picture stabilized. It showed a sea of white dots.

He knew it was useless but nevertheless strained his eyes until they hurt in an attempt to make out the dot that was the ship's destination. But he had no reference point whatsoever to work from in order to make any such determination. So, at last he just stood there with his gaze glued to the screen—without really seeing it at all. . . .

Concern about the authorities was naturally disappearing. At first they had tried using threats against the problem but without success. They had experimented with two-man crews—but found that as a rule only one of them was left alive when the ship returned. And when they tried replacing the dream machine with a dreamless lethargy, the number of applicants abruptly fell to zero.

It was the dreaming part that attracted applicants, dreaming and nothing else. The profession of starfarer was not for the career-minded, not for those who wanted to make easy money. It was a paying job, certainly—but at the same time it was a one-way proposition.

Because when you came back from a trip, you were an anachronism; everybody smiled at you behind your back, which made it doubly worse in every possible way. The way you talked, your tastes, your hairstyle, all the little details that when added up equaled a person, that were so common that they were not noticed except subconsciously, may have been a century out of date.

Everybody agreed that it was a pity about the starfarers—but nobody did anything about it, no one accepted them. And so they always had their dream machine. . . .

Yes, the dream machine was what attracted them. And the ones who applied were the ones who were ready to give up everything—just to have a little happiness which their own inhibitions or existing external conditions kept them from attaining in real life.

They actually had so many applicants to choose from that they could set their standards rather high—but they never got to the point where they could weed out the neurotics—because they were all that way.

The loss of ships and cargoes was terrible because the cargoes were of vital importance for supplying the growing colonies on star worlds.

They subjected all applicants to the most rigorous tests and after every time out they underwent psychological screening that had been perfected during the century since the first starfarer had ventured forth.

Occasionally they found suspicious tendencies and then the person concerned was forthwith discharged. And without anyone knowing for certain why, it was said that five times out was the absolute maximum.

Five times out.

He had adjusted to it.

And this was his fifth time.

He took his helmet off and went into the cabin straight to the dream machine. He stood there for a long time looking at it. A myriad of dancing shapes was reflected on the metal surface as if all dreams were forcing their way onto the surface in order to perform an enticing seduction.

Sweat beaded on his forehead.

Somewhere in there she was still standing and waiting for him to put his arm around her. Somewhere in there the band was still playing the opening bars over and over again waiting for him to come and take his place in the scene and bring it to life. He trembled at the thought.

He undid his suit in a quick motion and slipped it off.

He went back into the control room. He had forgotten to turn the screen off. He stopped as soon as he looked at it. Scintillating spots. But not only spots. Life. People who were waiting for him somewhere out there.

They were determined to make a new life for themselves and they needed his help.

What kind of cargo was he carrying?

Seeds perhaps, machines, medical supplies, news from the mother world.

He picked out a feeble pinpoint of light and studied it as if he had to have something to fix his eyes on, a symbol for those who were waiting for him. . . .

I'm sorry, he whispered. *I'm sorry.*

He moved quickly and purposefully. With steady hands he

rummaged around for the pair of small sharp snips which he had brought with him into the cabin. He went out to the dream machine and cut the thin wire that activated the wake-up mechanism.

He lay down and made a few small adjustments in the controls. The massage machine descended on him.

He turned a dial and with a quickly passing, annoying, tingling sensation it plunged small needles into his blood-stream.

With infinite pleasure he watched the room turn pale around him, felt his pain disappear, and he became young again.

Now he was seventeen once more.

He laughed at himself. What was the idea? Back again. He had now been standing and daydreaming again. . . .

"You're a real daydreamer," his mother used to say. And his father once said: "It wouldn't surprise me if you became a writer by doing that." Coming from him it sounded like something dirty.

The girl was still standing there. He laughed at himself again. Why shouldn't she have been standing there? It had only been a few minutes since he last saw her. . . .

She was wearing a pastel-colored dress which contrasted with her light suntan and her blond hair. She was the most beautiful girl he had ever laid eyes on and he stood there nervously wondering if he had the courage to go over and ask her to dance.

Finally he slowly counted to ten and hesitantly took a step. . . .

They got engaged two years later. It was at the same time that he had his first book published and with what he was paid for it he bought the most expensive engagement ring anyone in his family ever had—which seemed to make a bigger impression on them than the fact that he wrote a book and it was published.

A year later, approximately, they were sitting together under a blooming apple tree in his parents' orchard. He had just finished reading to her the first chapter in a novel he was beginning to write—when he heard off in the distance a faint ringing which in some strange way made him very sad.

She noticed it and asked him what was wrong. He smiled

tenderly, oh, the ringing, but had he forgotten it? Today was the very day they were to be married. . . .

And he pulled her to him and their lips met.

A starfarer never had any reason to feel afraid. He was protected by a complicated mechanism, the development of nearly a millennium of space travel, a mechanism which was designed for any and all eventualities known up to that time, and presumably a great deal more that would never happen other than in a space engineer's nightmare. . . .

Detectors discovered the danger and immediately activated the warning system.

Bells began ringing.

A relay tripped and a signal was sent out. But it never arrived.

Bells continued ringing for some time.

But they had grown silent long before the starship was swallowed up by the cold fire of a dwarf star.

DRUGS'LL DO YOU

KATHINKA LANNOY

Translated from the Dutch
by Joe F. Randolph

"Did you read that?" the woman asked.

With a weary gesture she slipped the dirty dishes and silverware into the garbage chute behind the dining table.

"Huh?" asked the man from behind his plastic newspaper, which would later on get folded up so that she could use it as a shopping bag.

"Well, did you read about the new drugs? I even heard about them on the TV. Drugs with no side effects, with no adverse effects."

"Don't believe a word of it," said the man.

Surprised, her eyebrows shot up. "Isn't there anything in the paper about them?"

"Of course there is." He shrugged. "So what? Any reason to believe it?" He sounded annoyed.

The woman turned on her dusting machine and then sat in her rocker, which immediately and obligingly began rocking.

"Well, some people will," she said in reply to his question. "In fact, most will, for that matter."

The man gave no response. The TV, the paper, the government, the citizenry, the people next door, they all interpreted it in their own way after hearing it. But the communications media were the message. Who knew for sure how ideas, ide-

44

ologies, ideals really get started? Everybody sent everybody else from pillar to post.

From doctor to specialist.

From one specialist to another, from one hospital to another.

From broker to broker to broker.

From one apartment building to another.

From one government agency to the next.

From one government worker to the next.

And nobody really knew any more than when he started.

Oh, yeah, you were alive, But you were programmed—even though you didn't know how it was done. You just didn't know whom you would have to fight—if you wanted to at all, if you were not fed up enough, or whatever the reason, to embark on such a course.

The Judges were the ones you would have to confront.

But who were the big shots?

The ones who decreed who, what, and how you are and exist.

And on top of everything else, how many kids you could have.

Plus how long a vacation you could take.

As well as where other people go on vacation.

Large-scale TV advertising campaigns roaring with laughter about the cool north, and vice versa. Beaming toothpaste smiles and nude young women with extra long legs.

Life—how long, and where, and under what conditions.

After a certain age, retired, cast aside, material for the chute, not worth a plugged nickel anymore. Life nipped in the bud, dragged out to a frequently undignified end.

Then who decided who was to live or die?

You just fall behind and see what happens.

"We're all like a piece of plastic," said the man suddenly. "We're getting to be just like a used newspaper, and we're not made for that."

The woman rocked back and forth. "What are we made for then?"

"How should I know?" said the man.

"What does it say there about the drugs?"

"Here, read it for yourself."

She rocked back and forth. "No thanks, just tell me. Reading is so tiresome. I've been up for almost a whole hour now."

"Get undressed again and go sun yourself."

"It's raining. The sun's not out."

She kept bothering him more and more. "Then turn on the sunlamp in the garden room."

"If you're reading about the drugs. . . ."

He squirmed around annoyed. The plastic rustled with a soft, old-fashioned sound like paper, but at the same time quite different.

"All right, already. If you'll just keep your trap shut. We haven't had an expensive garden room built for nothing. Everybody has his own private garden even though you live twenty-two stories up like we do. Sacrifice one room in your living space. Always traveling via the diversity of walls. They know them so well they can tell you every inch. We—"

"We have only two sets of walls," she interrupted him. "A beach wall and a moorscape. I'd really like to have a mountainscape or a forest scene or—"

"Just draw one on your stomach," the man said.

"On Mother's Day," the woman went on as if he had not said anything at all.

He snorted. "You ain't been no mudder not even once."

"If it hadn't been for all the abortions, I would've been a mother a long time ago. They just found. . . . But what else?"

"They should really have given some reason. Maybe they thought you were too unbalanced, too nervous, too unprepared."

"They who?"

"Well, they, the doctors or people like that, and then considering the motivation or some such thing."

"So do I get the walls?"

"If I could only get myself in gear to work," he said. "I've been waiting all month for some sign that I'm going to get moving."

"Maybe the computer's down or it must not be in the mood," suggested the woman. Half-thoughtful, half-dreamy, she closed her eyes. "A small swimming pool with lapping waves wouldn't be all that strange either. . . ."

He drowned out any more of her hints by reading out loud.

" 'A Way to Happiness' is the title. Professor So-and-so has invented some pills, pills or powders, I can't follow every word of it. All right, then, a drug. You don't get confused and you have no urge to jump out of the window or off the roof or to. . . . You don't get down from it, and there's not too much talk about tripping. You're quite different, you see everything in a different rose-colored light. 'People see the world with other eyes,' it says here. 'Cares, misery no longer hold people in bondage.' 'All pain disappears.' 'People learn how to be happy, contented, and. . . .' "

He broke off his recitation. "If you use it, you wouldn't want to have any more walls, or a swimming pool either. You'd be happy. You only have to try it once."

"If I ever get in the mood," said the woman.

"Everybody's always in the mood to get high."

"What is it like to be high, anyway?" asked the woman. "Would it be nice?"

"How should I know?" said the man again. "If it wasn't, they wouldn't be making any more pills."

"They who?"

"Well, them, of course, the common everyday-type them."

They were standing in a small, shabby lab. Sure enough, they were the common everyday type. The professor was a medium-sized man of indeterminate age, neither young nor old. He had a small bristly mustache and cold, insensitive, reptilian eyes. Excluding the cold look, his assistants still had the fanatical slavishness of all epigones. They were either young and had developed too weak a personality to be independent-minded, or else they were older and jealous of the younger ones who had not yet seen life pass them by without having lived it. It was the old shame and disgrace of criers who snuck around doing things on the sly and therefore had developed some inferiority complex or other that was centered around superiority.

The professor buttoned up his white lab coat and struggled up onto a high stool in back of one of the tables. In one continuous movement he brushed the hair out of his eyes and deftly pushed aside a couple of retorts.

The others respectfully gathered around him.

"We're all here now," said the big man while tapping on

the newspaper folded up before him. The letters in the head-
line above the drug article were jet-black.

"Is that further than we've ever gone before, professor?"
someone asked.

The professor nodded slowly. He raised his eyes and
looked at each one of his followers individually. It was a
fixed, serpentine look out of unblinking eyes.

"Yes, we've come a long way. In war there have always
been survivors up to now. In addition, it is increasingly
harder for people to come up with a good reason, a plausible
reason, for killing each other off. War is scarcely more than
mouthing off. The whole world has gradually become one
small country. The slogan 'For Your Country' doesn't work
anymore. Nobody willingly dies for that. Race against race is
ancient history. People have learned to get along with one another. What's more, there has always been a race left that
must continuously be indoctrinated with our ideas. No, it is
much too risky and not productive to play them off against
each other with their own bloodlust."

"What about a nuclear device?" asked a voice.

The professor looked in the direction of the speaker.

"A nuclear device would devastate both the Earth and humanity. That's what we don't want. And even with the neu-
tron bomb there could still be survivors."

"The Earth is ours, for our chosen ones," a woman's voice
cried out hysterically. "Can't you let them fight and starve,
sir?"

The professor did not reply. It was such an overworked argument. He waved his bony hand as if he were a king who
was declining the homage of his subjects in all modesty. But
there was no modesty about him.

"After Fascism came drugs, disputes between the agitated
people and the justifiably discontented youth and old people.
Hatred between generations, suicide, abortions, sex for the
sake of sex, which destroyed self-control. But there were always groups that were immune to our propaganda. Groups,
hundreds, thousands that went on living as they had. They
looked after one another and fathered children, they worked
at living. We've made those who are inferior increasingly
more so and the be-and-do-your-best philosophy less and less
attractive. We have undermined religion and in return given
an easy life of leisure with robots and enduring tolerance.

Crime and terror are no longer punished. Yet there are still some people who have not changed their thinking. But this drug, which is so innocuous and inviting, which you can mix with drinking water and add to food in short order, like 'Happiness for All'—nobody will be able to escape it. The aftereffect is so slow yet unrelenting that they won't know what hit 'em until it's too late."

"They'll all rest with you, great leader!" a voice cried out.

The professor again declined the gesture of homage.

"Possibly," he conceded, and his reptilian eyes narrowed to slits. "But even though some will pass away to God, the Earth will be depopulated for our Fourth Reich."

"Are my eyes getting weaker?" the woman asked. She pushed a couple of dishes past the garbage chute, but she couldn't have cared less.

"How so?" asked the man.

He wanted to raise his hand to the audio button to push it in, but he was much too comfortable and felt as high as if floating in space. So, he thought, later for that.

"Things are getting fuzzier all the time, fuzzier and fuzzier," said the woman.

"Sometimes I can hardly see myself in the mirror nowadays when I'm shaving."

"Why shave at all?"

"I've just about come to that conclusion," said the man and sighed with relief.

"So once again you see that we're being freed from all cares and troubles."

"Are we happy now?" asked the woman, and there was some doubt in the tone of her whispering voice.

He nodded. "Yes, we must be."

"I don't know for sure if I find it altogether satisfying to be happy," said the woman after a moment.

She sat down again in her rocking chair but failed to push the button. The chair remained motionless. "It's crazy, but every so often it's almost as if you've gotten completely transparent. I can see the stones in the wall right through you."

"Now you're talking," said the man and strained his eyes. "I believe I can see the rungs on the chair you're sitting in.

But the transparency is so clear, I mean. Before long we'll no longer need any clothing when it gets warm. That'll be a big saving."

"Could . . . could the drug be doing something else?" asked the woman suddenly, still a little anxious. "We're not going to disappear, are we?"

The man shook his head but was prepared for perhaps not seeing well anymore. "Nothing was said on the audio. There wasn't anything mentioned in the papers, either."

"We could occasionally black out exactly like an old-timey candle," ventured the woman.

But her voice was to be heard no more because her mouth completely dissolved.

The professor looked at the vacant stares of his helpers. As collaborators in his plans they had not drunk any of the water or eaten any of the food laced with the drug. But the toast to victory had been so spiked that one drink was enough.

"To our victory. Hail to our great leader!"

The echoes of their cheers had hardly faded away when the professor slowly stood up. He took off his coat, his shirt, his shoes, and socks. He also brushed the silly-looking bang from his forehead, that was very high and angular.

Then he pulled off his pants, dropped his tail with a dull thud on the floor, and his feet made a sound like goat hooves as he moved.

He stretched and walked to the intercom.

"Our people can land. The planet is finally clear," he said into the small box.

OPPORTUNITIES GALORE

(Cuestión de oportunidades)

GABRIEL BERMUDEZ CASTILLO

Translated from the Spanish
by Joe F. Randolph

When Mendoza opened the door, it seemed to him that no
one was sitting in the sumptuous leather armchair behind the
desk at the back of the room. Afterward he thought that it
must have been momentary blindness brought on by his nervousness since he right away realized that in the chair there
sat a tall blond beauty whose hair was the color of dark
honey and whose features were those of a movie or TV star.

"Please come in," the young woman said. "Come on in
and have a seat."

Noticing a typical tingling sensation in his fingertips (the
same as when he picked up a deck of cards before dealing),
Mendoza took a seat in one of the easy chairs arranged in
front of the big ivory desk.

"May I help you with something, Mr. . . . .?"

"Mendoza. Mendoza's the name, Ms."

"Very pleased to meet you. I'm Ms. Hollister, at your service."

"I was told," Mendoza mumbled in a low voice, "that you
people can arrange. . . ."

"Opportunities."

"Something like that."

"You've come to the right place. How about a drink, Mr.
Mendoza?"

"Yeah, thanks. Anything," Mendoza answered, beginning to feel more at ease. "I need one, to tell the truth."

"A Calixto Climb?"

"Fine, I'll have the same."

Mendoza tore his eyes away from the young woman's light-brown skin and blue eyes to carefully take stock of his surroundings. In addition to the magnificent desk, imitation ivory maybe, carved out of one of the tusks from the extinct Titan tyrannosaur perhaps, the decor was purely functional. Two easy chairs facing the desk; a big armchair occupied by Ms. Hollister, and a half-alive filing cabinet in a corner. The only window overlooked the barren Titan surface as well as displaying the gigantic planet Saturn with the thin edge of its rings turned toward Titan, as always.

Ms. Hollister's long hand put in front of him a spiral-shaped red-crystal glass filled with a cold liquid.

"Very good," Mendoza said after tasting it. "I—"

"You need money."

"That's it. . . . What—"

"Maybe it'd be better if I explained our system to you before we continue. I'm the representative of an organization whose duty it is to find work . . . an organization stretching throughout the known universe and part of the unknown. Our jobs are perfectly legal, at least on the planets where they are done. So that you don't have to talk in a low voice nor do you think you have to sneak around or hide. Not even the Licensed Gunmen of the Titan Autonomous State will try to initiate any legal action against us. . . ."

"The gunmen are . . ." Mendoza said with a sigh.

"We don't ask you for any kind of explanation, Mr. Mendoza."

"No. It's all the same to me. You know, I have a scrap iron foundry . . . a wife, Mary, and two children. I am also an inveterate gambler, and yesterday. . . ."

For a few seconds Mendoza's black eyes clouded over; he ran his callused hand over his prematurely gray hair.

"Yesterday," he said in a steadier voice, "I gambled away everything I had in the bank, eighteen thousand five hundred credits. And I lost every last one of 'em. The worst thing is that the major portion was funds from the Autonomous State to cast the rest of several ships of the line. You know how the Licensed Gunman treat whoever embezzles government money. . . ."

"Bad business, Mr. Mendoza," Ms. Hollister said with an understanding gesture.

"I was told about this. . . . Do you think I could get my hands on eighteen thousand five hundred credits, and *soon?* I have promised I'll never again gamble; never again, no matter how much my hands burn. . . . You can believe me, Ms. Hollister. Not another card game, nor a card, nor a die, no nothing. . . ."

"I . . ." replied the young woman, blushing slightly. "I cannot get involved in your moral conflicts, Mr. Mendoza. I can only give you information. Yes, you can get your hands on that amount of money . . . But pay close attention. Concentrate on what I'm going to say to you . . ."

A little more reassured, Mendoza thought the young woman had an eye-catching figure, set off quite well by her tight-fitting black and gold scale dress. A bit old-fashioned and conservative, just like the v-shaped neckline that plunged down to her navel; but he could see that she was a well-educated woman from a good family.

"Our office receives requests to look for personnel to do more or less hazardous jobs. The personnel can be human or any other species, and they can work when they wish, under certain conditions depending on the specific job. The more dangerous the work, the higher the pay. You understand, don't you?"

"I believe so. But what's the risk?"

"Only one, just about. Death. . . . Sometimes very serious injuries . . . but that's rare."

"All right. . . ." Mendoza said very thoughtfully. "If there's no other way out! If I don't come up with the money and cast the scrap iron, the gunmen will blast me to atoms."

"I don't wish to coerce you," she said sweetly. "Perhaps another approach, a loan from the Terrestrial Bank, from a friend. . . ."

"Oh, no! Nobody, nobody at all! I've already tried everything. I don't see any other way out. But . . . this . . . Ms Hollister . . . Does the work have to be completed beforehand? I need the money today!"

"Don't worry, sir. Even though you take one of our . . .

opportunities that'll last, let's say, a week, and as the transfer is immediate, a time stasis is produced."

She again blushed a little; he could see that she was repeating a speech learned by heart.

"All right. I understand now," he replied. "I'll come back here a tenth of a second after leaving even though I will have been working on a job for a month . . . wherever it is."

"Do you know anything about time travel, Mr. Mendoza?" Ms. Hollister asked, opening her beautiful blue eyes in admiration.

"In my line of work you have to know about everything," Mendoza showed off his knowledge. "OK. If I understand you correctly, the more dangerous, the more money. . . . Let's see. What kind of work do you have?"

It seemed that tears were about to flow out of the young woman's eyes.

"I'm sorry. . . . We don't have specifics about the type of work. We only know how much is to be paid, and the risk percentage . . . factor." ·

Mendoza downed the last drop of his Calixto Climb. A wave of warmth surged through his body. He felt very satisfied at seeing his problems solved; in high spirits because of the high alcohol content of the Calixto (maybe too high, he thought) and quite proud of the obvious admiration that Ms. Hollister had shown him.

"OK . . ." he said somewhat fearfully. "Why not get me a cheapie . . . and an easy one, to start off with? Just to find out what I'm getting myself into, you understand."

"I understand," she responded. "A lot of applicants do the same thing."

To Mendoza it seemed that the young woman's features took on a certain indifference as if she were thinking: *Too bad. So virile a man, and he didn't even dare* . . . She was indeed thinking that; he would have bet his solar furnace against a pebble that she was thinking just that.

"Come over here, Lorenzo," Ms. Hollister said affectionately.

The half-alive filing cabinet hummed, yawned, and came up to the table, putting its ugly gray form next to the young woman's fine features.

"Give me a low-probability one, Lorenzo. Between ten and twelve thousand."

"Not available," replied the filing cabinet in a harsh-sounding voice.

"Then, between twelve and fifteen thousand."

The filing cabinet emitted a revolting sound, like a drunk being beaten as he was throwing up, and ejected a gilt-edged iridescent sheet of Bristol board onto the ivory table.

"Let's take a look at this," she said. "Probabilities: one in twelve thousand three hundred eighteen. . . ."

"What does that mean?"

"That there is one chance of dying for every twelve thousand three hundred eighteen of coming out alive. Compensation for this . . . uh . . . opportunity: fifty credits per diem. When we say per diem, we mean that you're paid for completed days. If you come back in the middle of a day, you won't get anything for that day. Only completed days."

"Fine. I'll take it. . . . Let's see what happens."

"There is one restriction. Or rather two. You're not allowed to hide from the crowd or to throw money on the ground. If you do, you won't receive anything."

"What does all that mean?"

"I don't know, Mr. Mendoza. That's what it says on the card. But they don't explain it to us, you know. Now then. You must be sure you understand what is expected of you if you accept this . . . uh . . . opportunity. . . ."

"All right. I accept. No hiding from the crowd and no throwing money around, huh? Agreed. Oh, listen! Two things, Ms. Hollister . . . Do you people have to be paid anything?"

"No, sir. We receive our fees from the people or organizations that use our services; rather, those that request workers . . . In this case your payment, fifty credits per diem, is a net amount."

"And the other thing . . . Whenever I get tired, or if I get scared, what do I do to get back?"

"Look at this."

Ms. Hollister shook her lovely head of hair to show him a cheap plastic bracelet with a red button in the middle.

"Put this on. Like this. Whenever you want to come back, you just press the button. . . . And now. Do you accept the job?"

"Yep."

Mendoza hardly had time to see what the young blond woman's hands were doing on the top of the table. He disappeared immediately; and two-tenths of a second later he reappeared. The first sound he made was a long sigh of relief. There were no great changes in him; only his tired-out look, a bruise over his left eye, and a scratch on his right hand still dripping blood.

"Sir!" she gasped, pouncing upon a new chilled Calixto that had just appeared out of the ivory tabletop. "How awful!"

This time there was a clear tone of contempt in Ms. Hollister's voice.

"You only stayed one day . . . fifty credits, Mr. Mendoza."

The young woman's aristocratic hand deposited a coin on the table, beside the easy chair the man was sitting in.

"It wasn't very dangerous," he said after placing the empty glass on the table. "Do you know what the job was? Or are you prohibited from listening?"

"No, not at all. You can say whatever you like."

"Well. No sooner did I begin the . . . opportunity than I found myself in the midst of a bunch of green-colored beings with a type of crest on their heads."

"The planet Traskiliskar," she commented.

"The same. I was one of them, and it turned out that I was nothing less than a tax collector. . . . Everybody was rushing at me, screaming and yelling . . . . At first I thought they wanted to kill me, you understand. But then that was not the case. It seems that those people, the Traski . . . the Trasli . . . well, whatever their name is, have an absurd sense of things, you know. They were after me to pay their taxes! Nothing less! Then I understood the restrictions; I could not hide or throw the money around. It was quite obvious. But what foolishness! They hounded me, they pursued me, they shoved their money into the bags hanging from my belt; they grabbed receipts right out of my hands. . . . And yes indeed. . . . Do you know what tax I was collecting?"

"No, Mr. Mendoza."

"The tax on triple adultery . . . then I knew what it was, but now . . . well; I can't remember too well. It was horrible, believe you me. . . . Off in the distance I saw one of my fellow tax collectors fall beneath a mass of taxpayers; the poor guy got up and kept on collecting. . . . How awful! Right then and there I got sick, I really did. Listen, Ms. Hollister, I'd rather have another riskier job, with fewer people involved. . . . Can we try that?"

"Whatever you say. . . ." This time the woman's voice again sounded a tone of admiration; even her eyes looked at the man as if to say: *You're really a brave man* . . . "Let's see, sir . . . between eight and ten thousand. . . ."

"A little more, a little bit more," said Mendoza frankly feeling on top of the world by virtue of the Calixto he had just drunk. "Listen! What's to keep me from taking a cheap . . . opportunity like this one and sticking with it for a number of years if I can come back immediately?"

"Well . . . your physical age keeps increasing . . . you'd come back a number of years older . . . and then . . . eighteen thousand five hundred credits are . . . uh . . . three hundred sixty days at fifty credits per. . . . It would take another terrestrial year. . . . But if you're interested. . . ."

"No, no. Something quicker even if it is more hazardous. Right now I can assure you that I'm not a gambling man anymore. No more dice, no more cards. On my word."

"Then . . . how about something between four and five thousand?"

"All right."

"Lorenzo . . . something between four and five thousand."

Following the sound of a mechanical saw cutting through flesh-covered bones, the half-alive filing cabinet ejected a new card.

"Look at this, Mr. Mendoza. Probabilities: one in four thousand nine hundred fifteen. . . . You already know what that means. Payment: two hundred credits per diem. Restrictions: keeping quiet and leaving no door unopened. I don't understand, but I'm sure that you will. . . . Another Calixto?"

"No, I'd rather have a clear head. On with it, Ms. Let's get me there."

As fast as before he found himself in an unexpected place. A lead-colored sky, filled with storm clouds, stretched out before him. It was raining hard, and sudden bolts of lightning of a deep-blue sparkling color split the murky firmament asunder. He was standing on the deck of a ship; at least that

is what it looked like to him. Then he remembered the restrictions and started pacing from one side to the other.

He went to the gunwale and bent over it to look down at
the churning, foaming water continually crashing against the
vertical lead-colored wall. At times through the mist he could
hear weird clicks, the wail of a siren, and the deep rumble of
machinery, beating rhythmically like a huge heart, that
seemed to be coming from inside the ship.

The ship seemed to have no beginning or end. No matter
how hard he tried, he could not make out the prow or stern,
where the deck logically had to end. Suddenly, through the
mist, a rusty metal hatch with a humidity-covered locking
wheel appeared. He remembered the second restriction:
Leave no doors unopened. No matter what the reason, it was
obvious he was going to have to open them. He took the
locking wheel in his hands (he realized they were not exactly
hands but a type of fishskin-covered bulbs with four or five
sharp-pointed ends) and turned it. The hatch opened with a
swoosh to reveal a perforated metal staircase leading to the
depths. Nothing else happened, so that he thought his obliga-
tions had been fulfilled by that act.

He went on his way as he listened through the mist to the
dull slapping of waves. At times the siren was howling far
above his head, lost in gray-colored spirals of smoke. At
other times structures typical of a ship emerged; the white-
painted cranes and gangplanks of a freighter, the armored
turrets with two or three heavy guns of a man-of-war . . .
Every now and then a new hatch popped into view, or a gray
metal structure containing a door. Fulfilling his duties, he
opened them, at first fearfully and carefully, and then with
less care every time thereafter.

He lost all sense of time. There came a moment when he
got tired and sat down on the deck, resting his wrinkled back
against a ventilation shaft. He assumed that he was allowed a
rest period; it was logical since nobody was able to get by
without sleep and food. When he woke up, the scene was
unchanged; the same gloomy night rent asunder by bolts of
lightning, the howl of a siren, and the dismal sound of high
waves ceaselessly breaking against the metal hull of the
endless ship. Beside him there was a bottle of water and a
package of some yellow substance similar to hardtack. He
drank and ate; he felt restored and went on his way.

He seemed to hear far off, muffled by distance, slow cannonading. As he got closer, the noise that was drowned out by the sound of guns was replaced by thundering reports from heavy pieces of artillery. Red flashes began to appear in the mist; then a long wake of spray cut through the churning gray water headed toward the side of the ship, and a column of smoke and flames, punctuated by a splitting sound, rose up a hundred meters in front of him. . . .

There was a gray wall to his left with a varnished wood door equipped with a thick glass skylight and a bronze handle. He opened it and bent forward in order to see better the battle that was raging a short distance away, and that was what saved him. The door slammed against him violently, knocking him to the floor . . . a flood of yellow liquid surged from inside as if a dike had burst. . . . Terrified, Mendoza studied the liquid boiling and bubbling on the deck in astonishment; evidently it was a very potent corrosive acid. While he stayed calm yet filled with deep horror, he watched the wooden planking turn black, gray metal smoke, and the yellow liquid little by little, as its flow diminished, carve a wide path of destruction down the side of the ship. A short distance away the sound of cannonading was fading.

Up to then he had been walking glued to the gunwale, indistinguishable from the dark sea, which, without his knowing why, made him feel safe. But now there were too many dangers there, so he went inside to try to find the other side of the ship. He passed new structures, every now and then opening a new door. Two of them revealed no apparent danger; the first one was a long illuminated passageway that seemed to go on endlessly; the second a narrow room, poorly lighted and filled with rusty old devices.

"Have they found it?" he heard. "Have they found it?"

A shadow passed beside him; he tried to stop it, but his hand slipped against moist, sticky skin. The being disappeared in the distance, ceaselessly repeating the same words. He saw the being open one of the doors he had just investigated; suddenly a section of metal wall collapsed on the being and crushed him.

He slept again, ate, and drank. The next day a door shot a huge jet of flames at him, which he escaped only because of the many precautions he was now taking. He went by an elevated bridge on which ghostly figures were using old-fashioned navigation instruments and talking among themselves in inaudible tones. Little by little he was beginning to understand; the job was to look for someone, apparently hidden behind one of those doors. . . .

Another door tried to grab him with some steel pincers; the next one revealed a huge opening where massive machines hummed periodically between the times connecting rods and levers went into high speed; the third one made a section of deck give way under his feet. Fortunately he was able to grab onto the side of the trap and after a lot of effort to pull himself up to the deck again, still scared by the brightness of burning coal that he had seen in the depths. . . .

Occasionally other phantasmagorical figures crossed his path, forever opening doors. . . . That night, when he again felt sleepy, he cast one last look at the stormy sea, the gloomy structures on the ship, and what he was close to, a gigantic smokestack out of which clouds of black smoke poured. Then he pressed the red button.

"Three days completed," Ms. Hollister said. "That's six hundred credits."

The slender manicured hand deposited one sepia and one blue bill next to the previous money. Six hundred fifty credits in all, Mendoza thought. It was not much.

"I didn't reach the other gunwale . . ." he whispered.

"Beg pardon."

"No, nothing. Uh, thanks a lot."

There was another chilled Calixto, in a glass twice the size of the last one, on the table. Mendoza downed it in one gulp and felt the reviving warmth from the alcohol.

She looked at him with a doubtful expression.

"Shall we continue?"

"Sure. Right now . . . but I'd prefer a job for the same price as before. A little more. . . ."

"Dangerous?"

"Remunerative, if you get my meaning."

"Certainly. Lorenzo, give me something between two thousand and two thousand five hundred."

The half-alive filing cabinet howled like a wolf and spat out a new card.

"Let's see," she said, casting a cold look at Mendoza.

"Probabilities: one in two thousand five. . . . Payment: five hundred credits per diem. . . ."

"Restrictions?" Mendoza asked with an expression that said he already knew them all.

"Three. Do not remove transmitter; do not linger—"

"Same as on the boat, then?"

She gave him a searching look mixed with admiration and pity.

"And do not circle around in the same spot."

"Let's see. Do not remove transmitter, whatever that is; no going around in circles or stopping. Got it. . . . Could I have another glass?"

"Right away, Mr. Mendoza."

She got up a little to serve him another chilled Calixto, and Mendoza, who was slightly drunk, could appreciate her svelte silhouette enclosed in the flexible scale dress.

"Are you game?" she said in a hoarse-sounding voice.

There was something sensual in her look. . . . Mendoza was about to reply with: *That could be taken several ways.* But he remembered that there were several thousand credits to go, and merely said, while the filing cabinet seemed to be looking at him and humming dully:

"Sure, Ms."

It seemed to him to be a big planet rotating slowly beneath a sky of dark blue velvet. It was completely covered by thick forests, and there was not one single sea on it; only the silvery ribbons of some rivers. . . . Then he found himself firmly seated on a concrete surface. . . . He came to realize that he had four thick legs of a steel-gray color ending in several round toenails of polished bone. . . . Strapped with belts to his back was a metal box, most certainly the transmitter, and in his hand, or whatever it was called, he held a bulky rifle of bright metal. . . .

The forest surrounded him on all sides, and in front of him was a door with a flashing blue arrow on the lintel, pointing to a wide path that ran through the forest. Making a decision that stemmed from a desire to earn money and from the drinks he had had, Mendoza, in his new form, entered the dense forest growth.

Five days later he came to understand only too well the reasons the customer paid five hundred credits a day. He slowly

walked through a jungle of vines and bushes, treading heavily
with his thick legs through chocolate-colored mud beneath
the blinding light from a white sun that looked like the
mouth on a reverberatory furnace. The smooth elephant skin
on the creature now had scratches in various places, as well
as a wide but shallow wound, that was continually festering
with a scarlet serum.

The unknown customers had found an effective system for
exploring a planet and recording, examining, and checking
out the diverse dangers that could exist thereon with a view
toward ultimately colonizing it. Not only had another creature, similar to him, that he had come across two days ago,
explained that to him, but also the situation turned out to
be as clear as the light from the white sun. With each new
problem, with each new difficulty overcome, the transmitter
strapped to his back clicked and crackled for several seconds.
It was obvious that it was sending highly detailed precise data
back to some far-off mysterious recording center.

At first he found well-defined paths including a small
building in which to rest for a while. He had not been sup-
plied with any food, which made it evident that he had to
live off the land by sampling fruits off the trees or flesh from
animals that he could kill. He ate some green-colored stalks
that were as thick as human arms and that turned out to be
tasty and nutritious; also some round blue fruit which in spite
of their delicious taste gave him a terrible stomachache with
resultant sickness. He killed something that looked like a
cardboard box with a wheel of eyes on its outside that oozed
a revolting greenish goo. . . . He dared not eat it until he
saw a creature like him gobble it up heartily without apparent ill effects.

Naturally, certain tricks were possible. Always eating al-
ready-proven fruits or food, or killing the animals that had
shown themselves to be harmless. But it could not always be
that way. Sometimes his thirst and hunger were so overwhelming (perhaps artificially stimulated) that he saw himself
forced to eat the first thing that came along, or to drink
water out of a muddy pond filled with small black slugs.
However, what consoled him was the fact that each day completed represented five hundred credits more. . . . Taking
into account that the salary of a qualified worker on Titan

was, on the average, ten credits a day, he did not have much room to complain.

Every now and then the image of Ms. Hollister came to mind. The odd thing was that she was in the form of a pachyderm-sized creature with four gray legs and seven breasts ending in green nipples . . . in spite of which she was still as attractive to him as before. Every so often he promised never to gamble again, not to lift another card, a die, no nothing.

The day before, the other elephantine creature that he had paired up with had died by being devoured by a huge flower that anyone would have thought harmless. After passing close to it, his companion had been completely engulfed in a stream of amber liquid shot out by the flower when it bunched up its white petals. . . . Mendoza had run off in order not to listen to the creature's agonizing moans and screams as it dissolved in a disgusting magma.

And now he went on his way through the dense growth, through an absolutely unexplored area in which there were no longer any paths or small buildings to rest in. He had been forced to spend his nights out in the open, no doubt threatened by a thousand unknown dangers . . .

At those times he had a voracious appetite and a thirst no less excruciating. But there were only some of those damned blue fruit things within his reach and not a single drop of water . . .

He stopped. He had just heard a snap in the underbrush, which his hearing, now accustomed to the sounds of the foliage, easily picked out as an animal on the move. He waited, his large-caliber rifle at the ready.

A blue and black lizard with six legs worthy of any spider was crossing the clearing in front of him. The rifle shot immediately felled it, and its six legs raced frantically. Mendoza shot again, this time aiming at the head, and the lizard, after a last tetanic convulsion, lay still.

Mendoza could not hold himself back and tore into the animal, cutting it up into quarters with a small hunting knife that was part of his equipment. Then he built a fire while the transmitter strapped to his back was endlessly clicking, and roasted some of the meatiest parts of the lizard.

Filled up and satisfied even though still racked by a burning thirst, he sat down by the trunk of a low, spread-out tree whose kilometer-long horizontal branches reached out in all directions with clusters of green living matter on them.

A light sleepiness overcame him, and as he knew perfectly well that rest was permitted, and there was nothing in the way to stop him from collecting his daily salary, he let it take him over. After a few moments, the deep feeling of uneasiness which had been nagging at him since he began working on this planet got stronger than the drowsiness and with a start it made him fully conscious again.

It was time. The extremely long branches of the low, spread-out tree were slowly curving down toward the ground and forming a kind of cage little by little surrounding him. He got up in a rush and ran ahead, trying to escape from that green cage. . . . It was useless since the branches had spaced themselves in such a way that when he tried to get between them he was trapped like a butterfly in a sticky, living green web. He fought and struggled, feeling on his rough skin the burns caused by the acid secreted by the plant; he even fired his rifle at the branches and trunk in order to try to kill that terrifying vegetable creature. But nothing happened. He was on the verge of giving up when he remembered the lighter that was part of his equipment; with effort, he took it out of his backpack and lit it, turning the flame up to maximum. Little by little he managed to get close to some of the green clusters with the long white flame . . . With a mushy crackling the branches were withdrawn . . . Suddenly he was free and he ran wildly through the jungle.

Later he came across a large body of intensely blue water and drank some of it, thus assuaging his agonizing thirst. It was now getting close to dusk and he had to find a place of refuge to protect himself from wild animals. He noticed, as he was walking, that there were no spoors of other creatures like him on the muddy ground he was going across; it was clear that he was the only one that had managed to get this far.

It was fully dark when he found a thick-topped tree with a big trunk of red wood which from past experience he knew to be neither harmful nor carnivorous. He climbed up it, again feeling hunger and thirst pains, and settled down in the fork of a wrinkled branch. Fortunately he had kept some roasted pieces of lizard meat. He took them out and immediately threw them down on the ground when he realized they had turned into a kind of yellowish, foul-smelling gook. He could barely get to sleep; he felt feverish and out of sorts. Undoubtedly the funny taste of the blue water indicated a high content of laxative salts because he kept waking up all night long; and at dawn he counted twelve bowel movements, each one more painful and distressing than the last.

He felt extraordinarily sick the next morning. Weak, out of sorts, and just about ready to fall on the ground. His thick legs hung heavily on him, and his thick skin, previously gray, had taken on a dark bluish hue, no doubt a sign of some infectious disease. The transmitter on his back was clicking and snapping away as if continuously relaying multitudinous bodily states he was experiencing. He kept on feeling thirsty, but he had completely lost his appetite.

At noon he was lost in a quicksand swamp, into which he only sank up to his waist, fortunately. But he had to trudge through it for hours on end, burning up with fever, and shooting every now and then at some strange-looking beast peeping at him from the banks along the mire. The white sun shone down from the sky with dazzling intensity to blind him and increase his thirst. . . . Night had again fallen when he managed to emerge from the swamp, and by luck he chanced upon a spring of crystal-clear water flowing from a hole in the rock. He drank without stopping for a good long while with very little concern about whether the liquid was dangerous or not. But it turned out to be safe since not only did he get better, but also he felt his fever going away. . . . The transmitter clicked a couple of times relaying the position of the spring and its chemical composition in the same way it had done before with the quicksand quagmire.

"A good setup at my expense, you bastards," he said aloud. "All right. All right."

Before trying to get to sleep, he came across a patch of those big green-colored asparagus plants that agreed with him so well. There was a slight difference with these; they had a type of yellow bulb on the end. In spite of that, he tried eating one, and it came back up on him between his screams. . . . The yellow bulbs had broken open and spilled a caustic liquid. . . .

He had completed his sixth day. He pressed the red button without giving it another thought.

Ms. Hollister gave him a sympathetic look. Mendoza's arms were covered with scratches, his skin was sunburned, and it was obvious that a wicked fever was wearing him down. He had a bad-smelling running sore on one of his legs, and his mouth, burned by the liquid from the green shoots, was unable to quench his thirst.

"Six days," she said, "at five hundred credits . . . three thousand credits. You now have a total of three thousand six hundred fifty credits, Mr. Mendoza."

"I'm thirsty . . ." he said. "No, no Calixto, please. Something for thirst. . . ."

"Litag beer . . . doesn't have alcohol in it."

A sparkling pitcher of litag beer, crowned with white foam, appeared on the table. Mendoza drank and drank in big gulps only stopping to catch his breath.

"Do you have any photoaspirins?"

"Yes, Mr. Mendoza. I do think you need a couple at least. Was it very bad?"

"The pits."

"Did you leave it?"

"No."

Now it was a matter of personal pride. That damned outfit was not going to get the better of him; he would collect what little money he had coming; then they could. . . .

For the first time Ms. Hollister got up and came over to him. She really had a fine figure, and wherever did he get the idea that she had green tits? That was one crazy idea he had had!

She certainly had a superb figure; long, slender legs, encased in black and gold mesh stockings, and unusually feminine feet in a pair of silver-white high-heeled pumps.

"You didn't leave it?"

"No."

She handed him two photoaspirins and as she sat down on the arm of the chair, she rubbed her warm body against him. The filing cabinet let out a lion roar.

"Shut your trap, Lorenzo. Don't raise a ruckus."

"What's with him?" Mendoza asked as the two pills started to take effect.

"He's jealous . . ." she said, lowering her silky eyelashes and blushing, "of . . . well, you know, Mr. Mendoza. He's my lover—"

"Well, I didn't. . . ."

"Oh yeah! He knows that I . . . uh . . . get excited when a man as virile as you accepts some . . . opportunities as dangerous as these."

"Well, hell, what things . . ." he managed to get out without really knowing what to say. He was greatly aroused by the warmth coming from Ms. Hollister's slim body, and it took a lot of effort for him to take his eyes off of her v-shaped neckline and the golden-toned flesh it laid bare, but credits were credits, by Titan, and as the old chestnut went: "Anything not a credit is a debit."

However, Lorenzo was growling in a low tone and resorting to every art of seduction at his command. He was constantly giving off sweet-smelling scents, such as from fresh-roasted turkeys, garnished with baked potatoes and cranberry sauce, steaming with the smell of spices . . . the taste of fresh cut-up strawberries, sweet and juicy watermelons cut open and showing their red pulp . . . ginger, oatmeal, honey, and sugar dough (in equal portions, beat carefully, and five minutes in a hot oven), a fragrant Caribbean-rum mint julep.

But it seemed that none of that could dissuade Ms. Hollister. Her ruby-red lips were barely open in a sensual gesture, and her sky-blue eyes were glued to the worn-out Mendoza.

Right away he had seen that she was a well-educated young woman from a good family. If not. . . .

"Well, Ms.," he said. "Please find me something easy and quick. So that I won't have to go around opening doors or wading through mud. . . . If there is something risky that will let me be still . . . that's what Mendoza would like. . . ."

"Yes, yes, sir," she answered in a voice sparkling with adoration. "Lorenzo, darling. Something between zero and five hundred. . . ."

Lorenzo, howling like a wounded beast, spat out a card.

"No, not that. Give me another one."

Lorenzo wailed as if he were being skinned alive; he belched, moaned, and changed shape until instead of a filing cabinet a cross between a toad and a confessional appeared. But he finally coughed up a new card.

"Here we go, Mr. Mendoza. . . . What's your first name?"

"Ivan."

"My name's so unusual I'd rather not tell you."

"Please tell me . . ."

"It's Garifalia. But when people get to know me, they call me Gay. . . . You can too if you want."

"OK, Gay. What do you have there?"

"Yep, something easy. I shouldn't be telling you this, but other people have tried it and they told me something . . . . You don't have to do anything. There are no restrictions . . . . It says here that if you want to wave flags in the morning, you can but it's not mandatory. Probabilities: one in four hundred twelve. . . . Payment: two thousand credits per diem. Will you take it, dear?"

"Yep."

His fever was still burning when he found himself on top of a crenellated wall. Beside him several humanlike creatures, except for a horny crest on their head and a cover of reddish fur, held out flags to the orange-colored sky, cheered, and shouted. Someone thrust a flag into his hands and for the moment, while it dawned on him what was going on, proceeded to move it up and down.

"No, not like that," said a creature beside him. "You have to wave it."

"But what is it?"

"Are you new here?"

"Right. I arrived just this instant."

"Well, then, take a look here. You have to shake it with vigor, with patriotism . . . from one side to the other to make the country's colors stretch out and flap in the air. You can also let loose with some rousing cheers."

"Like what?"

"Well . . . like . . . 'Long live Sffigornia!' 'Ever onward with the slaves of Nikrator!' as well as 'Hooray for the three thousand twelve!' "

For a while Mendoza came out with some rousing cheers and waved the flag a little. He was beginning to tire when the show seemed to come to an end.

As he was performing that senseless job, he looked over his surroundings. It was a crenellated wall, almost a hundred meters high, on the lower part of which distant processions of beings like him passed, accompanied by steam cars that belched black-looking as well as foul-smelling smoke that in spite of the distance still reached his nose. When it was the proper time, the processions started up, and the creatures on the wall, after leaving their flags in the niches provided, began going down the stone stairs.

Mendoza had already noticed that the walls surrounded a city, the size of which, even though he could not tell exactly, was not very large. But he did observe that the buildings, every one of stone, and quite old, spread out along circular streets around what must have been a central plaza, since he could not make out any other structure.

He went down the stairs, feeling increasingly worse, while the one who had handed him the flag walked beside him and helped him when he semed about to stagger.

"Don't you feel well?"

"No, I've got a temperature. . . ."

"Come on with me. I'll fix you up. . . ."

They walked down a dank side street paved with wide slabs of stone while the other creatures drifted off among the ancient buildings. With his eyes clouded by fever, Mendoza saw that the houses were of a terribly antiquated style such as might have existed only in some ancient cities on Earth. Most of them were built with ocher-colored stone, some with brick, and every last one of them had a steep roof covered with slate slabs or clay tiles overlaid with moss. Small steel balconies, cupolas, minarets, and belvederes with dusty windows stretched out in every direction. The façades had dark-wood beams and low arched doorways; stone arches abounded as well as balustrades of the same material . . . The whole city exuded a musty odor as if of inconceivable age.

His companion stopped at the door to a red-brick dwelling with stained-glass leadwork windows set in Gothic arches. Four tall brick chimneys reached toward the sky, and out of one of them drifted a thin trickle of smoke. . . .

"This is where I live," said his companion. "You can stay with me. I'm Stringiamor . . . and you're . . . ?"

Mendoza, feeling a large swollen tongue in his mouth, could not answer. He rapidly started losing consciousness, and he only remembered, as if through a mist, that his newfound friend had helped him down stairs with uneven steps built with red tile and well-worn edges of wood while he barely supported himself on a black-wood handrail dripping with humidity. Later it seemed to him that he was laid on a

soft made-up bed, covered with blankets, and a hand covered
with reddish fur brought a refreshing drink to his lips. . . .

The last thought he had was the distressing possibility that
he might lose the two thousand credits a day because of his
sickness. . . . Then, there were only endless reddish clouds,
headaches, fever, and discomfort. . . . And from time to
time, there was a red hand that gave him something to
drink, or that tried to get him to eat some sweetened
dish. . . . Ms. Hollister, with an eye-catching horny crest on
her head and covered with abundant red fur that made her
even more attractive, flashed in and out of his dreams. . . .

One day he finally woke up. He found he was unusually
weak but totally free of the fever. Beside him, on a small
hideous-looking wooden table with revolting carved figures,
that represented nude creatures devoid of fur and heads covered with skin instead of a horny crest as was normal, there
sat a green-crystal glass filled with clear water. He was not
too thirsty, but nonetheless he drank a little, and sat up in
bed. It was daytime, judging by the pale light coming through
the leadwork windows, and from far off came the sound of
cheers and shouting that went with flag waving.

He was in a spacious vaulted room with stone arches that
intersected on the ceiling to form a cusp from which hung a
wide rock rosette similar to a stalactite. His bed was wood
with thick down quilts with a fabric similar to damask, which
even provided him with a little heat.

He wanted to get up, but he slowly went back to sleep.

When he woke up, the creature called Stringiamor was sitting beside him, handing him a brass tray on which rested
something like a chicken thigh if such a chicken with two
talons that size existed. But the smell was as appetizing as life
itself, and the tall glass of milky-white liquor that came with
the meal screamed to be drunk. Without asking any questions, Mendoza ate and drank, and at last felt restored.

"How long have I been here?"

"A week," answered his host. And his words clearly had an
edge of fear to them.

"I suppose I've lost the per diem rate. . . ."

The other one did not answer. But after a few seconds of a
threatening look from Mendoza, he shook his head no.

"Do you mean to say that I have earned fourteen thousand
credits?"

"If that's what they're paying you . . . yes."

"How much are you getting, then?"

"Twenty-nine gold pieces at present rate, per day."

"Is that your usual rate?"

"Yep."

Mendoza got up, feeling strong as an ox, and proceeded to put on his clothes lying at the foot of the bed. For five good Earth minutes he stood on the marble-slab floor, staring with increasing intensity at Stringiamor, who seemed to grow smaller under his wilting look. Very slowly Mendoza's expression changed from distrust to menace . . . and finally, like a released spring, he grabbed Stringiamor by his shaggy neck.

"Look," he said in a voice as sharp as a razor. "Nobody gives nothing for nothing, you know. You're gonna tell me what's going on around here, and why you've been taking such good care of me . . . or I'll break your neck."

Stringiamor gurgled some choking sounds and waved his arms right and left trying to make it understood that he was choking, by the very Sffigornia, and if Mendoza did not let up on the pressure a little, he could not explain anything. Mendoza released him, but positioned himself between him and the door in case he tried to get away.

"Now out with it," he said. "What's this all about, and what's the danger?"

"This is Worm City," answered Stringiamor, drying the tears running from his large, translucent eyes. "I'm sorry, but I'm so afraid . . . I promise not to mislead you, but don't hurt me, blessed be the three thousand twelve. . . . Look . . . the terrible curse of the worm has been hanging over the kingdom of Haranaskar for exactly two thousand years . . . and the city we're in is its birthplace and home, oh, partner in pain and peril! I've been forced to do a stretch for a few days in this place of horror because in Haranaskar artists aren't appreciated as people say they are on other worlds in the galaxy. . . . Pardon me for saying so but I'm a creator of plastic writing . . . and I know that your chaste ears will just burn after hearing such an obscenity. . . ."

As Mendoza's ears were not bothered either a little or a lot, he told the sensitive Stringiamor to make it short.

"Whatever you say, generous companion. Nobody really

knows how the terrible worm came into the kingdom, nor why it exacts such a tribute—"

"What tribute?"

"A human life every night, respected friend and partner. In the middle of this miserable city very few travelers return from, it rests during the day, sleeping the sleep of centuries, the terrible Haranaskar worm . . . If it didn't get its nightly quota of human life, it'd burst out of the walls and devastate the kingdom. . . . That's why those guilty of dishonest crimes, like this very humble servant of yours, they send here, and people still say that they hire offworlders to live in this land of terror and subject themselves to being devoured by the worm. . . . That's the kind and gist of the problem, esteemed friend in need. . . . It's our fatal destiny to stay until our sentence runs out, or in your case, your contract, and to subject ourselves each night to being eaten up by that terrifying worm."

Mendoza felt a chill run up his hairy back.

"And how many are there of us here?"

"Some four hundred, my friend. Any fate, struggle, or stormy sea loaded with unlimited hardships is preferable to this silent vigil during the long Haranaskar nights, waiting for the worm to wake up from its eternal sleep and crawl ominously down the dank streets, stick its terrifying snout into a house, and gobble up the dweller."

Mendoza remained quiet for a few seconds.

"Yes, indeed," he said. "Then the rest is clear, damn you. When you saw that I was sick, you brought me here because if that disgusting worm ever came by . . . it'd have me for dinner first. . . ."

"That was my intention, my noble protector . . . but I beg you to forgive me and take into account my overwhelming terror and my meager strength. As a creator of plastic writing, I am a person of great sensitivity and great fear . . . and may my weakness excuse my egoism if it is within your limitless generosity to—"

"Shut up, damn you!"

And a bruising punch to Stringiamor's jaw emphasized Mendoza's remark. The creator fell into a heap on the floor without Mendoza paying any more attention to him.

"I can assure you," said the artist, holding his face with his hand, "that that horrible worm will not eat you. . . . You

can believe me. Others have fallen prey to its damned maws
. . . and I looked after you with the utmost care . . . I fed
you and waved flags in your name . . . forgive me, worthy
lord of the universe! Give me your protection and help! Your
strong muscles—"

"Where is this worm, you turkey?"

"In the middle of the city, an amazing creature from the
stars . . . but you're not gonna see it since one look at it will
produce such dread that beings stronger than you have come
back mindless. . . . And I thank you for that unusual name
you bestowed on me, a word I'm not familiar with but it no
doubt must be some sort of unparalleled praise on the planet
you come from, for which I. . . ."

Completely fed up, Mendoza lifted his right foot and
landed a tremendous kick on the head of the creator, who
howled and finally sprawled on the floor with thick waves of
lemon-colored blood flowing from a wound in his forehead.

For some minutes Mendoza explored the rooms occupied
by Stringiamor. His bed was located in the front room so that
if the famous worm tried to get into the dwelling, it would
find him first thing. The rest was taken up by a bedroom for
Stringiamor, and a well-stocked storeroom.

Leaving the motionless creature to his fate, Mendoza went
out to the street. It was the middle of the afternoon, and two
flesh-colored suns were inching toward the west among horizontal shafts of gray clouds. Some creatures were slowly passing through the neighborhood, gingerly stepping across the
moss-covered slabs. On an impulse he stopped one of them.

"Tell me something . . . why do you have to wave flags up
there on the wall?"

"Leave me alone, fourthborn of a mungle," the other creature replied, obviously scared. "I'm a terrible murderer and I
terrorize everybody! Leave me alone!"

"Either you answer me or I'll break your neck," Mendoza
responded, grabbing him by the throat. "Tell me why!"

"Hodo! Hodo!" the creature exclaimed, pulling a curved
knife from his clothing. "Nurd of a wurd! To show our joy at
the sacrifice to the worm . . . damned crub . . . Hodo! Get
away from me, arcaner! Resuch your aber, crub! Hodo! May
the Furies devour your bulls, quedate!"

Maybe the change had given him musculature quite superior
to what was normal since it was evident that the creature with

the curved knife and sharp tongue was very frightened. However, there was no reason to keep him any longer, therefore
he let him go.

"Get lost, crub," Mendoza said.

The winding streets led him little by little toward the center of the city. Several times he stopped to admire increasingly more sumptuous palaces that appeared before him.
Magnificently carved colonnades, the gigantic sweep of balconies and eaves, the noble structure of walls covered with long
stone ribs all hid nothing more than desolate emptiness
beneath that endless finery. Nobody dared live so close to the
terrifying worm. . . . It seemed very clear that everybody
tried to move to the outer areas, thus believing that they
could escape as far as possible from the dreaded nocturnal
visit.

"Hodo . . ." Mendoza exclaimed, very moved, when he
thought about it.

The streets ended in a wide circular plaza surrounded by a
stone balustrade. Nobody was around. Solitude was complete.
Slowly Mendoza got closer to the railing as he felt a chill,
and with a certain trepidation he peered over it.

He would have liked to cuss, but his voice failed him.
Some fifteen meters deep down in a circular hollow lay,
coiled in on itself, the horrifying Haranaskar worm. He tried
to no avail to find words or images to describe it. . . . Saying that it was made up of rings, that it was slimy, that it was
abominable . . . served no purpose. Only the mind-boggling
image that he had of it when he looked down upon it there,
really, as a living thing, was enough to make an impression
on his mind; he even got to the point of closing his eyes for a
few seconds to try to recall it, and when he opened them, he
merely imagined a pale shadow of that astonishing creature.
It was huge and it took up about two hundred meters of
space, and its body was about as thick as two. . . . In addition, it had all the evil and repugnance that the human mind
could conjure up; it was slimy, a revolting green color, it was
covered with yellowish bristles clustered on the top of dark-
red chitinous bumps which came out of its filthy back in twos
. . . it had insect claws and pincers in some spots, and also
delicate horns facing backward that quivered abhorrently
with every shudder made by the creature.

A gentle breeze of cool air caressed Mendoza's face as he

stood there immobilized by terror. The sky had turned a black violet, and diamonds in unknown constellations began to shine in that growing darkness . . . For a few seconds Mendoza stayed calm until an ominous noise wrenched him out of his lethargy . . . In the middle of the plaza the head of the Haranaskar worm slowly started to rise up toward the firmament. In horror Mendoza watched as on one end of the worm a vertical crack opened, then was bisected by a horizontal crack, thus forming an open mouth with four sharp-pointed lips, the inside of which he could not make out . . .

With a scream, Mendoza turned, and staggering, he ran madly down the same street he had come up. He did not meet anybody at all, and at the height of his fright a thought that froze the blood in his veins crossed his mind . . . Would that spawn of hell be able to follow a trail? Because if it could, his no doubt would be the freshest one of all.

Breathing hard, he reached Stringiamor's dwelling. The artist was still stretched out on the floor in the same spot where Mendoza had left him. The pool of lemon-colored blood had gotten bigger, and the poor creature had labored breathing. He hardly had time to see that his reddish fur, previously sleek and silky as a mink pelt, was now bristled up and stiff, a sure sign that Stringiamor was in agony . . . Feeling a cold sweat dripping down his hairy forehead, Mendoza grabbed the artist by the shoulders and laid him across the door. Then, with his heart pounding like a triphammer, he hid in Stringiamor's room, closed the door, and piled all the furniture he could in front of it.

He collapsed on the luxurious silk and pelt bed and tried to calm his heart. He almost had when a hissing sound coming from the street again set him off. He did not even try to look out of one of the windows; just the thought of again gazing upon that loathsome Haranaskar worm caused him such terror and nausea. . . . Trying not to make a sound, he headed toward Stringiamor's well-stocked larder and grabbed a bottle that seemed to hold liquor. . . . He took a swig; it was liquid lava and it did not pep him up, it just made him feel even more fearful.

A strong musky odor filtered through the walls while a dark curved shadow spread across the leadwork glass in the Gothic window. . . . Mendoza wailed, threw the bottle on the floor, and found himself, without knowing how, under the bed. . . .

"Nurd of a wurd . . ." he whispered in a faint voice. "Don't take me, you quedate!"

Blood-curdling sounds came from the adjoining room. Something terribly powerful was pushing things around, moving beds, knocking over chairs . . . and the smell of ants, bugs, and reptiles got stronger by the second to the point that Mendoza found himself heaving and throwing up the little food he had eaten.

Then there was just a moan, promptly cut off, and the sound of dragging. . . . Something fell booming down the stairs while something else, or other things, slithered down the street, scraping against the walls with spine-covered ribs.

At the height of terror, Mendoza lost consciousness.

When he woke up, it was bright daylight. Somewhat calm, he took down the pile of furniture he had put up against the door and opened it. The unfortunate Stringiamor's body was nowhere to be found, but a trace of sticky slime that uniformly covered the walls, the furniture, and the threshold of the front door told only too well what had carried him off.

He lost any desire he had to wave flags and cheer Sffigornia, whatever or whoever that was . . . He bided his time until the eighth day was up, and when the sky again started turning dark, he pushed the red button.

He immediately felt weighed down by a female body that was sitting on his knees. Ms. Hollister, exuding an overpowering perfume, had his face in her hands, and she was giving him a look that was enough to wither stone. Lorenzo, the filing cabinet, was hiding in a corner and letting out loose low-pitched moans and shedding some big scarlet tears.

"Oh, you're a dear!" she said. "What a great big marvelous man!"

And she kissed him. Mendoza, in a highly emotional state, let her do it, thinking that if she had not been an educated young woman from a good family, he would not have permitted it, obviously.

Finally she got up, blushing a lot and with her blue eyes shining at him like two first-magnitude stars. He could clearly see that she was aroused and in love and was ready to do anything for him. . . .

"Eight days," she said, "at two thousand credits . . . sixteen thousand credits which, added to your previous earnings, equals nineteen thousand six hundred fifty credits! Oh, Mr. Mendoza, oh, oh! How could you go through eight days that were *so* terrible? I'm *so* impressed! How did you do it?"

"It was simple, with a little courage, Ms. Hollister. . . . That's not hard for a real man, believe me."

"You now have everything you need, Mr. Mendoza. You'll be on your way . . . won't you?"

"Sure will be," he answered, eyeing the bundle of bills and coins that Ms. Hollister had deposited on the table. "And I will never again gamble, I have promised myself. After all . . . By the way, just out of curiosity . . . do you have anything more . . . difficult?"

"Do you mean . . . uh . . . better-paying opportunities?"

"Right. Just for the sake of curiosity, right now."

"Sure, certainly. . . . If you'd like, I'll show you one of the best. . . . Lorenzo, give me the two in one. . . ."

Lorenzo had a fit of crying and withdrew farther into the corner, having become a gray-colored ball, at one end of the room.

"He's still jealous, you know. I'll have to threaten him a bit. . . . Come on, Lorenzo! Give it to me! If you don't, I'll strip and surrender myself to this extraordinary man right here before your very eyes. . . ."

The wails with which the filing cabinet issued the new card would have moved a mountain.

"Probabilities: two in one. . . ."

"One chance of death for every two—"

"No, no, Mr. Mendoza. The opposite. Two chances of death for every one of life. . . . Restrictions: no moving around. Payment: fifty thousand credits!"

"Per day?"

"Per hour, per hour completed, that is, Mr. Mendoza."

Through his mind for a second passed a thousand thoughts that entirely erased the image of Ms. Hollister, disheveled and exuding desire everywhere. . . . Fifty thousand credits an hour! A fortune! The salary of a lifetime! No, he did not see the young blond woman with the provocatively open mouth, tongue rubbing ruby-red lips, eyes almost bulging out with arousal, the stacked body breathing hard and fast, wiggling, anxious to be taken by him. . . . He saw a stroke

of luck, a grand house on the main drag, a private
spaceship. . . .

"I'll take it," he said without giving it another thought.
"Go for broke."

"What?"

"I want to go . . . just for a single hour. . . ."

He found himself completely naked with his arms spread
on top of a high, steep mountain. His feet were resting on the
summit, which was just large enough to accommodate
them. . . . All around him the sides of the needle of rock
fell away precipitously into unfathomable chasms whose bottom he could not make out. Overcome by a frightening dizziness, he realized that on other needles of rock stretching to
the horizon were other human beings naked like him and
with their arms spread like his, and that hundreds of electri-
cal cables passed within a centimeter of their open fingers,
arms, body, legs, just as if a knife thrower had outlined their
figures. . . .

His brain and nerves continually throbbed from the uninterrupted instructions the bosses were issuing. . . . He realized he was being used as a living computer to control,
through his nervous system, the strength of the current passing through the hundreds of cables. He understood that they
carried terrifying amounts of voltage that could fry a human
body in a microsecond . . . just one part of his skin rubbing
against one of those copper cables would be enough to. . . .

Off in the distance one of the naked figures went up in a
sudden white flash of flame. . . .

Feeling sweat dripping down his forehead, Mendoza tried
not to move a muscle, nor even to look down at the dreadful
depths. But they seemed to attract him, to be tugging at him.

After eight minutes and thirty-two seconds his index finger
touched one of the thickest cables.

In the Titan office Ms. Hollister waited in vain while
Lorenzo chuckled sardonically in his corner. When a half
hour had gone by, the young woman, with a sigh, put the
nineteen thousand six hundred fifty credits in an envelope,
cast an indifferent glance at the chair Mendoza had been sitting in, and put the sum of money away.

The door opened.

Ms. Hollister disappeared immediately.

The newcomer, a fat woman, with heavy makeup, wearing a plume dress and arms loaded with bracelets, looked into the room in surprise. For a moment it seemed to her that no one was sitting in the luxurious armchair behind the ivory table; then she realized that a young black-haired man with seductive eyes was sitting there.

"Please come in," the young man said in a pleasant baritone voice. "Come on in and have a seat. . . ."

The woman took a seat in one of the easy chairs arranged in front of the ivory desk, staring intently with her blue-shadowed eyes at the good-looking young man.

"Well, look," she said in a somewhat hoarse voice. "I was told that easy money could be had here. . . . It's just that . . . you know. I messed up the other day. . . . I'm, well, I'm a *fille de joie*, you know, and a woman friend of mine talked me into servicing one of those Deneb octopuses. No need to worry, it can't give you anything, they don't have the same chromosomes, or more like . . . bullshit! I got pregnant because of him, you see, and they say to get this over with I have to go to Deneb, and it's expensive, you don't know how expensive! So that . . . are you certain you people have—"

"Opportunities. . . ."

"Whatever you call it. . . . I'm Krasga de Nar, you know."

"And I," he said with a captivating smile, "am Mr. Hollister. How about a drink, Ms. de Nar?"

FILL IN THE BLANK(S)
(Les Colmateurs)

MICHEL JEURY

Translated from the French
by Joe F. Randolph

With sails furled the *Dehekahar* was cruising under engine power. The four people on board had already crossed several hundred miles of the Indian Ocean. Jimenez was playing the role of captain. Barano was asleep in the tiny cabin. The black, Ney Varagan, was at the helm. And David, the only passenger aboard, was sitting up front scanning the horizon.

Ney Varagan stated that they were now getting close to Lohenwa, the mysterious isle.

Focus! Discard! Project! Fill in!

A mechanical voice recited the Four Commandments in David's head. And these words, so often heard, so often repeated, were the only link that the division head, David Nadun, had with reality.

Focus! Discard! Pro. . . . He had to make an effort to return to the boat he was on.

Focus! Dis . . .

The sea now showed its alarming blue-green depths. You might say that a sky filled with big scudding clouds was reflected under the water. But the sky above the small craft was clear, cloudless, and unmarred. Lohenwa was located, they said, at the extreme southern end of the Maldive archipelago. And as the *Dehekahar* steered toward the southwest, there was land dead ahead.

Lohenwa was barely a few hundred hectares of sand and rock, mainly birds and shellfish, with about a fifty-person leper colony and a handful of adventurers . . . Who would ever have dreamed of putting these seven letters down on a map in Jules Verne's day? To guide what travelers? But for the pirates in search of a base, the island was the perfect spot.

The *Dehekahar* tacked, always under the guidance of the black, Ney Varagan, as it entered an almost-invisible channel that a Terran would not have noticed . . . David could not make out either bank or channel and he never caught sight of Lohenwa that Ney Varagan and Jimenez were now searching for with troubled looks in the violet mist, with hands over their eyes.

"By Nemo!" Jimenez exclaimed. "You have to be a real shark to get to that bastard of an island. A real shark, ha, ha."

"There's something I don't understand," David began.

The two Spaniards glared at him. David preferred not saying anything, and he regretted the two hundred fifty araboes he had paid for the trip. Varagan was smiling mockingly.

"Let me off at the nearest Lion Hotel!" David said.

Barano, who had just stood up, was in a growling bad mood. He started getting the chain ready to drop anchor. Lohenwa had finally appeared, ringed by a pale mist, two or three cable lengths from the boat. Long afterwards, the black told David:

"About the hotel, buddy, all you have to do is ask Captain Komar. He's the hotelier on Lohenwa!"

David Nadun had found this weird trio thanks to a Gulf Union employee with whom he had become acquainted during a stay at the Ramaville ashram. Ahmed Gupta's description was accurate. From a distance in a Trivanderam bar he had recognized Juan Jimenez—heavy-set, bald, cool, and composed, ageless—then Pablo Barano—big, muscular, hirsute, bronze-skinned. . . . Lastly, the young black, Ney Varagan—thin, handsome, strong and smiling, his hands powerful, his face intelligent and cold. . . .

Were the three men equal partners? Jimenez sometimes gave the impression of ordering the other two around. Barano readily talked like a born leader; but most often the initiative seemed to come from Ney Varagan.

Jimenez had set the price of the voyage, food included, a

round trip, trusting in God (if He exists). Two hundred fifty
araboes, the price of a superjet ticket to Paris and two-thirds
of the fortune David Nadun now had.

But David wanted to see Lohenwa.

The mysterious island was tiny, sandy at the southern end,
on the shore where travelers disembarked, rocky to the west
and north in the leper colony. The island vegetation was neither beautiful nor lush. Some coconut palms, however, grew
on the central plateau, a spot about a kilometer in size. Fortunately, fish were found in abundance in coves, and the
coastline was a rich source of several species of shellfish.

Jimenez and Barano were into a very profitable trade, gun
running. The island must have served as their warehouse.
There had been some talk about the cargo ship that had just
unloaded its radiation rifles, lasers, and atomic grenades. . . .

Focus! Discard! Project! Fill in!

*With the tips of his tobacco-stained fingers, the head of the
projection division, David Nadun, drummed on his wrinkled,
feverish brow. He was not in a projecting mood. He was content with just following an old movid. However. . . .*

Movid: a highly sophisticated action show, done with a
psychord by using subliminal suggestion on the viewer, who
generally gets the impression of being among and around
the characters in the story and more or less taking part in the
action.

Some psychiatrists accused movids of being at the root of
schizoid or hallucinatory-type mental problems.

And some geoprogrammers were of the opinion that movids might be at the root of the slight breaches through which
light or enticing elements had begun filtering into the real
present toward the end of the twenty-fourth century.

The Mysterious Island was an adventure movid, like the
hundred or more others David had seen on the *Ring*, at the
archives, or at Geosouth Base 5. Once again the projection
mechanism had worked to a tee. David no longer found himself ensconced in the comfort of his inflatable chair but in a
regular dreamworld with heroes in a story cast against the
background of an earlier century, all done by creative technicians under the supervision of a less-than-original specialized
computer.

David Nadun walked across the white sand on the island,

accompanied by an anxious trio of gun runners. He was now asking Ney Varagan about life on Lohenwa. But Jimenez butted in.

"Yeah, buddy, you can live here with some lepers and Captain Komar!"

"Did you say Komar . . . not Nemo?"

"May the Virgin bless me!" exclaimed Jimenez. "It's Komar for sure. Komar the Dark. . . ."

For the first time since David had met him, the black started laughing at the top of his voice, his eyes bulging.

"But I'm darker than the Dark," he roared.

By Nemo! David mused, this does not jibe with Jules Verne no matter if screened and edited by some movid maker!

Focus! Discard! Project! Fill in!

Focus! Discard! The division head, David Nadun, focused and discarded the images invading him, but only existing in his mind, and he found himself back in his chair.

He rubbed his eyes and got his memory back together. He suspected that the Lohenwa lepers were in reality (in reality?) victims of a mysterious war who were suffering from radiation sickness. . . . But hadn't he figured out the role of Captain Komar, Komar the Dark?

Whatever the danger, he had to dive in again so that he could make his report to the geoprogrammer, Jonathan Groomb.

The house the adventurers lived in was located a hundred paces from the shore. It was the old skeleton of a ship with no masts, half buried in the sand and surrounded by a wooden fence. Carlos, a huge watchdog with drooping lips, greeted the travelers with affectionate, rough-sounding growls. Jimenez asked the dog in a grating voice if he had eaten his food. The Spaniard asked his question by moving his jaws in imitation of chewing.

"He ain't even touched his dried fish!" Jimenez yelled. "Look at that fat slob! You've been putting it away over at Captain Komar's, huh? Eating off the man!"

"Does Captain Komar give human food to your dog?" David asked. "Where does he put it?"

"We're not short on human food here!" Barano said.

"Who's Komar?"

"A crazy who was taken in by the master of Lohenwa!"
Varagan said.

"May the Virgin forgive me!" Jimenez said. "He's not a
crazy, and I'm sorry I said it."

"I'd like to meet him," David said.

Then he immediately thought—DANGER!

Focus! Discard! Project! Fill in!

A touch on the armrest stopped the projection. At the
same time he instinctively applied the Four Commandments.
Light flooded the inside of the movisphere and slowly went
out. David *focused* on the dark spot that came after the flash
of light. He *discarded* some lingering images. He *projected*
the neutral setting of a room in Geosouth Base 5, and in vain
searched for a blank to *fill in.* . . . Any gap. . . . It was almost a crying shame.

He regained consciousness little by little. He, David
Nadun, was the division head, and he had just been viewing
some excerpts from an adventure movid, based on one of
Jules Verne's novels, *The Mysterious Island.* A movid considered very suspect by the analysts, therefore their investigation. And analysts were not wrong!

This particular movid had no doubt been *invaded.* Following it to conclusion would have been dangerous. Even for
him, an experienced projector. Maybe what was needed was
to order all the existing copies destroyed. Or all those that
could be found. . . . That is what was needed no doubt, but
David was sure it would not do any good. For one hole
plugged up here, two or six opened up somewhere else, in
space or time or whatever else. He glanced at his watch. He
was to meet Groomb, the geoprogrammer, in just an hour.
He allowed himself a moment of thought.

He had read all of Verne's original works. Or almost.

The books could hardly be tampered with. At least for the
moment, David thought. There was nothing to indicate that
some obscure novel hidden away at the bottom of some forgotten library was not being breached. . . . Jules Verne's
work seemed to be a preferred way for *light elements* to filter
through, above all because of the numerous movids that had
been adapted from his novels during the second quarter of
the last century on the anniversary of his birth five hundred
years before. In fact, he was the one most often adapted but
very freely and highly modernized.

The Lohenwa in the movid had nothing to do with Jules Verne's mysterious island. But it would be purposeless to compare the plot of the novel to the film version. He would have to have the movid script. The *Ring* archives might be able to find it. Anyway, that was an analyst's job, not a projector's. And David did not need the script to feel that this *Mysterious Island* had been completely invaded.

On the door a flashing sign said: *John Grant, Geoprogrammer.* John Grant? A name a little too Jules Verneish. And the geoprogrammer David had to see was named Groomb. . . . Good God!

Focus! Discard! Project! Fill in!

Even here, in the very heart of the impenetrable Geosouth Base 5. . . . After twenty years of practice, the art of projecting was entirely instinctive to David. He focused on the tampered-with sign. He discarded the name John Grant. In its place he projected *Jonathan Groomb.* He carefully filled in the fuzzy blank left in the surrounding scenery, the hallway, the door. . . . The door opened in front of him. The process had not lasted more than a second. Quick action was the secret of filling in the blank(s). That is what he told his students over and over again. Six seconds to zero in on a mirage, to pursue it, to put in its place the real image, and to close the breach? Yes, indeed, that was six seconds too long.

Deep down inside of him, he no longer believed like that, but young people did not need to know that. Focus, discard, project, and fill in, my children, that's life. . . .

"I've just heard your coded report," Jonathan Groomb said. "Does it seem that we're really up against a new form of invasion, Nadun?"

"In short, ultralight elements?" David suggested.

"And strongly enticing. . . ."

The geoprogrammer was a stout man with a square face and a heavy black beard. He was rarely seen to smile, but a geoprogrammer does not smile. Nor a division head either, for that matter.

David sat down, and Groomb looked at his fingernails as if afraid of seeing them turn into cat claws or deer hooves.

"So, there's no doubt?"

"None whatsoever," David said. "I don't know where this movid came from, but it has holes in it like a sieve."

"An investigation is under way to find out where it came from."

"Is there a copy in the archives?"

"Yep."

"Do the analysts want to go over all of it?"

"What do you think, Nadun?"

"There are risks. Analysts are not projectors even if they do have good theoretical training. If it were me, I'd destroy the copy we have here. Although it would be somewhat of a pity."

"Why a pity?"

"I'm a bit intrigued with this island of Lohenwa. I'd love to know who exactly Captain Komar is."

"We can't destroy an invaded vector without studying it first."

"I know. The general geoprogrammer is convinced that the breaches are the result of a concerted action by some mysterious enemies. He wants all the invaded vectors analyzed thoroughly in the hopes of identifying the adversary."

"All right. What do you think about it?"

"You know what I think, Mr. Groomb. It's no secret. I believe the invasion is due to a large-scale psychosociological imbalance. Or, if you will, it's a phenomenon caused by pollution in the Earth's infosphere!"

"You told me. But if your idea is examined a little closely, it means that we're all crazy. That's the drawback."

"I don't agree. I'd rather compare the invasion to a fever. Fever is an attempt by an organism to combat the disease. The infosphere's sick. It's struggling with the invasion."

"That's hardly an orthodox viewpoint. But you're an excellent projector and. . . . Oh, and another thing, Nadun. I have some bad news for you."

David closed his eyes. Then he opened them and looked at Groomb with a sarcastic expression. *Focus! Discard! Project! Fill in!* For one or two seconds he toyed with the idea of treating his superior as a mirage. He projected himself into his place. But he could not close a reverse breach. Reality came back full speed. Even so, it was a partial success.

"I see," he said. "My training in geoprogramming has seen better days. Once more. The last time, since I won't ask anything else.

"Will you recant? That is probably the best thing to do. I

repeat what I've always told you. You're a top-notch projector and one of the best division heads I have ever known. But you're a man of action. You're not an idea man or an organizer. I don't see you—"

David stood up.

"Our meeting is over, sir. I won't bother you any more with it."

"I just might have an interesting job for you pretty soon."

Before leaving, David turned around.

"I must admit that I'm very pessimistic about the future."

He found himself standing in front of the door to his apartment without being conscious of a change of floors. Geosouth Base 5 had twenty-six levels. It was a manmade island floating in the Atlantic between Africa and South America. . . . The light flashed on when he entered his graywalled living quarters and lit up the dubious antique furniture which Maria had chosen and he hated. The couch was in poor shape, and the fabric hung like rags over the worn and dirty red carpet.

"What did I accomplish?" he asked out loud. "Have I been hit on the head, was I on a drunk, or what?"

Then he remembered. The invaded movid. After being present at the viewing of a contaminated medium, there was always some disorientation for a few hours. The phenomenon showed up during crises occurring at a viewing which were not without risks. . . .

Maria was not there and she had not left any message. He popped a normostat pill with half a glass of tap water that tasted like brine. Maybe a desalinization plant was out of commission. Or it was a new type of invasion. He roamed around for a moment aimlessly in the two rooms where a suffocating heat prevailed. If he had been a geoprogrammer, he would have had six, or eight, or ten rooms. But geoprogrammers belonged to the planetary ruling class. There was a gap between their caste and the projector class.

David Nadun knew that his career was at its height. He would never have a six-room apartment at Geosouth Base 5. But. . . . Oh, well, he could always be offered a breach!

He rummaged around in his library hoping to come across a book by Jules Verne. He had to have one or two. Impossible to put his hands on. Anyway, it did not matter. Jules

Verne did not have anything to do with the invasion. He was just a man with imagination among so many others.

The telephone rang. He answered it grumpily.

"Ney Varagan?" the caller asked. He had a harsh voice and strange accent.

"Which Varagan?" the division head inquired.

"Are you Ney Varagan, the pilot?"

"Nope. Varagan is black," he said. "It happens that I'm white. And not prouder because of it."

"You want to clown around or are you trying to make a fool out of me?" the unknown caller grumbled and then hung up.

David shrugged. Phone breaches were hardly considered dangerous; they were also very hard to fill in. He decided to let the matter drop.

He automatically looked down at his hands. They were black! Focus! Dis . . . No. This was the time to open up a breach in geoprogrammer Groomb's health! He ran to look at himself in the bathroom mirror. He was a young black, big, slender, muscular—and handsome, unbelievably so. Ney Varagan. . . .

He would have been able to discard the image and put in its place his pale, forty-year-old picture with its haggard features and puffed-up eyes about a second sooner. Plus a second to fill in the background scene. Easy. But for what purpose? For a few seconds or a few minutes he accepted the fact of being Ney Varagan.

A serious professional error. Refusal to fill in by a high-ranking projector; that was one way to spend the rest of his days going around in subjective circles. But time would tell. . . .

The light went out. David ran into a hard object and lost his balance. The light came back on. He got back up rubbing his sore knee. Maria was standing in front of him, nude, her hair let down, her breasts erect; she was alluring, yet mocking.

"What's with you, David dear? You're talking up a storm in your sleep! Are you becoming a sleepwalker or something?"

"But I wasn't asleep!"

"You're *very* tired out, aren't you, dear?"

"Yep, I am tired," David conceded. "I'm a bit discouraged too."

"Is it your training course?"

"Try to get used to the idea that I'll never be a geoprogrammer."

"Oh!"

He fell flat on his face on the bed and hid his face in the pillow. Something warm and sticky touched his hand hanging down. He turned over with a howl.

"A dog! What the hell is a mangy mutt doing in here?"

Huh, a dog in an apartment on Standard Island? Standard Island . . . no . . . I'm confusing it with a Jules Verne scene!

Focus! Discard! Project! Fill in! It was a breach. . . . The dog refused to disappear. Something was not working. By Nemo!

"I'm the one who brought it!" Maria said in a thoughtful tone of voice.

"How? Where'd you find it? What. . . ?"

No, it was impossible. Governor Bikerstaff did not allow animals on Standard Island . . . on Geosouth Base 5! Had Maria also been invaded?

David burst out laughing.

"It's not a house dog, by Enoch!"

Carlos was a big rawboned watchdog with a skittish look, a drooping ear, and eczema plaques on its back. . . .

"He stinks, dear. He stinks like a pig. Put him over there by the door since he obeys you!"

The dog seemed to understand; it went over and lay down under a piece of furniture, an antique sideboard. An object that should have been plainly visible crashed down on the floor. Then another one from higher up. David thought about guns with a look of bitter hatred. But he did not attempt to discard the scene nor fill in the setting.

The breach was filling itself in, as the projectors said in their argot.

"Good God, where's that stuff coming from?"

The stench coming from Carlos was turning his stomach. *I'm gonna be sick,* he thought. A division head who pukes because of a noisome blank. . . . Just the thing to laugh at all the way to Geonorth Base 11!

The telephone rang. Watch it, David Nadun, you only have two seconds. . . . Focus! Discard! Project! Fill in!

There was a double link between the dog and the guns. Lohenwa, to begin with. Carlos and the gun running; then a semantic connection in the old expression "gun dog." Focused, buddy. And now, damn! The animal and the guns disappeared simultaneously. Mentally David blocked out the breach effortlessly by pressing the comset button.

The ship helix, symbol of the governor, geoprogrammer of the first rank, Jack Simcoe, appeared on the screen. The man's face remained hidden in dark-blue shadow.

"This is the governor, Nadun."

"At your service, sir."

"It seems that we've been invaded. What do you think? Is it serious?"

"Is your name Simcoe, governor?"

"What? My name? Of course my name's Jack Simcoe! I—"

The screen went blank. David recalled that the governor's name was in reality Adam Reith. By Nemo! We've been invaded. . . .

The screen lit up again. The governor appeared, his eyes blinking, his forehead wrinkled. He stroked his blond beard and said:

"Very well, Nadun. Everybody knows that my name's Kiku Abendsen. There are breaches all over the place. That's why I'm mobilizing you. What are we going to do?"

"I at least know a source of contamination," David said. "No matter what the general geoprogrammer thinks, the crystal copies of a movid entitled *The Mysterious Island* should be destroyed immediately by laser!"

"Jules Verne again!"

"A version of Jules Verne that the author would certainly not recognize."

The most messed-up movid I have ever seen!

"Thanks," the governor said. "What you suggested will be carried out. No matter what the general geoprogrammer thinks. After all, it's a matter of our security. I'll be waiting for you in a quarter of an hour on level 23, station 1!"

Kiku Abendsen or Adam Reith or Jack Simcoe, commander of base 5, whatever his name was, broke the connection, and David rushed to his kitchen-unit bar to pour himself a glass of kakelune.

He was offered the luxury of playing two parts. In one he was division head Nadun, the uncompromising projector who did not hesitate when it came to asking for the destruction of contaminated material despite official orders. In the other he was the disillusioned veteran who made his own breach and took pleasure in putting himself in the skin of a young black, playboy, and adventurer.

But there was something worse. From now on, the vector was no longer the movid; it was David himself. The majority of theoreticians denied the phenomenon since they could not explain it. David had come to the certainty that the human brain could be used as a vector as well as any other electronic, magnetic, or crystalline medium. It would be better for him if the base authorities were not aware of the danger he represented. The general geoprogrammer would have fewer scruples about turning a laser on a pesty projector than a century-old movid!

Maria was sound asleep. An ordinary enough condition to be in after an invasion, especially after the first time. David got dressed, took his projector gun, and left.

It was October 26, 2426 by the calendar if you could trust it. The invasion that night was an isolated incident. The faulty movid had been disposed of by laser. The name of the governor of Geosouth Base 5, Paul Haderach, had been posted all over the place in order to foil any new attempt at mental invasion.

They had been informed officially about the loss of Geosouth Base 1. The projectors had for a long time known that that island, invaded in 2417, was rotten to the core and no doubt unrecoverable. David had taken part in two assaults in 2418; in 2425 he had conducted a reconnaissance operation to no avail. They wondered how the base, or whatever remained of it, could still be afloat. And also why the general geoprogrammer did not have it sunk by the satellites.

When David arrived at his training class on floor 14, it was the main subject of conversation among the students. He came to the conclusion that the young people had no knowledge of the night invasion. In addition, new information on the subject of former base 1 had come in, and he himself was still not privy to it. They had managed to bring

the island close to the coast in geoprogrammed sector 944,
and it had run aground in shallow water. Starting then,
speculation was rampant. The students, some fifteen boys and
a dozen girls, surrounded the division head and besieged him
with questions.

*"What do you think, sir? Is it going to be destroyed? No, if
they wanted it destroyed, it wouldn't have been run aground
along the coast. . . . Do you think they'll try another assault? If so, would you take part, sir? And what about us?
What about us? If they want volunteers, would we have a
chance? What. . . ."*

The golden tunic of a geoprogrammer appeared at the
door to the room.

"Focus!" David yelled.

"Discard!" the students continued in unison with the usual
right-arm gesture. David noticed a girl who had discarded
with her left arm, and he wondered if that mistake was entirely unintentional.

"Project!" geoprogrammer Jonathan Groomb said softly.
The students stressed the Fourth Commandment by clapping
their hands in beautiful harmony.

"I've come to tell you not to attach any importance to the
rumors about an invasion going around. . . ."

Jonathan Groomb watched the raw recruits without expression and added:

"My friends, there is not one unprepared person on this
base! Any hint about anything like that can net the perpetra-
tor an hour of subjective punishment!"

"Having your mind tapped?" a girl asked.

The geoprogrammer searched the student's eyes.

"Having your mind tapped," he confirmed. "And if it happens to you, I'll be there with pleasure."

This witty badinage provoked an outburst of general laughter, and the tense atmosphere relaxed.

"I'm personally doing my best to round up volunteers in
case base 1 is to be assaulted," Groomb said. "It could be
that a certain number of students would be part of the assault
force. Who here would *not* volunteer?"

Only the girl who had already sparred with the geoprogrammer raised her hand.

"Very well, miss. You can clear out right now. By the way,

let me point out to you that sector 944 is crammed with food and desalinization plants. You'll be left along the way!"

He turned to David.

"While we're on the subject, my appeal also goes out to veterans, even division heads!"

"At your service, geoprogrammer!" David said while going into a First-Commandment mode.

After this incident, it was no longer a matter of giving a normal lecture. David ensconced himself in the midst of the students and started thumbing through handwritten notes. Writing was considered the medium the least susceptible to invasion. On the other hand, it was never a direct vector. . . . The division head smoked a lot. When he lit up his third Shumway of the session, the students were so bold as to imitate him. The room was soon immersed in smoke conducive to images. But no breach appeared.

David recounted some of his projection experiences. He answered a certain number of questions. The line of questions tended toward a history of invasion and projecting. David recalled that the first heavy elements started infiltrating at the beginning of the last century. A full-strength German panzer division right out of the middle of the twentieth century had appeared in the area of the cape. But according to certain historians, invasion and breach phenomena started much earlier, since the birth of the planetary infosphere, so to speak.

The infosphere was created during and after the Second World War (1939–1945) because of the massive use of radio. Then TV starting broadcasting. The world entered the era of mass communication, mass media . . . and unidentified flying objects! UFOs were no doubt the first invaders of the terrestrial infosphere. Where they came from was a mystery; they belonged more to present-day light elements, the make-believe right out of the movids or from some other source, than the heavy elements, the historical ebb from the last century. The heavy elements were not enticers—the German panzer divisions, the Japanese battleships, the Warsaw Pact armor, SAC airborne squadrons all did not deceive anyone. No one took them for real except for a practical joker or some schizophrenic who had greeted General Sepp Dietrich at his place. . . . In the twentieth century witnesses had had contact with little green or blue men from flying saucers; some honestly told stories of being taken away or being attacked; tracks left by the invading craft were noticed. . . .

"That's what we today call *deterioration*," David explained. "The light elements, quite penetrating, filtered into reality, starting with what are called vectors, and they sometimes left lasting traces of their invasion on beings and things . . . These days, new-type breaches are cropping up. They're most often produced by Jules-Verne-type vectors, in particular the five-hundred-year anniversary movids turned out in 2325–2330. They're very heavy on pure make-believe, which has nothing much to do with Jules Verne, and the enticing draw of these elements is considerable. It also seems that certain light elements show some resistance to being filled in. I therefore wonder if they aren't ready for a change in their invasion MO just simply because of our action. If you compare the breaches that appear during our time in the infosphere with the big invasions of the past, the surprising thing is the consistency of the latter as opposed to present-day inconsistency. For example, the big wave of UFOs during the period 1980–1990 was a phenomenon as widespread, as important as the present-day invasion of make-believe. But at that time filling in did not exist. Flying saucers and extraterrestrials of every breed could then appear without being suppressed. Therefore the similarity of sightings. Now, the invading elements are continuously being pursued all over the place. In order to penetrate an infosphere as protected as ours, they are in some way compelled to change their form, appearance, and vector constantly. The invasion is an increasingly complex and subtle phenomenon. . . ."

"You talked about UFOs," a student interrupted, "and you said that the infosphere did not exist before the middle of the twentieth century. But what about ghosts, obsessions, all the things that showed up since the beginning of time, aren't they also breaches, invasions, disturbances in the infosphere?"

"You're right," replied David, who was in an agreeable mood. "The modern infosphere effectively started in the twentieth century with the mass media, above all with TV and data processing. But, in a broader sense, the infosphere can be thought of as a psychic veneer overlaying the biosphere. During the first two millennia of our era, there existed a religion-oriented infosphere that was invaded by ghosts and other phenomena of that type. You might say that exorcists were the forerunners of projectors. Their methods hardly seem rational, but they perhaps had a certain amount of effectiveness in a religious infosphere!"

David thoughtfully looked at his watch. The end of the training period had arrived, and it was even a little past it. He did not have the courage to recite the Four Commandments that ritually ended each session. Those words he had been saying with conviction for twenty years, the method he had applied many times without hesitation, all at once seemed to him devoid of sense, out of date, and bad.

The girl who had sparred with the geoprogrammer and who had refused to volunteer for duty in sector 944 raised her hand. David smiled at her as he waited for her question with a certain feeling of pleasure and not a bit of anxiety.

"All of you projectors, geoprogrammers, and I don't know who else," she said, "you people act as if you're the angels of goodness whose job it is to get rid of the wickedness invading our world. *Vade retro, Satanas?* That's what the exorcists used to say, your forerunners, right? And what would happen if the suppression was stopped? I mean if the forces and images trying to penetrate our world were not held back?"

That was a question that David often pondered. A question that was being asked more and more often, especially after last night. What would happen if the projectors went on strike and let the make-believe worlds invade all of reality?

Would it be utopia or death?

In any event, the planet would not stop turning!

"Take a walk through sector 944," he said. "You might be able to see Jules Verne's heroes demolish the desalinization plants . . . although it may not be their thing!"

The troops of the 77th Division of Marine Projectors stuck to the edge of a tropical forest, deployed in two or three confused lines.

"By Nemo!" said the platoon leader to the right of David.

Impossible to recall his name. . . . Idiot, you never knew it! You don't know anybody's name around here. Are you even no longer sure of your own name, division head David Nadun? Provided that it lasts!

The sector seemed unusually quiet, without one iota of decay. David knew that you couldn't count on it, but. . . . He slipped the heavy triple-action DPF rifle off his shoulder, the rifle he was carrying when he joined the troop. He was not in the habit of dragging around equipment that weighed this much. DPFs were designed to discard-project-fill-in important breaches. They were equipped with a device that synchronized the firing among several dozen or several hundred shooters.

The diminutive officer took off his helmet, then his glasses. This equipment, linked to a computer, was useful in applying the First Commandment. . . . David considered the effectiveness of this equipment, triple-action rifle, helmet, and all the rest, extremely doubtful. It might be suitable for use against the heavy elements. But an invasion by the light elements was much too subtle, individualized, and interiorized for the heavy equipment to be used. Evidently, all this rigmarole reassured the soldiers.

The platoon leaders were running in all directions, noses in the air, looking for the breach. Some had reached the beach and floundered around in the water with silly looks and mirthful gestures. The officer frowned and brought up to his mouth a small megaphone he had concealed in his palm.

"Listen up, platoon! Focus! Discard! Project! Fill in!"

The soldiers obeyed the Four Commandments mechanically, took up their positions one after another, brandishing their triple-action rifles with less than enthusiasm. The routine. . . .

"What exactly is going on?" a slightly faltering feminine voice asked.

"Oh, there you are!"

David smiled at Loryn, the young student from base 5 who ended up by volunteering for the sector 944 mission and who was there not by chance at all.

"Nothing," he said. "For the time being nothing's happening. We're getting closer to the objective while waiting for the enemy to show himself. If he exists, that is!"

"If he exists!" said the platoon leader indignantly.

Loryn put her hands up to the bottom of her helmet to take it off. There was no chin strap to hold it on, but a magnetic lock. The officer got closer to help her. A soldier began laughing as he tramped across the sand.

"Keep your helmets on!" David said.

It was only meant to annoy the platoon leader, and he knew it.

"Just one minute," Loryn pleaded. "I feel as if I'm on vacation!"

David raised his eyes. The sea and sky resembled two huge mirrors reflecting the image of one on the other. Tiny sailing vessels could be seen sailing way above the horizon and ungainly birds swimming with big wing strokes under curling waves. Was that normal? Focus! Dis . . . Aw, ignore it. Time will tell.

He adjusted his glasses to look at the sun, that was almost at its zenith and was sending down on beach 944 31D a flood of vertical light and an almost-electric warmth. But when he raised his head, as much as the space in his helmet permitted, the scene changed. The sky became dull and the sun, a large pale disc, an enormous ball pasted on smooth space, was steadily slipping toward the horizon as its rays came down obliquely and covered the sea with small, dancing golden flames. . .

A breach. Project! Fill. . . . No! David summoned all his strength to resist his instinct. He looked at Loryn, who had fallen on the sand, her long legs and arms crossed. The men were watching her too. By Nemo! She was wearing a pair of pants much too tight-fitting to be regulation. . . . But David was especially thinking about what she had told him at base 5. "If the forces and images trying to penetrate our world were not held back. . . ."

Well, what would happen? But why did the platoon leader not realize that the countryside had been invaded? Oh, that idiot had taken his helmet off. And then if I, his superior, am the vector and some distance away, he cannot be suspicious. . . .

David took his field miniord out of the chest pocket on his shirt and punched up a map of the sector on the screen. He turned to the young officer.

"Overlieutenant, I see that you have everything under control here. So we're going to leave. I'll continue with my inspection over toward the west."

"As you wish, sir. Your platform—"

"No. The student and I will go on foot. On a platform, even flying very slowly, we could fly into a breach and be swallowed up before we knew what hit us."

"I understand," the overlieutenant said.

Much too long to be regulation, Loryn's Titian-red hair

flowed down her back, over a very fancy green shirt. Officer and soldiers alike would love to start out on an inspection tour with a student like that, either on foot or platform. For the briefest second the overlieutenant gazed at her pointed breasts that the shirt hardly hid, then he looked below her belt visibly searching for the breach. . . . David shouldered his triple-action rifle.

"Come on! We're going!"

"Focus!" the overlieutenant cried. David replied, "Discard!" in unison with the soldiers. Smiling, Loryn had the last word.

The division head and the student headed toward the west along the beach, toward subsector 944 32A, where ex-base 1 was temporarily grounded.

"Put on your helmet!" David ordered Loryn.

"Are you trying to make a fool of me?" the girl said. "Watch it!"

The platoon of marine projectors occupying the terrain between subsector 31D and 32A seemed to be as unmilitary as possible. The men had all taken off their helmets; many had peeled off their shirts or their uniform jackets; some had stripped down to their skivvies, two or three had completely stripped down. . . . They were coming and going all along the length of the beach, running down the shore or swimming clumsily near it. Several were roaming along the edge of the forest, bamboo and coconut palms or some such things. And their abandoned triple-action rifles littered the ground.

"You see?" Loryn said. "What do you really care about what goes on around here, David?"

"As you know, two hours ago I was promoted to division head, special rank. Furthermore, it's because of the promotion that you're with me. At the same time I became inspector general of the marine projectors. And here we are, you and I, on an inspection tour!"

"I like this well enough," the young student agreed.

David looked at the forest more closely and found it strange. The first trees looked normal; some species of coconut palms with thick jungle beneath. But beyond them rose increasingly higher clumps of shade pines, eucalyptus, fir, and sequoia. While he admitted that such a mixture was possible, it hardly corresponded to sector 944. They must have started invading the forest too. . . . We are right in the middle of a breach! And these idiots who think they're on vacation. . . . Oh, they are right after all.

"Loryn," he said, "what if we stop and make love. To me the occasion seems—"

"Well, I suppose it's a rule of the game," the student said.

"No," David said. "It isn't. But I wish it were."

"I agree."

The girl threw her helmet off and with one hand on hip and the other like a visor over her eyes she looked over the countryside and the people there with a critical eye.

"The forest or the sea?"

"It's up to you. This forest doesn't do a thing for me. But at the edge of the sea we would have a lot of onlookers. . . ."

"Why not here? A hole could be made in the sand, and let the invasion come!"

David and Loryn were walking along the beach. They kept heading west, and they were out of sight of the projector troops. Not another soul around. They were alone with the birds, crabs, and worms. Big pink worms that burrowed through the pink sand. . . . Pink-colored beams of light drifted on the pale beige sea, over and under a huge salmon-colored sun. Murky white and yellow clouds colored the sky a milky shade.

A small pink bird landed on the ground, its wings half spread. A worm tried to catch it while standing up but it missed and fell down, hissing violently. The bird landed by the water and started drinking—not the water itself, but a pink-looking liquid, somewhat viscous, that oozed from the sand in thin streams.

An invasion in pink. Even Loryn's uniform had taken on that hue. Love had now become the invasion vector. David and his young companion had willingly let themselves be influenced. The breach was open right up to the horizon. . . .

Too beautiful to be true? Too beautiful to last, in any event. The sky was melting like grease. The horizon was coming to pieces. Space was cracking.

On the ground crabs and worms were increasing in number. They were becoming increasingly nasty and aggressive.

The pink-looking liquid oozing out of the sand was turning stickier and more foul-smelling.

David and Loryn walked slowly. Their bare feet—bare?—made a path that was filled in by the pink-looking liquid seething with worms. The sand was changing into mud. David's helmet weighed down on his aching head, injuring his neck. Sweat boiled between hair and helmet liner.

"Get that thing off!" Loryn said.

He obeyed like an automaton. He no longer had his rifle. His uniform had changed color. It was now an almost-white gray. In contrast his hands and arms were very rapidly turning brown.

All that, of course, was nothing but an illusion. Or to be more precise, a suggestive phenomenon. Even if he had wanted to, David would not have been able to resist the invasion, especially since he himself in conjunction with Loryn was the vector of contamination, and also since the two of them had penetrated too deeply into the breach. They could only continue to look for the answer to the question posed by the girl back at Geosouth. "What would happen if. . .?" They came to the sea.

They found a big engine-powered sailboat at the head of a sandy cove. David recognized the *Dehekahar*. Ney Varagan, the black, was busy on the boat. Jimenez and Barano were standing on the beach. They seemed to be waiting for the travelers. . . .

That damned old movid! David thought. Par for the course. He had been contaminated by the film. He himself had become the vector for *The Mysterious Island*.

"Come on, let's get aboard!" he told Loryn.

The girl followed him, her eyes glued to the black.

"Welcome aboard, sir, miss!" Jimenez said.

"We're bound for Lohenwa!" David said as they jumped on board.

"It's more than an island!" Barano said. "It's just a peninsula on this rotten coast!"

David burst out laughing. "You said it. Rotten!" Loryn was entranced by Ney Varagan. She only had eyes for the young pilot who was black and handsome. David was expecting something like this. But he knew what to do. All he needed was to let himself be invaded. He looked at his hands that were getting longer and browner. He took a deep breath, being careful of the swelling in his chest. His shoulders were broadening out. He was getting taller. . . . Without being concerned he saw Varagan make preparations to get under way. When the time came, he would take his place at the helm and in Loryn's heart. It would thus turn out to be the most beautiful breach in his life. Maybe the last one too.

Even while in the illusion he still remained lucid. No doubt the assault by the marine projectors was faltering. From one minute to the next the general geoprogrammer could decide to have ex-base 1 bombed by satellites. Ex-base 1 and the surrounding area at the risk of destroying some food and desalinization plants as well as the vacationing projectors.

They arrived at Lohenwa. David took an old Jules Verne-era rifle out of the ship's magazine. Then he jumped on the ground. Carlos, the dog, rushed up to greet his masters. With a flick of his thumb, David cocked the rifle. Loryn grabbed him by the wrist. He shoved the girl away. Almost without aiming he shot in the direction of Carlos. Neither report nor recoil happened, just a dazzling flash. He put the rifle to his shoulder again. Loryn put a hand over her wounded eyes and screamed. The dog had disappeared. A smell of burned flesh permeated the beach air.

"What's happening?" Loryn yelled.

"This is the answer to the question you asked me back at Geosouth. We've stopped holding it back, as you said to do. We've been invaded, we're not sure about the breach anymore. We're right in the middle of it all! What I just did was simply a test. . . ."

The girl did not ask him how the test came out. She ran to take shelter near Varagan. David shrugged. The shot and the death of the dog did not prove much at all. Things were slightly out of synchronization. The old Winchester had an effect a little more like a modern heat weapon. Anyway, the terrain was contaminated; it had been invaded. Loryn too. The dog had never existed. David wanted to shoot over Varagan to confirm whether he was an invaded vector or simply an illusion. He did not dare. He could not risk killing a living being with a weapon that did not really exist. At least in principle. But he might traumatize Loryn and lose any chance to fall in love with her by becoming Ney Varagan. . . . Whatever he was, the rules of life in an invaded world were entirely his to make.

Shrugging, he moved away from the shore, his hands in his marine pants pockets. He walked around the boat that was used as a house for the adventurers. A cardboard Lohenwa. . . . But Lohenwa had doubtlessly never existed even in a Jules Verne story. Head projector David Nadun for the first time in his life found himself in an imaginary world!

"Take me to Captain Komar," he told the others who had rejoined him.

"May the Virgin bless me!" Jimenez said. "If you want to keep on living in peace, don't say—"

"I can take you!" Ney Varagan said.

"Let's go."

They rushed toward the island interior. Jimenez and Barano followed far in the distance. Loryn was holding the black's hand. Very quickly they made it to the central plateau where some thick underbrush and scrawny-looking coconut palms grew. Birds flew up from among the rocks and crags. David searched the sky. With Loryn and the others he was certainly on ex-base 1. Base 1 invaded by Lohenwa. He needed to know who this mysterious Captain Komar was. After that, he would try to get off the island as soon as possible.

Because the geoprogrammers could sooner or later decide to destroy that contaminated piece of real estate.

"That's their intention!" said the man who was approaching to greet them at the threshold to where he lived. "So far, I've managed to keep them from doing so. But I also expect to leave. The last one, naturally—"

"Captain Komar?"

"The same!"

He was a big, strong, young, and lithe man. There was a close family resemblance between him and Ney Varagan; but his skin was a well-suntanned white. He had very bright green eyes. He was wearing a tight-fitting pair of black overalls and short red boots. Thick black hair covered his long, narrow head. He seemed to be living in a deep cave, luxuriously appointed, right in the middle of the island.

"I've been waiting for you, David Nadun," he said. "I'm not disappointed. I believe we'll be able to work together—"

"The Mysterious Island—"

"Was also a message. For you and some others. . . ."

"You're Komar, the geoprogrammer, aren't you?"

"Yes. I was base-1 commander. One day I decided to let a breach fill itself in, as you projectors say. I've been invaded for several years and I'm quite satisfied to be that way. Even you—"

David turned around. Jimenez and Barano were staying some distance away. Ney Varagan had disappeared. He felt Loryn's hand in his. Captain Komar led them into a very dark room with sculptured walls, a big aquarium in the middle, carpets and cushions on the floor. Loryn kneeled and started to stroke the furs. David sat down on a bench hewn out of the rock. Captain Komar lit up a long cigarette, and its burning end glowed in the darkness.

"We're entering the decisive phase of a battle that's been going on for centuries, David Nadun. The big flying saucer invasion of 1980–1990 all but succeeded. But it would have been worse than geoprogramming. The present-day invasion is much more enticing. Have you ever wondered who made, who *imagined*, all those *light elements*, those hallucinations that burst into our reality through numerous breaches?"

"Everybody's asked that question," David said. "Beginning with the general geoprogrammer! In any case, it was neither Jules Verne nor extraterrestrials—"

"No!"

"I think it was people. All the people!"

"Or almost all . . . Unconsciously, for the most part. Quite consciously on the part of some. The imaginary expressed a revolt burning more or less secretively in the hearts and minds of hundreds of millions of beings for centuries. A revolt against the mediocrity of existence and against the omnipotence of the forces of oppression—"

"Geoprogramming!"

"Geoprogramming that is the outgrowth of totalitarian power. The more their power increased, the more the dreams of revolt were held back. But the more they became insidious and dangerous—"

"Enticers!"

"Right. And you were enticed, David Nadun, just as I have been!"

David went up to a big oval mirror in a golden frame hung on the wall and half covered by a purple tapestry. The image reflected back to him was a familiar one, the young pi-

lot Ney Varagan. He looked at his long black hands, puffed
up his powerful chest. . . . Yes, it was Ney Varagan. Loryn
appeared in front of him!

"David," Captain Komar went on, "we'll now go into action. The height of the invasion is occurring now. It will not
last forever. It'd be advantageous to destroy geoprogramming
and all the structures of totalitarian power. Do you
want. . . . You have to help me. . . . No, it'd be better if
you take my place as the principal vector and spearhead our
struggle!"

"Why should I take your place?"

Captain Komar did not reply right away. He was at the
back of the room, on a high, straight-backed chair. A reddish
lamp cast its light vertically and kept the room in shadow.

"I have other. . . ."

He corrected himself.

"The one who has invaded me has other projects. But he is
ready to share with the one who has invaded *you* certain
powers that have given rise to religion and legend."

"Who has invaded you?"

David felt Loryn's hand squeeze his.

"Look at me closely and maybe you can recognize me!"
Captain Komar yelled.

He slowly raised his talonlike red gloves to his face. His
golden-green almond-shaped eyes stretched out under his
wide forehead and resembled orbs of fire. With a long-gloved
finger he brushed aside the mass of hair covering his left
temple. An almost metallic-looking point flashed for an instant. Then the hair fell back into place.

"Focus! Discard! Project! Fill in!" David shouted.

The image did not even waver.

"Too late, friend!" the Dark One said. "You're my son
now. I've always dreamed of having a black son."

WHERE NEUROSES THRIVE
(Ou fleurissent les nevroses)

RICHARD D. NOLANE

Translated from the French
by Joe F. Randolph

Redford arrived at the center along with the rain. The sky
had been overcast ever since he left Los Angeles—a threatening, ill-omened black sky. Under the light filtering down
through the clouds, the buildings in the Puerta del Mar Center for Mental Rehabilitation took on a morbid-looking hue,
close to the color of bones dried out by a relentless sun.

It took Redford a while to look for an empty spot in the
parking lot landscaped with trees whose branches had grown
out in such a way that they clasped to form a sort of green
roof above the pavement. He finally found one all the way at
the end of the lot. He had to maneuver several times to park
the big Oldsmobile facing the Pacific. He sat several seconds
looking out at the ocean before shutting off the engine. He
told himself it would be a spectacular view in nice
weather. . . .

He glanced at his watch. Two-thirty—he was just in time
for his appointment. Outside, big drops, heavy as his worries,
gradually covered the windshield. Redford decided to get out
of the car before the blues came back to get him down.

Once outside, he made an effort not to run toward the reception area. He recalled his visit here less than a year
ago—eleven months, to be exact—when Margaret was going through her worst crisis, the one that had in the final anal-

ysis been the determining factor in having her committed to the center. He had come into this same parking lot behind a huge ambulance that would have no problem in passing for a hearse had it not been painted a dazzlingly clean white. But in a sense, he had taken part in a cortege for the mental burial of his wife. . . . The speed at which the chain of events happened had left a deep mark on his memory that still troubled Redford's mind.

He then noticed the rain getting increasingly heavier, which made him quicken his pace. The electronic doors to the reception area soundlessly opened at his approach.

He went up to the reception desk where a well-built, good-looking young woman was sitting. A new one. She raised her head.

"May I help you, sir?"

Redford took her all in within a second with the same efficiency that a spectrogram would have recorded some star. The absorption lines from the good-looking receptionist were completely imprinted on his libido. . . . Redford tried to imagine her undressed by having salacious thoughts of her behind her desk. He hastened to erase the image from his mind. The woman looked at him with the outline of a smile etched at the sides of her mouth. Redford pretended not to notice.

"I have an appointment with Dr. Simson," he said.

The receptionist nodded and scanned a list lying on her desk. Her finger paused at a name two-thirds of the way down.

"You must be Professor Redford."

"Right. I've come to pick up my wife."

She picked up the telephone receiver.

"One moment. I'll inform the doctor that you're here."

Five minutes later Simson entered the reception area. He was a broad-shouldered man who looked more like a football player than the director of a psychotherapy center.

"Pleased to see you again, professor," he said, extending his hand to Redford.

"Same here. How's Margaret doing?" he asked. He knew his answer to that from way back, but the question was now the opening line in a sort of tacit ritual between him and the center. It had become a sort of open sesame to the door of madness.

Simson made his response with the other half of the sacred ceremony.

"Not too badly. . . . Would you follow me, please?"

Redford nodded. They took a padded, sound-proof elevator to the third floor. They got out in a corridor such as is seen in the best hotels in the country. As they approached Room 325, Redford slowed his walk. Simson got to the door well ahead of him. He knocked and went in. Redford stopped in front of the open door. With a shrug of his shoulders he took the plunge.

Like every other time, he was shocked a little more when he saw his wife.

Margaret had not changed much since she had been there. At the very most, she was not quite as thin as before because of a lack of exercise. . . .

Redford felt ashamed at not being able to experience one iota of joy at coming to see his wife. But there was something about her—or something that emanated from her—that made him afraid. That even scared the hell out of him.

Sensing Redford's lack of enthusiasm, Dr. Simson took Margaret's hand and helped her to get up from the rocking chair where she was sitting and taking in the sun.

"Your husband's come for you, Margaret," he said in a cheerful tone of voice.

Redford was not taken in by the doctor's game, but he was grateful to him for making the situation easier and smoother. He smiled and kissed his wife on the cheek.

"You're looking fit as a fiddle!" he said in order to strike up a conversation.

Margaret said nothing. Not one muscle in her face betrayed the slightest movement. This was the precise moment when Redford took stock of the knowledge that his wife had not uttered a single word in the space of eleven months and the fact that he was now going to have to put up with this for a whole week. He had a sudden urge to take Dr. Simson aside to tell him that he had just changed his mind. . . . He had to make an effort not to do so.

He saw Dr. Simson go into the bathroom just to come back almost immediately with a leather bag. The doctor handed it to him.

"Here, take this. The infirmary gathered up her belongings

this morning. To them I added her medications with a sheet
of instructions so that you would know when and how to give
them to her."

"Thanks, doctor."

"How are you doing, dear?"

Margaret remained as motionless as a statue. Redford had
to take her by the hand to lead her out of the room. Crossing
the center to his car was a real trial. Simson helped the
young woman to get seated in the car. He put the seat belt
around her and closed the door. He came around from the
other side. Redford shook his hand, then got in. He started
the engine.

"She's all yours now," Simson said to him. "Call me at the
slightest problem, okay? Don't forget. See you later."

Redford waved to him and quickly rolled up the window
since the rain was still coming down hard.

A short while after leaving the center, he got back on the
freeway to Los Angeles. As soon as the Oldsmobile had
reached cruising speed, he glanced over at Margaret. She
stared at the road in inhuman silence with an expression of
no longer being in touch with the world. Only the seat belt
seemed to be able to keep her in the surrounding reality.

It took Redford a good hour to reach the forty-story tower
where their apartment was located. At the moment he shut
off the engine, he suddenly turned to his wife to gauge her
reaction. Life in that tower had deranged Margaret's mind.
For the first time since they had left the center, he was almost relieved to see her motionless, never showing any reaction.

"Do you understand?" Simson said to him a month before,
"your wife feels smothered and beset by life in your tower to
a greater degree than what an average human being would
have been able to endure. In fact, I believe she would have
been able to put up with this pressure even longer without
this episode of attempted rape in which she was victimized
right before her first crisis."

"I have still tried everything to change her outlook. . . ."

"I don't doubt it. But, you see, once the harm was done,
there is present in this type of case a type of geometric pro-
gression of effects. In her they are quite far advanced since

she has fallen into a tetanic coma. She very nearly died. . . ."

"In a sense, wouldn't it have been better if she had? Whenever I see her like that, I get sick over it."

"I must confess that I have exhausted all the resources of ordinary medicine. I have come to wonder if it wouldn't be a bad idea to try shock—putting her back for a certain length of time in the situation that caused her crisis. It's risky, but since she has nothing to lose. . . ."

"If I understand you correctly, you're asking me to take her back home?"

"I regret burdening you with this experiment, but it's a last-ditch hope of seeing her return to us."

Redford never stopped replaying the conversation in his mind. He had put Margaret to bed—the sight of his wife naked disturbed him—and he went to get a drink. He was on his fifth glass. Under the influence of Jack Daniels, Chopin's *Grande Polonaise* was becoming almost psychedelic. Thinking it over, he decided that distortion of the music had gone on long enough and that it was time to retire. A single question still remained in his mind when he stretched out on the bed in the spare bedroom. If Margaret were to have some type of reaction, what would it be?

Simson called first thing the next morning. Redford told him that nothing in particular had happened.

"She's not talking?"

"Not a thing. Quiet as a tomb. I wonder if you weren't a little too optimistic when you told me that she was going to experience some shock. . . . Yesterday, when we got here, she didn't have any more reaction when she saw the tower than if I had taken her to visit a laundromat."

"You have to have patience, professor. . . . You still have six days to go!"

"Yep, if things continue like this, you can come after both of us before the week is up."

As soon as Simson had hung up, Redford went into her room. He found Margaret sitting on the edge of the bed slipping on her mules. She got up to go to the bathroom in a zombielike trance. It was only when she had shut the door that Redford realized that he had not needed to say anything to her or to help her. He held back for several seconds before thinking that Simson might not have been wrong after all. He decided to wait a little while before calling him with the news.

Along about noontime John Winterman came by to see him. Winterman was the director of the lab for spectrum studies at the California Institute of Space Research, and Redford had been loaned from Mount Palomar two years ago to help him out when CISR had just opened its doors. In time they had become the best friends in the world.

Winterman shook Redford's hand. As was his habit, he was wearing his perennial black-velour suit reeking of cigar smoke.

"She here?" he asked in a low voice.

Redford nodded.

"May I see her?"

"Sure thing. She should be in the living room."

He motioned Winterman to follow him. Margaret slowly raised her head when they came in. This time Redford was convinced that her eyes lighted up when they met Winterman's.

"I'm sure she'll come out of it," Winterman said as he was leaving the apartment. "I get the impression that Janette will soon have to get along without you, old pal. . . ."

Redford's face clouded over. Throughout the scenario Janette had been the weak point in his armor; she had proved to him that he was unable to live without really putting down roots somewhere. He felt no blame for Margaret's condition insofar as he believed he was sure of always loving her as before. No, he only regretted stating his personal weakness for women in general. Besides, Janette made love so well. . . .

Winterman patted him on the shoulder and left. The rest of the day went along smoothly. Redford was now on the lookout for any signs of a reaction from his wife. Late in the afternoon he called Simson to inform him of his discoveries. The only thing that he did not tell him was that Margaret always caused him so much uneasiness by her mere presence as if she gave off an evil aura.

Margaret spoke for the first time the next day around six in the evening. Redford was busy helping her get ready for bed when she abruptly stopped to stare straight into his eyes with a sudden piercing look. Right away Redford thought that she was ashamed of being undressed like this in front of her husband whom she had not seen in almost a year. He was about to turn around when Margaret put her hand on his forearm. He felt her fingers tighten, racked by nervous spasms.

"I'm afraid . . ." Margaret said in a hoarse, cracked voice.

Astonishment left Redford speechless.

"You . . . you're talking!" he exclaimed after a period of silence.

Margaret opened her mouth—no doubt to reply—then she suddenly shut it again. Her eyes gleamed for a few seconds, then the brightness diminished in intensity and disappeared altogether. Redford felt the resurrection of his wife elude him like smoke dispersed by the wind.

He took her hands in his. Deep down inside him, he felt a growing urge to weep, which he restrained with pain and difficulty. When his urge faded away completely, he got up again, still staring into Margaret's eyes.

Redford felt he had to do something, make some gesture that would dispel the unreality of the scene that had unfolded before him. He decided to leave. He flipped off the room light as he shut the door.

A little bit later with a can of Schlitz in front of him, he wondered several times if he had let slip through his fingers the very moment when he failed to act, a little like a poker player who does not have a royal flush because of a wrongly played card. A good quarter hour of pondering went by before he came to the conclusion that he should try to make love to his wife.

He went in, in total darkness, and headed to where he thought the night stand was. He ended up putting his hand on the bedside lamp switch. The filtered light found Margaret, as always, sitting on the edge of the bed. She had not moved an inch.

Redford walked around the bed. When he was almost opposite his wife, he gently put a hand on each of her breasts. He began to stroke them until he felt the nipples harden beneath his finger tips. Then he leaned close to her to kiss her.

It was terrible. Never had Redford been so awkward when making love to a woman. Margaret's body had responded to his caresses, but he had the bitter impression that every sensation he had perceived had been born and had died without even touching Margaret's mind. He was beating his head against a wall of insanity. Until it was bloody.

He stayed stretched out beside her, his sight riveted on a long crack shaped like a streak of lightning that ran across the recently redone ceiling. The crack even encroached on the top of the wall as if it were trying to carve a road through the plaster to the bed.

Margaret moved. She turned her head away from Redford. He made an effort to look at her.

"I'm afraid . . ." she said.

Redford got goose bumps. He got up to call Simson.

"You say she's talking?" Simson exclaimed.

"Right. . . . Listen, doctor, I want the experiment to stop right now. You see, Margaret gives me the jitters!"

"Don't think such a thing! She might be in the process of getting cured, and you dare to ask me to take her back!"

"But—"

"No but about it. Go to sleep and call me tomorrow. I hope you think about it overnight."

Simson hung up.

Redford remained in front of the phone, bewildered. Finally, he decided to go to bed. As he passed by her room, he glanced inside. He caught sight of Margaret stretched out, both her legs spread in a provocative position and her big eyes open and staring at the ceiling kept him from entering. He did not have the courage to go in and turn off the bedside lamp. He was satisfied just to close the door.

He plopped down on his bed hoping to find refuge in a dreamless sleep.

"I told you not to come!" Redford spat out while trying not to raise his voice.

"I just couldn't resist it," Janette replied. "I haven't stopped thinking about you, alone with that crazy woman!"

Redford cut her off.

"That's my wife you're talking about, Janette. . . ."

"So what! That doesn't keep her from being a complete idiot and me from being afraid for you. . . ."

Everybody is really up the wall in this dump! Redford thought. *All because of that fool Simson. . . .*

"I love you. You know that," the young woman went on.

Redford watched as she came up to him. Her lips met his before he had a chance to make a move. He could not resist the temptation to stroke her jet-black hair.

A sound in the hallway made them both turn around.

"I'm afraid . . ." Margaret said, stark naked and framed in the doorway.

Janette's eyes widened in terror and her nails dug into Redford. She stayed like that for a few seconds, frozen with a distraught expression on her face, then she screamed. Several times before fleeing toward the elevator.

"Oh, shit . . ." Redford mumbled.

He wordlessly closed the front door. Margaret watched him do it without moving a muscle. She waited until he came back toward her before starting back to her room. Redford let her since he obviously saw that he did not have to say a word. . . . His wife had been back for less than three days, and the situation was deteriorating to such a degree that it was already beyond his control.

All of a sudden he made the decision to take Margaret back to the center as soon as possible. All Simson had to do was see for himself!

When he came into the room to tell Margaret, he found her standing on the bed following the twisted outline of the lightning-shaped crack in the ceiling with her fingertip. The bed was quite high up, and she could touch the ceiling. She was humming in a low voice like a kid with a doll. Redford got closer to see if he could make out what she was saying. He felt his body tense up when he heard:

"I'm afraid . . . I'm afraid . . ." Margaret relentlessly mumbled on.

"Good heavens, is that all you know how to say?" Redford yelled.

Margaret let out a scream of fright, slipped, and fell on the bed.

"Tomorrow you're going back with the rest of the whackos, understand? I'm fed up with seeing you wander around here. . . . I've had it!"

Margaret's eyes turned a darker shade. She opened her mouth but not a sound came out. Redford took advantage of her surprise to grab her by the arm. He forced her to stand up.

"And now you're gonna get dressed. . . . I've had about enough of seeing you parade around here in the nude!"

He gathered up the clothes lying on the chair and tossed them through the open bathroom door. Terror-stricken, Margaret watched him. She was trembling all over. Redford did not even notice she was when he pushed her into the shower.

He started straightening up the room in a sort of frenzy as if it would speed up his wife's departure. As he was smoothing out the bedspread, he knocked against the glass bedside lamp and it shattered on the floor.

The sound of the light bulb breaking produced a shocking effect in him. He thought he heard the sound continue to echo in him. He stayed motionless until the feeling went away. Finally, he stretched out on the bed and listened to Margaret having problems getting dressed.

His sight settled on the crack as it had the evening before. To calm himself down, he tried to follow the fracture in the plaster right down to its tiniest details. After he finished with his inspection, it seemed to him that it was longer than before and shaped more like a bolt of lightning. He smiled, telling himself that he was beginning to talk nonsense.

When Redford felt definitely calmed down, his thoughts went back to Margaret. Maybe he would wait a little, after all, before sending her back there. . . . He closed his eyes to think better.

Winterman lit up his cigar before knocking on Redford's door. He hated getting mixed up in other people's business, but Janette had had such a distressed look on her face that he had to promise to come and talk to Redford. He would love to know what to say to him!

He knocked five times without sign of an answer. He began to get worried because Redford should not have left his apartment during his wife's stay. He was going to knock a sixth time, but he changed his mind and turned the doorknob.

The door was not locked. Winterman tried to allay his disquiet by telling himself that Redford most likely must have taken Margaret back to the center immediately and that he had forgotten to lock the door. After several seconds of hesitation, he finally decided to go in.

Right away he sensed that something was amiss. He rushed into the hallway. Moans were coming from Margaret's room.

He found her kneeling at the foot of the bed, half dressed. As for Redford, he was sprawled out in a ridiculous-looking position.

With bated breath he got closer. He carelessly bumped against Margaret and put his ear to Redford's chest. When he got back up, the blood had drained from his face. Several times his eyes traveled from the busted lamp—with bare wires—to Margaret and back again. But why had it electrocuted him?

Margaret stood up. With her hand she pointed at the ceiling over the bed.

"The lightning is gone, and I'm not afraid anymore . . ." she mumbled.

Winterman's eyes followed her movement. A sudden frown showed on his face while he searched in vain for a flow in the spotless and uncracked plaster that Redford had had redone just recently.

Then his sight returned to the young woman's face.

"You shouldn't have done that, Margaret. . . ."

She did not appear to understand. Winterman backed out of the room. In the hallway, he picked up the telephone. He hesitated only a second between calling the center and the police.

BACK TO EARTH, FINALLY
(Retour à la terre, définitif)

PHILIP GOY

Translated from the French
by Joe F. Randolph

"Wake-up time. Code pink, number 10,212. Urine: 408 milliliters. Stool: 293 grams, nothing indicated. Weight: 74.3 kilograms. Temperature: 36.9° C. Pulse: 102 per sandglass. Meal: 132 grams of CP21 pseudomeat protein with 3 grams of salt (pure NaC1) + 87 grams of CL72 bacteria-fortified yeast scented and salted with 60 drops of soya sauce. Liquid intake: 250 milliliters of jar A water along with a spoonful of instant coffee and sugar (pure $C_{12}H_{22}O_{11}$)."

"Song of the Earth," *Das Lied von der Erde.* I remember it very well. It was while listening to the very rendition by Bruno Walter with Kathleen Ferrier that everything began. . . . How long ago?

I was stretched out on the floor, on my back, arms and legs spread out, eyes staring at the ceiling, literally immersed in Gustav Mahler's music, with the loudspeakers as high as they would go. I had had some incredible luck; my one-room apartment at that time was in the Latin Quarter and was in fact an old basement to a bookstore that had been closed for years. Both in broad daylight as well as in the middle of the night, it was impossible for that throbbing volume to disturb anyone at all.

Later on, a restaurant was built on the site, which transformed even my apartment into a pseudomedieval room with candles, fake beams apparently well wormeaten, and all the trappings that reflected the tastes of that era. At that time I was still interested in the world. I tried to understand the whys of fashion. So, there was not a single restaurant, for example, that did not try to make its decor antique, whether Louis XIII, Louis XVI, or the latest being 1900. . . . The labels on wine bottles were all printed in Gothic letters with a lot of seals, coats of arms, and fleurs-de-lis. French citizens liked all kinds of things from the old order with their meals!

Philosophizing like that, I had no idea that my expulsion was going to turn out to be dramatic and that it was a very private part of my being that had been torn from me—or rather the veneer of my personality, the shell protecting my melomaniacal soul. (That is also the reason I am here.)

The break in my good luck was to take place a little before the disaster. On that still-melodious afternoon when I was in my basement apartment letting "Song of the Earth" flow through me, it showed up like a new scratch on an often-played record. It was irreparable; the scratch would not go away, and it came out as tick, tick, tick for a moment. Later on it could never be enjoyed anymore without anticipating that part, a cut waiting to make noise. "May I have your attention, please. It is now . . . tick, tick." The expected source of annoyance became suspense.

A sunbeam struck the surface of the LP, and my eyes followed with fascination the reflection traveling across the ceiling. Slight warps in the record caused a surprising change in the reflected spot while the network of grooves broke down the white light into colors of the rainbow. There's a list of credits right at hand, I thought, the lines passing in front of the spinning background. The action went right on while the spot got farther and farther away (like a zoom lens being adjusted) then swung back toward the record or the melomaniacal character (me). It's easy to have ideas. How come films are so badly made?

I'm quite satisfied with myself. *For me anything is possible!* I thought. Vertigo.

And then, brutally, the truth, the fall. I'm not a Mozart. I'll never be a Monteverdi, or Wagner, or Debussy. . . . So what? Is life worth the trouble to live???

Suddenly I felt very sick. I got up again. A not-to-be-held-back nausea rose in me; a veil came down in front of my eyes. I had to lie down.

Later I tried to convince myself that this upset really came before the rush of grim ideas, all due precisely to the strange state of my body. No matter, it had definitely marked me, like the dreams that my mind believed could be made bearable: "This is nothing but a dream, after all. No need to wake me up." But dreams that also took possession of me subconsciously.

I do not like to remember the period of time that followed, my problems with an apartment overlooking a courtyard resounding with every one of the TV series, in a room next to the street where I got all the noise. It was when my fiancée ran off with my best friend that I somehow became attuned to the fact that there was nothing good to expect from humanity. . . .

"I changed the belt on pump X5, which was cracked over more than 40 percent of its surface. The air-conditioning unit is working perfectly. However, the voltage output from the atomic generator fell to 47.8 volts. When it falls to 47.6, I'll renew the electrolyte. Drank 360 milliliters of jar B water with 2 tablespoons of instant tea and 2 unrefined sugars. Ate 190 grams of CP33 dough. Urine: 256 milliliters."

Many considered, I felt, me to be an unfortunate person. In my mind the word misfortune had about as much meaning as success. Certainly, people are not worth much, present company included since I am not a Mozart (nor even a Rossini!), and life did not have much meaning. Nevertheless, I ended up by achieving some sort of balance thanks to my outside work, and most of all thanks to a very simple change in my habits at my place. Let's say that I had to go through almost two years of suffering before thinking about it!

It had become unbearable. Either I could listen to my music—but it was all messed up by a lot of background noises such as a squeaking air pump, whistling kettles, backfires from countless internal-combustion engines, or the silence of the night and the thin walls in dumpy living quarters kept me from good listening, that is, high volume.

I now realize at what point the great principles of a good education can be misleading. Adversity neither molds character nor does it excite the imagination. Just about deprived of music, I went half out of my mind. I all but failed an exam. In spite of everything, I wound up by finding a solution, the obvious cure for my torments, listening with earphones or, as the far-out sound-equipment salespeople would say, being plugged in.

I wanted to buy the symphonic poem by Richard Strauss, *Thus Spake Zarathustra.* The person who usually sold to me, a charming young man, discriminating and cultured, liked my true melomania but also dreaded my requirements, which he called my fickleness. How many records did I exchange for defects which he thought very minor, but which according to me ruined the expected pleasure with unbearable tortures? "Karajan!" he told me, "you can't do without this recording." Karajan? Mmm . . . I thought, Boehm to me seems more like an authentic Strauss. Karajan is too brilliant to be true.

The sales clerk had already put the record on the turntable. However, he did not have me listen to the record in its resounding brilliance! To our left a suburban couple was being persuaded that their status required the purchase of such a series with a good supply of the unavoidable *Ninth Symphony.* To our right *Sun Ra and His Magic Arkestra* was turning two longhairs on. Without saying a thing, the sales clerk put a headset on me, but not without grazing—ever so pleasantly—my neck.

In a flash.

When I closed my eyes, I was right in the middle of the orchestra. The music—it was more than something in my ears, in my head . . . the music—it was me. As at a concert, as at the opera, I cried.

No doubt the stereophonic effect can be very true-to-life if the loudspeakers are of good quality and well placed, if the room has the right shape and echo, if the listener is in the right spot . . . that is, never. As soon as you listen with a headset, it is perfect right away. It is better because the headset isolates you acoustically and mentally. It is still better because the power can be cranked up to the threshold of pain without polluting the environment with noise!

I left with the record . . . and the headset. The certainty that musical waves were again going to wash over me was enough to reestablish quickly my full identity.

My studies immediately improved, and I finished them successfully with two diplomas in science and one in psychology. A spot had just opened up in the Circadian Rhythm Study Group. This lab had connections with several biomedical services and . . . the army. There was plenty of money. We tried to be open to all kinds of experiences by studying the influence which the day-night cycle had on plants, animals, as well as volunteers—us in particular. We followed a 24, 12, or 48-hour cycle in a number of activities.

Without expecting anything at all, living completely alone, I had a lot of freedom that I put to good use in this work. Soon my reputation as a researcher put me in the forefront of the group. My bosses began to open my eyes a little.

For an astronaut traveling through space, the waking-sleeping cycle is completely arbitrary. There is no need to adhere to the (nonexistent) alternating day-night cycle nor to the activity of any other man (too far away). It is possible that a cycle different from the normal 24 could be adopted for humanity in general, in any case to someone in particular. I have easily verified this theory on myself. During my youth I never felt sleepy, for one thing, and I never woke up immediately, for another. As a result, my first "free" night was 12 hours long, after which I still had less sleep and woke up later proportionately so that my second night was 14 hours long. Very quickly I adjusted to a 48-hour personal circadian rhythm. It is probable that this value, exactly double the terrestrial norm, came about because of lingering synchronization with the environment.

A truly convincing experiment needed a completely atemporal environment such as a capsule traveling through the void of space, or a cave so deep that it was devoid of any time-keeping mechanism. Several projects along these lines had already been done with differing results both in France and the US. Now they wanted to go to the next step, a true time test for an interplanetary trip, say Earth to Mars and back. Obviously it could last for some years. . . . The traveler has to be in good physical and mental condition, all the while living in a closed vessel with a restricted area and completely artificial environment, poor in stimulating factors and devoid of any time cycles, even those of Earth.

Authorities attach the greatest importance to the mental balance of the traveler. They pay special attention to his ability to reestablish without problems human communication after silence for an undetermined length of time. This communication most often takes a single form, an order to follow. I can easily understand that not only will there be astronaut missions in the bargain, but also military missions in space and at the bottom of the sea. . . .

"Urine: 456 milliliters. Drank 350 milliliters of water from jar B to which was added 44 tablespoons of powdered milk without sugar."

Volunteers to live alone for an undetermined length of time several hundred meters beneath the ground while drinking recycled urine and eating hydroponic cultures were not all that numerous. It dawned on me that my scientific knowledge and my strong personality made me the ideal subject. To put it more matter-of-factly, I was the only single person in the research group . . . I was put through all kinds of tests and I still remember what I saw in the enthusiastic psychologist's look: "This guy's certain that he's gonna like it down there! He's completely out of his mind!!!" Man, is he not, a social animal. A schizophrenic of my caliber, a rara avis, a godsend!

Dubbed the MOTIONLESS TRIP, our project aroused the interest of the press. For some time I became sort of a national hero. But the attention of the public and journalists was abruptly shifted to subjects of quite another serious nature. After the destruction of the Middle East, international tension reached a fever-pitch stage.

I finally went down into the hole that I had long had a hand in getting ready, without any fanfare, without the press, without anybody looking on.

I was connected to the outside by a telephone. It came in handy twice. The first time to let them know that I had arrived at my post. The second time to make sure that it was still working.

Now I have an idea that the phone is out of order. Every now and then I make a move to pick it up. "This is just to be sure that it's not working anymore," I tell myself. But what if someone answers? On the other hand, if I verify the fact that it's not working anymore, wouldn't that say it all? I'm scared to death of the phone. I recall the telegram informing me of my mother's death. I was sure about what it was going to tell

me; however, to this day I have still not been able to lay a
finger on it, and Mélisande was the one who opened it for
me. I don't have Mélisande here with me now. She ran off
with Marcellus quite some time ago. . . .

"Urine: 378 milliliters. I'm going to sleep."

"Wake-up time. Code pink, number 10,213. Urine: 459
milliliters. Stool: 321 grams, too soft. Disagreeable odor. I
took three M3205 pills. I walked 15 kilometer equivalents on
the exercise bike without too much effort. Pulse then 158 per
sandglass. Meal of 300 grams of CA03 algae cooked at 130°
C and ground up. Took two pills of vitamin compound
M1056. Drank 250 milliliters of water from jar A with two
tablespoons of instant coffee and one sugar (pure
$C_{12}H_{11}O_{22}$)."

How many years have I been here? My reflection in the
mirror makes me look 45. Has it therefore been more than
15 years that I have been down here? I recently changed the
heads on my tape recorder for the third time. The factory
guarantees them for 15,000 hours. If I admit that I have been
in this capsule for 15 years, then that would mean that I
have spent just about a third of my time listening to music. It
is conceivable even though I seem to be listening to music
with increasing frequency. We must be nearing the end of the
twentieth century. We? I may be what is left of humanity. . . . Another reason to say us, is it not? I am the king,
the emperor of a vast world, the only survivor of an all-out
war on the surface. Because the war, after pondering it, to
me seems quite likely.

Hello, up there on the surface! Are you all dead? I'm not
picking the receiver up, it's too easy! Hello, God, is this when
I die? Hello, doctor, am I dying or simply sentenced to
death?

Dying without knowing it, me, the thinking humanity?
There the mute telephone sits, but it just might be answered,
it does work in reality as long as I do not use it. This telephone is the symbol of my hope, my own little everlasting
hope.

God exists. The proof of His existence is that He does all I
ask of Him. Obviously I am not going to bother God with ev-

ery little whim of mine; I ask nothing of Him. God does nothing, therefore God exists, or at least He exists as long as I ask nothing of Him. Like the world outside.

The existence of God is my telephone.

"Tests T1225 and T1226. Each one requires less time than a sandglass. The answers are 'right, then left' for the first one, 'never' for the second one. Next, I had a little difficulty with navigation problem P708. The course to take is 68°22' North, without knowing for sure that the path in that direction is clear (my map of that area is not detailed enough). Used 2,000 milliliters from jar C to take a bath. Drank 250 milliliters of water from jar A to which was added two tablespoons of instant tea with two unrefined sugars."

I have some books in my subterranean space vessel; no novels (they bore me—variations on the same theme of human vanity, and silly stories of contacts between skin and mucous membranes) but books on art, science, philosophy, and well-written history. And exactly as viewed from the bottom of my hole, history comes up with some almost-infallible laws. For example: *The causes of a war are to be looked for in the way the previous war turned out badly.* If you think about the world situation right at the moment when I left the surface, you should recognize that all the conditions for a new world war were merging, socioeconomic tensions, unstable conditions of all types, a universal need to hate.

Down with the enemies of the people, the country, and freedom!!!

They do not want to recognize us as a nation, as men . . . I have been chased from the sacred earth of my forbears! Not mine! Mine! I am condemned to shoot the first one! Compelled to assassinate the hostages in order to put an end to oppression!

They reject any agreement! They refuse to talk about it! Be quiet, kiddies, or else you'll get spanked. Up yours, kiddies, we the biggies are always saviors of the world. Hello, Mike? Hello, Ivan, you clown! . . . A popping noise on the phone. . . . Did you say bang? Not bang? Wham? Bang? Bang? Bang?

I escaped the Third World War, I see it as if I were there myself. The neutrons, infrared radiation, the shock waves. . . . The alpha, beta, and gamma rays!

I have apocalyptic visions. I look down at vast cemeteries on a super missile. I perceive waves of pain about the end of the world. My brain has just bored through tons of earth, right at the bottom of my impregnable bunker. . . . Telepathy? Bull! For some time, if it has blown up without leaving anything behind, then the less suffering there will be. Barring . . . ghosts? Ha, ha! I raise my glass to my invisible guests. I see myself playing the role of Dr. Praetorius in *The Bride of Frankenstein*, not in the least surprised at the arrival of the monster in the subterranean cave, soon trusted, even clinking glasses over corpses. To your good health! Health for the burn victims, for those blasted out of existence, the hideously disemboweled! A toast to those quartered, the tortured crybabies!

Every now and then I get uneasy. This long confinement can disturb me. Will I go crazy? But how is my sparkling humor to be explained, the irresistible way I do away with all my fellow humans with a thought? Boom! Boom!

"Urine: 420 milliliters. Stool: 278 grams, appearance and odor not improved. I again take four M3205 pills. My weight: 73.9 kilograms. My temperature: 37° C. My meal: 320 grams of bacteria-fortified C172 yeast without soya sauce. Liquid intake: 250 milliliters of water from jar A to which was added two tablespoons of instant verbena."

I have to tell you about my work. You might get the wrong idea about my behavior. There you go! It's well known, it's rejection of the world, withdrawing into oneself, a return to the womb. My descent to the bosom of the round, peaceful, and warm Earth—what an analogy! This amounts to denying the enormous scientific interest in the experiment (and if you don't believe in the value of knowledge, I don't know what you can believe in, in our century). Then there is my work, my creation! You think of me as someone completely passive, only interested in music—as a listener. I am not a Mozart, but I did discover that I am a great painter. A very great painter. Underground!!!

I paint spheres (earthwomen) giving birth to armies of children (rocket bombs), faces rotting away into legions of skeletons, genitals tied up with an umbilical cord sutured with a telephone cord. . . . I paint the world and the end of it. I am a painter of the Apocalypse (and of myself as well?).

I paint for hours on end. How many hours in my clockless living quarters? One morning, I mean after I got up, I painted without stopping while listening to the entire *Der Ring des Nibelungen*. A rough (exact?) estimate: 2 hours for *Das Rheingold* + 4 hours for *Die Walkyrie* + 5 hours for *Siegfried* + 6 hours for *Die Götterdämmerung* = at least 17 hours. I then ate and did my chores. Next, I went back to my painting, again listening to *Der Ring des Nibelungen* from start to finish. This music is as dangerous as any drug. In it there are so many overt forms which emerge only through other overt forms . . . and always pleasurably. It's like eroticism, you constantly want to go further, you never get to the end.

Climbing up and up with no end in sight!

I must limit myself to a minimum of interruptions. I used to sober up with the Viennese school. But Schönberg is a bridge. Starting out with *Pierrot Lunaire*, I went to *Gurrelieder* which gave rise to Richard Strauss's *The Woman Without a Shadow*, then to Mahler and Brahms: I was lost. Now I've found solid footing, the absolute antidote—Debussy! *Pelléas*. . . .

Twice through *Der Ring des Nibelungen*, plus hours of work and eating . . . have I reached a circadian rhythm of more than 36 hours? It would be easy for me to confirm it. For example I could suspend a Foucault pendulum from the immense arch covering my capsule. I would then see the track of the pendulum in the sand returning in the same direction every twenty-four hours. This kind of trickery does not interest me any more than the others do.

There is a subterranean lake quite near here. I could quite easily drink water that does not have the musty smell of my recycled liquid. I could even go swimming in the lake!

In fact I have never left my capsule. I have never gone beyond the canvas lock to the outside. I did not even make an effort to walk around to breathe in some natural air. However, none of the authorities in the program felt it necessary to prohibit me; that would not affect the results except in a negligible way from the physiological viewpoint. But what a difference in mental outlook! If I could go out, take a few minutes' vacation, but the astronaut can only live inside his capsule. Outside is the void.

Outside is death.

"Drank 300 milliliters of water from jar A to which were added two tablespoons of instant tea and three unrefined sugars."

Every time I drink my foul-smelling water, I can't help but think that I no doubt owe my life to it. It is likely that the subterranean stream has been contaminated by radioactivity or something else. The cave air, except for the air in the rigidly controlled system in my capsule, had perhaps become temporarily toxic. . . . My space capsule, my nylon tent in its deep grotto, an incomparable cocoon! A super bunker!!! My motionless trip, fording the river of universal death! Who else will get across it but me? My lab is very well equipped; but they did not think it necessary to issue me a Geiger counter. . . .

"Urine: 467 milliliters. I'm going to bed."

"Wake-up time. Code pink, number 10,214. Urine: 554 milliliters. Calisthenics: 20 of exercise 521 in the manual. I feel fine. The generator output is 47.6 volts. I renewed the electrolyte, and the voltage went up to 48."

OUTSIDE IS DEATH.
This is the subject of a sketch I'm doing at this moment. I have hung on the walls my paintings on this theme; a circular, or clearly ovoid, spot where all kinds of things go on, surrounded by an absolutely black surface.

The first one was reminiscent of the Cambrian sea in whose depths so many primitive forms of life swarmed as the land was emerging and the air was totally devoid of life, without one plant or insect.

The second one represents a drop of milk as seen under a microscope.

The third one is a spaceship in sidereal space.

The fourth one is the Earth in its orbit, a canvas quite similar to the previous one.

The fifth one reminds you of a fetus in the womb.

The sixth one is a symbolic view of my capsule bathed in light in its totally dark and almost-lifeless cave setting.

On this last canvas I originally encircled the black ring representing the cave with a bright green border to represent the outside world. I finally painted over the green with black. Only for reasons of esthetics? I have felt rather remorseful about that act. If I doubt life on the outside, I express it as more improbable; if I no longer believe in it, I blot it out.

Whatever it is, my sketch has been an enormous success. I have written several highly laudatory reviews of it. Therefore, you could say that I am most likely the greatest painter alive.

"Food intake: 250 grams of pseudomeat protein CP21 scented and salted with 50 drops of soya sauce. 100 grams of bacteria-fortified yeast CL72. Liquid intake: 300 milliliters of water from jar B to which was added two tablespoons of instant tea and two refined sugars (pure $C_{12}H_{22}O_{11}$)."

Every now and then a subtle doubt nags at me. Does creation exist apart from all communication? Am I really a painter if there is no public to view my work?

On the one hand I could be considered the public, that is (maybe) the entire human race. On the other hand, if you think of all the works of Schubert that were never played during his lifetime, would you consider that they only existed from the time of their being played after the death of the great composer? That's absurd!

"Code pink, number 10,215."

Is there any better music to jerk off to than Beethoven's? Brahms did almost as well, almost. . . . But only Beethoven could lay claim to a genius totally lacking in imagination. These hard-to-find themes, heavily used, this desperate tension, what strength!

One of the great concerns of the officials in this research program as well as, I must say, the almost-exclusive interest of the public centered around the sexual activity of an isolated man. Nothing like saltpeter has been added to my food. Even though my sphere of existence sometimes resembles a hospital, there is not a drop of bromide in my liquid intake. I live like a normal man if you disregard the moot theory: *Man is a social animal.*

In my capsule there are many devices that automatically monitor certain aspects in my day-to-day (cycle-to-cycle?) existence. Besides, I have to record certain of my activities on a dictaphone that simultaneously enters the day and hour in code. I pretend that I am one of Samuel Beckett's characters by talking through a toothbrush. . . .

After I leave this capsule, all they will have to do is hook up some magnetic tapes to a computer to get a synthetic view of Project Motionless Trip. There is even a machine that will tape the report! I will sign only the pages titled *Subjective Impressions of the Test Subject.* The subject's subjective feelings!!! Data processing certainly has some verbal progress to make. . . . I'm talking disparagingly. This computer is in effect my judge of last resort, my God. An IBM Godot.

"Drank 300 milliliters of water from jar A to which was added two tablespoons of mint syrup."

It was well established by preliminary experiments that sexual behavior is to a large degree modified if done in the light of cold scientific study, after the event (if I can say that!). There is a basic idea in quantum physics: Observation destroys what is being observed. It is odd to state that that principle—having to do with infinitely minute atoms—can just as well be applied to the human condition. How many discoveries were made by prehistorians at the same time that irreversible damage was done? "The ideal excavation," wrote A. Leroi-Gourhan in 1950, "is the one where after twenty years the smallest object, the tiniest splinter of bone, and the most minute grain of sand can all be put back into their proper place. Since such a feat is unrealistic, any prehistorian is more or less a vandal. . . ." How many such primitive societies have been destroyed by being studied? The best ethnologist is the one who does not leave his room. Look at Lévy-Strauss.

Regarding the sexuality of an astronaut on a long trip, there was total contradiction between unrestrained desire, which revealed knowledge of it, and the fact that this desire even rendered it unrecognizable. So a compromise was

reached. The test subject (that is, me) was to write down in
a special notebook (with a pink cover) each and every erotic
activity, each one to be assigned a numerical code. Just the
number code was recorded on the dictaphone entry; that way
certain numbers would correspond to nothing at all in order
to cover up the trail. Every sexual act is thus tagged, but
nothing can be inferred from the code numbers alone, from
their date, or their frequency.

The test subject has total freedom to:

(1) destroy the pink notebook;

(2) turn it over in whole or in part for analysis;

(3) analyze it himself and reveal it in his report in the
way, whether brief or detailed, he judges appropriate.

This privacy enables me to set down with ease in the pink
notebook any detail about my depravity. That is where I
write down with satisfaction my fantasies, my jerk-off objects,
my pleasure toys. For some time I have been adding to it, I
have thought up all sorts of terribly obscene visions, unlikely
impulses. . . . I take delight in rereading those pages, in spic-
ing them up with suggestive styles, in making them hot reading with juicy additions. That's my movie, my panoramic
delirium!

As far as the project officials and all of you, possible readers, WHAT THE HELL DO YOU CARE about my intimate titil-
lations, my bursts of pleasure?

"Urine: 375 milliliters. Stool: 273 grams, nothing indicated. Food intake: 250 grams of algae CA03 ground up and
cooked at 130° C, mixed with 100 grams of bacteria-fortified
yeast CL72, the whole business seasoned with 90 drops of
soya sauce. Liquid intake: 400 milliliters of water from jar A
to which were added 5 tablespoons of instant tea and four
sugars (pure $C_{12}H_{22}O_{11}$). Two pills of vitamin complex
M1056."

The fact is that I prefer music to anything else. Even
Mélisande set me on edge when she felt the need to talk after
just a few hours of listening together.

Marcellus had a theory all ready for me. I knew it was
false and ridiculous, but I thought he was successful in getting Mélisande to admit it. He claimed that my reticence

about human contact, my libido influenced by my melomania, could be explained by unconscious homosexuality. As
an only child, did I live too long hanging onto my mother's
skirts? Was my father's image too negative throughout my
childhood and on into my teenage years? As a result, I was
unable to leave the Oedipal nest. Naturally, I was afraid that
my true inclinations would come to light. This alienated me
even more from society. In order to hide the direction and
force of my impulses from my own eyes, I opted to sublimate
them in an excessive love of music. In addition, that's where
I found myself in good company. . . .

At the concerts of counter tenor Alfred Deller, Marcellus
turned to the audience and snapped his fingers at me. "Look
at the men in the room!" At the Aix-en-Provence festival he
dragged me down Mirabeau into Les Deux Garçons cafe,
laughing derisively at the affected behavior of the white-din-
ner-jacket set on *Cosi* or *La Flute*. He went with me to the
record stores. "Have you seen this? What about this one?
What about all the salespeople?" I summed up his exasper-
ating talk in the following way. Homosexuality leads to melomania; melomania leads to homosexuality.

On the other hand Marcellus was far from being a fool.
His sharp, original mind often gave him in-depth analyses
(unadulterated by any sophism, except that which concerned
me). He had quite a handsome face and an interesting
body. He was even capable of loving music! That perhaps explains why I blindly put up with his little game for so
long. . . .

Afterwards, it seemed evident to me that it was Marcellus's
fabric of slander about my alleged tendencies that drove
Mélisande away from me. Otherwise it would not be under-
standable. She sincerely loved music as much as I did.

"Urine: 207 milliliters. I'm going to bed."

"Wake-up time. Code pink, number 10,216. Urine: 269
milliliters. Stool: 270 grams, nothing indicated. Arterial
pressure 12/8. Blood sample: all results within normal except
blood count with leucocyte count up 10 percent. Drank 300
milliliters of water from jar B with two tablespoons of instant
tea and three unrefined sugars. Ate 50 grams of CG28 gel

and 350 grams of protein source CS01. Visual acuity tests: 10/10. Five kilometer equivalent distance peddled on the exercise bike."

The space set aside for personal belongings is very limited in my capsule. As used to headset listening as I was, I gave up my loudspeakers without regret. Alas, there was no room for thousands of records. I was able to record my record library on compact magnet tape. My precious records are waiting for me at my place on their shelves. Provided that. . . .

Provided that they haven't melted. My treasure trove: a black flood of polyvinyl chloride. . . .

What a shocking vision!

THE ABSOLUTE HORROR.

But I am really too morbid, I let myself go to extremes. . . . Completely perverse! I go to the edges of human cruelty. Why such a disaster? A black flood???

What the hell, let's be optimistic! God is alive and well. The telephone works. It does even more—it does not disturb my peace and quiet. A smart telephone. An object endowed with a soul. A true miracle! (Proof of God's existence. . . .)

Let us therefore suppose that my records are waiting for me. There is a certain pleasure in cheating them with their copies, I who was so loyal to them. Wait, Penelope, I still don't remember. And even if I leave here, will I no longer be able to touch you? Well, well! It is so delightful to be able to understand three successive renditions of *The Art of the Fugue,* followed by two interpretations of *Boris Godunov* without having to adjust anything, without those annoying interruptions during the whole 25 minutes on each side of the record. There are some leading women singers who have a lot more breath than others. . . . How in the world can you not prefer them?

Come on, now, Penelope, don't be all that frightened, I'm kidding. And you have so many qualities for a lover such as I who endlessly repeats acts, to be sure, but who might need some sudden contact, some new piece of flesh with great impatience. My complete madness! An untiring Ulysses. A temperamental Ulysses!

My cherished treasures, my records, I will certainly keep watch on them. Because each record is easy to pick out. For sentimentality. You don't sell your nurse, your old mistress, in the slave market. . . .

"Code pink, numbers 10,217 and 10,218."

How can they be enjoyed for so long?

Human nature is so constructed that it gets tired of any-thing. Sex, taste, or hearing are all threatened by monotony more than by old age.

The remedies are time-proved and well known. Change your situation, your associates, vary your diet. Verdi—Stra-vinsky, Schütz—Offenbach. Arabic music intrigues me just like Richard Wagner's music. I haven't gotten burned out on it. Even more so with Indian music. . . . I pretend that I'm the reincarnation of a maharajah in a film by S. Ray; this pas-sion made him sacrifice everything for his *Music House*, his palace resounding with Ravi Shankar's magic.

I do not know how long I have been here, but the length of time—however long it is—has not diminished my love of music at all, purposely aroused by the arrangement of my choices. The silence itself is charged with unheard-of poten-tial, I relax, I smile, I enjoy all these operas, all these sym-phonies, all this chamber music, available whenever I wish! My sudden, instant harem! And never any distraction to fear, no bad-smelling kid to bawl during *The Good Friday Spell*.

Literally speaking, nothing keeps me from my music, noth-ing can ever keep me from it. No more favorable circum-stances can be imagined for a sumptuous life. I ask myself: "Should I listen to this or that?" Excerpts pass freely through my head. All these recordings are available for play. Music is so constructed that it does not live except when played in the dimension of time. The scores beg me to be reborn, to throb once again in the air. The competent and ruling listener, I am their supreme judge!

I soothe myself with my power. I delight in uncertainty. The delicious silence is prolonged. Even Mozart and Bach have to wait for a little sign from me in order to be revived.

I have time! I have all the time in the world!!!

"Drank 350 milliliters of water from jar A to which were

added four tablespoons of powdered milk and three sugars (pure $C_{12}H_{22}O_{11}$)."

Snap.
I heard. . . . In the deep silence punctuated by the quiet humming of soundproofed vacuum pumps I heard. . . . I was shocked to hear a noise!
Snap. Snap.
A strange noise?
Snap. Snap. Snap.
Like a human step, that's impossible!
Snap.
For the first time since I have been here something unexpected might be going to happen. . . .
Snap. Snap.
A paralyzing terror gradually grips me. A "thing" is out there threatening me.
Snap.
Someone! A fly in the ointment, a hideous fly introduced into my vessel, my own little functioning universe, attuned to my own rhythm; my musical paradise, my shell of rationality and pleasure.
Snap. Snap. Snap. Snap.
Crazy! I've gone crazy! This noise *cannot* exist. I've been sick too long. . . . I'm hearing things!
I yell, "Who's out there?" The sound of my voice echoes in the cave like a tremendous peal of thunder.
Silence returned, still tense with the vehemence of my call. Fear has made me a Thundering Jove! The impossible menace is gone. I cannot hear a suspicious sound anymore.
I regain my confidence. It is so simple, an acoustical phenomenon. . . . My musical orgies have sharpened my hearing. Anything can be explained. Let's forget about this ridiculous incident. The sleeping tablet dispenser has given me the maximum dosage.
I'm falling asleep.

"I'm awake. I made no record of when I went to sleep; I have taken four M302 pills. Urine: 196 milliliters. Drank 150 milliliters of water from jar B to which were added two tablespoons of instant coffee and two sugars (pure $C_{12}H_{22}O_{11}$)."

I have slept very badly.

I get the impression that something is canceling out the strong narcotic—as if several battles were being fought in me between the forces of sleep and wakefulness. The latter have come out on top. However, the strong dose of sleep medicine still continues to have effects; my mind is hazy, my reactions slow, and I can hardly feel my lips—as if numbed by cold. I know the feeling quite well; it remains as long as the drug stays in my system.

Before coming down here, my sleep often had to be artificially induced. Then an alarm clock woke me up. Finally, a cup of strong coffee eliminated the last traces of it. Breaking the infernal downer/wake-up/upper cycle has been one of the important reasons I was prodded into trying this *Motionless Trip* experiment.

Here music is my pride and joy; the lack of a schedule, my freedom.

Until this last sleep, I have had nothing but perfect "nights," soothing naps in the view of eternity without distress or uneasiness about the "next day," which only exists if I wish it to. If my last sleep was rough, it was no doubt because—for the first time—it was artificial.

I still have not yet had any reason to use the dangerous drug dispenser. When some dose of one of those drugs is dispensed, a mechanism engages and cuts off the supply for the minimum amount of time so that the next dose can be taken without danger. In the case of sleeping medicine, the system is obviously geared to preventing suicides. . . .

I try the sleeping medicine dispenser; it is shut off. Then it is true that I have been getting little sleep. I try to remember. It's a repeating signal that wakes me up—I'm sure of it. A light . . . A smell? . . . A sound???

Snap.

That's the sound.

Snap. Snap.

I'm having a nightmare! I try to scream; no sound issues from my mouth. I try to get up; objects dance before my eyes; the ceiling goes round and round. I collapse onto the bed.

"Wake-up time. I have not been recording my sudden lapses into sleep. Urine: 283 milliliters. Stool: 225 grams."

I have a terrible taste in my mouth.

Oh, yeah, the sleeping medicine, and that horrible dream. . . . Was it a dream? I'll punch up another dose of sleeping medicine. The machine spat out the pill. This time, at least, I slept for a good long while.

I had to get up again. A good cognac (my secret reserve) washed away the aftertaste lingering in my mouth. Hm! Not bad. . . . Another little glassful. There you go! That's much better. I feel fine, ever so fine . . . completely euphoric, to tell the truth. Well, well! What was bugging me?

Snap.

That's it, I remember.

Snap. Snap.

The noise. The famous, mysterious noise.

Snap. Snap. Snap.

Weird snapping, like a human footstep. I'm no longer afraid of anything. "Hello?" Let's be friendly with this visitor! "Come on in, dear friend. Have a drink with me." I pour two glasses. He stays quiet, he doesn't move around anymore. I look at the two glasses. But, am I a fool, he may be a stranger. "How are you, dear?" Silence. "Sprechen Sie Deutsch?" Silence. "E' pericoloso sporgersi." Silence. "Credo in unum Deum (this time I sing) factorem coeli et terrae, visibilium omnium et invisibilium. . . ." Invisibilium. No mistake about it. "Well, you loony, I'm gonna go have a look at your puss!"

I grabbed hold of a flashlight and dashed out of the airlock. How amusing it was to pass through those canvases! Would you believe a tiger in a circus?

Here I am in the cave. "Now, sweetie, are you going to show yourself?" My flashlight swept over the stalagmites, stalactites, searching every nook and cranny. . . . The noise did seem quite close.

I made a circuit of the capsule. . . .

Nothing, not a soul.

"Not only did you stir me up, but you don't exist!" Furious, I went back in. I plopped down at my table. I'm crazy! I heard it nevertheless. I'm crazy! I downed another two small glasses.

Snap.

"Keep quiet!"

Snap. Snap. Snap.

Go away, noise, you don't exist.

Snap. Snap.

I'm at the end of my rope. This is dreadful! I've not been able to stand up to the strain. I'm a pitiful case. Mélisande ... Marcellus! You guessed it—I'm unable to see it through to the end. That's part of my nature! It's in my blood! Age-old despair. . . . A long line of flash-in-the-pan forebears. An outstanding family of stillborn geniuses. And coming down through time, increasingly hardy, they live on sacrificed generations, the impulse of self-destruction, our thriving demon ... finally my conqueror!

Everything has now been played out; I am a failure in life. Furthermore, I am no Mozart (not even a Cimarosa!).

My eyes glanced absentmindedly at my colored scrawls, the canvases in my exhibit. Outside is death. Outside is the noise, madness! Unconsciously my sight was riveted to the black surfaces. I felt drawn in by these dark records, these bottomless holes. . . . Fortunately my tears came to confuse this irresistible call from the depths. My subconscious descended into oblivion. Once again I was lucky enough to avoid meeting the monster face to face. I made no reflection in the mirror just like a vampire.

My stomach is swelled up. I feel very tired, eager for another small sign of mercy. A wave of cowardice completely inundates me. . . . I kneel. Even lower: I crawl! I confess my sins!!!

It'll be hard, but I have to confess my sins.

"Well! Uh . . . I believe I'm . . . hearing things. I'm hearing . . . it seems to me that I'm hearing . . . uh . . . a kind of snapping that sometimes has the cadence of a footstep . . . a human footstep. I—"

Snap.

The modulation meter moved. The noise did exist, the dictaphone has recorded it!

Snap. Snap. Snap. Snap. Snap.

There it is again!!! It's quite clear, a noise coming from very close to the airlock. . . .

A rat!

It was a kind of rat, a dormouse. The poor little thing came up to the edge of the capsule in small leaps, frightened at the plastic sheets. It must have fallen down into the access shaft and then was attracted to me by the smell. It ran away whenever I got close, but it came back—the poor thing, it must be dying of hunger. I left it 250 grams of CP30 protein on a plate.

Friday has changed my life. Ever since the little creature has been sharing my existence in the capsule, everything has taken a new turn.

With infinite patience, I had to appeal to it as a master, teach it like a child. The feed has won it over to me. She came to feed closer and closer to the entrance, then in the lock, finally in the capsule itself. I have gotten her used to my touch. Friday lets me pet her, and she sleeps in my bed just like a well-bred pussy cat! It has been hard for me to be her master, and I would so much not like to remember by what means I came to be here. . . .

Friday is a friend. She spends long moments looking at me with her intelligent eyes. I believe I can see in her the small rodent that outlasted the most terrifying dinosaurs. What is more, they were our common ancestors, both hers and mine. We are close relatives; she is my aunt, so to speak, and it is not surprising that we understand each other so well. She listens to me when I talk to her. When she wants to tell me something, she acts it out with gestures and motions that I readily understand.

The marvelous exists in a living being. It cannot be reduced to an organism made for needs alone. If you expect to understand anything at all about her, you must consider more than intelligence, more even than sympathy. . . .

Friday, I love you.

I believe you love me too. If not, how could you explain the impatience you show when I'm engrossed in my thing, when I'm listening to my music? You run between my feet in a frenzy; you climb up my legs; you come up and stare at me right under my nose; you go so far as to nibble on the headset wire. (Fortunately it is insulated!) You're jealous.

My existence has taken an altruistic turn. Instead of my asking every instant, "How can you make me happy?" I inquire of Friday with a look that says, "How can I make you happy?"

I have changed the makeup of my food so that Friday can better partake of it with me—and so that she can enjoy it, if such mixtures appeal to her.

I have reason to believe that even my circadian rhythm has been upset, most likely in the sense of being sharply curtailed. The little creature could not have survived except for a short time beneath the ground so that her rhythm is no doubt still more like a 24-hour cycle.

At last, so much in love that I give up music increasingly often.

Since I met Friday, there has been so much rearranging to do that I haven't had the time to devote to my melomania. The seductive inveigling by my lovely friend requires me to be more mobile than the headset allows. On the other hand, listening to music always takes up a large part of my consciousness, and so I want to give my full attention to it. I have spent hours, days (how many days?) outside my living quarters, outside the capsule, then in the big open lock.

When Friday became my completely separate companion in the capsule, I believed I could get back to my old pleasure, my ears to be soothed with music while she gladdened my sight. "Happiness, nothing but. Double happiness as if it no longer existed. . . . Who would want more than someone who has nothing! You can't have everything, that's the way it is and that's the way it was. It is forbidden!" She has the duty of reminding me of the moral in *Histoire du Soldat*.

After appealing to my heart, Friday did the same to my reason. She gives the impression that she thinks recorded music is no more music than the movements of an automaton are life. I do not agree with her on that score since music does not mimic body movement but translates the movements of the soul. It hardly matters that the sound reaches us long after it is played—the light from stars that we see is real even though it takes years to get to us!

However, I must recognize the fact that Friday is more alive than all of the music combined. . . .

I never grow tired of looking at her so expressive, so delicate face. I laugh at the charming way she eats. Both the round and elongated shape of her body fascinates me. Her short-haired coat is a small wonder, soft to the touch, a subtle color that quietly changes with shifts in the light. But wonder of wonders is her tail, a sort of small ghostly feather that is out of place! There is an exuding sexual attraction that has several times failed to affect me; nevertheless, she seems so delicate, so fragile . . . I dare not touch her.

"I must apologize for neglecting my reports for some time. Furthermore, it is possible that the atmospheric balance in the capsule has suddenly been upset; I left the two big airlock doors open. . . . Friday—I mean the dormouse—is motioning to me. I'll finish this report later."

It has taken me some time to think about Friday's last gesture. I should say it has taken me some time to admit that she could ever ask such a thing of me.

Friday wants to leave here!!!

It is not that she is not cared for or fed or that she's tired of my company (she has clearly restated her friendship), but she seems to have an uncontrollable hormonal flow, an irrepressible urge to carry out the duty of breeding for the dormouse species. . . .

Friday has already caused me to rethink all the details of my life in the capsule. She has disputed all my tastes, upset all my habits. She is my bad conscience, my political commissar, a merciless dialectician!

On the subject of my painting, I have seen the refined estheticism of my previous work take on a declining meaning in Friday's eyes. She expected better from me. She wanted me to go beyond simple statement, the static and desperate style of my *Death is Outside* series. The role of art is by its very nature always in a state of flux. A work of art does not have the right to describe a definitely hopeless situation. The artist must fight with and drag others into the struggle. He must get a message across! And if death is outside, there is no possible way to communicate!!!

I have taken down the canvases in my exhibit to replace them with a series of portraits of Friday, first very stylistic, then increasingly realistic. My love for painting, based on the absolute concept of "Art for art's sake," has given way to my passion for Friday. I used to play at the act of *painting*. Now my pride and joy is *painting Friday!*

Friday appreciates the new direction my work has taken. For one thing, communication has been established, since I paint a subject completely outside myself, an independent being. (Up to the present, I only painted representations of my own anxieties; now my pictorial vocabulary has enlarged beyond my problems with the world.) For another thing, the development of my style in an increasingly pronounced vein of realism seems encouraging to her from the viewpoint of helping creative dynamics.

Meanwhile Friday still voiced serious reservations about my art and, it seems, about any form of artistic creation in the past. She sees—with good reason—that the artist's attitude is right away a withdrawal into himself. The pleasure an artist gets is a type of dangerously individualistic self-satisfaction. This can only lead to consequences—affecting the artist's body—as bad as masturbation, practices that are roundly condemned in pure, progressive countries: excessive brain stimulation, dizziness, insomnia, general loss of strength, and, finally, diminution of creative energy. Friday has tried to break me of my solitary tendencies by suggesting an extensive study of works by the great thinkers of the French Revolution. Friday now demands that I renew contact with my peers, that I honestly submit my art to judgment by the people.

I resist her arguments. The artist's sacred egoism is always seen quite justified not only by the artist himself, but in succeeding generations of the entire human community. It is very possible after all that Constance had an urgent need for paper to cover his jars of preserves; however, every opinion poll approves Mozart 100 percent for soundly beating his wife whom he surprised in the act of destroying his masterful sheets of scored music. After him, who among us would not be ready, with pleasure, to punish his guilty wife more, in the hopes of retrieving traces of Wolfgang Amadeus's heavenly inspirations?

Let us think about the last quartets by the great Ludwig. It is easy to say that art is so much greater than the artist's isolation is complete—Beethoven the deaf, Moussorgsky the drunkard. . . .

As far as any wish to have me find my peers (if they still

exist . . .), this stubborn wish to get me back to the surface, this wish to reintegrate me into the proletarian masses,
Friday does not even realize that it comes from her urge to
mate. All this dialogue is a result of chemical reactions taking
place in her glands! This does not detract from the fact that
her arguments are valid, far from it. But, after all, what is
Friday's present ideal? To give up her dignity and independence, to rent her body to strangers, to get pregnant, let her
graceful curves swell up to a grotesque size, to nurture like
precious plants these small living cancers that are devouring
her womb and breasts, then discarding her like suddenly useless packing. . . . Friday, my dear.

But she keeps on by using my passion for her as a lever to
break down my last mental barriers.

She has just hit me with the decisive argument. "Your
creations, your painting, imagine it all buried with you. En-
tombed forever! And no small boy to discover by chance the
entrance to the gallery leading to the treasure. . . . The Las-
caux never discovered?"

Now there are no longer any details. I am facing my re-
sponsibilities. Have I the strength to be a new man, to make a
clean break with my individualism?

I try to argue; I try to justify our presence here. But what
can I say?

No monastic life-style pushes seclusion to the point that I
have put up with it. I have been mocked, my credulity has
been exploited. I have been used like the dogs that were shot
into space without any hope of return. At least they did not
agree to it! As for me, I am a consenting victim of exploitation of man by man, an objective accomplice of the old order. . . . And for what experiment, great gods? Can you call
this science, the weighing of dung, urine, and sperm? So
many grams, milliliters. . . . Quantitative analysis. Qualita-
tive analysis too. "Is the substance needed?" You can believe
fully in Molière. . . .

Interplanetary travel?
Man in space?
Let me laugh!
First of all, man will never leave the solar system.
Secondly, if man takes a small step to Mars (it is quite im-
probable at the present time, but we must admit it is very
feasible), there will be a clock for it, or rather ten, one

quartz (you know the gold-plated space stopwatch on sale everywhere), three cesium, fifty super standards!!!

And do you believe that there will be only one? Certainly not! There will be at least three.

Could everyone freely organize his use of time? Are you kidding? It would be like anywhere else, three eight-hour shifts: Al on duty from 0600 to 1400 hours, Bert from 1400 to 2200, and Charlie from 2200 to 0600. Circadian rhythm? 24 hours! Well, let's see. . . . The fine young men go from here to the other end of the solar system; if in addition they have to be exiled. . . .

Have you seen a haywire chronometer, a musician, or simply a stargazer? Nothing except for a few kazoo players, almost. Waiting for orders. Waiting for the order to push the button that. . . . In fact, I too was waiting for the order. I am here for that reason: "Reestablish human contact after an indeterminate period of silence." Contact? I have already said they want to know if I am ready to obey blindly. There's a good boy scout for you: *Always ready!* after all these years of spent youth at the bottom of this deep ditch. . . .

I am going to reestablish human contact right here and now! Oh! But wait a minute!

The phone!

The phone!

If I could only yell at them TO HELL WITH ALL OF YOU!

Hello!

Hello!

No juice, no doubt—the line has been cut.

What now?

Am I really the only member of humanity left, and everybody up there. . . . Boom! Boom! Bang! Bang! . . . Mortibus? Have they done one another in with all-out nuclear warfare?

Keep calm. Friday seems to think that the silence on the phone does not prove a thing. Without having to resort to it, the people (the ones who dispatch repairmen) on the surface are unaware that it is no longer working. Most certainly the phone is out of order, but that does not indicate that God does not exist. I agree with you, Friday.

"Well, are we going back up?"

I believe I heard the small sneering voice, now impatient.

"Well, are we off?"

Go back up? The surface? The land, the water? An image
flashed before my eyes, an old memory of Venice, the city on
water. It was dusk. On Piazza San Marco the orchestra was
playing tango after tango for some old society dancers. On
the Piazzetta a band was playing Verdi arrangements. Veneti-
ans were listening attentively, tears in their eyes. Patriotic
emotion was at its height. There was life! I was ready to
chuck into a canal my ticket for the evening concert at the
Doges Palace. Marcellus was calling me. "Well, are we off?"
Let's go . . . I found myself in a room filled with oils by
Canaletto showing Venice in the eighteenth century, eternal
Venice. . . . Music: Monteverdi's madrigals. . . . A prodigy!

"Well, are we off?"

I would like to know if Venice has sunk for sure. I would
like to know if everything has sunk. . . .

"I'm choking in here, let's get going!"

"All right, let's leave!"

"Ah! I can finally breathe! For an instant there I thought I
was going to get lost in these enormous caves. I was just
about to drop. In the caves the air is close and humid like
lead dew, and the deep darkness like poisoned pastry. And
now, all the air was like sea air!"

. . . All the air from the whole earth! . . .

"I tried using the phone. It's out of order. Everything else
is in good working order. The lock plays its new role of isolation. I carry with me my pink notebook and the dormouse. I
am going up to the surface again. End of report."

I have stashed some provisions in my backpack. Friday is in
there too where she has enough room. My flashlight cuts
through the darkness of the subterranean gallery. I am a bit
apprehensive about stepping into a hole. Oof! The ladder is
still there—the nylon has not aged.

Beginning the endless climb. . . .

I cannot yet see daylight. . . . However, I recognize the
signs. . . . I am right before the top now. I put out my flashlight. No light. Maybe the entrance is shut up with a
door. . . . Has it been walled in?

Buried alive!

I have been buried alive! Already tired from the long

stretch of climbing, my heart is racing. An overwhelming anxiety racks me. A never-ending vertigo is on the verge of swallowing me up in the black vacuum surrounding me on all sides. I switched on my flashlight just in the nick of time. The light calmed me down somewhat. I painfully made my way again; I could only climb very slowly, step by step. Suddenly I felt a breath of warm air. Saved! I no longer felt tired. I clambered up very quickly and emerged without realizing that I am on the outside. . . .

It is pitch black, just that simple. I am assailed by an avalanche of familiar feelings almost forgotten—the smell of wood, the caress of wind on skin, the softness of grass where your feet press it down. A section of sky revealed itself momentarily.

Stars!!!

For me this was a rebirth into the world! I rejoiced, I hugged the ground, I gave thanks to the earth, our fertile mother goddess. Then I lay on my back and waited for God.

It was black, all was quiet.

I could believe I was still in my capsule. However, I know the unconquerable force governing time and light here. I gladly gave up my solitary rhythm. I was ready to submit myself to the laws of the sun god. Beforehand, I humbled myself before his splendor. . . . The first light of dawn saw me prostrate in ecstasy in the direction of the rising sun. . . .

Green.

Everything is green.

A thin veil of clouds filtered the sun and blotted out the blue of the sky. Only the plant life shone. The forest covered the hills as far as the eye could see. The trees, the ferns, the thick weeds all have partly overgrown the old entrance path. Here and there the remains of the telephone line show that it has been abandoned for a long time. I walk a few steps in the road leading toward the plain.

No human sound disturbs the air. No plane, no lumberjack in the woods. It does not prove a thing; I am still too far from the small village. Nevertheless, the lush plant growth gave a disquieting impression of nature returning to the wild state. . . .

Woof! Woof!

Barking in the distance. A dog! Men *still* exist since the

dog is a strictly domestic animal unable to survive in a wild state!!!

Men. . . .

I am afraid. I sat down on a tree trunk fallen across the road that had apparently died of old age (is it possible?).

Friday was making increasingly frenzied movements in my backpack. She should have been fed long ago. I fixed her food and put it on the ground. "Friday, will you stay with me?" If I take her out of the pack here in her natural surroundings, she will obviously try to get away. On the other hand, if I meet a man, if I go back to life in society. . . . I sensed that something irreversible was going to happen.

"Well, are we off?"

It was too late to go back. Friday was no longer imprisoned, I have freed her. . . .

It all happened so fast!

Friday hesitated a little, staring at the food, then she scampered down the road like a streak of lightning. The barking got quite close. I saw the dog rushing in my direction. Friday was literally sucked up into its snout.

It was horrible.

The spaniel broke her neck with a single bite. Crazy with rage and hurt, I collapsed, cradling my head between my hands. Panting quite close by made me open my eyes. In an act of submission the dog had started licking me on my legs and watching with moist eyes for a sign of approval from his new master. I kicked him as hard as I possibly could before running away.

Death is outside.

"I have come back."

TAKE ME DOWN THE RIVER

by Sam J. Lundwall

A man was preparing to go over the edge of the world when they came down the road from the hotel. He worked doggedly with some detail on his contraption, a dull metal cylinder resembling an oversized beer barrel richly adorned with projecting boltheads and spidery rods, stolidly refusing to meet the eyes of the few spectators that stood around him and his vehicle, offering him and themselves joking advice and wisdom. The man, an elderly, surly fellow with small piercing eyes and a thin, disapproving mouth, finished tightening a series of bolts, crept with amazing agility into his contraption, and banged the lid shut with a loud crash. The sound of more bolts being tightened from the inside could be heard for a while, then everything was quiet again. An expectant hush fell over the dozen or so spectators around the metal barrel. The incessant roar from the wide river falling over the edge and into space seemed to swell and engulf the group on the riverside.

"He is inside, now," said one of the bystanders, a woman in her sixties with unmemorable features but piercing voice, one of those eternal summer resort people always lured to scenes of madness and death.

"So he is," said her companion, a somberly dressed man who for the past minutes had been staring at the new couple like a lonesome dog looking at possible new and kinder owners.

"Someone ought to help him over the edge," declared the woman. "He can't lie there all day."

"He should have thought about that before he got himself into that thing," said another bystander. "*We* didn't ask him to do it."

"He could suffocate in there!" said the woman in sudden alarm. "He might die!"

"He *will* die when he falls over the edge," said an unseemly cheerful young man in garish clothes and very shiny hair. "He can wait. If it was *me* in there, I could wait forever, I tell you that." He turned to the newcomers, a fortyish man in sports jacket and a much younger girl. A mistress, thought the garish young man who had never had a mistress but always had longed to. Or a daughter. He smiled at her. "What do you think?"

The man shrugged his shoulders. The girl smiled shyly and looked away.

"Someone ought to *do* something!" appealed the woman.

The barrel lay immobile on the riverside, only a few feet from the rushing water, its various projecting rods and pins sticking out like the legs of an overturned beetle. Several hundred yards away the river, at this point almost a mile wide, had eaten its way down through the hard rock at the sharp edge of the world and went in a gently curving slope down to a point some fifty yards below the plain until it fell over the edge, down into an abyss that literally had no end. Standing at the outmost cliff edge, one could see the face of the cliff drop straight down into nothingness, and far away distant stars, even in the middle of the day. No one was near the edge now. It was off-season, no fruit vendors, no souvenir hawkers, only a dozen people staring with varying degrees of interest and boredom at the unmoving barrel.

"He should have done it last month," said a sage old man, underlining his words with energetic nods. "A lot of people come here during the season, a damn waste to do it like this, if you ask me. No one here who can appreciate it, no . . ."

The barrel started rocking back and forth, like an overturned beetle trying to right itself. The surly man inside threw himself forward, then backwards, shifting his weight in impatient, jerky movements. The bystanders ooh'ed and aah'ed as

the barrel turned slightly, rocked back again, then fell over
toward the frothing waters. One projecting rod caught in the
muddy ground, bent a little but got free when the barrel
slowly rolled down to the edge of the river. The surly man inside banged furiously at the metal with hands and feet, anxious for the indescribable, vertiginous moment when the barrel
would start its unending fall through space. The man in the
sports jacket nudged the girl (*Mistress?* wondered the garish
young man. *Daughter?*) with his elbow and made a gesture
toward the outmost cliff. They went away, unnoticed except
by the young man who gazed wistfully after them, dreaming
of forbidden carnal love, or any carnal love at all.

"Some summers they come by the thousands," said the
sage old man, blissfully unaware that no one was listening.
"They do it in barrels and boats and riding on logs or just
swimming, but all go over the edge and no one ever sees
them again. Only foreigners do it, though. None of us who
live here, they come from all parts of the world and just fall
over . . ."

The barrel finally fell into the churning waters of the river
and was swept away. A boy ran alongside it at the bank,
shouting joyously. The rest of the bystanders just stood looking after the glint of metal bobbing on the waves.

"I really don't understand them," confessed the sage old
man. "I really don't."

The man and the girl had just reached the outmost edge of
the world when the barrel flew out in space. It shot straight
out for almost a hundred yards before it started falling; the
midday sun gleamed in polished metal and glass. The crafty
old devil inside must have started working as soon as the barrel left the world; the projecting rods turned into wide metal
wings; a large parachute suddenly burst out like an enormous
flower over the gleaming cylinder. It checked the fall somewhat, but could not halt the descent. The barrel slowly sank
down into the eternal night.

Behind them, the little group of bystanders had scattered to
tea and slow, meandering talk. They sat at the edge of the
world, with their feet dangling over eternity. Faint stars
gleamed down there, far beyond the cliff which fell down into
gathering darkness. The world ended abruptly at the edge. Inside was still autumn, off-season, the sleeping hotel at the
edge of the world, old people noisily drinking tea at the worn

lawn where summer's croquet wickets still stuck up above the grass. Outside was unending, cold, black space. A hundred yards to their left the river fell roaring out in the gulf, water drops flashing like precious jewels in the sunlight until darkness swallowed everything a few hundred yards down.

"I wonder what there is down there," she said, leaning dangerously far out over the edge. Her thin forearms bent sharply outward from the elbows, long fingers dug into the soil at the edge of the world.

"Nothing," he said curtly, and immediately regretted it. "I don't know," he said. "Something . . ."

"Something different," she said, looking down into space.

"Perhaps."

She was shivering in her light dress. There was winter outside the world. She was thin, almost scrawny, very freckled, very blond. The light eyebrows stood out in startling white against the skin. She seemed very young.

"I have never seen the river before," she said shyly, as if revealing a shameful secret. "I have heard so much about it, but never seen it."

"No one sees it twice," he said.

"Except those who live here," she said, practically.

"Except those who couldn't go on," he said. "They don't count."

She looked down the slope at her left where the mile-wide river fell down into space. A big red-brown bird dived into the churning water only a few yards from the fall, reappeared with something glittering in its beak and flew heavily back toward the world.

"I wonder where that man is now," she said. "The one with the barrel, I mean."

He shrugged.

"Falling," she said. "Still falling. He'll never stop falling. What do you think?"

"That parachute won't help him much, that's for sure," he said.

"No."

"Or that barrel." He smiled. "A crackpot. Going over the edge in a barrel!"

"Yes."

"A *barrel!*" he repeated incredulously. "The world is full of nuts," he told her. "And most of them come here sooner or later, dragging their barrels and diving suits and one-man submarines and God knows what else, and then they go over the edge, thousands of them every year, and that's that . . ." His voice trailed away. He looked at the river which fell out into endless space in the most graceful and natural of curves. A faint rainbow hung above the rushing water; the scene was painfully beautiful.

"I wonder what he sees now," she said.

He shrugged and, without thinking, put his arm around her shoulders. She leaned against him, still looking out over the fall.

"Yes," he said slowly. "Yes. I wonder."

Dinner was being served when they got back to the hotel. The talkative woman with the piercing voice sat at a window table, talking to her somberly dressed husband.

"It is a shame," she told him in a voice that would not accept any contradictions, "letting that poor man suffocate inside that . . . *thing*. And no one cared. No one! What is the world coming to?" she wanted to know, "when a man can die like that right in front of so-called respectable people?" She observed the man and the girl sitting down at a nearby table and turned to them. "Is that," she asked, "right?"

The girl smiled at her. The woman turned back to her husband, obviously pleased.

"He was mad," the husband appealed, looking around for support but finding none. "Crazy. And in off-season, too. Going over in a barrel like that . . ." He threw out his hands. "What could *I* do?"

The woman turned to the girl again, hanging over the back of her chair like a huge, trapped animal reaching for an unreachable prey. The girl smiled mechanically at her, not really seeing her. "The problem with me," she told the girl, "is that I am too kind. I care too much for other people. I can't let a poor madman die like that, in a barrel, without air, trapped like an animal. But some people," she continued, turning back to her husband, "some people couldn't care less. Now, a nice secure boat," she said, suddenly shifting track, "*that* I could understand. A boat like ours, a decent little thing, nothing ostentatious. I could understand *that*. But a *barrel!*"

The man and the girl ate slowly, saying almost nothing,

while the woman at the other table kept on her interminable monologue. The hotel stood on a small hill right by the edge of the world. On the other side of the narrow veranda the bottomless gulf yawned at them, immensely enticing and terrifying. The depth tugged at them, whispered, persuaded. They ate slowly, without looking out through the window, and then went up to their room, grateful to get away from the persistent, lamenting voice of the woman.

The garish young man would have been gratified to learn that they were neither lovers nor relatives. In fact, they hardly knew each other. There was a mutual feeling of trust, maybe of sympathy, but that was all. They had met two days earlier, on a train speeding across the immense fertile plains that ended at the edge of the world, and decided to go together to the hotel at world's end. One hotel room is cheaper than two, and both were almost out of money after having traveled across the world to reach this place. Fellow travelers with a common goal, they went the last bit of the long journey together, ending up in a cheap room in the last hotel, off-season, paying the room in advance each day, spending the unchanging autumn days walking by the fabled river. They were both kite flyers; indeed, this was what had first brought them together on the train, both recognizing the familiar package carried by the other. Now they waited for the wind, the beautiful, strong wind at world's end which would carry them along and away. That night, they sat at the window in the hotel room, looking out at the changeless plains. Nothing moved.

Long after the girl had fallen asleep, he lay awake and stared up at the ceiling. She lay fully dressed close to him, with her right arm across his chest and her right knee shyly drawn up a bit over his legs, seeking a comfortable position but not quite daring. The gesture was very intimate and very trusting, much more so than the simple lovemaking of two strangers. He held his arms around her, rocking her gently, thinking of the wind. The ever-present sound of the river falling over the edge of the world was clearly audible and he remembered a song she had recited to him on the train:

Take me down the river
To ever-green and fragrant meadows

Where blindfolded maidens praise
The subtle light of dawn—

The deep tugged at him, whispered soothingly, promising
peace and bliss beyond the understanding of man. He clasped
the girl's thin body like a drowning man reaching for safety.
She sighed in her sleep, settling more comfortably with her
right knee drawn up over his legs, at last. He lay still on his
back, holding her thin body close, listening to the slowly
swelling sound of the river as it triumphantly fell into eternity.

The wind came during the night. The garish young man
saw them coming out from the hotel at dawn, carrying their
strange packages, opening them, unfolding majestic and wonderful kites. His was shaped like an enormous black bird,
with a wing span of almost eight yards. Cold, painted eyes re-
garded him as he snapped together rods, tightened paper-thin
canvas, readied lines and handgrips. The wide, black wings
flapped in the wind, trying to soar up and away from the
ground. He worked quickly and methodically, assembling his
kite with a skill that spoke of long practice. The girl's kite
was a mess. A many-colored butterfly, much larger than his
bird of prey, delicate and beautiful, but broken and torn during the long journey. The sparkling gossamer wings were broken, rods and edgings hung dead in her hands, strips of wood
jutted out like broken ribs. As he finished assembling his
magnificent, proud bird, she sat listlessly, staring down at her
dead butterfly.

The wind rose. He sat for a long time, looking back and
forth between the girl and his bird. On the veranda of the hotel, a few hundred yards away, a small group of residents re-
garded them with disapproving eyes, talking among
themselves. They saw the man and the girl (Daughter? Wife?
Mistress?) talk, with many imploring gestures, like all foreigners do, over their childish playthings. This went on for
quite some time. Then they rose, and the man strapped the
big ugly bird to the girl's back. She ran up against the wind,
spreading out the great black wings, and suddenly took off
from the ground. She soared up toward the overcast sky,
clumsily at first, then with growing skill as she used the wind
and the thermals to gain height. She made a pass around the

man, dipped her wings and then steered out over the wide river. The talkative woman at the veranda followed her flight with disbelieving eyes.

"Madmen!" she said breathlessly as the slim white form under the black bird climbed up toward the sky, leaving the lone man standing silent and still on the ground far below. "How could you let her do it? Why didn't anyone stop her? Why doesn't anyone *care* anymore?"

That night, the man in the sports jacket ate alone in the dining hall, under the hostile gaze of the talkative woman. She talked incessantly to her husband and the garish young man, who thought of the slim white figure dwindling in the distance, borne away by the black bird. The man in the sports jacket pretended not to hear; he ate slowly and methodically, talking to no one, and then went up to his room. That night, and the next day, and the day after that, he worked with infinite patience on the girl's broken butterfly. He worked slowly, repairing strips of wood and torn gossamer gauze, glued and wound and strapped. The dazzling wings grew and strengthened until he had to move outdoors with his work. He slept alone at night with one forearm over his eyes, as if to protect himself from unknown and unseen dangers. He went out in the first gray light of dawn the third day, carrying the wonderful butterfly in his arms like a loved one. The wind was rising over the immense plains; he strapped on the exquisite butterfly and lifted gracefully, almost without effort, from the ground. No one saw him when he soared up over the frothing river, circled around a certain spot once, as the girl had done, and then steered out over the edge of the world where thundering water crashed down into the total darkness and emptiness of space. The wonderful butterfly carried him far out, shimmering like a precious jewel in the dark. As the world dropped away beneath and behind him he smiled, for the first time since the girl went away over the edge. Then, when the frail gossamer wings gracefully folded and broke, his lips moved soundlessly. He fell into the endless darkness, following the girl, whispering as she had done, as she perhaps still whispered somewhere in the darkness where there was no beginning and no end and no distance, where the surly man's metal barrel still tumbled clumsily down and the wide, strong wings of the black bird carried the girl down, down, down:

Take me down the river
To ever-green and fragrant meadows
Where blindfolded maidens praise
The subtle light of dawn.
I'll dream you as the shadow
On the softly singing grasslands
In a never-never dreamland you can't pawn.
I'm walking down the alleys
Of my memory, don't disturb me.
I might smile at you and whisper: "Please
    be kind."
But there's really nothing to it,
I'm far away, a-strolling
In the self-contained universe
And the wastelands of my mind.

TURNABOUT
(Røtter)

INGAR KNUDTSEN, JR.

Translated from the Norwegian
by Joe F. Randolph

The people back home thought he was a fool. He understood that much. The quick look between Helga and cousin Jonas, uncle Stein's grin. . . . A fool who had lost his last few dollars, the entire sum for damages from the insurance policy's face value, and Marianne after that, and he was left with the responsibility for Little Marianne.

Cato Thorsen straightened up and looked out over the greenhouses, beyond them and up at the Amenthes range of hills. His hand automatically wanted to go up to his forehead to wipe the sweat away and somehow brush the stiff blond hair out of his eyes. He could not do that through the oxygen mask. Instead, he turned down the thermostat on the suit heating element a few degrees.

He had been on Mars for three years, and had settled down in Moeris Lacus, well placed in Mars's equatorial farm belt, as a farmer. What it meant was that he had started out the first year as a prospector, but gave it up for Little Marianne's sake. In addition, his bad foot bothered him more as a prospector than as a farmer. At fifty-six he hoped to have enough money put away to be able to go back to Earth—and still have a little left over. At the agricultural secretary's last inspection his small farm had been praised, and he had been promised preferred orders from the government. Which meant both a higher and more certain income.

"We need people like you, Thorsen," inspector Jamies had said. "Honest, loyal working people who will help us to colonize this stubborn planet."

Cato understood quite well what the inspector meant by "loyal." It had been a personal success story for him, everything considered, to go through the red tape and rigmarole in colonial administration on Earth.

"Mars," cousin Jonas had laughed derisively. "You're out of your mind. Besides, you'll never make it past the tests. That leg of yours. . . ."

"I *have* made it through the tests," Cato had replied. "They didn't give a damn about my leg. They were much more interested in my political ideas." And for once he had had the satisfaction of seeing Jonas Thorsen's arrogant expression twist up into a stupid-looking gape.

"Daddy! Daddy, can you hear me?"

Cato pushed the transmit button in his helmet.

"Yes, Marianne, what is it?"

"There's a TV call for you, Daddy. From Gagaringrad. Somebody wants to talk to you!"

"I'm on my way."

Cato left his tools and went over to the main building, a low-rise gray standard B house.

Inside the air lock he took his helmet off and hung his suit up.

Marianne came up to him when he entered and he squeezed her in his arms.

"The man says it's important, Daddy."

"I'm coming already."

Cato smiled down at Marianne's flushed face. At the same time he felt a stab of bad conscience. So dull was her life on the farm that a TV call was a big event. Especially when it came from the capital.

The man on the screen was a stranger to him. A pale, narrow face with dark eyes.

"Mr. Cato Thorsen, I believe?"

"Correct. And who are you?"

The man made an impatient motion with his hand.

"Secretary Urisow of SIS."

Cato just barely managed to hold back a surprised whistle. The security service! But what. . . .

"I'll make it short and sweet," Urisow continued. "We've checked your military record and found out that you used to be in the Politicomilitary Corps back on Earth and were discharged because of a service-related injury. Your record's perfect, and additional remarks label you absolutely trustworthy—"

"Thank you," Cato cut him off abruptly. "But what has all this to do with me? It's been a good five years since I was in the corps."

"I was coming to that. But first a question. Have you ever heard of MSO?"

"The Mars Space Organization? The rebel-rousing organization? Obviously I have."

"Do you know what it stands for?"

"Having Mars secede from the mother planet, and a revolutionary economic and political program, but what in the world—"

"We believe that MSO agents are active among the farmers in Moeris Lacus and Nephentes right now according to what some things indicate. And they have also been having a certain success from what we can gather."

"But why tell me this? I can't possibly undertake political work again. I still have a hard time with my leg, and besides, I have a daughter to take care of."

"Aren't you still loyal?" His voice turned brusque. "Don't you want to make a contribution to Earth's cause?"

Cato turned red.

"Sure, of course. I'm willing to do anything within reason to fight against a bunch of troublemakers here on the planet. I just have certain things I have to consider, and those are the things I'm referring to."

"Well." The narrow face with dark eyes smiled again. "We ask nothing more than to keep your eyes open. And if you come across something important, don't forget that we reward our helpers for their services." The narrow face paused expressively before continuing. "Take down this number."

A seven-digit number flashed on the screen.

"Did you get it?"

Cato nodded. "Right," he said. "I have it."

It was a rather irritated Cato that ate supper. Outside, a fire-red sun was setting among the scant crater rims in Syrtis Major and making the Martian sand look like blood. The sky was also redder than usual, a salmon-red hue which indicated that there was dust in the atmosphere. It could mean that a dust storm was on the way. Cato doubted it since it was not yet the right time of year for them.

He tried to rid himself of the bitter taste in his mouth after his chat with the SIS man. It was not that he did not want to do anything and the money was perhaps more enticing than he wished to admit, but for his part he did not know what he could do. He had hardly had anything to do with his two or three nearest neighbors since he had come there, and he could not imagine either Elin and Ezra Greshko or the Gomez family having any connection with the MSO. Nor the woman hermit Lydia Erness, for sure. Cato had intentionally shut himself off from the others, and saw no need to change the situation now. The only daily contact he and Marianne had with the outside world was with the Carter City school center, and it was necessary primarily for Marianne.

Thoughtful, he began clearing the table. The food on Marianne's plate was almost untouched. Cato looked at her, surprised. He had been so engrossed in his own thoughts that he had not noticed that she was quiet and pale.

"What's wrong, Marianne? You've hardly eaten a thing."

"I have a stomachache, Daddy," she answered evasively.

Guilt-ridden, Cato helped her onto the sofa and put a blanket over her. He sat down to hold her in his arms. It was a big responsibility to take a child to Mars, but he was so fond of her and could not bear the thought of leaving her with strangers at an orphanage on Earth. Yet he was often uncertain if he had done the right thing. He had come to Mars, he had not sought out any active contact with neighbors so that she could have other children to play with. . . . Everything considered, *he* had always been the one to make the decisions for both of them on his own terms.

He discreetly squeezed her hands.

"Does it still hurt?" he asked.

She did not answer but just nodded. Her hands were cold and she was running a slight fever.

"I have to go and do my chores in the greenhouse," he said. "But I'll be back soon." He put a CB unit over on the sofa. "Give me a call if something comes up, but try to get some sleep and it just might pass. Are you sick to your stomach?"

"No."

"I hope not, but if you have to vomit, just do it on the floor. I'll clean it up when I get back."

The sun had set and the stars shone down on the desolate plains and craters while the dust which was blowing in from the northwest made them glitter and sparkle. Cato turned on the light in the greenhouses. Phobos was high in the sky, an oblong giant-sized rock in space, which, even though fully illuminated by the sun, hardly managed to cast more than a shadow.

Cato's relationship with this planet which he made his livelihood from was largely marked by indifference. Somewhat like his relationship to his Antarctic home. A place where you could go and make good money only to turn around and spend it. His earnings had probably been a good deal less than he had expected, but it was mostly his own fault that he had chosen to become a farmer rather than going on as a prospector.

The Earth government had had a use for Mars's resources, they needed the planet as a way station to the asteroid belt and the moons of Jupiter. They had invested billions of dollars and had only recently begun to reap what they had sown.

And right in the middle of it all MSO had appeared, originally a space-travel cooperative started by the Mars colonists with the intention of protecting Mars and its profits derived from the wealth which had been brought up out of the Martian land and out of the asteroid belt.

Two years ago the organization had been outlawed after stealing property that rightfully belonged to the colonial administration and repeatedly abusing the right to use natural resources. . . . MSO had reacted by going underground and gradually changing its nature to become an organized center for all kinds of subversive activities, a rebel-rousing organization with declared revolutionary and anti-Earth goals. "Anarchist" used as an insult had no effect on them, they accepted

the name and propagandized for a positive meaning to the
word as they saw it.

In spite of his being on Mars, Cato felt more like a specta-
tor to what was going on. A person traveling through a land
with problems that only concerned him indirectly, a tour-
ist. . . . And that is probably why he could control his enthusiasm about getting involved in security service work no
matter how slightly. Cato Thorsen grew up in a big city on
Earth and had been taught to mind his own business, except
when he worked in the political corps—but it was a job.

He finished the potatoes in greenhouse 9 and left. He
closed the air lock door behind him and checked to see that
the green light was on. With a slight hobble he trudged back
to the main building.

During the night Marianne got worse. She lay crouched on
the bed with her knees up under her chin, weakly complaining with every breath. Her forehead glistened with sweat.

Cato called the Gagaringrad medical center.

"Hello. Medical center."

The young pimple-faced man at base headquarters
grumpily looked at Cato on the TV screen.

"I'm calling from Moeris Lacus, District 121. It's about my
daughter. She's sick. She has bad pains in her stomach and
back—"

"One moment and I'll connect you with the mobile unit,"
the TV operator interrupted.

Cato waited a few seconds before a roly-poly man's face
appeared on the screen. He introduced himself as Dr. Poul
Girard. Cato began to explain the situation.

"It doesn't sound too serious," the doctor interrupted.
"You'd better keep us informed about her condition. I'll try
to send a vehicle over there in a few days in case she doesn't
get better. Dust clouds have been reported in the air between
Hellas and Syrtis Major, so for the time being we've issued
orders not to send any ambulances out in that direction.
However, if you can bring her in yourself, of course do so,
but at your own risk."

"But I'm afraid this is serious, doctor. She's really having a
hard time. Can't you send an aircraft?"

"An aircraft?" The doctor's forehead wrinkled, and his

tired voice turned brusque. "They have been reserved for emergency cases."

"But this may be——" Cato began with increasing irritation.

"We don't think this is an emergency case," Dr. Girard finished. "There's an epidemic of intestinal flu in the Elysium district at this time, which could well be what your child contracted. But, as I said, look after her and let us know if she gets any worse."

Cato swallowed the rage building up in his throat—he was dying to say something he knew he would later regret. He glared at the doctor for a fraction of a second before lowering his eyes.

"Yes, indeed," he mumbled. "You damned hardhead," he added after breaking the connection.

"An epidemic in Elysium." Oh, hell. Neither he nor Marianne had been breathing any other air than their own and eating their own food either stored for weeks and months or homegrown from way back. So where could Marianne have picked up the infection? It was absurd.

In the west the faint mist of dust in the salmon-red sky was the same. Higher up the color of the sky was turning violet, some thin white clouds passed across the face of the sun.

Cato hurried to get ready for the toughest outdoor work so that he could come back in and sit with her even though there was not very much he could do for her. She had not shown any signs of throwing up. Her fever was not all that high, but it did not mean anything because he had given her a couple of pain-relieving tablets, which at the same time brought the fever down. So now she was finally getting a little sleep, and Cato felt relieved about it even though he knew that the improvements the tablets induced were false, and that she would be just as ill when the effects wore off. He wiped some beads of sweat off her brow. The love he felt for her pained him like a needle in his chest when he saw her lying there like that.

A dust cloud down in a small valley toward the Lowell chasms made Cato put his hand over his eyes. Reflections from the sun on the double plexiglass covering the greenhouse made it hard to see. It might be the people from the medical center. . . . He rejected the thought. And now the vehicle had come close enough for him to recognize Lydia Erness's green and yellow desert car.

Lydia Erness flipped up the catches holding the visor down on her oxygen mask when she came into the greenhouse.

"I came over to ask if you could lend me some fuses for my TV phone," she said right off the bat. "The thing is all out of sorts, and I have to fix it. I've already used up three fuses and I don't have any more. As soon as the people in Gagaringrad spot a little dust in the sky, they use it as an excuse for not budging a centimeter outside the Hellas district."

Cato's mouth opened wide.

"Repairing a TV phone connection yourself . . ." he repeated. "But do you have a repair license?"

"Pfah," Erness snorted. "Those bureaucratic bumpkins only manage to cause more trouble. They should listen to a word of truth or two." She looked at Cato with her impatient, light-blue eyes. "Do you have a couple of fuses or not? If not, Gomez can certainly lend me some."

"Of course I have extra fuses," Cato said quickly. "Stay here in the greenhouse and I'll go and search around for some. I know I should have some out in the workshop because I removed the old outlet here when I moved into the house."

Erness was standing in the house and waiting while Cato went into a back room. When he came out again, she was standing over the sofa Marianne was lying on. She turned around to Cato as she pointed to Marianne, who had now started moaning in her sleep.

"And what ails her?"

Cato held back a smart retort. The woman was so hardhearted that nothing at all would affect her.

"Stomach cramps," he said curtly.

"Stomach cramps!" coming from Erness's mouth it sounded like cussing. She bent over Marianne, who looked up. She tried to smile at Lydia Erness, but it was just a grin. Her face looked dismally pale compared to the black hair which lay spread out on the blue pillow. She willingly let Erness's fingers explore her.

"Does it hurt there?"

Marianne nodded.

"Yep." Her voice was barely above a whisper.

"Does it hurt the worst there?"

The grimace on Marianne's face answered before she could get out another yep.

"This kid needs a doctor, and right away. It may just be intestinal flu, as you say, but I doubt it. It looks more like an inflamed appendix, if you ask me."

"Appendix . . ." Cato repeated, and looked at her in alarm. "I called up the medical center, but they couldn't send anybody out here."

Lydia Erness busied herself with the pillow and gave a short, hard laugh.

"Obviously. Because of the 'severe dust storms,' right?"

Cato helplessly nodded.

"I'll call them up again," he said. "I'll have them do a diagnosis over the TV phone."

"Don't bother. They'll give you the same runaround. Their indifference to us has already cost human life both here and in other farm districts. They need us to cultivate the food they gobble down so that they won't have to import it at expensive prices from Earth, but no simple country yokel is gonna ask them to risk anything in order to lend a helping hand when it's needed."

"Wait a minute." Cato began an exasperated protest, but she brushed it aside with a hand gesture.

"I'll get your little girl a doctor," she said. "A qualified one."

Cato looked at her for a long second before he came up with what he wanted to say.

"You . . . you," he stammered. "How? Where from?"

"That's my business." Erness opened the air lock door. "What do you say?"

"Yeah, thanks. I say thank you very much," Cato said, bewildered.

"Good."

She closed the air lock door right in his face. He opened it back up.

"From the MSO?" he asked.

Erness smiled, but did not utter a sound.

A plan, an idea took shape in Cato's mind. He tried to reject it, but could not. So he tried to find something wrong with it, but could not.

He punched up the number he had been given for the SIS headquarters and asked to speak with Urisow.

Urisow's narrow face flashed on the screen.

"Yes?" His voice sounded impatient. So he recognized Cato. "Oh, it's you. That was quick. Have you anything to report?"

Cato savored the situation for a moment. For once it was he, Cato Thorsen, who was killing a flock of birds with one stone. He combined a patriotic, law-abiding act with a sure reward for himself.

"What do you say to arresting one or more MSO members?" he blurted out.

Urisow's eyes got big for a fraction of a second before they became narrow and sly again.

"Explain yourself."

Cato gave a short summary of what had taken place.

"And you insisted?" Urisow's face was impassive now, after the first surprised look.

Cato found that he had a liking for this man. He smiled.

"Well, Mars'll be an unlivable place for me after this. I'll have to have free passage back to Earth, and some money— is fifty thousand too much?"

Urisow did not bat an eye.

"You got it, provided that it really is an MSO doctor who gets caught in the trap. I'm counting on the fact that a doctor will have a lot of information he could divulge, names . . . Oh, well. We'll show up. You can count on that."

"One more thing. The most important thing on my part. Send over another doctor for my daughter."

"OK."

Urisow broke the connection.

Cato Thorsen heaved a surprised sigh of relief. So soft it was gone in a flash. Presto! All his problems were over. And besides, he could be proud of doing society a service by contributing to the rounding up of a dangerous terrorist organization.

The MSO doctor introduced herself as Dr. Vanda Minescu while the two armed militia people, dressed in camouflage suits, who accompanied her merely shook hands and mumbled indistinctly.

The doctor had just begun to examine Marianne when the SIS people emerged from the back room.

One rebel soldier tried to pick up her weapon which she had carelessly leaned against the wall behind her, but got a terrible blow on the neck with a rifle butt. She fell straight to the floor and writhed around. The other one raised his hands over his head. He looked Cato up and down.

"Coward," he spat. "You damned coward!"

"Shuddup!" SIS officer M'boto snarled and raised his pistol threateningly.

Meanwhile the SIS people snapped handcuffs on the soldier on the floor, and were busy holding Dr. Minescu's hands behind her back. She did not utter a sound, she just looked at Cato furiously and accusingly, as he irritatingly knew he was red in the face.

"You've learned your lesson, doctor," the officer sneered. "There are still average farmers and prospectors who are completely and fully loyal to their mother planet. But you people have preached so long and loud about yourselves as 'the people's representatives' that you've begun to believe your own lies." He turned to Cato. "Thank you, Citizen Thorsen, this was easier than shooting fish in a barrel. Have you packed your things?"

"My things? No—"

"Then go and get a suitcase and throw everything you're gonna need into it if you don't want to be around here when these people's cohorts come calling."

Cato shook his head speechlessly.

"All right, let's get a move on," M'boto growled impatiently. "Come on, come on!" He snapped his fingers to emphasize his last order.

"Hold on," Cato protested. "In any case, one thing I have to insist on is gonna come before anything else. My daughter. Urisow promised to send a doctor who could both examine and treat her if need be. That comes first."

The officer exchanged glances with one of the SIS soldiers.

"Corporal Groeder here, he's a trained doctor, right, Groeder?"

"Yes, sir," the diminutive corporal bowed.

"So go on in now and look at the young 'un. And get it out of the way!"

There was a pause while Groeder examined Marianne,

who was too groggy and exhausted to have understood very much of what had transpired. She whimpered quietly while Groeder was busy with her. Then he got back up.

"Nothing seriously wrong with your little girl, sir, that I can see. Just some strong gas pains."

Dr. Minescu laughed loudly and scornfully.

"The child has an inflamed appendix and should have been operated on long ago. I doubt she'll survive being transported to Gagaringrad even in a flyer."

"Bull," the SIS officer snarled. "From now on keep your trap shut until you're spoken to." He slapped Minescu on the face with the flat of his hand. A thin stream of blood ran down from her lips and onto her chin. "You can interpret that as a foretaste of what's in store for you." M'boto turned to Cato again. "You heard what the corporal said, Mr. Thorsen. You can rest easy about everything. Go on and pack your things, and, as I said, make it snappy! And then you and your kid will be in Gagaringrad before you know it."

But Cato was only half listening. As if half asleep, he lifted Marianne up and carried her out of the workshop with him.

What Dr. Minescu had said was swirling around in his head. He carefully laid Marianne down on a bench, but he wrapped her up well in eiderdown. He kissed her on the forehead.

"Your daddy's a fool, Marianne. Even what I'm gonna do now may well turn out just as foolishly."

He went back into the room and put on his pressure suit.

"I have to get something out in the greenhouses," he said. "Be right back."

Out in the greenhouse he turned on the light. Experimentally he lifted a long cutting knife. It certainly was not much of an arsenal he was holding. . . .

"What are you doing? Honing knives in the middle of the night?"

Cato spun around and stood face to face with Lydia Erness. She had crept up on him so quietly and he had been so wrapped up in his own thoughts that he had not heard her come in through the air lock. He bit his lip.

"Take it easy, man," Erness said. "You're really dog-tired. What is it . . . I hope it's not . . . Marianne?" A hint of apprehension crept into her voice.

"No, Lydia," he said. "That's not it. Not yet. I've gotten everything into a terrible mess. So terrible. . . ."

And then the whole story came pouring out of him, words rushed out of his mouth helter skelter.

When he was finished, Erness looked at him with a troubled face.

"Well, you certainly turned out to be a nice one. . . ."

She drew her pistol. Cato reached back behind him and found the long knife.

"I've changed my mind, Mr. M'boto," Cato said. "I'm not going to Gagaringrad. Not while Marianne is so sick. I'll be along in my own vehicle in a couple of days if she's better by then."

"What? Are you crazy? Don't you know what risks you're running if you don't come with us right now? This morning it's going to be swarming with rebels around here, and they'll hardly be satisfied with the answers you come up with when they ask what happened to the doctor here and her two bodyguards."

"I'll probably be able to talk my way out of it," Cato said.

"Go with them, Thorsen, and take your daughter along," Minescu butted in unexpectedly. "I'm not saying this for your sake. You can be buried alive in the desert dust for all I care—but she at least has a fighting chance if she gets to Gagaringrad by tonight."

Cato defiantly stared at the floor.

"I've made my decision. And as a matter of fact I believe you gave a wrong diagnosis, doctor. The appendix is not the only thing wrong."

"OK. It's your funeral." The SIS commander put his finger to the side of his head to show Cato Thorsen what he meant. "We can't waste any more time on this guy, men. It's been a long night tonight if I'm not too mistaken. But certainly with its bright spots." He looked at Dr. Minescu, and what he was thinking was clearly written all over his face.

Cato turned the air lock wheel and locked it. Next, he turned to the TV phone and punched up a number.

M'boto cussed impatiently while two men tinkered with the engine desperately to find out what was wrong. In an agitated

state he looked at his watch then at the soldiers working on
the engine and back again, and then over at the prisoners
whose faces he could barely make out behind the lattice-cov-
ered windows in the holding room. Some other soldiers were
busy rolling up the camouflage tarpaulin. The temporary
work lights cast a yellow Spartan glow on the scene down in
the small round meteor crater on the other side of Cato
Thorsen's greenhouse. The shallow hole in the Martian landscape had offered itself as the perfect hiding place for the
flyer.

The foolish Cato Thorsen had also come out and was
down in the crater trying to help with the repairs while all he
actually did was get in the way.

Corporal Groeder climbed down from the cockpit and
saluted stiffly.

"The radio's on the blink, sir," he said. "And if you ask me
what I mean, I think it suspiciously looks like sabotage."

"Sabotage? Sabotage!" With that the commander came
alive and cussed to himself *sotto voce*. "Corporal, go in with
Thorsen and use his TV phone to get in touch with headquarters. We gotta have reinforcements on the double!"

Fifteen minutes later Groeder came back crestfallen. His
helmet radio crackled as he turned it on.

"Thorsen's TV phone is out too, sir."

"Yeah, I don't understand it," Cato babbled. "It was working fine yesterday afternoon when I—"

"Thorsen!" M'boto pointed his index finger at Cato.
"There's something funny going on around here."

Nobody ever found out what he was going to say because
right at that moment lights from ten desert vehicles pierced
the darkness, and bathed the craters and farmstead in light.
Concealed by darkness and the thin air that carried no sounds
to the SIS people, the vehicles had surrounded them. And immediately Lydia Erness's voice burst out of the loudspeakers
in all helmet radios.

"You're surrounded and trying to shoot your way out or
trying to harm the prisoners will lead to a shoot-out in which
no SIS personnel will be spared! Lay down your weapons and
get up against the flyer!"

They obeyed hesitatingly. M'boto fiercely stared into the
lights and raised his laser gun.

"Put it down, commander!"

Cato's voice quavered, but the pistol stayed in his hand and pointed right at M'boto's chest.

In the vehicle lights armed MSO personnel moved down toward them.

"Cato," Erness's voice again sounded over the radio. "Unlock the doctor and the others, will you. The commander has the handcuff keys. We can only hope Minescu's hands aren't too shaky to hold her operating laser steady. Furthermore, I'd be happy to have my pistol back."

The trick Cato played on Urisow was so outlandish that it almost had to succeed.

Urisow's sharp eyes glared at Cato.

". . . haven't gotten there," he repeated softly. "Haven't my men gotten there yet? But we got a radio report that they had landed . . ."

Cato shrugged.

"Neither they nor the MSO doctor has shown up around here. Luckily nothing serious was wrong with my daughter. She's a lot better already."

Urisow completely ignored his last statement.

"The misfits," he chewed it out. "The dad-burned hoodlums have in some devious way managed to elude us again!"

Dr. Minescu chuckled in the doorway when Cato broke the connection.

"You've just been written off as spy material for SIS," she said. "But for that matter there was one thing you were right about in what you said yesterday evening. You're a super bluffer!"

Marianne was quietly sleeping after the operation when he went to check on the greenhouses for the night. You're alone again, you two, but not the same way as before, that he knew.

Yet he felt unaccountably easy in his mind. The course of events had thrust him out in front. In a confused moment he had changed sides and thereby changed his future for all time. And without still being sure about what was right and wrong.

Deep down inside, would he prefer to remain a farmer forever?

He had certainly gone through enough these last two days, but what had he lost?

His heavy, coarse boots left deep furrows in the loose Martian soil. In the sky a big blue-white "star" beamed down. It was almost as bright as Phobos—it was Earth. But Cato Thorsen forced himself not to look at it.

ARUNA

ERWIN NEUTZSKY-WULFF

Translated from the Danish
by Joe F. Randolph

I

". . . these bases cannot be tolerated under any circumstances," the president concluded. "If they aren't shut down, it'll be interpreted as an overt military action against this country, and complete retaliation—"

Martha turned off the car radio. For the time being she was still too worried to be in any mood for listening to music. That was not like her at all. Was the danger of war as imminent as the newspapers were screaming? Well, you could hardly keep from speculating about it. Arthur was now sitting and moping in his bomb shelter, of course. What a price it had cost! He wanted to "get used to it just to be on the safe side." Good Lord! All Martha could see was Arthur's case of hopeless nerves. It did not occur to her for an instant that she would ever wind up like that.

And those terrible dreams!

If it had been just a nightmare about the impending war—who did not have them these days?—but it was about black stuff and monsters and princesses not to mention even more ridiculous things. Arthur had no sense of reality.

Lately it had become quite bad. Psychoanalysis had not

helped, and she had jumped at the latest, desperate way out.
Hey, there's a parking place.

She had made an appointment with Dr. Allen, who was no
doubt a quack, but it would not hurt to try him out. In any
case, Allen was charming and listened very attentively to her
tale of woe; it was certainly nothing to ignore, as her husband yelled and screamed.

"Excellent!" he finally said. "I'll be glad to see your husband. I'll do what I can for him!"

It was the best news Mr. Mannering had heard in a long
time.

"You really do believe you can help my husband . . ."

"I didn't say that, ma'am. But I promise to try." Dr. Allen
stopped his fidgety pacing around the desk, sat down behind
it, and started looking through his appointment book. "Your
husband's sickness stems from a traumatic experience in his
past. He—"

"But, doctor, the other shrinks said the same thing. But
which one? Arthur had a very *happy* childhood."

The doctor dismissed her objections with a gesture of his
hand.

"I'm not talking about Arthur Mannering's childhood," he
said. "I'm talking about his previous life. With hypnosis I can
perhaps—perhaps, mind you—make him remember and relive the traumatic experience. This is actually the only type of
therapy, I believe, that has any chance for success."

"But . . . reincarnation. Isn't that a bit farfetched?"

Allen shrugged.

"You know exactly how I argue with my detractors ad
nauseam. The patient does not relive his previous existences,
but on the contrary, what I impute to him with suggestions.
Well, people were saying the same thing about hypnosis not
long ago, and psychoanalysis on a par with it for that matter.
You mustn't forget that *you* came to *me*. You can take it
from me. I won't con you into anything!"

Ms. Mannering got some time to think it over, but she
hardly used it. Right after Arthur's next nightmare she agreed
to Dr. Allen's experiment if he made the dangers abundantly
clear. Arthur himself was anxious to be pulled around by the
hair to a few dozen different shrinks, ready to do anything.
He had always been so in other respects as far as Martha was
concerned. His problems were still far from over.

In order to get the right response under hypnosis, the analyst had to go through countless sessions with his patient, who was possibly less enthused about this soulless routine. The preparations took so long that in the end it was hard to believe the day had finally come.

"If everything goes all right, Ms. Mannering—and God forbid it otherwise—tomorrow your husband in thought will be not a hundred, not a thousand, but close to *ten thousand* years back in time, five thousand years before the first pyramids were built."

That last night Arthur did not have any bad dreams. It was annoying up to a point for Arthur to wake her up all the time with his screaming and yelling, but that night she still could not get to sleep. She lay awake and thought about the experiment. And about the doctor. An impressive man, very attractive. Almost too good-looking to be true. Well, she would come to grips with all that in the morning. Maybe, she thought, she should not have married Arthur. He was a weakling, always nervous over nothing. If he were only an interesting case of neurosis, but there was nothing more exciting about Arthur than a Beschauffer ulcer.

Martha went to sleep.

"You may come in now. I've brought your husband back, and he should begin talking any time!"

"So did he go . . . back so long ago?" Martha sat down, looked at Arthur, and remembered what she had thought about the night before. If she had only been right. She did not object to the thought that Allen had taken her for her money. She could have financed his experiments! But would the doctor be interested in running off with her on Arthur's disability pension?

"I. . . ." It was Arthur who had made a sound halfway between a disappointed grunt and a whistling snore, and the doctor looked triumphantly at Martha, who immediately gave him a weird look in return.

"I . . . am . . . Sri . . ."

Martha turned up her nose. Rather undramatic. And thus still not completely realistic.

"I am Sri . . ."

II

He was lying down watching the sun come up. He was not interested in the sun. But shortly after sunrise animals came to get a drink. They came straggling in, sniffing and blinking at the red disc. They laid their ears back and came closer with lowered heads, they spread out around the water hole, walking around unconcerned at right angles to each other. Sri waited. He saw the glossy manes, and the wind, which was blowing in his direction, as it should, was bringing him the smells of fur and piles of sun-baked excrement, reminiscent of a crackling fire which made these kicking things edible. He focused his eyes at the right moment. He raised himself up with a sudden movement and at the same time thrust a spear under the ear of the nearest kid. When the kid stopped struggling, he was once again alone. He climbed up a tree after covering the kid with leaves and lay down to rest. He did not fall asleep but rested, he swung his legs on either side of a branch with his eyes closed. He lay in the sun, which came through his closed eyes in a red hue. Thoughts flowed through his mind, and he no longer noticed the hard branch against his back. He got up and floated away, he rolled into the water, he went to sleep, he twitched, the tree limb was hard again, and he rubbed against it. He thought and dozed and thought. He slept. He floated away. He was going up a plain that was tilting away from him, but which he could not see. A blue ball flashed in the distance and showed part of its surface; it took off with the same speed as he approached it with. He simply realized he was headed north.

The blue ball suddenly exploded and rained golden apples all over the landscape, which came into view. Slopes and hills, steel-blue without any irregular features or spoors of any living thing. They rose up and up before his eyes, and over it all was a reddening hill of blood-stained ice flattening out on top. On the plain of plains stood a woman in black clothing, and golden balls spun around her head like a halo. Her golden hair was spread out wide over her shoulders, she had red eyes like a beast of prey, and below the female features glowed a sensual mouth, almost a congenital deformity, in the opening of which two pointed white teeth gleamed. There was such strength in that face, so much feminine force that

Sri did not have to think that he would ever forget it; he had always been aware of it. The earth came up to him in the space of a bewildering second, and he landed in the grass under the tree. It was something that had never happened before. His ankle hurt, but it did not feel broken. He put the kid across his shoulders and headed home.

The next day he started north.

III

What a bunch of nonsense.

"Aruna?" That was what her husband kept on repeating. She shook her head at the thought. Martha had given the good doctor the brushoff. If it cost twenty-five bucks an hour to treat Arthur's nightmare, then he had better get used to it.

Hadn't these sessions already helped?

Sure, Arthur had not had any dreams the last couple of nights. But what proof was there? Martha had given up on Arthur. She had other plans. Arthur's pathological nervousness had yielded something—or could—if she played her cards right. Suppose he went and died on her? He was indeed a nervous wreck haunted by his continual nightmare, in fact he had often talked to his friends about the best way to do away with himself. Suppose he carried out his threat? Arthur was a coward. But then she could help Arthur on his way with nobody the wiser. Not even Arthur. Anyway, not before it was too late to do anything about it.

Insured for $100,000. That was not half bad. A new life. What about the doctor? Nope, he was not good for anything. Something better. Something better than Arthur would hardly be difficult to find—with one hundred grand in your pocket. Arthur had to go. And he had to die in such a way as to make it look like suicide. Martha thought it over. And so she began complaining. Going around apprehensive—he could not put up with that. All those burglaries. Wouldn't he buy a pistol?

That would look good, she thought. *Arthur Mannering Buys Pistol and Shoots Self Next Day.*

And so Arthur Mannering went out and bought a pistol.

IV

Sri had been heading north for three days; that is all it took him to reach areas he had never before seen. He came across a village where the inhabitants greeted him in a friendly way, and he was shortly lying in a bed in a hut and counting the stars through the window. He found it hard to fall asleep, and when he finally did, he woke up not long afterward. It was a never-ending night. He wanted to go back to the stars, but they were not there. Only a couple of specks just below the top of the window. He tried to remember and came to the conclusion that the missing stars formed a ball-shaped outline in the lower half of the carved-out window. He squinted and could *see* the sphere; not far from where he was there was a huge dome blotting out the stars. But it had not been there earlier that night. He got dressed and went out. Several of the villagers were standing around and staring the same as he was. They shrugged it off and went to bed. Only Sri was left standing there and staring. Then he followed suit.

The sun lit up the sky and contrasted sharply with the sphere, which was black as night, when Sri woke up again. He was the first one up, and he went to awaken a couple of the other young men. Together they set out toward the sphere, which was smaller and closer than they had thought, about ten people high. They got their courage up and touched it. Its surface was smooth though not shiny; even, but tough and resilient. It did not take the villagers much more than an afternoon to gape at it. By the time the most skittish in the population had touched the thing for their own amusement, they decided it was harmless. When they could not find any use to put it to, they gave up on it as of no interest to them. In the meantime Sri had left.

Five days of travel later Sri understood that he was on the right track because he found five of the very same gold balls the size of apples as he had seen in his dream. In the next village he found out that all the villagers had picked up the golden apples. Certain women found them enticing, some of them had two or three, which they hid under their bed. They were, it was said, shot out of a strange volcano, which had suddenly sprung from the earth a few days ago. Sri understood what they meant. Not far from the village sat one of the black domes.

The golden apples had aroused great excitement in the small village. They were traded for enormous amounts of food or clothing. Everyone wanted to own them. One girl had become a murderer to get her hands on some from a younger sister who had quite a few. She was banished from the village for her transgression, and when Sri had to move on the next morning, she urgently begged him to take her with him to the next village on his journey. Sri consented. The girl had had her apples confiscated, but she had managed to bury one outside the village before she had been caught. She retrieved it, and the little village disappeared beyond the horizon.

They did not come upon the next village right away, and one morning when they woke up, the apple had turned black and soft. The girl—Eni was her name—became a bit disappointed, but still did not have the heart to part with her treasure. In the end the ball melted into a blob on the ground, impossible to carry.

Sri was at his wits' end. They could not take the black blob with them, but Eni did not want to leave it behind. A little slap was all the murderer needed. Sri could still not bring himself to leave her behind as quarry for beasts of prey. While he was thinking, the sun set, which got rid of his problem for the time being.

He was awakened by something cool touching his hand and thought that it must be Eni, who was still romantically inclined. But it was the black stuff. It was moving around and shifting, writhing like a snake, stretching out and contracting like a piece of white-hot iron on an anvil. In between times it lay perfectly still as if to catch its breath. Sri moved farther into the woods and again lay down to rest.

The sun rose, and Sri went over to wake the sleeping girl. Before he managed to do so, he glanced over at the black spot, which was motionless but had taken on an unmistakable form. It was clothing of some sort. Eni woke up and looked at it with suspicion and surprise. So she suggested that they should leave the thing and continue on their way, which made the hunter tremendously happy.

He went down to the river and washed. Here were many animals, and he thought it would not be so hard to obtain the morning meal in that place. He had taken his spear with him to the river. Now he was holding onto it tighter—a deer was in sight. Cautiously he slipped closer. The animal did not seem to spot him, but it nevertheless moved around so much the whole time that he could not reach it with his spear.

Much to his annoyance, it led him back to camp where Eni would certainly frighten it away. He was quite right. There she was, only she did not see him yet and she was shooing the deer away! No, she was apparently busy with something else. Sri's attention was distracted, he had his eyes on the girl, he felt uncertain, was sure that the deer would still eventually discover him, but he kept lying in the underbrush.

Eni was walking around the strange clothing in smaller and smaller circles. Finally she stooped down and touched them, but immediately drew her hand back as if she had been burned. Yet she touched it again.

The deer began moving away, and Sri loosened his grip on the spear. Now he only saw the girl and what she was doing, fascinated for a while and unable to disturb the weird scene. Eni undressed and held the clothes up in front of her, then she began putting them on; they covered both hands and feet, they were tight around her, they sparkled when she walked around, they fit like a new skin over her whole body. Finally her face disappeared along with her limbs as if there had never been any. He thought she must be choking, and she soon began struggling, she was floating in the clothing, she almost tied her own body up in knots as she desperately rolled around on the dew-wet grass. Then she lay still, but she was breathing regularly. She was out of breath, but she could obviously breathe in that garb.

She hardly looked like a woman then. He got the impression that her body was missing under the clothing, completely replaced by the black stuff. He thought about how it would be to touch and knew it right away. He threw the spear aside, grabbed onto a tree limb, vomited, and came hard at the same time. That is why he crossed fields heading north, trembling and sobbing like a freezing child.

V

The next village Sri came across was deserted. The black sphere which he had learned to recognize towered over the land. All around lay the golden apples, some had burst and left blobs, others had completely turned into ready-to-wear clothing waiting for their female victims. So what? When women put on the clothing, who cared? They became irresistible to the village men and they could take them wherever they wanted to—no, wherever *it* wanted, the big round thing whose damned offspring were now shooting up all over the countryside.

Sri studied the sphere. If there had been an opening in it, it was now gone. And Sri could guess why there must have been one.

The village men had left their clothes in a little pile.

Sri hardly got any sleep that night. He woke up at dawn, but still felt tired out and went back to sleep. He again saw the plain, the blue ball or globe, which was first like steel, then black, then shiny, then dull, the golden apples, the red hill, and *Aruna*, who was beckoning him silently. The dream consoled and invigorated him, and he resumed his journey.

He walked through a crumbling world, but he walked in its loving embrace. That there would be other worlds after this one did not interest him. Only Aruna, Aruna who was waiting for him, way up north at the end of the world.

Worlds upon worlds would disappear into the black stuff, into a big weak oneness. Everything will be like that, smooth, but not radiant, even, tough, and dead. But every time it happened he would be there on his way north, toward the blood-stained ice and Aruna. She wanted to see him—he dreamed of her bestial eyes, her mouth dripping with blood, fresh red blood, never the damned black stuff. He left and headed north to Aruna.

VI

The pistol he had bought did not let him sleep any more peacefully than on any other night. He woke up bathed in sweat and to his relief determined that he had not awakened Martha.

What kind of a dream was this? Shadows of the past? The present? The future? Everything was so different and yet so strangely familiar. The dreams reflected a half-forgotten love, but also a hatred that was especially current. Hatred for Martha, who resembled his mother so much and in a terrible

way. His mother who had never let him be a man. Martha,
he knew, hated *him*. And the war! He was walking through a
crumbling world.

The next day his wife tried to do him in. She suddenly
shoved the pistol against his temple and pulled the trigger.
Only a reflex movement saved his life, so he got away with a
singed temple. Terrified, he rushed out of the room and down
the basement stairs. He locked himself up in the bomb shelter.

Martha pleaded with him to open the heavy steel door. It
had all been a joke. He could understand that! She gave up
after a few hours.

For days on end he did not hear from her. Then she was
suddenly there again with a new line.

"Arthur! Lemme in . . . listen to the radio—the bombs'll
be here any minute now! Arthur! Aaarrrthuuurrr!"

It was as if a steel and concrete vessel was being juggled
by a huge fist, Arthur was being thrown around, and it made
his ears ring, then he immediately lost his hearing. An invisible force tugged at his insides and pulled them to pieces, his
eyeballs bulged, and he could hear his heart thumping in
rhythm to the last bars of one of Shostakovich's symphonies
before it stopped working.

When he woke up, his hearing had been restored and probably his sanity as well. But there were only his own footsteps
to hear and wonder at. He stayed in the room as long as he
had food, most likely around three weeks. Then he warily
opened the door.

VII

He could not go up the basement stairs because there were
none. But there was really no need to. The ground on which
his house had stood looked like an empty bathtub.

The big city looked as if it had been blown away by a gust
of wind leaving hardly any rubble in its wake. There was not
a living being to be seen.

He searched for food for two days.

Three days. He found nothing.

On the fourth day he found the body of a neighbor. The
poor man had made it through in a bomb shelter; he had had
it built at Arthur's suggestion, only to die of hunger and

thirst. Arthur looked out over the steel-blue landscape almost without any irregular features or traces of life. The sun beamed down from a black sky and dusted the landscape with golden drops like a wet dog shaking itself. The black, thin, smooth shell that had housed him and his for so long was missing. It had been a shell, and something had broken it.

The egg had hatched.

The body was still warm, and he drank the red, life-giving liquid. Then he turned and started northward where a shape rose up. The dearly beloved, long-desired Aruna waited there with open arms.

RED RHOMBUSES

(Screziato di rosso)

LINO ALDANI

Translated from the Italian
by Joe F. Randolph

It all happened last year in Cascina Torti toward the end
of summer. Cascina Torti is the only spot not shown at all on
local maps. Maybe land-office records mention it or military
maps, which are meticulous and detailed to the point of being
ridiculous, those voluminous sheets folded thirty-two times
that also indicate the names of ditches, elevations, wells, and
small crumbling hill forts. Cascina Torti has sixty-five inhabitants, a handful of houses at the foot of a barren hill, similar
to Calvary, one of the many located almost on a ridge between the Pavian and Ligurian Appennines.

An out-of-the-way place, as I was saying, forgotten, a tiny
cluster of hovels that some whim of the Earth could swallow
up or a cyclone uproot, and nobody would know the difference. Nevertheless, last year that bunch of humble little
houses, that geographic gem was the scene of a drama, ordinary if you will, but also intense and fascinating. At least for
me.

I'm talking about the time. . . .

There is a before and there is an after. There always is.
And between the before and after, like a splinter, or a mem-
brane, or like a thin, quivering piece of tin foil, there is the
now, the present.

The story of time is all here. Generations of men have racked their brains and bodies looking for an answer to this infamous riddle. There was one man who talked about groups without batting an eye and one who was made a saint for having said that time, like every other thing or idea, is divine work, one who talked about spirals and knots, one who amused himself by making up paradoxes, one who drew chronosynclastic funnels, and one who coldly quoted *tempus quod aequaliter fluit.*

I almost envy the last one. He was the sleepy sort who as soon as he could took naps out in the open field, an apple or some such thing fell on his head, and he thus made some very important discoveries, gravity, infinitesimal calculus, et cetera. The day he mumbled about time, maybe it was a pumpkin that hit him, or a tile, something heavy that would have knocked him out cold. But looking back, the one who eclipsed everybody was the bard of Stratford when he said that the best way to waste time is just to wonder about the nature of it. A magnificent observation! Especially when you consider that our dilettante friend usually put those seven little words in the mouth of the stupidest person in the cast.

And so. . . . And so there is a little confusion. Rather, a whole lot. After all, since it is a big problem and the points of reference a bit fleeting, the image of a piece of tin foil seems to me the most appropriate. Open a package of cigarettes, take off the little silver square—usually PULL is printed on it—put it anywhere on top of a table, and with the thumbnail flat rub it a little, making the bubbles disappear, those tiny bumps dotting the paper until just before you get down to the backing sheet, smooth it out until it goes zip-zip like a fast-flying mosquito or a taut string.

Well, time, or that fragment of time that defines the present is that very piece of laminated paper, zip-zip, zip-zip, a little metallic heart, like a transister, throbbing and pulsating, pulsating and throbbing, while time passes, or better yet, while *we* pass.

It all happened last year toward the end of summer in the place I have already said and that I would prefer not to rename. However, for anybody who wants to, it would not be hard to look it up later. You can go up from Canneto, or else, if you wish, from Montebello or Rivanázzano. One road is as

good as another, they all lead to the place. And they are
roads that I know every meter of by heart. I traveled them
for the first time before I was twenty but eager to carry a
weapon. And whistling a tune popular back then, a song
about a certain woman by the name of Fortune and a dame
obviously game, to make it rhyme. Most of all I liked the beginning: *There's a road called destiny leading into the
hills.* . . . But I was not looking for destiny up there, or love
either. I was motivated by hatred, rebellion, that crazy emotion that churns your insides and makes your blood boil at
the sight of injustice, continuing outrages, and violence di-
rected at an ideological system.

And so last year, in September, when I came back to travel
up those same roads I trod more than thirty years ago, my
memory reluctantly went back in time. The Volkswagen
tooled along around curves and I was watching out for
pedestraisn, gulleys, and plant life as I sniffed the air, the
scents, and I drank in the blue sky which seemed to be the
same sky as the one of the crazy years of my younger days.

It was at that time last year while I was going up the
mountain that derivatives and integrals seemed to be drawn
on the windshield and back window. The future is a derivative, I mused. And the past, an integral. A scent was all I
needed, the chirping of sparrows, a flash and in an instant,
with the help of an enormous store of memory, you can
reconstruct the primitive function.

I am using the language of mathematics that might seem to
be out of place. However . . . While I was looking around,
for a moment I felt the absurd inclination to see the bars to
certain equations smashed. I suppose that all men my age
have felt or must have felt something similar sooner or later;
the sudden and violent urge to break free of the trap, namely
the chance to *really* go back in time, or else to get around it,
cheat it by escaping the abyss of old age, beyond death, into
a future that might exist.

I am still talking about the time. . . .

When I got to the Swede's inn, Wind was not there yet.
Not that he was late, maybe I was a bit early. We had a
standing appointment up here twice a year, in May and September, the two best months for mountain-water fishing.

Wind, officially Dario Vailati, a bank official, from Genoa.

I, a middle-aged university professor, from Milan. I teach numerical and graphical calculus, a subject I do not care one way or another about; I would like to get into something more familiar that I know, like topology or non-Euclidean, Riemann, Lobachevski geometry, just between you and me.

Wind is a nickname. Or rather, an alias. Just like mine, Fortune. He would have preferred the name Folgore or some such thing just as I would have liked Turbine, or Bixio, something that reproduces the sound of a saber slash. Instead, because of two songs then popular that he and I used to sing at the top of our voices. . . . In short, we came out Wind and Fortune. In reality, it was the whole bunch that dubbed us with those monikers.

The oliveless Martini hardly had any taste to it. And the Campari was as hot as a pepper. I looked around and I could not figure out if the ten other people in the bar were paying me no attention because of a respectful sense of discretion or indifference.

Ermete, the village idiot, was playing with toothpicks, breaking five at once and stubbornly arranging them in a fan pattern on the plastic tabletop, then poking a finger in a glass of wine and letting a drop fall in the middle, convinced that it formed a star; it was a little trick I had shown him on more than one occasion, but which he with his simple mind could not manage to repeat.

On my right, seated at a table next to the window overlooking the yard, a middle-aged woman with a still-youthful appearance was eating sullenly, her eyes glued to the plate. I could see her out of the corner of my eye and watch her when I stood up to look out the window periodically at the sound of an approaching car.

When Wind arrived, the woman had come to the fruit course and was lazily chomping on a banana. I spotted my friend in the middle of the parking lot. The car was not his. He was digging around in his wallet. The other one, a swarthy young man wearing a checkered shirt, was unloading the fishing rods and an overnight bag. He pocketed the money and left, putting forefinger to temple in a salute.

That goddamned Wind. Always in shape, always rock hard, a big handsome bunch of muscles without an inch of fat, a gray head of hair still quite thick.

"My brakes failed on me," he explained. "It was a close

one, a few inches more and I would've wound up at the bottom of a slope. However, the young guy who brought me here is a mechanic. He fixes everything and tomorrow evening will bring me my wheels. . . ."

"Where'd it happen?" the innkeeper asked.

"About five or six kilometers from the summit. Fortunately I was going up." He looked around, patted himself on the stomach, and said, "God, I'm hungry."

The Swede served bone marrow. And so we ate. And then he wanted a big onion to dip in oil and salt. And he showed me his teeth, rolled back his gums, and remarked, "Look, I'm missing another one all of a sudden. And over here I need a crown. I'm getting old, my boy. . . ."

I pointed out to him that he still had all of his hair.

"Oh, yeah, a beautiful bush, but I can't chew with hair. I'd rather be bald as a billiard ball and still have every last one of my teeth."

The woman sitting at the table on the right burst out laughing. And he immediately took advantage of the situation. Wind is like that, but he is neither a ladies' man nor one of those slick characters who make a pass at anything under any circumstances, even during a shipwreck. Wind is different, well bred, reasonable, but if a woman encourages him, he can't help himself.

Five minutes later he was sitting by the window and moving his hands on the table, engrossed in a rapid, nonstop monologue.

The Swede served two cognacs. Wind and the woman drank a toast while looking into one another's eyes. It seemed that they were not interested in anybody else. I drank my coffee alone. Then Ermete came over to me with his toothpicks. He mumbled that he wanted me to repeat the usual trick and insisted until I gave in.

"Your name's Sil," Wind said in a sweet voice. "It's a nice name, but something's missing. How about an a? I like Sail better."

"Sail?" the woman said. "But that doesn't make any sense. That's not a name."

"Names are what you make of them. My name's Wind. What do you make of that?"

"I know your name's Wind. A very nice name."

"All right. We put in an a and you're Sail. Get it? Sail and wind can only work in unison, they're made for each other."

Sharp guy. Oh, yeah, Wind is quite capable of defending and sustaining an absurd opinion just to look good and make his point.

On the plastic tabletop a star took shape. Ermete watched it open-mouthed, his eyes wide like a kid's, shaking his head, and then all of a sudden he beat his fists on the table and made the glasses dance around.

Four old men came in. I knew them right away. Moreover, the oldest, almost an octogenarian, whom I knew quite well, had spent fourteen months in the resistance with us in the mountains.

"Partisan and Knight of Vittorio Veneto," he shouted. "The war of 1518, always manning the wall."

The others in the back of the room had finished playing briscola. One started singing "Monte Canino." The knight of Vittorio Veneto, his voice rheumy and slobbery, answered him with "Kerboom." Then they motioned to me. And so I sang too, but *my* song, the only one that I knew from start to finish, "Lady Fortune."

They showered slaps on my back. "Hey, Fortune, you remember when we helped to create the republic?" and another slap on the back. "You remember when we charged six lire for a kilo of bread?" and add another pat.

They were referring to Varzi's free republic, which lasted from July to September of '44 right under the noses of the Germans and Socialist Republicans in Salò.

The Swede brought over a basket of bottles. Ermete was the first to get drunk merely because they forced him to drink against his will. There was a moment when, getting excited, he tried to sing the "Katyusha." "The wind's whistling, the storm's blowing. . . ." And everybody, some with fingers, others with their minds, were pointing at the window. But Wind pretended not to notice. He was there talking away and clasping the woman's thin white hand between his large smooth hands, and he seemed to be in complete control of the situation.

Hopping around like a monkey, Ermete tried to distract him. But he got rid of him rudely.

"Let's drink to everybody!" he yelled, turning to look in our direction.

The revelry went on for a good spell. Then the old men left the bar, unsteady on their feet, holding each other up as a group. Ermete did not want to leave. The Swede then gave him a swift kick in the seat of his pants.

The woman also got up to leave, wrapping a long black-wool stole around her shoulders. I caught a glimpse of a very quick, puzzling gesture, but it was clearly a sign of agreement. Next, Wind sat down at the bar.

"Another cognac," he told the Swede. "This is the last one, then upstairs to bed. . . ."

The innkeeper closed the shutters.

"Ah, yes, the big beautiful woman Sil," he said pouring out some glasses. "She's lived a little, Turin, Milan, but right now she's tired, she's been getting her head together. . . ."

"How old is she?" I asked as a matter of conversation.

"Forty more or less. . . . Don't you remember her? She was an eight or nine-year-old lass when you two passed through here with a submachine gun on your back. And you two were clapping your hands. . . ."

Time. . . . A thing that passes which nobody dares to stop. A diabolical invention.

I took off my shoes and remained seated on the bed, moving my feet to get rid of the weird tingling that for some time had been bothering my extremities, especially after a drink.

"Tonight," I said. "Tonight coming up. . . . Strange thoughts have been bouncing around in my head." I talked to him about time, the crazy urge that came over me all of a sudden, the urge to ball up the piece of tinfoil and stop everything.

Wind was standing next to the chest of drawers. He turned around suddenly.

"Me too," he said in a tone that revealed surprise and uneasiness. "The same thing happened to me right at the moment I stopped a hair's breadth from the edge of the precipice with the brakes gone. . . . Bah! Humbug! Andropause side effects." He laughed and unexpectedly changed the subject. "Tomorrow morning," he said. "Would you mind if Sil tagged along with us tomorrow morning?"

I shrugged, but I could not help teasing a little. "What's with you, Dario?"

"Nothing. Nothing's wrong with me. Sil knows how to

make a fire, serve drinks, cook on a grill, and anything that needs doing. We'll have a fine outing, you'll see." And then he added, "I'm interested in that woman."

"Granted, but you don't want me carrying a flashlight up there."

"Come on! Let's check out the flies and lures and go to bed."

The flies and lures. Wind and I have the same equipment, perfectly interchangeable if need be. Therefore, one more reason to be fussy. Or not to be. Only Wind, especially when it came to fishing, was exacting to the point of being ridiculous. With weapons, too. In '44 I remember the Mickey Mouse inspections and the chewings out he used to give anyone who did not have his Stein thoroughly oiled.

So, I had to go through the ceremony. I opened the fly case and waited in silence. On the other side of the bed and now standing next to the chest of drawers, he was inspecting the fishing lines, the spare fishing hooks, and the ends, then began:

"Alexandra Jungle Cock."

"Check."

"Blody Butcher."

"Check."

"Bromley Light."

"Check."

"Silver Doctor."

"Check."

"Silver Dunn."

"Check."

"Soldier Palmer."

"Oops, that one I don't have."

Wind rummaged around in the box for two or three seconds, then flung a Soldier Palmer at the foot of the bed.

I was also missing a Zulu Silver and Mustads Fancy.

Wind got all steamed up. "Christ, you're missing the best lure, the one that's indispensable in fall. Fishing in September without a Mustads Fancy . . . You should be ashamed of yourself!"

The onslaught went on for another five minutes all because of March Brown, Olive Dunn, Miller, May Fly, Scott Jock and Red Tago, Silver Professor, Bromley Dark, and Greenwell's Glory.

Finally, he closed the box. He undressed and threw shirt and pants at the wall.

"What were you saying about time? A piece of tinfoil that goes zip-zip. . . . Well, you're not wrong. The fact is that time screws us all sooner or later. It's not a matter of andropause, we're really screwed."

He put out the light, said *ciao*, and immediately started snoring.

Fog arose unexpectedly right in the middle of a beautiful morning. Even today I dare not try to explain it to myself. Even today, by now almost a year later I dare not try to understand, understand anything because the weather could never have turned rotten like that in the wink of an eye. I know several newspapers published accounts of it, everybody was indulging in flights of fancy in some of the more abstruse and odd comments, and Cascina Torti, a fly speck nestled on a ridge of hills, was the big news event for several days. Then, as is often the case, the topic fades away, and no one talks about it anymore. Anyway, none of us around here understood anything about it. For Ermete and Sil it was different. Perhaps at that moment they were aware. But not all the rest of them. There is no science that can explain the phenomenon of fog coming in a sudden torrent, at first thin and vaporous, and then in the space of a few seconds thick and dense as a curtain.

The sun grew dim; only ghostly reflected light remained. And then there was that strange noise, piercing, unbearable, like that of a taut iron wire suddenly cut by snips, the long, drawn-out hum, the electronic zing of an intense, deep vibration.

Something exploded in my head. I fell into the water seat first, stunned, in the middle of the fog hungrily enveloping me, my eyelids heavy and my limbs no longer mine, for an instant (maybe longer, maybe a minute or an hour) beyond my control.

"What happened?" Wind cried, shaking my shoulders.

I swam up from the depths of unconsciousness and looked around like a little boy. The fog was dispersing, we were no longer surrounded by it. It had stopped like a wall a few meters away to hover over the water in the stream. And the wall ran through valleys and across mountains in a smooth, vaguely circular curve that disappeared behind the silhouette of chestnut and fir trees.

A wall. A wall of fog. It shed a diffuse light that cast no shadows. I looked at Sil sitting on the bank, her face terrified and twisted.

There was a long silence. Then the birds resumed their singing. Mechanically I avoided the wall to retrieve my line. Water had gotten into my boots, and I was soaked up to my waist. I let Wind take me to dry land. I stretched out on the ground between the smoking embers in the grill and the backpacks. Exhausted.

The birds likewise. They were not exactly singing. Rather, it was a muffled peeping, monotonous, the same tune, as if every note were dying in their throats.

Wind swore.

"Let's get out of here," Sil said. "This place gives me the creeps. . . ."

"Yeah, let's get out of here," I echoed. And my voice no doubt sounded full of apprehension because Wind gathered up the utensils and bags in a flash and rushed to put them all in my Volkswagen.

I tossed him the keys. "You drive," I said. I took off my boots and got water all over the car floor.

Wind swore again.

The fog was no longer there. On the contrary, the air had become fairly clear, but it was like a hood over our head, a dark dome originating in the sky. A hothouse. I had the impression of breathing and moving around as if in a hothouse, under an overheated opaque-glass roof.

"You can think what you want about it," said Wind, his hands gripping the wheel and face straight ahead to avoid potholes in the back road. "That wasn't any heat mist. It wouldn't have come up all at once like that, not at this time of year. You both heard that noise and also felt that whack in the middle of your brain. . . ."

I shrugged impatiently. What worried me was the persistence of the phenomenon, the dark dome over us that was now casting bluish shadows all over the surrounding countryside.

"Let's go to Cascina Torti," I said. "I have an idea that the storm might let loose at any moment."

"It's not a storm," Sil retorted. "You know better than I do that it's not a storm. Something's happening around here!"

"I'll agree to that," I went on. "It's not a storm. But right now let's step on it. We can discuss it later!"

Wind pressed down on the gas pedal. We reached Cascina Torti at a pretty speedy clip while disregarding the most basic rules of safety. An extremely thin old man with a dark vest over a white shirt was standing in the middle of the road. He was looking in our direction, but did not make the slightest move to get out of the way even when the Volkswagen got within a few meters of him.

Wind slammed on the brakes. There was a long squeal of rubber against dusty asphalt, but the old man did not budge.

"Hey, you!" Wind addressed him, sticking his head out of the window. "Tell me something, buddy. Is that any way to go for a walk?"

No response. The old man remained motionless, half a meter in front of the hood, staring at some point in space, mouth trembling, arms waving around, his hands groping for who knows what.

I got out of the car.

"Come over here," I said, taking him by an arm. "That's it, this way."

I hardly noticed a confused babbling. Evidently he must have been drunk. In Cascina Torti it is not such a rarity, even in the morning. But that explanation did not quite leave me convinced. There were other people along the road who were acting like dolts, for the most part they were standing quietly in front of doors and windows. Also, on the faces of those I knew personally I observed the pale and unfocused features of mental deficiency.

When we entered the Swede's inn, I was astonished. It looked as if the place had been the scene of a brawl right out of a shoot-'em-up western.

Ermete was behind the bar on a platform and amusing himself by smashing glasses and bottles to pieces. The inn-keeper was standing there in silence with his elbows resting on the counter, on the other side of the bar where customers were served. And there were three or four others seated at tables, half asleep. On the floor were shards of glass and big pools of liquid.

Ermete then turned around. I was dumbstruck, my mouth

dropped open, I was unable to move, as if I had been punched in the solar plexus. Wind and Sil were right behind me, but I knew they were also shocked. Because Ermete. . . . In short, Ermete was no longer himself. The person was to a large degree the same, the same clothes, the same hair, face, the well-known face, but the eyes were gone, the eyes shone with such an intense light of intelligence that he was rendered unrecognizable. The mouth, too. The lower lip no longer drooped and drooled, but was tightened up into a virile grimace revealing certainty and contempt.

"Look who's watching who!" he said with irony. "Signor Fortune and Signor Wind. And 'Segnorina' Sil!"

He said it just like that, "segnorina," the way the Americans did in Naples and Rome after the Anzio landing.

I never heard Ermete talk so fast. And above all, never in Italian.

Wind went by me and headed toward the bar.

"What's going on?" he asked.

Ermete got down from the platform and came up close, his body erect and chest pushed out. Christ, what had become of his feeble, limp figure? I saw a big handsome man, straight as a ramrod, taller than Wind, *stronger and more decisive*.

"Nothing's happened," Ermete said with a very clear, sharp voice devoid of accent, a little like the old TV announcers. "Everything's normal for me. Just a half hour ago the fog came and everybody turned stupid." His index finger went around in a circle beside his head and he nodded toward the window overlooking the yard. "Look at what a sight!"

"What about you?" I said. "How come you're not asleep like all the rest?"

A flash of wickedness appeared in his eyes. Instinctively I retreated a few centimeters, but he latched onto my arm—a strong, decisive vise—and dragged me toward the corner table. In the center there were five toothpicks arranged in a star.

"I was standing here," he said without releasing his grip and almost weighing every syllable. "Half an hour ago I was standing over here, engrossed in that trick that I could never quite get the hang of. And all of a sudden a light bulb flashed on in my head, I dipped my finger in the wine, and right away a star formed. Next, I was told: Ermete, your suffering is over. And everything I had inside, all that I alone always knew albeit indistinctly came surging to the surface. A wonderful discovery, especially when compared to the state those imbeciles around here are in. . . ."

I tried to get loose, but he tightened his grip, and said: "Listen to me, beanbrain. Don't try to get curt with me, otherwise I'll break your little arm to pieces."

"Call the carabinieri," Wind said, turning to Sil.

Ermete burst out laughing. "The carabinieri! You'd do better to call the men in white coats. There're enough around here to fill up a nut house. Anyway, if you don't mind, I'd like to amuse myself a bit."

He went over to the liquor shelf and took down two bottles of cognac. One he tossed at the bars on the window; he broke the neck on the other one by slamming it on the edge of the table and poured a drink for some guy who was sitting off to the side.

"Cheer up," he said. "It's a beautiful glassful, but you'll go ahead and swallow it all, won't you?"

The man stayed as motionless as a statue. Next, Ermete put a finger under the man's chin and forced his head up. "Drink, you first-class turd. Don't you remember the times you got me drunk? Drink, you piece of shit!"

And the one he was talking to downed it all in one gulp like an automaton. Then he put his head on the table.

"Oh, no," Ermete remarked. "Now drink another one, another beautiful glassful. I want to see you crawl like a worm. Don't you remember how you laughed when I pissed all over myself?"

Wind was about to intervene. But at that moment Sil came out of the telephone booth. "Nobody answers," she said. "The phone's out of order."

Ermete delicately put the bottle on the table. "Out of order? What do you mean when you say out of order?" and then he split his sides laughing. He said, "Very well. If we're cut off, that means that I'm the one in charge, and you are three to many. I wonder why you three escaped being idiots like all the others. Maybe you used to be three idiots like me, or maybe. . . ."

"Maybe we're alive and kicking because we were caught on the fringes of the fog," Wind said. "At any rate, you're in charge of a whole lot of nothing, right?"

Ermete gave a small snort. "That's why you'd like to be in

charge! Oh, no, my good man, the partisan wars were over with a while back. Haul down your flag and roll it up."

I saw Wind flare up and stiffen like the hair on a dog's back. Sil put herself between the two. Delicately Ermete raised his arm and stroked her cheek with two fingers. "I wish you well," he said, "because you never made fun of me. But right now do me a favor and leave this place."

"Let's talk about it," Sil said. "Come on, Ermete. Let's discuss—"

"Ermete's not going to and never has. Get out of here, pretty woman. I said I wanted to amuse myself."

It was impossible to stop him. Waving his arms, he moved away from the woman and in rapid steps went up behind the Swede, now standing still beside the counter. Ermete gave the innkeeper a swift kick in the seat of his pants, which jolted him all over. One of his elbows slipped off the edge and he was just about to lose his balance, but Ermete quickly grabbed hold of his shirt.

"That's for the brutal kick you laid on me, Ermete, the Cascina Torti idiot, last night. . . ."

He threw him on the nearest chair like a limp rag, put a foot on his knee, grabbed the Swede by the hair, and forced his head down. "Kiss my shoe, you lousy bastard!"

And the Swede kissed his shoe. Next, Ermete opened his hand and spit in it. "And now swallow that spit, my spit!"

Wind glanced at me and we were on him in an instant and managed to drag him to the corner where the table with toothpicks arranged in a star was. Oddly enough, Ermete seemed to calm down right away.

"I hate you," he hissed. "I hate you all, you miserable runts that have made my life hell. But the tables are turning. . . ."

"You're right," Wind said in an extremely even-toned voice. "You have a reason to want to take it out on somebody. But right now how about settling down?"

"Why?" Ermete asked, raising his head with a lingering bit of unbearable bitterness. "If there's a lame chick in the henhouse, all the other chickens will peck at it and make it suffer until it dies. Don't you believe stupid people suffer?"

"Keep calm, Ermete. And forgive me, forgive everybody. We've erred, but if you truly understand now, don't make the same mistake."

He shook his head three times, then stuck his finger in the toothpicks and with a weary gesture destroyed the star. He had glossy eyes, almost a veil of tears.

"I'm talking," he said. "I see clearly and I understand, it's as if the hand of God has touched me here, in my head. And my blood is like the roar of a . . . a jet. Is that the way you say it? I should be overcome with happiness, but now I don't know . . . grief has set in, maybe because I see things that you people never have. You've never been lame chicks. But I have. I now perceive certain things in the air, and walls, and objects, and your persons scare me. . . . They ooze with disgust!"

A fine fix to be in. We still had not returned the mental defective back to reason by the blow. It was not that I disliked talking to Ermete or listening to his way of speaking that had unexpectedly become fluent with imaginative approaches. Quite to the contrary. Just because so much had happened in here and on the outside the most minute details had to be looked at closely. In addition, a slobbering idiot who starts talking like a philosopher does not turn up every day.

That's what happened. I like to analyze, think about, and look for the causes, and extrapolate. Wind, on the other hand, is the hasty type, ready for action, oriented toward practical and efficient organization. I remember the time he booed the political commissar, a pale little man who wore glasses and had come up into the hills to talk to us about Gramsci and Matteotti. As ignorant as I was of such things, I listened to him with great interest. In contrast, Wind lost his temper. "You're a good speaker," he told him, "but words are no use against the Germans. It takes these things." He picked up his machine gun and two hand grenades and threw them at the commissar's feet. "Rather than tramping over hill and dale to give political lectures, you'd do better to stay here with us. Give up on Gramsci and learn how to handle weapons instead."

In short, Wind seemed perfectly cut out to take charge. At first he coaxed and cajoled Ermete into a calmer state. Then, when he saw Sil start to cry, this time due to hysteria, he slapped her.

The telephone was out of order. And the TV was not working—no electricity. Then he tried the battery-powered transister radio. The dial lit up, he tuned up and down the length of the dial, but nothing came out.

"We don't even have radio reception," Wind remarked. "We're in a bad situation. Damned if I know what's up. Anyway, let's get busy. First thing: We need to round up everybody in one spot to keep them safely in sight. I don't want any rampages or injuries. The yard out in front here seems suitable and large enough to me. Second thing: We need to inspect the houses to see if anyone's sick in bed, turn off the gas stoves, care for the animals. Ermete and Sil will think they are the ones for this in Cascina Torti. Third thing: Take the car and drive to the next town to round up some help, provided that they haven't all turned into imbeciles there too."

I was disturbed, nervous, and discouraged by a flood of thoughts. And yet I felt nothing but admiration for my friend.

"Here we go again," I said. "Just like in the old days. We've gone back thirty-two years—"

"Shit. This is 1976, and this is a different problem to solve. Take the car and do what I told you."

I could still see ahead. But when I got over the crest of the hill, the fog closed in around me after a kilometer or two. I kept going along on a false route, a straight road, and all at once I saw myself forced to reduce speed, not so much because of the power visibility—the wayside stones could still be made out—but rather, due to air resistance, the physical medium that I was going through. The engine was laboring. I shifted from third to second, and after about a hundred meters when I realized the Volkswagen was on the brink of stalling, I got scared.

The wall. The wall of fog. I downshifted to first and the car lumbered along for a few more meters, but the fog was getting increasingly thicker and worse, like sticky mud, and the car finally came to a halt, the motor conked out, with me there in the middle of that dismal pea soup pressing against the windows, a living thing eager to creep in.

With my stomach turning somersaults and heart pounding like a hammer, I put all my trust in reverse. It was not easy to pull myself out of that gook, back up until I found a side road to turn around in, and go back.

They were all there, seated in a row like kids in kinder-
garten, or perhaps . . . like inmates in a concentration camp.

They were not even paying attention to me. I gave them a
cursory glance. I got out of the car and dashed to the inn in
spite of my unsteady legs.

There they were, Ermete, Wind, and Sil. They were sitting
around the double table, the one in the middle of the room.
And there was somebody else. At first I was unable to make
him out. I had come in from outside, and the place was all
bathed in faint light. Then, as my vision adjusted. . . .

He was a gigantic black with round, bovine eyes. He
had. . . . He had red hair. And he was wearing a costume,
or a pair of overalls, now I don't remember what that silky
fabric was wrapped around him, something that gave off red
rhombuses at the slightest movement.

"Who's this?" I asked.

Wind looked at me askance. "That little ole fog maker,"
he explained. "As far as we can judge, he had this whole
place staked out."

Ermete got up, came over to me, and pushed me toward
the window overlooking the fields. "He came in that," he
said. And he pointed at a large silvery sphere parked in the
middle of the alfalfa. "He travels through time and came
from the future. . . ."

I said nothing. I went behind the bar and took a hard-
boiled egg out of the basket. I shelled it slowly after hitting it
hard on a bottle of mineral water. The red-haired black
glanced at me from time to time, but kept talking to Wind in
a voice so low that I couldn't catch a word.

"He travels in time," Ermete said again, also taking an egg
for himself. "He's the one who caused the fog, he came from
the future and cured me, understand? He cured me!"

I grabbed the bottle of mineral water and was ready to
break it over his head, but Sil stepped in. "Ermete's right,"
she said. She smiled, almost in satisfaction.

Then I lost my temper. I came out from behind the bar
and went up to Wind and took hold of his collar.

"What's this tale I hear? And who is this joker? Where did
he blow in from?"

Wind pointed to the silvery sphere sitting in the middle of
the green field.

"But you're crazy!" I yelled. "Crazier than Ermete and sillier than this slut. . . ."

"Calm down," the black man said. His voice was sonorous and shrill with a hint of Tuscan accent. "I've already explained everything to your friends while you were away trying to escape from the *Umwelt*. . . . Oh, I'm sorry, that's what we call the electronic umbrella over us, an impenetrable envelope against which an H bomb would be . . . ineffective. Isn't that how you say it?"

"Ineffective hell! I'm gonna flatten your ugly mug, you illusionist, black my foot. . . ."

And I don't know what else I said. I felt a rage growing inside, and what I was saying seemed to be what somebody else was saying. I jumped. But the black sprang up, raised his hand, palm open, pink-colored like a baby blanket.

All of my energy drained out of me through my legs. I was breathing with difficulty.

"Calm down," said the black man speckled with red rhombuses. "I've already explained everything to your friends. I have a peaceful mission here. I have to go now. I have some problems to solve because something is malfunctioning. I have to go back over the program. . . . I'm going back to that silver sphere out there, but I'll return in a couple of hours and I'll want your decisions."

He left, tall, ramrod straight in his clothing that blinked with scarlet lights.

We started off with a bottle of Fundador. Wind poured himself a cup of coffee and milk and dunked some rusk in it. I drank absentmindedly and scribbled mathematical formulas on paper napkins.

Ermete and Sil were outside taking care of the people assembled in the yard.

"He said there's no danger," Wind mumbled. "The dome'll be removed as soon as he leaves with three or four of us. . . ."

I drank and started laughing.

"He talked about traveling without returning. . . ."

"That guy's loony or else he's a second-rate trickster. I caught him watching his clothes with all those little red lights, a sham, a device to make hypnosis easier."

"That man comes from the future—"

"That guy's a liar."

"The fog's not a lie. . . ."

"Not the fog. But the fog can be explained several ways, and so can the out-of-order telephone and the radio that doesn't work. And there will also be an explanation for that black devil."

"He comes from the future," Wind repeated monotonously, this time only half believing it. "He's come to take three or four of us back to his time. But he's not forcing anybody, he said he will not harm any living person. And then he said it's an important experiment."

By that time we were talking about two different things. A conversation between two deaf people or two drunks since Wind was drinking like a sponge and I was doing no better, and so after Fundador it was Bourbon's turn, and then Ermete opened other bottles and from that point on I don't remember. I no longer remember all the absurd discussions, suppositions, conjectures . . .

My head was on fire. "That sphere," I said pointing out of the window. "Is it for real?"

"Sure it is! I touched it with my own hands and so has Ermete. It materialized there in the middle of the meadow a couple of minutes after you had left on your excursion. Then the hatch opened and he came out."

"Is he by himself?" I asked while trying to overcome the drowsiness washing over me.

"He seems to be."

"In that case we can clobber him. When he gets back, we'll jump him and—"

"That I've already tried. And so have you, to no avail. He comes from the future, is more advanced than we are, and is stronger."

"Stop it," I said. And I poured myself another glass. "Time travel's impossible. Time is linked to space, the Earth rotates on its axis and revolves around the sun, and the sun is heading toward Sirius. Then you have conic movement, Copernican perturbations. . . . Moving through time means moving through space. . . ."

"That machine out there seems to be able to."

"But who said so? Look, let's reason it out." I took a paper napkin and filled it up with diagrams. "Imagine getting aboard that sphere and wanting to go back in time ten years.

You'd have to have immense amounts of energy at your disposal. Well, I'm God Almighty and I supply you with all the energy you want. But before you can push the return button, you would have to figure out what point in space the Earth was at ten years ago. Understand what I'm saying?"

"Nope."

"Jesus H. Christ, how can you sit there and say you don't understand? You need to move the Earth in space and reposition it in the exact spot where it was ten years ago. Furthermore, you need to rearrange the entire universe, every last celestial body and put them back in their places ten years ago. There's no reference point, understand? And then imagine we went back and arrived at that precise instant ten years ago when we came here to fish. We come out of the sphere and see . . . us two with fishing rods in hand. Where are you now that we need you, Saint Anthony? But ubiquity would not be enough, I would also have to swallow the bitter pill of simultaneous reality. My friend, please leave these things to the kids, the science fiction freaks."

I believe I said that, or something like it.

"You're talking way over my head," Wind said. "I don't understand what you're driving at, and it'd be useless to shove formulas and sketches under my nose, I'm not a mathematician. But yesterday evening you. . . . Weren't you talking about time travel yesterday evening?"

"I was talking about a dream yesterday evening."

I have confused memories of what else transpired. I know that I stood up dead drunk. I wanted to get out, go down the valley and try to find a way out in that direction since it was not possible through the mountains.

But Wind and Ermete prevented me. Sil was napping in a corner with her head on the table. Wind continued to drink, Ermete was busy fooling with the espresso machine. All at once he uttered a little shout of joy.

"It works!" he exclaimed, quite satisfied. "Now I can fix us some coffee."

I went on scribbling on the paper napkins.

I remember—this is a clear, very sharp memory—that at a certain point I jotted down Schrödinger's formula. Wind was twisting his neck and following my explanation with a dazed

look, his eyebrows rising and falling as if he were making
faces in front of a mirror.

"See this x?" said the drunkard talking inside me. "The x
represents the spatial coordinate along which the infinitesimal
particle can be found. We are in the microcosm, in the sub-
atomic area, but put into proper perspective, it can serve as a
very good model for that sphere out there in the middle of
the meadow; m represents the mass of the elementary particle, or if you will, that sphere; h is the Planck constant: W
stands for the total energy of the particle, V the potential, so
that the difference W-V stands for pure kinetic energy. . . ."

"What about this doohickey here?" said Wind pointing his
finger into the middle of my scribbling. "What does it mean?"

I scratched behind an ear, extremely perplexed.

"That's psi, a letter in the Greek alphabet. Nobody knows
what it means, not even Schrödinger, and he's the one who
put it into the formula just to make it come out."

"Convenient," Wind remarked. "In order to make an equa-
tion balance, he resorts to values that nobody even knows
what they stand for!"

My friend was the one doing the reasoning this time. And
I was the one lost. Caught in the net that I myself had
thrown out, I tried a different tack.

"Maybe the psi represents probability, the probability of
finding a particle in a defined space."

"Shit. What probability are you talking about? You don't
know nothin', but on the other hand that guy's solved everything, he's from the future and has known about it longer
than we have. . . ."

I drank another glass and stopped. I rested my weary head
on the back of my arm, and dozed off in a caramel cascade
of numbers and equations, with Ermete every now and then
coming to shake my shoulder. "He cured me," he said. "You
want to see me do the toothpick trick for you?" I was drowning in a sea of cotton. Wind belched two or three times; I
couldn't care less about the black or his silver sphere or the
bird that perched for an instant on the window sill. It was so
pleasant that I slipped back into unconsciousness. I slept like
a log.

It looked like a crumb, minuscule, like a miniature toy. To
be brief, a very tiny black man. Then, when I fully opened

my eyes with difficulty, I saw him in front of me, impressive, slim and tall like a basketball player. In his hand he had my scribbled-on paper napkins. And he was laughing.

"What foolishness," he said. He was slightly startled when his sight fell on the Schrödinger formula, he frowned, and for an instant I caught an incredulous expression flash across his face. But only for an instant, a very fleeting batting of the eyes. He rolled the scraps of paper up into a ball and threw them into a corner. "What nonsense," he repeated.

The sun beat against the glass in the window facing west and a stream of reflected beams grazed his person. His hair, not at all kinky or woolly but rather straight and silky, shone with an intense, dazzling red.

It's been dyed, I thought. I had never seen a Black with red hair. I had the impression that the rhombuses on his clothes were blinking faster right at the times when he stayed perfectly still.

"Now, what have you people decided?" the Black inquired.

My head was nodding and I could not keep it up. I collapsed on the table again, in a drowsiness sometimes wakeful, sometimes torporous, with voices coming and going and a piece of tinfoil, zip-zip, my heart and temples pounding like crazy.

Wind: "None of us will go."

Sil: "What if we do come along? What sense would a life in the future make to us?"

The Black: "You'll find a better world with so many problems still to be solved. . . . However, a better world than this one."

Ermete: "Will the fog go away?"

The Black: "Yes, as soon as the ship leaves."

Then a whole lot of stupid paradoxical remarks, a bunch of madhouse conversations.

"What about those out there?" Sil asked. "Will they be as they were before?"

"Exactly as they were before," he stated. "I've consulted the computer. There's room for four on the ship. We're not forcing anybody, but you who've seen and understood . . . it would be fine if all of you came."

Wind bristled up. He said ironically: "You're not forcing anybody! When the fog set in, one mental defective was cured, and that was not in your program. You wanted us all

to be simpletons so that you could operate unhindered. Three
other people escaped you when the fog set in because they
were on the edges of the affected area. Another unforeseen
circumstance. But there's something I'd like to know. How
would you choose your guinea pigs in the middle of a bunch
of dolts? How would you round them up without resorting to
violence?"

"Some more talk," the Black said. At that moment I raised
my head again and opened my eyes wide. The Black was
holding a little black box.

"This is a psychic probe," he explained. "It would enable
me to single out the most suitable people in the group, those
who would accept my proposal if asked in a state of lucid-
ness."

"Perfect!" I said jumping up and overturning the table.
"Then why aren't you going to choose your guinea pigs from
those in the yard? The ones out there waiting, as docile as
lambs."

"The computer has rejected this approach," the Black answered with the utmost calm. "Here are you four who have
seen and understood. If you stay, you won't be believed, but
the best course of action is not to run risks. The most suitable
would be you four. Though, you're free to choose for yourselves."

"Nobody's moving from this spot," Wind declared stead-
fastly. Wind always turned out to be the one to take charge
and make quick, well-informed decisions. "Nobody," he repeated.

And everything seemed to be finished at that point. The
image of the Black would disappear within moments, the
people of Cascina Torti would awaken from a long sleep, and
then, maybe, an all-out drinking spree in order not to remember anything.

On the other hand . . . Ermete might upset the applecart.
I saw him get close to the Black, grab onto his clothes like a
leper holding onto Christ's raiment.

"You said that when you go, the fog will too and everything will be like it was before. Tell me what will become of
me? This light that's burning in my head . . . this light that
made me see and understand and feel and enjoy . . . will it
go out?"

"Maybe," said the red-speckled Black. "I don't know. I can't say."

"Then I'm coming with you. You've cured me. And the woman's coming too, *my* woman."

"You're crazy!" Wind shouted. "If you want to leave, go on. Get out of my life! But Sil stays here."

"Sil's coming with me. And you'd better not stop me, or your partner either, that highfalutin' look of mock shrewdness he goes around with just because he's a professor. . . ." He turned to the woman. "He even called you a slut," he said, "and the other one who was trying to make out with you last night slapped you this morning. You did right. You have your head together, but if you go with him, sooner or later he will throw your past up to you. We're branded, Sil. For these people you will always be a little of the good, I the eternal village idiot even though I'm cured. . . ."

He ended on that note, a truly unforeseen epilogue. Wind plopped down defeated into the chair, put his elbows on the table, and buried his head in his hands. The red-speckled Black stopped for a moment, indecisive, then he headed toward the exit. Ermete followed him, holding Sil's hand.

I don't remember any more. I saw the three as they made their way across the alfalfa field, I saw them go into the silver sphere and right afterward . . . a flash of lightning, a yellow beam and that was all. It all disappeared as if in a dream.

"They're gone," I said. And I rubbed my eyes.

"Bring me a drink," he responded. "And start your song, please."

I did not understand.

"Your song," Wind insisted. "The Lady Fortune song."

"Don't you remember the words? *There's a street called destiny. . . .*"

"No, the other verse."

"This time Lady Fortune shut the door on me. . . ."

"That's it." And he started singing, but grief choked his throat and I could hardly hear his voice. "I liked Sil," he interjected. "I really did. And that birdbrain by the name of Ermete stole her away from me!"

He drank half the glass. I finished off the other half. And then we started all over again, and we again downed two, three, four glasses. And finally the people in the yard came

pouring into the inn, the women were bawling, the Swede
was cussing, there was a mess of glass on the floor, seats were
overturned, the bar was in disarray. A little five or six-year-
old boy was complaining in a loud voice about the red-
headed Black. And then everybody burst out laughing at
those incomprehensible words, they gave him some caramels,
but I also realized they were laughing at us two, me and
Wind, as we kept pouring drinks and chugalugging.

And then . . . we heard the howl of a siren, and the carabinieri burst into the inn.

Well, I could end here. Because nothing peculiar happened
afterward. The lieutenant, a thin little character with a pen-
cil-line Douglas Fairbanks mustache, seemed to be uptight,
was in a bad mood, and was conducting the investigation
without good sense.

The Swede was there talking with his arms. "I don't know
a thing," he repeated while Wind and I went on downing 'em,
chugalug fashion.

The lieutenant came up to our table.

"You two . . ." he said.

Wind answered him with a cuss word. That's when the
little lieutenant blew up, threatened to haul us in to the station on a charge of being drunk and disorderly, brawling, and
I don't know or remember what else.

"The fog," the lieutenant said. "Where were you two when
the fog set in?"

I was on the verge of answering when Wind kicked me under the table.

"What fog?" he replied in a seemingly ignorant voice. "The
weather's been beautiful here, a beaming sun all day long.
We were out fishing. Come along with me, lieutenant, I'll
show you some trout. . . ."

The lieutenant was fuming. And at that moment the little
boy tugged on the side of his pants. Evidently, the fog had
not affected him because he seemed to remember everything.

"A black man," he said in blissful ignorance, "there was a
black man with red hair here, and there was a silver ball, and
everybody broke bottles and upset tables. And there was Ermete who wanted to control us, and Sil who was crying . . ."

The lieutenant was still fuming. He mumbled, "Ermete,
Sil. . . ."

"Ermete's the village idiot," Wind explained. "He's gone on a long, slow walk along the stream, but he'll be back by this evening. Sil . . . Sil is a cheerful little woman. She left this morning on the seven-thirty bus."

That's how the lieutenant put together his report. The next morning reports of fainting spells were published in the newspapers. The story went on for a good week. Everybody put in his two cents' worth. One daily published statements by Coronel Bernacca, who gave the weather report on TV every evening, others talked about radioactive fog, decorative fog, and other such nonsense. Ermete was reported as missing, most likely drowned in the stream. They're still looking for Sil in the seedier sections of Milan and Turin. But the funniest story was published in a small provincial paper. In order to explain away everything, the journalist expounded on nothing less than ergot. He just talked about "terrible bread." He dug up an old article about a similar incident in France some fifteen or twenty years ago when an entire village went out of its mind seemingly because of bread contaminated with ergot, a hallucinogen, something that makes you see big lizards, monsters, and other such devils. So the circle is closed.

Wind and I have an agreement not to talk anymore even between ourselves about what happened in Cascina Torti last year toward the end of summer because—I distinctly remember saying these exact words—the problems of the present are solved right here in the present, not by escaping into a future of dreams, a future that doesn't exist since we have to built it ourselves day by day.

Sure, every time I open a pack of cigarettes and pull off the tinfoil, a slight shudder runs up my back. I run my fingernail across the tinfoil and then put it next to my ear. Zip-zip, zip-zip. The mystery of time is contained all in that vibration.

Wind and I still meet to go fishing, but you can believe far from Cascina Torti. A long, long way away.

THE MANY MINIWORLDS OF MATUSCHEK
(Matuscheks Welten)

THOMAS ZIEGLER

Translated from the German
by Joe F. Randolph

Matuschek impassively gazed at the bright patch of light on the wall. It was an odd patch, the size of the palm of your hand, amorphous and blown up, with countless angles, edges, and indentations, with things jutting out, holes, and fringed borders.

"What do you see?" Rescor asked in his monotonously babbling voice.

Matuschek blinked and closed his smarting eyes. If the pressure would only ease up! "A sailing ship," he said at last. Unintentionally he nodded. Yes, it really was. Now he could make it out clearly. A ponderous, creaking schooner moving ahead hesitantly with flapping sails, lapped at by stinging salt waves, frozen wet and stiff in the ice-cold sea air.

"Amazing!" Rescor remarked with interest.

Matuschek did not respond. He sat motionless and limp in the upholstered swivel armchair; finger-wide plastic tapes lay across his thigh, waist, and chest, and cold, dully glistening electrodes were attached to his forehead. Only vaguely did Matuschek perceive the deep drone made by the diagnostician, a huge metal and plastic monster which electronically monitored his reactions to a tee.

The patch disappeared and a new one took its place.

"What do you see now?" Rescor asked again.

How many more times? Matuschek thought in a daze. Fifty, a hundred, or a thousand? What had become of time? And what did they intend to do with him? Why this examination?

"What do you see this time?" The analyst's patience seemed to be inexhaustible.

The spot on the wall had a soothing and calming effect in some inexplicable way, and Matuschek suppressed the chuckle growing irritatingly in his throat, moistened his parched lips, and swallowed to clear his throat.

"A bird!" Matuschek decided. "A bird! Resilient plumage, wide white wings, in the distance against the setting sun. A bird floating on the wind."

For a while silence reigned. Matuschek heard his heart pounding.

"I think we know enough," Tribeau said impatiently. He glanced around questioningly. "Or is one of you still uncertain?"

Persson, Hellmann, and Kleijinken all shook their gray-haired heads in earnest, looked at Rescor, and waited for his approval.

The chief analyst rubbed his eyebrows lightly with his finger-tips. It was a mannerism which Matuschek had often caught him at. It produced a put-on, artificial effect, and was only meant to camouflage Rescor's pervasive callousness, which the lines on his face showed clearly yet subtly.

"Escapism," Tribeau went on enthusiastically, "has, in my opinion, turned into the dominating neurosis and is already affecting the defense mechanism of his subconscious. Quite ideal I would say! Quite ideal!"

Rescor got up, went to the diagnostician, and threw some switches.

It went *wham!* in Matuschek. *Wham! Wham! Wham!* The deafening noises ceased in his skull.

Rescor dipped into the roomy pocket in his silky grass-green plastic uniform and brought out a pack of cigarettes. "*Would* you merely say that the patient Matuschek is quite ideal, or really mean it, Dr. Tribeau?" he asked ironically.

Tribeau turned red. With a curious clarity Matuschek could follow the path of blood flow, which distended his cheek venules so that they tightly covered the white of his bloated skin. Tribeau cleared his throat. "The patient *is* ideal!" he corrected himself by way of apology.

Rescor nodded and pursed his lips in delight. "The problem of our day," he philosophized sarcastically, "is the progressive weakening of the scientifically exacting term precision, Dr. Tribeau! Only with precision is it possible to control the state, the society, and the individual and to keep them developing in the only right way." He thoughtfully puffed on his cigarette and blew a quivering cloud of smoke at the ceiling. "We still remember! For ten years the dominant political and moral chaos has proven quite plainly the rightness of this way of thinking!"

"Of course, Dr. Rescor," Tribeau hastened to affirm. "Excuse me!" He bowed his head.

Rescor shook his head in disapproval. Then he walked over to Matuschek. "The test is over," he informed the man sitting there in restraints, without a change in mood. "In conjunction with your previous criminal history, your antigovernment and antisocial behavior indicates a clear-cut, unquestionable, and conclusive diagnosis."

"Dr. Persson!" The small, thin-limbed psychologist with the big grotesque-looking ears quickly got up. "Dr. Persson, you may begin!"

Persson cleared his throat and started his statement with an awkward bow. "Criminal tendencies have already been recorded in patient Matuschek's early years. According to information from the National Data Bank, at the age of nineteen he did a four-week jail term for violating the drug laws. After the revolution and the subsequent creation of a union of states the patient repeatedly and deliberately failed to carry out his basic civic duties.

"He rebelled against the economic advancement law by encouraging his fellow workers to start an illegal strike against a branch plant of the EUROpharma Chemical Company.

"He publicly protested against the essential city reconstruction program and erroneously stated that the quality of life would decrease because of it.

"He insulted the new government by calling it exploitative, dictatorial, and quote: The personal property of a clique of greedy and corrupt politicians and their accomplices in the military-industrial complex: unquote.

"For these slanderous statements prejudicial to the government and contributing to the breakdown of morality the patient was sentenced by a special court in the central region to one year of public service. Next, he was enrolled in a social-stabilizing course of treatment at the Institute for Psychoresearch. Following his discharge he lived for several months in Brussels and got mixed up with a group of notorious troublemakers whose influence he fell more and more prey to.

"Because of a terrorist act against a secret military research facility operated by the national militia he was captured by the security forces and incarcerated here at our institute for personality analysis." Persson moistened his upper lip, which was wrinkled and cracked from dryness. "The analysis proves that patient Matuschek's criminal tendencies stem from a mental defect. Patient Matuschek has a neurotic need for independence, which in the course of his life has developed into a neurotic flight from reality. The patient interprets the government's concern and effort to guarantee security, law and order for all citizens as an ever-present threat to his person.

"Mentally patient Matuschek takes flight from reality in a monstrous delusion of persecution, socially in the illegality of criminal and antigovernment acts of violence." Persson smiled thinly. "A cure at this advanced stage seems to me to be out of the question!"

Matuschek held his tongue. A debilitating weariness slowed down his thoughts and kept him from expressing his indignation. The reasoning process of this gnomelike man were based on an odd comprehension of psychology.

Naturally he was suffering from paranoia, but was it not logical in a country whose inhabitants were being spied upon by an all-seeing, all-hearing, all-knowing Medusa, a many-headed control apparatus? Big Brother? In a country whose media preached lies and edited the truth, suppressed grievances, and labeled every opposition to the dictatorial regime a criminal act? Where the courts did not administer justice but handed down rules of conduct for mental behavior? Where psychology, sociology, and philosophy stood for legalized murder and institutionalized terror? In a country where many must obey and not own anything, but few command and have control of everything and everyone?

Law and order—*naturally* he viewed these two things as a

personal threat! Yet was this really a sickness when dehuman-
ization stood for oppression, law and order? When the aim of
the government was to make every man, woman, and child
mute and compliant?

When you include these facts, was he then truly sick and
criminal, or were they simply bent on *making* him so merely
in order to ignore these facts?

"Your psychology," Matuschek said slowly, surprised at his
mouth and energy as he spoke, "your psychology is bullshit
that reduces social problems to mental disturbances."

The doctors smiled, showing their teeth and radiating expressive looks. Rescor clapped his hands. "Dr. Tribeau now,
please!"

Tribeau's nervous system seemed to be permanently under
strain, and this incessant internal strain erupted in physical
overreactions. While he was speaking, nervous pink spots covered his neck and hands, his shoulders twitched constantly,
and his almost-bald cranium shook. Tribeau arched his
mouth and trumpeted his delivery.

"The social origin of patient Matuschek can shed some sig-
nificant light on his personality. Growing up among thieves,
dope fiends, anarchists, drunkards, and similar antisocial elements, he increasingly became more of a member of a socially unacceptable subculture whose most outstanding
features were moral chaos, shiftlessness, and political fantasies. After the disaster ten years ago and the conditional re-
organization of society, every last subculture was weeded out,
as you well know. Their intractable advocates underwent
reeducation and coupled it—when compelled by necessity—
with cooperation.

"The mental damage, however, which was inflicted on the
patient during his life in the subculture is apparently irrepar-
ble. By way of example, his psychodiagram and his role model
show a radical deviation from the government norm. To say
nothing of his illegal activities!

"Patient Matuschek declined the normally settled life of a
citizen because he had never experienced social health, moral
hygiene, and a regulated existence. He lived in fear of it, and
as a result always took refuge deeper in an egocentric world
of visions and oriented his life to their unreal norms valid
only to him.

"Such behavior is psychopathic, potentially dangerous to the government, and an obstacle to strengthening the coming new world as represented by the union of states.

"Like my fellow doctor Persson, I can see no chance for reintegrating patient Matuschek back into society!"

Tribeau's explanations, Matuschek thought, were even a bit more farcical. For him mental disease seemed to present itself as a deviation from fixed social modes of conduct. The question of whether or not the norms themselves were psychotic or the cause of psychopathology since the needs of men like him were suppressed had never occurred to Tribeau.

As mentally sound as the conformists, the say-nothings, the obeyers, the obsequious ones, the lackeys and oppressors, the yes people and sycophants, the rich, the powerful, the powers that be, the haves, and the complacent all were.

Stunned, Matuschek noticed that his field of vision was little by little decreasing. He was getting weak; was he being knocked unconscious by umpteen different drugs, by truth pills and energetics, by tranquilizers and hypnosis, barbiturates and amphetamines?

Some drowsy nook in his brain was replaying a tune heard long ago, and it oozed along his ganglia and tinkled underneath his sweat-dripping cranium.

Get in shape easily with Valium!

Tribeau's voice had by then become so faint and hollow that Matuschek imagined it oozing out of a cheap headset located some distance away.

"In conclusion," Rescor, the chief analyst, looked pleased, "in our judgment, upon examination, the patient and test prisoner Volkmar Matuschek is suffering from an escapist psychosis combined with symptoms of paranoia. Since this abnormal behavior by patient Matuschek has been acted out in antigovernment and antisocial ways and there seems to be no hope for a cure to Analyst Committee Three of the Institute for Psychoresearch, we cannot recommend returning patient Matuschek to life on the outside."

The black edges to the right and left of Matuschek's eyes flowed together like thick molasses, plunging his vision into total darkness. The weakness in his limbs was chilling, and the drilling pain in his head was hot and burning.

Never had Matuschek expected forgetting to take so long

and be so painful. And then, at some point in time, his thoughts ceased.

"Your last report on the situation has created a certain uneasiness in the presidental palace.

"A basically optimistic and decisive approach is missing. They wonder if the immense budget of the Institute for Psychoresearch is only enough to paint a bleak picture and come up with fatalism.

"Confidentially, the Secretary of Security is pushing for a personal shake-up. You understand?"

"Up to now I made it my business to keep the government informed. I didn't know that only hard information was requested, coordinator."

"Evidently the government sets great value on facts, and it's still waiting for solutions or at least proposals for solutions, strategies, and plans."

"Solutions? Proposals? Strategies? What for? How can they keep the number of mental patients from increasing thirty percent a year as it has been up to now? How can they cure eight million cases of acute psychoses and prevent upward of at least twenty million mental breakdowns?"

"We're not asking for any cures, just loyal behavior. We're not interested in whether someone is well or sick, we're interested in whether they're *functioning*."

"I see."

It was quiet in the cell. As far as Matuschek knew, it was quiet in every other cell in the entire wing. You could not hear a thing. Not one sound. And the beating of his heart did not even reach his ears, but was suppressed, absorbed somewhere around his shoulders, or at his chin, his lower lip, the trembling end of his nose.

Every four hours a white-painted plastic flap atop the low square table next to the sink would open and eject a paper cup containing nutritive gruel along with a hard-rubber spoon lying in front always ready to be used.

The nutritive gruel tasted bad like dust and stale air, tobacco smoke and snot. Nobody could stand it. Neither could Matuschek. But you had to eat it. Morsel after morsel, one spoonful of green slime after another spread on a resisting palate. You had to lick the cup clean with the tip of your tongue right to the bottom and lap up every carelessly spilled speck of pap.

At first Matuschek had refused, and the nurse and security guard had tightly strapped him to his bed, shoved a transparent tube in his vein and left him alone. Matuschek waited motionless and cowed, waited and thought and watched pearl-shaped drops roll into his arm. He started counting the drops, breathed in rhythm to their movement, he counted and breathed and meditated, until his thoughts were only small drops, which an invisible tubule squeezed into his brain convolutions.

Matuschek hummed a tune. It was off-key and uneven, his voice rough and distorted, but that made no difference. Matuschek hummed, and it sounded good.

" 'We shall overcome . . .' "

The door opened. "That song is on the proscribed list," Dr. Rescor said. His poker face showed life only in the movement of his pupils.

"I couldn't care less," Matuschek replied calmly.

"But you know that every one of your actions and reactions is being recorded and may be used as incriminating evidence in setting a sentence at the regional court."

"Yep, I know all that."

Rescor shook his head. "You needn't entertain any hopes that they will take your illness into account as a mitigating factor."

"I am not sick!" Matuschek contradicted.

"That's a mistake!"

"I am healthy!"

"That's a lie!"

"You, Doctor Rescor, you're the one who's sick!"

"That's slander!" Rescor put his arms akimbo and stared at Matuschek coldly and without any visible indignation. "What are you mistakenly talking about?"

"Nothing," Matuschek mumbled. "Nothing at all."

"Why are you keeping on then?"

"Because that's the way it is!"

"An erroneous idea!"

Matuschek kept quiet.

Rescor sat down with a groan in the backless chair at the eating table and studied Matuschek. "How many years at hard labor are you facing?"

"I'm not facing anything." Matuschek searched the barren wall with his eyes. *No patch of light?* he thought to himself. *No questions?*

"Hopes? Wishes?"

"Nope."

"Fear?"

Matuschek squeezed his lips together.

Rescor contentedly lit up a cigarette. Like a volcano shortly before an eruption, a blue-black funnel steamed out of his mouth. "You obviously are afraid, Matuschek. You *have* to be afraid! You know all about hard labor, the prevailing conditions there, the violence, the pain, the despair. Twenty years is the maximum penalty, Matuschek. Twenty years is a long time. Nobody has yet survived it."

"What do you want from me?" Matuschek asked angrily. "Does it turn you on to torment other men?"

Rescor flicked his ashes on the floor, ground them out with the soles of his flat shoes until only a light gray dust soiled the chalky white of the plastic flooring.

"No, I'm just doing my job! It's just my job, Matuschek!"

"Whatta you want then? Out with it? Or else leave me alone!"

"We're planning an experiment!" Rescor said.

"An experiment?"

"An experiment. Maybe it'll help us to find a solution to a serious problem."

"What do your problems have to do with me?"

"For the past few years," Rescor continued undisturbed, "neurotic and psychotic symptoms have been spreading through the population of the six states of the union like an epidemic. Nervous breakdowns, crime, and uncontrolled outbreaks of violence are keeping the police and medical profession busy to such a degree that it's threatening to cause breakdowns in both police and health service agencies."

"The shock waves from the reactor disaster a decade ago are now being felt for the first time. During the time of privation with millions dead and the old order breaking down people suppressed their dread, their mental pain, but now since that's all behind us and law and order are reestablished, they're beginning to feel suppressed alarm."

Matuschek laughed humorlessly. "Do you really believe what you're saying, Dr. Rescor?"

The chief analyst knitted his brow indignantly. "Meaning?"

"Don't you think it more likely that this wave of neurotic phenomena merely represents the reaction of the human psyche to an intolerable, existence-threatening situation? It's not the reactor accident, but the oppressive political reality that's causing mental imbalances."

Rescor smiled in a superior way. "Excuse me for again bringing the conversation around to your basic topic, but your absurd imputations have only gotten us off the track!"

He didn't want to hear about it! Matuschek thought. No hear, no see, no think, and no believe! "You're a robot, Rescor," Matuschek determined matter-of-factly. "You only jump when someone pushes your button. You just repeat what you've been programmed to say. Your head is empty."

"You're sick, Matuschek," Rescor retorted mildly. He held the burned-down cigarette butt under the spigot and waited patiently until the thin, cloudy jet of water had smoked it. He turned around and explained, "The Institute for Psychoresearch has been ordered by the union government to come up with measures against the growing flood of illness cases.

"This has caused problems.

"Our new psychiatry is still in its infancy. Up to now eccentric behavior has been suppressed by administering psychoactive drugs. As long as the number of cases was low, they helped fine and produced acceptable results. But quite recently we've had a million patients who can only work and function under the influence of drugs. A fast decline in production figures, a barely financed rise in expenditures for medical supplies, and a damper on economic growth due to millions of man-hours lost are the results."

"In other words," Matuschek calmly added, "you're helpless."

"Not completely, Matuschek!" Rescor corrected. "Because we haven't been idle, and the resources we have at our disposal have made wide-ranging research projects possible. And one of these projects looks promising."

"Why an experiment then?"

"You see, Matuschek, madness is a dialectical process. Extreme situations of stress or shock burden the conscious, affect the subconscious, and arouse suppressed fears. It causes enormous mental pressure, which backfires through the entire system of the body and—as the specific makeup of the mental load may dictate—sets in motion certain hormonal processes. The body's balance of hormones is altered, which in turn affects brain activity.

"To make a long story short, insanity occurs when external stimuli trigger suppressed fears whose mental pressure alters the balance of hormones in such a way that the brain can no longer function normally."

"Change the illness-producing environment, then you'll also cure the patients!" Matuschek suggested.

"The key to solving the problem," Rescor coldly pointed out, "thus lies in controlling hormonal balance. By way of example, if we block an over or underproduction of serotonin or noradrenalin, we also inhibit eccentric behavior!"

Naturally! Matuschek thought, discouraged. *You only do away with the symptoms, not the causes. You reject that social and political insanity must also lead to individual insanity.*

"However, in order to control hormone production, we need data on what concentration of hormonal substance leads to what psychosis. If our supposition proves correct that schizophrenia is caused by too much aminooxidate in brain tissue—it's produced by a psychotic subconscious—then we need only inject lithium carbonate, which lowers the level of aminooxidate, and the schizophrenia disappears.

"And in exactly the same way we can also cure all other such mental disorders!"

Either Matuschek was having an alarming vision or they were able to exercise control over him and his feelings and inclinations, and make him meek and obedient so that he would happily work for them and contentedly die among the ready-made parts all jammed together on a conveyor belt.

"We have made large-scale tests," Rescor informed him. "Ten thousand patients analyzed inside and out. But the results were too insignificant to give an exact conclusion.

"By accident we stumbled upon the Ruthland Principle. A stroke of good luck, a spin-off from another series of tests, at first unnoticed, not taken seriously, at last rediscovered and developed.

"The Ruthland Principle states that the same hormonal changes can temporarily induce psychoses in the conscious such as impairment of the conscious, which originates naturally through a failure of the subconscious defense mechanism.

"We seized upon the idea, built a device, and hooked a highly sensitive probe up to a computer.

"This device is capable of simulating all mental diseases supposedly known up to this time. We leave the subconscious untouched, and only take possession of the consciously felt fears. Do you understand the significance, Matuschek?

"We connect you to this machine, push the buttons, and suddenly your brain explodes! Even the slightest impulse of psychotic thought breaking out of the chains of the defense mechanism will swell up to the size of an ocean. Fear becomes outright terror, it determines your thoughts and the image of your environment as you see it!

"The consequences, Matuschek, the consequences! Every person carries a time bomb around with him in which all potential distortions of the mind are waiting for something to set them off. We're not going to detonate it, but we are going to make a few adjustments and defuse it to make you more productive and your hormones dance and go around in circles, and indicate to us what we have to do to cure paranoia, catatonia, phobias, and all other psychoses through hormonal reduction or increase!"

Matuschek shivered and studied Rescor's expressionless face. "I decline your offer!" Matuschek whispered. "I'll resist, fight. . . ."

Rescor grinned, inflated his nostrils, and rubbed his thin eyebrows. "You're powerless, Matuschek," he reminded him in a friendly way. "You're in our hands. You have to obey."

Several hours later—long after he had stopped wringing the chief analyst's neck with both hands like a piece of wet cloth—Rescor's screams still echoed in his head. Not once did he notice the blows from the billy club wielded by the fast-moving security guard.

"Have you made any progress?"

"I think we're on the right track, coordinator. Have you read Report Number Seven?"

"The Ruthland Principle?"

"That's right. At the institute we're going to make an experimental application shortly!"

"Your prognosis?"

"According to the high estimate by the National Data Bank, 63 percent."

"That's a bit low!"

"The matter of a multiple-aspect problem—"

"Even so, the difficulties get bigger every day! If something doesn't happen soon, the unrest and fear in the population will erupt in violence! That cannot be allowed! The government is hardly calm and collected!"

"But we need time. . . ."

"Which you have, within reasonable limits, naturally! The Sociology Institute has already prepared a large-scale campaign to divert attention away from the problem."

"What kind, coordinator?"

"Space travel! We're making space travel popular again!"

"Ah, the wide-open spaces, heroes, the waiting stars. . . ."

Matuschek sat in a busily buzzing wheelchair, his hands and chest tied down, and was being pushed down the corridor by a security guard.

"Where am I going?" Matuschek asked.

No answer.

Matuschek moved and rubbed up against the armrests. The blue flash of an electrowhip slapped across his chin as a warning. The air was filled with the smell of just-milled metal filings. Matuschek sat still.

The black-painted elevator seemed like a plastic coffin. "Down?" Matuschek asked.

Yes, down. Matuschek closed his eyes, and dozed his uneasiness away. The elevator stopped, shoved him and his wheelchair out into one of the wide main corridors, past glass doors, around subway entrances and yellow-green plant boxes whose plants hungrily stretched out their bright, luminous leaves.

In the lab soft light predominated.

Rescor was again smoking and grinned with yellow, nicotine-stained teeth showing. "Science needs a lot of servants," he mumbled desultorily. The strangle marks on his throat turned reddish.

Tribeau put a wire-thin metal headband on Matuschek, garnished him with electrodes and probes, adjusted some sliding regulators, and threw switches.

Wham! Wham! Wham!

It's clicking in me again, Matuschek thought faintheartedly. And even though the gleaming band on his forehead was soon warm and comfortable, Matuschek's lips trembled.

"All systems go!" Tribeau cheerfully announced.

"I have a headache!" Matuschek said hoarsely. "Heavens, my skull's about to burst!"

"No reason to worry," Rescor soothed him confidently. "A completely harmless and normal side effect." He turned the knob and signaled Tribeau. "We're ready to start."

Matuschek braced himself and waited—for what? Breathless tension showed on the analyst's face.

Rescor, Tribeau, the lab, the diagnostician all melted.

Click!

Matuschek repeatedly went over the answers from the onboard computer. Could it really be possible? An error? Now? Out here? At this crucial point?

It was only a minute variation, not even a thousandth of a degree, but at this distance . . .

How was it possible? A discrepancy? Human error? Or . . . or what if somebody had falsified the coordinates for Epsilon Eridani?

In his armpits Matuschek felt warm, moist sweat cooking.

But who? Such a recomputation of the flight plan could only be made by someone on board.

Who?

Rescor? Unlikely, the doctor did not know enough about electronic systems.

Tribeau—he seemed to be the only one! The technician! Matuschek balled his hands up into fists. He must have come on board shortly before!

How the scales fell from his eyes.

That odd cunning look . . . His nervousness . . . The furtive footsteps, the uncommunicativeness, the hacking cough . . . The sharp, cutting, sneering insidious tone of his voice . . . The ironic gestures . . . The pointed, killing snout . . . And hard eyes, no feeling except hatred. . . .

Matuschek felt panic, a helplessness, as if he were an insect fearfully struggling in the invisible web of a transformed spider.

But what did the technician intend by it? What was he after? Why was he trying to keep the Epsilon Eridani expedition from arriving? Only a lunatic would plan to let a survey ship speed aimlessly through interstellar space without fuel supplies, without a chance to get back, lost and forgotten for all time. . . . Only a lunatic. . . .

The realization left him groaning. Matuschek saw his fingers shaking. *What was he to do?* his thoughts rushed. How was he to react? His heart skipped a beat.

Rescor! Rescor must help him! He must help to outwit Tribeau, he had to give him a shot, make him talk . . . Rescor! Where was Rescor?

Matuschek switched on the intercom, tried to give his voice a bored tone, and muttered Rescor's name into the microphone.

No response.

What had happened? *What had just happened?*

My God! Of all the things to happen! Had Tribeau somehow put Rescor out of the way? Did the saboteur have any idea of Matuschek's discovery? If so, then. . . .

Anxiety mounted. Panic. A stone weight, paralyzed limbs, taut muscles, rushing blood.

Matuschek flinched.

Crouching down and sniggering, Tribeau snuck through the open bulkhead onto the bridge. In his right hand he held a small laser.

Matuschek swallowed. "What's this all about? What's the meaning of this?" he asked unsteadily.

Tribeau grinned. He grinned only with his mouth, not with his eyes or cheeks. Tribeau grinned at fear. The laser was aimed at Matuschek's chest.

"Rescor!" Matuschek screamed and threw himself at the control panel. "Rescor! Help me! For heaven's sake, help me!"

A thinner shadow appeared behind Tribeau. *Rescor!* Finally! He had heard his cry for help. Rescor was there. Everything was going to turn out all right. That brave old Rescor!

Rescor tapped Tribeau on the shoulder. His voice was painful, it sounded tinny, strident. "Should we shoot him dead on the spot," he bared his pointed teeth and smirked obscenely, "or should we have a little fun with him beforehand?" The scalpel gleamed like burning magnesium. "You know, I like it when they howl, whimper. . . ."

Click!

"Organic diagnosis—within the load limit. Circulation

somewhat uneven, stabilized but fast. Blood pressure high."
Tribeau leaned over the diagnostician slightly. "Restabilization
of the hormonal balance immediately followed termination of
electronic stimulation . . . Evaluation is still on-going, but
the information is, as you can now see, plain and clear." He
looked over at Rescor. "The computer is checking it over now.
Should we continue, or. . . ."

The chief analyst snapped his fingers impatiently. "What
are you waiting for?"

Tribeau lowered his hand.

Click!

Matuschek listened to the sound of his body, the rasping
breathing, the surges of blood, the heartbeats. He cautiously
pressed the palms of his hands against the wooden planks
right in front of his face, pushed with all his might, groaned,
moaned, drank the sweat from his skin.

In vain. Solid, immovably solid, riveted, nailed, sealed, and
reinforced by twenty miles of concrete.

Matuschek could not move, the closeness was choking him,
his head was burning up. Air! Breath! He needed air! The
closeness was squashing his thoughts to pulp.

Matuschek felt the pressure on his body increase, felt all of
the millions of tons of weight pressing down and crushing his
chest.

He could not stand it anymore. The pain, the agony. . . .

Matuschek wanted to scream, call for help, but something
or other was flattening his throat, grinding down his vocal
chords, pulverizing him, making him speechless, weak.

Click!

"We must repeat this simulation should the need arise,"
Rescor said, lost in thought. "The data are rather inconclu-
sive."

"It's relatively harmless. . . ." Tribeau studied the close-
spaced computer printout, which he slipped off the paper
pins. "Matuschek's ego world is little by little taking over his
body. Surprising, this sensitivity! When we raise the energy
supply, we have to be careful of a psychosomatic reaction.
And what if that overrides the defense mechanism of the subconscious? Look at his skin. Over there, the blue pressure
points. They'll disappear gradually, but they still cover almost
his whole chest!"

Rescor went over to Tribeau, studied the scales and diagrams. "Wait a minute," he ordered Tribeau. "I'm going to
talk to the section analyst!"

Matuschek was breathing hard and fast. His thoughts crept
along stubbornly and sluggishly.

Something or other was going on here. Where were his
memories?

Faded, bleached out, whitewashed away. . . .

"The Secretary of Education inquired about your results
this morning."

"All secretaries are being kept constantly informed by us
on the latest status of our research."

"No rebuke intended."

"I did not take what you said that way, coordinator."

"The Secretary of Education has a hunch that Project P is
a failure. He expects the institute to concentrate more on the
promising experiments with Ptyramon derivative.

"Quick, effective, and manageable supervision of the populace by conscious-controlling psychoactive drugs also seems to
be a pressing priority of the presidential palace."

"We have more than one line of research, coordinator. Our
Ptyramon findings are not yet sufficient to apply them on a
large-scale test. And as far as Project P goes, no one could
possibly hope to obtain precise results after such a short
space of time."

"I see. I can wait."

Click!

Matuschek was standing on the canyon rim, staring down
at the rocky pinnacles, the scarred chimneys, the rocky ledges
and the sparsely overgrown terraces, the rushing mountain
stream flowing through the distant valley.

A shadowy evening, as cold as Matuschek's thoughts. A
howling winter wind, as bone-chilling as Matuschek's feelings.
The empty crying of a gust of wind, as hopeless as Matuschek's prospects.

So it must be true! Matuschek thought. *If the stars don't
fall and the ground doesn't cave in, then humankind must
fall and tumble to the ground. That is truth, that is fate.*

A teardrop rolled out of his right eye and froze into a rigid
globule.

The rocks nodded to Matuschek.

I'm leaving everything! Matuschek told himself. *I'm leaving everything behind! The grief, the pain, the fear, the agony. Just one step, and a long fall.*

From the summit of a huge mountain nearby the moon stared down silently at Matuschek.

The only way out! Matuschek pondered. *The only chance to escape failure and worry, the all-devouring despair. A quick rush through the air, and it's all over and done with.*

Matuschek raised his foot.

Click!

"At the last possible moment!" Tribeau sighed anxiously. "And that was a 50 percent energy flow! If this damned computer—"

"Control yourself, Tribeau!" Rescor ordered, expressionless. "It has nothing to do with the computer. It's functioning perfectly. I suspected earlier that something or other was amiss with Matuschek."

Matuschek? thought Matuschek. *Isn't he . . . dead? Dead? How did I wind up dead? I'm Matuschek, Matuschek lives. Why do I think he/I is/am dead? Why?*

"Should we end it now?" Tribeau seemed to be startled. "The diagnostician cannot detect any variation."

"No, of course we're not stopping. The section analyst has given us a free hand. The project has priority, especially in regards to a political criminal. You very well know that!"

"But all the same . . . Matuschek's a good test subject. We don't want to endanger him needlessly."

"What does the hormone count show?"

Tribeau pushed a few buttons, adjusted a few sliding regulators. "Regeneration this time took longer than the first two tests," he nervously explained. "But that was to be expected."

"As before, the strain is geared to the tolerance level. And up to and including the state of excitation in the vegetative nervous system the organism functions normally."

Rescor made a motioning gesture.

Click!

"You're unmasked, Matuschek!" the middle shadow said.

Matuschek shivered, shrank back, hands and forehead chilled with horror.

"It won't do you any good to deny it, Matuschek!" the shadow on the right remarked.

"Denying it makes your situation worse, Matuschek," the dark shape on the left concurred delightedly.

"You're unmasked, Matuschek," the middle shadow repeated.

The wall behind Matuschek was thorny and unfriendly, it scraped his skin and burned his nerve endings like fire.

"I'm innocent," Matuschek stammered. The moisture in his mouth evaporated.

Slowly the shadows came up closer to him.

They have no faces! Matuschek was quaking. *My God, where are your faces?*

"Innocent?" the middle one scoffed.

"In—no—cent?" the left one mimicked Matuschek's word.

"Look at yourself, Matuschek," the shadow on the right shrilled. "Look at yourself down there, Matuschek."

Matuschek bent his head forward. He froze.

Naked!

Naked, unclothed, fish-pale skin. And *there*—Good heavens! he was *also* naked *there!*

Matuschek collapsed. A hundred thousand fingers were pointing at him, a hundred thousand mouths were sneering, laughing, laughing at him.

"Innocent!" the huge tottering shadow foamed at the mouth over him. "Innocentinnocentinnocentinnocent. *And innocent!*"

Matuschek sobbed from fear and shame. He hid from the leering, whispering eyes.

"It's not all that serious!" he screamed. "It's still a part of me! It can't be bad! Don't you understand?"

Matuschek twisted and ran his hands over his nakedness, went lower. . . .

"Don't touch it!" bellowed the shadow. *"It's sin!* Away from it! Dirt and filth!"

Matuschek's small limp hand scratched his stomach, scratched. . . .

"Don't touch it!" screeched the shadow throbbing with hatred.

Matuschek grabbed. . . .

All over the place, their voices choked with seething rage, and the thin, red-lacquered claws of the shadows attacked his throat, they sunk into his flesh just like sharp razor blades.

Click!

"Are you out of your mind, Tribeau?" Rescor yelled full of rage. "What good is this junk? Are you trying to sabotage my work?"

Tribeau stood speechless before the hectically humming and blinking diagnostician. "It . . . I . . ." he stammered.

Cussing, Rescor shoved him aside and worked the controls.

Amazed, Matuschek noticed that out of the countless small wounds on his neck trickled a warm, sticky fluid, and it was staining his clothing dark red. What had happened? What had they been doing to him?

A flexible, tentaclelike arm came out of the diagnostician, carefully cleaned the finger-deep cuts with its padded extension, and sprayed a bandage over the wounds. Then it gave him a shot in a vein. Right away Matuschek became calm and drowsy.

Tribeau hit his hand against his forehead. "Unbelievable!" escaped from his lips.

Rescor snorted. "Spare me your remarks!" he snapped back in a surly tone. "Who gave you permission to alter the program and arouse subconscious body taboos? Nakedness, or anything else?" The chief analyst read the computer record on the monitor. "That's it! A sexual neurosis! Do you want to kill the test subject? You know full well that is why the energy the device puts out is only so high while blocking of the conscious is being *simulated!* Such intense stimulation of currently existing neuroses automatically leads to a reaction in the systems of the body!

"There! Look at Matuschek! His growing feelings of overwhelming guilt have almost done him in! We can thank our lucky stars that we managed to cut off the energy supply just in the nick of time!"

"But that's inconceivable to me!" Tribeau helplessly justified himself. "The instrument settings faultlessly indicated that the computer was supposed to induce agoraphobia, fear of open spaces, in the patient. And not this nudity complex!"

Rescor was not even listening. "Don't make a fool of yourself," he hissed. "That's impossible! I had a hand in the development of the device myself." He started lecturing with his hands. "The computer overloaded the conscious with definite enticements and impulses, which according to what is selected engenders a particular psychosis. When you simulate schizophrenia, the test subject *becomes* schizophrenic and not manic-depressive. That's exactly why—only while we simulate psychoses, the subconscious is left untouched—we can work with so high an energy level.

"If we destroy the subconscious defense mechanism and stimulate the currently existing psychoses contained up to now, we only need a fraction of this energy. Otherwise," Rescor folded his arms, "the subconscious gets overloaded, takes control, a wave of panic overwhelms the organism, and finally brings on its self-destruction."

Tribeau was taken down a notch. "I have no explanation," he said hesitantly.

The chief analyst looked at Matuschek.

"How do you feel?"

Matuschek overheard the sound of his voice. *Feel?* he wondered. Did he feel?

"I don't feel," he serenely stated. "No, I don't feel."

"The diagnoser . . ." Tribeau began, but Rescor curtly nodded no.

"Let's call it a day," he decided. "Anyway, the sedative gives false readings."

"The situation's getting critical."

"Our efforts—"

"Your efforts get the attention they deserve. But they're displeased over the continuing delay."

"It's the first experiment. Problems are merely par for the course."

"Let me repeat it. Problems are avoidable. Do you perhaps have the wrong test subject?"

"Not very likely. The psychological tests—"

"I'm familiar with. That's why I also suspect that the experiment started out on the wrong hypothesis."

"Meaning?"

"I mean the machine is no good for the stated goal. The attempt to simulate mental disorders in order to discover something about illness-causing hormone fluctuations did not pan out. Judging by the report, only latent symptoms were reinforced."

"But a large-scale test—"

"There's no longer any need for a large-scale test. Project P is immediately canceled."

"But—"

"No buts! We're changing our approach. Prospects about the use of Ptyramon derivative gamma conclusively show that this psychoactive drug will be adequate to eliminate our problems.

"I've already given orders to have Ptyramon G slowly added to the Ruhr subdistrict drinking water. If the calculations hold true, mental illness will rapidly decrease within two weeks.

"Moreover, criticism, discontent, and passive resistance in the populace might also be reduced. Understand? We control emotions. . . ."

". . . we control thoughts."

Matuschek woke up looking into Rescor's face. The light in the cell was dreary yellow.

"How long have I been asleep?" he wheezed.

Rescor glanced at his watch. "Only four hours. Remarkable, that dose of barbiturate the diagnoser shot you up with."

Matuschek was frightened by his dim memory. "They wanted to come after me and. . . ."

"No." The chief analyst shook his head, sighing resignedly. "The experiment's been stopped. The institute management and governing authorities are of the opinion that we're on the wrong track. The results are way off expectations."

Matuschek got up holding his numb head in both hands. "What now?"

Rescor frowned. "Nothing. The institute no longer needs you. Tomorrow you'll be taken to the Lyon penal facility. I don't know when your trial and sentencing take place."

"My head," Matuschek whispered. "Something's wrong with my head! Something's happening to my head! What have you done to me? What have you done?"

Rescor stood up. "Side effects," he explained. "They'll go away."

Matuschek opened and shut his eyes. "Something's wrong with my head," he said feebly. "If I could only remember! My thoughts . . . They're swirling and buzzing. I can't get a grip on them, it's so hard. . . .

"*Rescor!* You've got to help me! You have to take a look at me! My brain—something's out of whack with it! I feel it! I feel it!"

"Don't worry yourself with it, Matuschek," Rescor calmed
him absentmindedly. "Psychoactive drugs can temporarily
disrupt the thinking mechanism. Any kid knows that! It's the
tranquilizer, that's all! Lie down and go to sleep. You've just
gone through a hard time." He laughed without a trace of
friendliness.

"Rescor!" Matuschek cried. "What's going on? What is it?
What—"

Click!

The path was narrow and covered with sparkling hoar-
frost. It was vibrating under Matuschek's footsteps, and his
feet were time and again slipping off into emptiness. Fog was
rising. The sky was starless.

Matuschek hurried down the path, paddling with his arms
to keep his balance. He rushed and ran, slipping on icy
stones, constantly looking behind him and blowing into his
numb hands.

Matuschek stopped, blinked at the cloud of fog, at the fear
in his head. The narrow rocky ledge came to an end, jutting
out broken and miserable into darkness.

Behind him Matuschek heard the sounds of his fast-ap-
proaching pursuers.

Matuschek! they howled.

The fog got thicker. It lay clammy on Matuschek's skin
aflame with fear.

Matuschek staggered, looking at the ground in horror. A
rock slowly came unlodged, rolling off into the abyss, clatter-
ing like a gravelly waterfall.

Matuschek! they whispered.

Then—all at once—the fog disappeared. Matuschek whimpered. Twittering, the serpentine bodies crawled toward him.
Prickly teeth were slavering, they jumped at his face, they
bore into his calves.

Click!

"Rescor!" yelled Matuschek. "What are you doing to me?"
Everything was going around and around in him and getting
blurred.

Unbelieving, Rescor stared at the finger-deep bite wounds
on Matuschek's leg. The gushing blood had already collected
in a thick puddle on the floor. The chief analyst jumped for
the door and hit the alarm button. Shrill high-frequency hums
whined excitedly.

"A relapse!" Rescor said aghast. "How can—"

Click!

Matuschek crawled back deeper into the narrow corner be-tween the desk and bookcase, squeezing the damp, black-stained handkerchief against his mouth, coughing and spitting, his bulging eyes glued to the crackling, forward-creeping flames.

The heat almost choked him, it singed his eyebrows, his hair, it roasted his skin painfully red, scorched his clothes, blackened his mind.

Matuschek moaned.

The flames danced in triumph. A section of the ceiling crashed down, showering glowing sparks on the burning rug belching thick, pitch-black choking smoke.

The wall of flame curved around the melting plastic chairs a bit hesitantly, stopped, got its bearings, spotted Matuschek, and shot thin yellow incandescent tongues at his chest.

Matuschek screamed and tore off his flaming jacket.

Click!

Matuschek broke down. His parched hair fell out and struck fast to his injured facial skin.

Rescor was choking. He had turned gray.

"Orderlies!" he yelled helplessly through the open door above the sound of the alarm siren. "Where are the god-damned order—"

Click!

"We'll get you, Matuschek!" the table knife threatened. It fell out of the silverware drawer in the cupboard and reeled in circles on Matuschek. In the faint daylight it flashed its blade like a rusty sheet of metal.

"We're gonna kill you, Matuschek!" the meat fork heckled, hopping over the sink, just missing his neck.

"We're gonna do you in, Matuschek!" jeered the meat ten-derizer pounding hatefully on the refrigerator, taking a big leap and hitting Matuschek's knee excruciatingly.

Snip! went the scissors, clicking with its blades, clicking and cutting off Matuschek's right ear with a lightning-fast swipe.

Snap! went the table knife, shaving Matuschek's chin, slic-ing his skin into confetti streamers.

Click!

Rescor got sick and threw up a soapy jet of half-digested

food all over the disarranged bed in front of which Matuschek was squirming and squeezing his ear stump with his
hand while screaming.

"Tribeau!" groaned Rescor, grabbing the arm of the bewildered analyst rushing up and looking in. "A shot! A tranquilizer shot! Quick! He's dying! Psychosomatic relapse . . . A
tranq—"

Click!

Panting, Matuschek was running across the black, smoking, endless plain, his lungs eaten up by the acid fumes spew-
ing out of the crater at him. He ran and ran with no feeling
left in his legs and helpless fear in his spasming heart, and
behind him he heard the stomping and roaring of the pur-
suer, feeling the snapping at his ankles and smelling the sweat
from its body.

And although panic-stricken, Matuschek was unmercifully
pushing his flayed, exhausted body ahead with his remaining
strength, he paid no attention to his cut-up feet and blood-
whipped legs, but he ran and escaped as he had once before
in his poor, short life,

when the orderlies arrived

and although he swore and cussed in anger, infuriated and
shaking with loathing, he screamed threats, and ran and ran
and fled, kilometer after kilometer, leaving that black lifeless
plain behind him,

*a double dose, you look around at them like an idiot and
you go faster*

and although he wondered why they wanted to kill him
and what he had done for them to pursue him so relentlessly,
and what sense did his life make if he died here between
the crater and the bubbling acid pool.

we have to hold him down and give him the shot

and although at that moment above in the pale-green sky
the needlelike gleaming silver *Syringes*, Syringe of the escaping spaceship piercing the jagged cloud banks,

he's dying

even though everything in that one single second occurred
to him, he still knew with complete crying certainty that he
had finally and forever lost.

Staggering, he fell into the dry powder.

END OF AN ERA
(Zusammenbruch)

RONALD M. HAHN &
JÜRGEN ANDREAS

Translated from the German

by Joe F. Randolph

Rogier landed in Cologne in the morning, and just as he was getting into his car to be driven over to the head offices of McDonnell Douglas Chemicals, the whole country started to disgust him.

The noise, the closeness, the hundreds of thousands of brutish, stupid-looking workers who overflowed into the streets of Leverkusen like torrents. He could not stand it.

"Drive faster," he ordered the uniformed chauffeur. The man behind the wheel visibly winced. He mumbled something unintelligible.

They reached the MDC building in just under fifteen minutes. The driver guided the gleaming chromed car into the underground garage. Two employees who were waiting for Rogier zealously dashed toward him and opened the car door. A third man was standing at the elevator door.

Damned chalk faces, Rogier thought, infuriated. He shot the employees a contemptuous look without deigning to speak to them. They trembled in his presence, which was what he wanted, and he enjoyed it. They were like small bugs that he could squash underfoot.

The elevator took him up. The air was to some degree breathable on the topmost floor if, of course, not compared to what he was used to breathing in his Bahamas villa.

Pestilence, garbage, disease, filth. That was Europe. Rogier shuddered.

The employee who had introduced himself as Salzmann in obsequious tones remained standing hesitantly in front of Corcoran's office.

"Well, what are you waiting for?" snapped Rogier, annoyed. "Open the door, man. I have serious business to attend to."

"Uh . . . yes, sir. Of course." He knocked timidly. Nothing. More knocks. Still nothing.

"Buzz off," Rogier snarled. The man bowed and hurried off. Rogier put his right hand on the doorknob and turned. The door flew back as well as the bare-bosomed platinum blonde who had been sitting on Corcoran's lap.

"Oh . . . uh . . . hello, Rogier." Corcoran shot the girl a withering look and straightened up his clothes. With a crestfallen look the girl disappeared through a second door.

"Been having a little fun?" Rogier grinned cynically. He laid his attaché case aside and sat down across from Corcoran. "What was she doing here?"

Corcoran laughed. "Oh, God, she's just some office girl who thought she could manage to get liver treatment through me. My brother's the head doctor at the NEW Clinic. As far as I'm concerned, why should I believe anything she says?"

"Let's skip that." Rogier put his fingertips together and scrutinized the man opposite him keenly. He wanted to get away from here as soon as possible. At home a half dozen women were waiting for him. Beautiful, charming young women who read his every wish in his eyes, who adorned his existence until they got too old or until he got bored with them. Not a one of them would dare go against his wishes as long as they knew that he could demote them back to the plague continent just as fast as he had sent for them. "The latest profits leave a lot to be desired, Corcoran. What's going on around here? At home they are displeased with the way you do business. The stockholders demand more."

"Conditions are getting worse by the day," Corcoran defended himself. He was a rather stout man with a slightly receding forehead. And his suntanned face was not genuine but came from a sunlamp. "We've been having too much fallout. People are forever calling in sick. I can't supervise everything all by myself."

The last sentence was an admission to Rogier of business ineptitude. "I can't supervise everything all by myself." That meant that Corcoran was either not the right man for this job or his energies were being wasted elsewhere. On office girls, for example. Maybe he was even taking drugs.

"The privileges which have been granted to you are not to be sneered at, Corcoran," Rogier stated coldly. "In Leverkusen I believe there are a lot of people who would give their right arm for your job."

Corcoran winced. He turned red right up to his hairline. "I didn't mean it that way, Rogier. I—"

"Mr. Rogier to you," Rogier said caustically. "We're still not buddy-buddy. The stockholders are only interested in facts. Any problems you have and how you deal with them are your concern and yours alone." He glanced at his watch. "But I see right now that I have an urgent appointment."

Without giving Corcoran, who wanted to babble on with his excuses, another look, he got up and left. Outside in the hallway he took out a small pigskin-bound appointment book. On the still-empty page for the next day he jotted down: *Fire Corcoran.*

Hungry, he went into the MDC dining room. Outside, heavy trucks rumbled past as he sat by the window and studied the menu. A waiter who had recognized him from a distance rushed up and bowed servilely.

"You'd better not try and serve me this hog slop," Rogier said. He flung the menu away and stood up. The man turned red as a pickled beet. "Don't you have anything to do?"

The waiter vanished confused and humiliated. Rogier snapped his attaché case shut and strolled down the hallways, through the reception area, and toward his waiting car. On the outside, which he saw through the large square window, it was gloomy and misty. A cold, damp wind was blowing. The workers filling tank trucks outside the MDC buildings were wearing heavy oilcloth and oxygen masks.

Rogier smiled. Like flies after honey, he thought. With his right foot he arrogantly kicked over a bucket a cleaning woman had left there. Serves her right. What in the world was that bucket doing right in his way?

The Federal Republic was an uninteresting field of operation for him. Here there were no more challenges for a real man. Everything was regulated, such as how and when you crossed the street. The video stations warned the pedestrians so that they would not venture out on the street during fallout time. You had to carry gas maks in many areas. Being led around by the nose like this got on Rogier's nerves. Something more beautiful should be waiting for a free man. He recalled his last safari, which Wellington had organized. The old Wellington. The GFC company belonged to him; it was McDonnell Douglas's biggest rival. Industrial spies from both firms were beating their brains out to discover each other's secrets and thus have their own share of the market. In the meantime old Wellington amused himself in Rhodesia-Zimbabwe along with the MDC stockholders on an elephant hunt.

Rogier passed the first inside checkpoint without showing his ID to the security guard. The slim pimply man blanched under his greasy uniform hat, but he dared not utter a sound.

The car that had picked him up was no longer there. There was another in its place, a model from the year before driven by a severe-faced chauffeur. He had certainly never cheated on his wife. Even the car was a surprisingly filthy bucket of bolts. Inside it reeked of gas, cold ashes, and sweat.

"Take me to the Glass Palace," Rogier said irritably. That was the only spot here in the city that he could put up with for more than a day.

Look over here. Just look at yourself, our city. Anyone can live here as he pleases. Neither oppression nor intolerance is the order of the day. We have built our city—a present-day metropolis. Our work is beginning to pay off little by little. Everyone can live here as he pleases. We are prepared for the future.

Just look at yourself.

The uniformed men rudely made a path through the crowd of people. Individual shouts rang out here and there that were lost in the general murmur. Somewhere a siren was wailing. The white-helmeted squad leader pushed a thin man aside and said: "Make way, people! Out of the way!"

"Coming through," a weary-looking uniformed man added. "Be reasonable. Get to the sides."

The squad leader, a broad-shouldered man with a square

face and fiery eyes, surveyed the crowd with a stubborn look and then asked: "Who called us?"

A policeman stepped forward. He was pale like all the other bystanders, short-winded, and wearing glasses. His right hand shook in a restrained way as he put it up against his headgear.

"Sawitzki, SP 2965–87. With Patrol Helicopter 412."

The squad leader pointed with his head in the direction Sawitzki had come from. The crowd of people hid the object he had been called about.

"Is it over there? This shadow?"

"Yes, inspector," Sawitzki said.

"When did it appear?"

"We've been here about ten minutes, inspector. But the . . . shadow is believed to have been here . . . for a good fifteen minutes, the people say."

The squad leader looked around inquisitively. The crowd parted automatically.

"Which one of you people saw it first?" The bystanders began coaxing each other at random. Someone yelled, "I did!" another, "I was one of the first ones here," still another, "I was near here when it appeared!"

The squad leader took a few steps forward. Obligingly the people made way. Before him was a three-meter-diameter sphere, apparently composed of pure energy, at the center of which the figure of a man was outlined in shadow, a man who seemed to be sitting in a chair and whom the crowd was watching with interest.

The squad leader shook his head. Then he realized that a young man had appeared beside him.

"Your name?"

"Ralph Meinhard, inspector."

"Tell me what you saw."

Meinhard cast the bystanders an ill-at-ease look as if he felt self-conscious to be speaking freely in front of a large group of people. Then he said: "I was on my way to the next subway airlock at Albert Station five minutes from here. I was going down the other side of the street when something out of the ordinary caught my attention. At first I thought it was an unusual neon sign and being curious, I got closer be-cause—because it was flashing so strangely. And then . . . I saw . . . this thing, this man on his odd platform, just like now, but at first it was a little clearer—diaphanous, if you understand what I'm trying to say."

The squad leader shot Meinhard a look of disapproval. "And you haven't seen anything else unusual that we haven't seen *ourselves?*"

Meinhard blushed and bit his upper lip. He had better stop talking.

"No, I haven't, inspector."

"Give my partner your personal data. I'm finished with you." He moved away and said to his assistant: "That man under the energy dome is dressed oddly, don't you think? Like someone out of the past, like that Grandpa Methuselah, right? He seems to be sitting on a machine and moving very slowly. Has anyone tried to touch it?"

His assistant shook his head. "You can't get near it. A strange, impenetrable wall surrounds him. You can't get through it."

The squad leader walked a few paces closer to the misshapen structure which had appeared out of the blue.

"He's clearly trying," he then said after he had watched the man who was sitting in the energy dome for a long time, "to tell us something. But you can't hear a thing, not even up close. Is there anybody here who can read lips?" The squad leader wandered around looking at the crowd questioningly. Suddenly the people opened their eyes wide. Several people pointed at the object behind the police officers.

"It's disappearing!" someone yelled. The squad leader rushed up to it. The energy field began to dissipate and with it the human shape inside.

"He's turning transparent!"

"The image is fading!"

"Now it's gone!"

The squad leader had stood there without saying a word. This phantom was beyond his ken.

With shaking fingers he lit up a cigarette and said to his assistant: "Write up a report, Steiner, and deliver it to me pronto. Ten copies."

"Sawitzki!"

"Yes, inspector?" The 'copter pilot was there in a flash.

"Disperse this crowd! I have to get to the Interior Ministry right away!"

Dr. Kern was washing his hands. When he took hold of the towel, he said: "You may get dressed now."

The slender pale woman sitting before him reached for her clothes. Without looking at the doctor she said: "I've known you from day one, doctor. When you talk like that, hell's waiting for us."

Kern shrugged in resignation. A deep wrinkle creased his forehead. "I'm sorry for you, my child."

"Is there no hope, then?" the woman asked.

Kern shook his head. His eyes were expressionless.

"Nope. The diagnosis is unmistakable. There's really no other alternative left to me. You must go to the clinic today." He handed her a printed sheet of paper. "Here's your transfer. I want you to get it over with today no matter what. The earliest you can manage."

The woman looked at him with weary eyes. Kern noticed her jaw trembling slightly. "It's so easy for you doctors. Go to the clinic. . . ."

"No, it isn't, Gilla," Kern somberly replied. "I'm ashamed that our medicine has advanced only so far and we can help humanity increasingly less." He smiled worriedly and placed a finger on his cheek.

"I can't even help myself. Look at my face. It's been eaten away by cancer, the same with my lungs and liver despite all the excising laser therapy over the past two years. Or my left eye, blind from acid cataract, one of the many new diseases which strike quicker than we can actually diagnose them."

He sighed. "What have we done to this old world? Instead of expunging disease, infirmity, death, and poverty from the history books, we've made them our closest allies. We've been dumping filth and sewage water on our heads by the bucketful and are proud of it."

The woman, who meantime had put on her last piece of clothing, replied: "He's coming out of the NEW Clinic this afternoon believing that we're among the fortunate ones on this earth, believing in several years of health for us both, in the nights with me and the child he made for me. How should I break the news to him that the kid is a cancer-ridden creature that can't survive and that I won't be able to have any more children?"

Kern sat down behind his desk and cradled his head in both hands. It was painful for him to have to listen to these

words, but it was more unpleasant still to have to give an
even tougher answer.

"It sounds so brutal," he started out. "You'll have to live
with this reality that you've mostly forgotten during the short
time of your dream of happiness." His voice lowered to a
hoarse, broken whisper. "A kid isn't the whole world. You
two still have a couple of years of comparatively good health,
you still have the nights. Believe me, woman—nine out of ten
people are worse off than you are."

Gilla looked at him wordlessly for a while. Between his
spread fingers she saw the doctor's eyes fill with tears. But she
did not utter a word.

The reception area of the clinic smelled strongly of an-
tiseptics as Meinhard got off the paternoster elevator and
moved around the u-shaped area. The man sitting behind the
desk was not the one who had checked him in.

"Excuse me," he said. "I've been told that I can get my papers here in reception. My papers."

The man looked up. "Name, please."

"Meinhard, Ralph Meinhard."

The man's face lighted up. "Oh, yes, I remember. . . ."
He fingered through his card file. "Mann . . . Manders . . .
Marwitz . . . aha, here you are . . . Ralph Meinhard, twenty-
eight years old, a traffic engineer. . . ."

The man cleared his throat. "You're in luck," he then said,
"a NEW patient, right? I wish I had this kind of luck just
once, my friend."

Ill at ease, Meinhard responded. "Only one in a thousand
applicants receives free treatment in the NEW Clinic, right?"

"There used to be less than that. And besides, the five and
ten-year guarantees are only for the big shots, believe you
me. Anyway, it's a fact that *I* can't get out of my wheelchair.
Diagnosis: progressive paralysis. Pathogen unknown."

"I'm sorry," Meinhard said, taken aback.

"No need to be, my good man, no need to be. It gets us all
down . . . Just lookee here at your guarantees: three years of
cost-free care—if needed—for heart, circulation, liver, kid-
neys, GI tract, lungs, larynx, and genitals. My heartiest con-
gratulations! But also read the fine print, and keep in mind
that the human body can also make use of the organs not
listed—not to mention the brain."

Meinhard thanked him.

"Lot's of luck," the receptionist said. "And don't forget your supply of nose filters! Over there—in the rack, right next to the exit lock. The nearest subway lock is ten minutes from here, on the right, just follow your nose!"

Meinhard hurried off. Thought after thought went through his brain in rapid succession. I should really be happy, he thought, guaranteed health for three years, in love, loved in turn, Gilla is to a certain degree healthy and is expecting my kid. And yet, no matter where you went, you ran into the sick and invalid, the unfortunate and the dying.

He thought about his pals that he had not even said good-bye to, and he did not even know if they were still alive or not. He did not even know if anyone else's organ was in him. Detmar's liver maybe.

"The doctors believe my liver is just about the only thing in me that's healthy," he had said. "I'm donating it to you, Kumpel, but there'll be hell to pay if you mess it up with cheap rotgut liquor!"

How could a person look forward to death so calmly? Meinhard thought. Detmar had probably been under the influence of drugs. It must have been terrible to know that you only went on living because you had a couple of healthy organs that somebody else needed, and that you had entered a lottery to win a healthy body or lose everything.

Somebody was yelling. "Hey, is there a subway airlock somewhere around here?" Meinhard discovered that he was the one yelling. A passerby showed him the way.

He bought a ticket and went into a compartment on the subway train that was passing the revolving platform without stopping.

A booming voice assaulted Meinhard. It lasted a few seconds before he could understand what was said. "Freeloader! You're risking denial of a body repair in all private and public NEW Clinics for up to five years!"

He could not help grinning.

The teenager rose up threateningly to the extremely old man, put his fists on his hips, and said grinning cynically: "Spit it out, grandpa."

"Shut your trap, you sassy brat," Methuselah answered, gnashing his teeth. "I'll talk when *I* want to!"

"We've paid you to babble, you old goat," said a second teenager forcefully as he pushed his way up with determination.

"You go well with this lousy world, you asshole. It's as stinking and disgusting as you are!"

Methuselah's answer caused a storm of laughter. The onlookers did not know whether this dialogue was genuine or staged by the management.

Methuselah eyed the crowd for a while, then said, "I want to tell you about the time I was a young man. You can safely believe me. At one time I was as young as you people, and I was a damned sight more handsome than you people. And healthier too. No damned cancer cells anywhere in my body, no bleary eyes and amputated limbs, no puffed-up face, no mechanical larynx, and no shortwindedness like I see in you people. In those days there were old people too, and they weren't put on display—like today—at the animal meat market. They were quite ordinary then and died some time or other. But until their death they were people like anybody else, doing their job or living on a pension alone, with family, or in an old folks home.

"When I was a young man, people were full of high spirits and carefree although—God knows—there were no better times to rave about. I came here from West Prussia. I was a fugitive, I had suffered what the Nazis had done to others. They were nothing but miserably hard times, then. A lot of times we had nothing to eat. We had to gather and eat stinging nettles. You people naturally can't imagine anything along those lines since you only know about trees and shrubs from TV. Nope, in those days plants still grew wild in the ground—and stinging nettles were a species of weed.

"And when we were really lucky, we got soup from the butcher, it was kind of like dishwater he had cooked his sausages in. It was a feast when a sausage had burst and little pieces of meat were left floating in it. . . . Frankly, it was bad for us in those days, but not as lousy as today. At least we still had sun and fresh air. You people can hardly imagine what it's like to walk around on a dyke, see green grass and white sand, and cool blue-green seawater and a blue-white sky with a shining golden sun—and then a spicy, salty fresh wind from the sea blowing right in your face. . . ."

Methuselah nudged the teenager who was now standing

silently next to him and hanging onto his every word with mouth open.

"Hey, you brat, do you know another kind of wind other than this never-ending miasma of fumes and chemicals? You don't—and that's why I feel sorry for you even though you're stupid. If a person left the city—in those days—he came across meadows, tilled fields, and woods with tall pines and the smell of resin and ozone. On the ground lay a cushion of fallen pine needles and leaves that absorbed the sound of your every footstep. And there were animals! Insects, birds, hares, deer. Butterflies hovered over blooms, beetles scurried across the ground, ants carried pine needles into their hills, and there were mice and rabbits everywhere!"

Methuselah's voice increased in volume. "That's all long gone now!" he exclaimed. "Humanity has ruined everything for us! The profit seekers, the speculators have gambled away the Earth and land from under the feet of the unborn; the exploiters and milkers, the bloodsuckers and the nature despoilers, the unscrupulous and irresponsible, and the simply stupid! The powerful who could abandon everything on a large scale because they long ago had their private oases set aside that they could retreat to; those who could buy their health if the environment made them sick—or those who were indifferent to everything because they were pursuing other interests like power, fame, seeing others brought down; the satisfaction of kicking them when they were down. *We* are the ones who let them get away with it—and that was our downfall. And I could tell you all the times—"

The booming voice of an automatic announcer cut into Methuselah's last words. "That was Methuselah, the oldest man in the world! The man from out of the past! The man from the time machine! Eighty-seven years old and naturally aged. Without any need for parts replacement! From the beginning days of the twentieth century! Please tell your friends about us! Amuse yourself with Methuselah, the oldest man in the world. . . ."

The regular clatter of the subway train caused Meinhard to be overcome by a slight weariness. Again and again he caught his chin falling against his chest. His eyelids were suddenly as heavy as lead.

It was in the air. It was stifling, warm, and smelled stagnant. With difficulty he forced himself to stay awake, but it was in vain. The next time he opened his eyes, he found that he had passed the station that he had to get off at.

At the next stop he got off and took the escalator to the surface. Although it was getting close to noon, the streets were overflowing with people. Meinhard spotted housewives who, armed with see-through handbags purchased at department stores (to prevent thefts), were walking along rows of store windows. From somewhere scratchy music blared, accompanied by the voice of two amputee beggars. They held out their holey hats to the stream of people going past, but their business seemed to be worse than it should have been.

In front of the checkout lines a bunch of people had gathered around a shoplifter caught in the act. From a distance Meinhard watched how a store detective brought the man to his knees with a police grip while another one beat him with his billy club.

Meinhard could truly be content. He had been given three days' grace after his release from the NEW Clinic; what it meant was that he did not have to go back to work unless he was losing more than twenty-five percent of his net salary for this time period. He could look around town for a few hours more before meeting Gilla in the afternoon. He was standing in front of a porn shop, in front of the window of which some peaked out-of-work people were standing and cracking jokes, looking over the set of male-female sex dolls with a simulated human appearance displayed there, and shook his head. A thin man in an olive-colored suit that was obviously a uniform for the store's sales personnel was insistently tugging at his sleeve.

"Look over our assortment, sir," he said suavely and licked his thick lips at the same time. "Just arrived from Paris. Paris —ooo-la-la." The man rolled his eyes. It was quite obvious that he had never been to Paris because Meinhard knew only too well that the Seine metropolis in the space of the last twenty years had disintegrated into a slum without equal in the entire world. In France not too long ago an immense exodus to rural areas had begun because it was almost impossible to walk the streets of the sixteen-million-inhabitant city without an oxygen mask. Paris, always associated with a charming life, was testimony not only to ignorance but also to extreme stupidity.

"Thanks," Meinhard said. "But no thanks." The salesman still did not give up. "These models are exceptional," he whispered with a conspiratorial look. "You can just about do anything. . . ."

Meinhard declined with a shake of his head and went on his way. There were really more important things to invest your money in.

His thoughts returned to yesterday morning. The energy dome . . . the man who had been sitting on his strange, arm-chairlike platform. A time traveler? He recalled the annual fair and a man by the name of Methuselah that the newspapers occasionally had an article about. He was also an alleged time traveler. Something had plucked him out of the past and cast him into the future, which made him the leading topic all week long on the video press. The man was reputed to be the oldest living man on Earth. Lately he had fallen somewhat into oblivion even though short pieces about him still appeared. Methuselah had gone against some influential institutions which were not well disposed toward him on that account. He had attacked the Order of Butchers and reproached it for making a business out of despair. He had referred to the order as a bunch of bloodthirsty vampires.

All right. Meinhard stepped out into the street without paying attention to where he was going. Suddenly brakes squealed. The line of cars came to a halt.

He was instantly wide awake. He was standing right in the middle of the street in front of a taxi in which someone was rolling down the window and shouting something at him.

"I . . . I . . ." he stammered, startled.

"Get out of the road, you idiot!" The man shouting at him was dressed in good taste and seemed highly irritated. He was sitting in the back seat waving his arms excitedly. "Out of the way! Get lost!"

Meinhard was too confused to make any decisive moves. Free treatment, death, disease, the shadow, Methuselah, the Order of Butchers. He took two steps forward and then turned back again, thereby making the man in the taxi stare in amazement. The car sped off. Meinhard wanted a drink.

After he had spent two and a half hours in the Glass Palace, Rogier could not stand it anymore. Sure, the proprietor had gone to great pains to get the best-looking woman on the continent for his customer, but according to his pampered taste Rogier had been offered nothing but cheap, average merchandise.

Rogier paid his bill with the tips of his fingers, making sure that the cashier's hand did not touch his. The whole place suddenly sickened him. He had most likely been away from Europe too long. He simply could not live there anymore.

He spent a good long while in the ostentatiously furnished lounge while the man at the reception desk worked desperately to call a taxi.

In the inner city traffic tie-ups were bound to happen at any moment. It was the height of the swing-shift rush hour, and traffic was stalled. It was time this scum was buried six feet under. But his concern was that he would be leaving this municipal dump in two days.

Irritated, Rogier grabbed his attaché case and left the Palace. The charges were always exorbitant—compared to what he was offered.

What if he took the subway? Just the idea of the air quality that existed there turned his stomach. Jammed in between unwashed, bleary-eyed commoners. The odor of stale air and sweaty feet. He would rather not. He went a few meters out into the street. A taxi. Thank heaven.

He gave the driver the name of the hotel where he always stayed whenever he paid MDC an official visit and leaned back in the seat.

He could not tolerate natural—natural?—air for long. He longed to take a hot bath and massage his body with lotion. He decided to get roaring drunk that evening.

The taxi driver slammed on the brakes. A man who a moment ago had tried to cross the street between two cars kept standing there like a statue.

"You asleep?" Rogier cranked the handle to lower the window and stuck his head out. It was a young man, about twenty-six and oddly enough he presented a healthy appearance. Such men were a rarity.

The man stared at Rogier in shock, and moved but not out of the way. Apparently he had been deep in thought out of which he had been wrenched by the taxi's screeching brakes.

"I . . . I . . ." he stammered.

"Get out of the road, you idiot!" Rogier spat at him in irritation.

The air was beginning to get to him. It was absolutely inexplicable to him how people put up with it. "Out of the way! Get lost!"

The young man took two steps forward and then turned back again with Rogier watching him every second. The car sped off. The driver let him off at the hotel and disappeared. A bellboy whose left eyelid had a nervous twitch and whose right leg was shorter than the left rushed up to Rogier to relieve him of his bag.

"Hands off!" Rogier pushed past the man, who turned red in the face, and hurried to the desk, where he was given a key to his room.

While he was standing under the shower taking great pains not to let get in his mouth or nose the water that smelled of all types of possible and impossible chemicals, he thought about Corcoran and MDC.

That man had to go, and ASAP to boot. With the argument that working conditions were at fault, that the workers could not maintain the previous tempo, nobody had yet dared come to him. What if Corcoran had gone crazy? That the conditions making production fall off were not the best was definitely a fact of life that Rogier's grandfather had worked under. After all is said and done, you had to do something to correct the situation. A couple of new machines brought in, a couple of useless workers gotten rid of. That was the solution, and he had always taken it. It was, he thought, only due to the declining wealth of the company heads and their technical managers, as he understood the problem, not because of profits.

Rogier went down to the lounge and ordered something to eat. The sight of dinner made his stomach grumble. It was a colorless gruel that tasted like he didn't know what and supposedly it contained everything that the human body needed in the way of proteins and vitamins. Well, it should have. Anyway, it was just for two days.

A shadow fell across his shoulder. He looked up. Before him stood the man his driver had almost run over a short while ago asking: "Is this place taken?"

"No," Rogier said bluntly. He looked the young man up and down. "Haven't we met somewhere before?"

"I don't know . . ." the person opposite him replied, then a look of recognition swept over his face. "You're the guy that was yelling at me out on the street a few minutes ago, aren't you?"

Rogier grinned. If the brat got sassy, he would make short work of him. He did not look rich enough to stand up to Rogier.

"You're an impudent, petty me-first aristocrat, aren't you?" the young man was now saying. He was getting ready to sit down at the table across from Rogier, but at the last moment he seemed to reconsider. "I didn't come here to have words with you when I don't even know you, Mr. . . ."

"Rogier," Rogier helped him out. He was flabbergasted at the insolence of this man and infuriated that he was near him without being given permission.

"My name's Meinhard, Mr. Rogier," the young man said. "And I've come into this restaurant because I intended to—"

"I'm not interested in your intentions," Rogier said and beat his fork on the table. "Why not be a good little boy and buzz off?"

"That's fine with me," Meinhard said. His hands opened and closed nervously. He would have loved to give Rogier a flat nose, but he knew that he would no doubt wind up on the short end of the stick in an argument that turned into fisticuffs. The man in front of him was a *financier*. He belonged in these surroundings as little as Meinhard did. The hotel might have a well-known reputation—this guy had grown up in clean air, had drunk nothing but pure, clear water his whole life, and eaten tasty, unspoiled meat. No, he could not do a thing against him. One word from him was enough to put Meinhard out of food and a job.

He chose the best course open to him. "Maybe we'll meet up again somewhere else."

"For your sake, I hope not," Rogier said *sotto voce*. But Meinhard had already crossed the dining room and was looking for an empty table.

For a time he thought about the clean-shaven, well-groomed, and previously unknown man who smelled of perfume and then forgot about him.

His attention turned to other things. The haggard-looking waiter who was frantically trying to cut a good figure in his thoroughly conservative uniform; a one-eyed man the right side of whose face carried a recently healed scar (his job probably required him to work with acids); a dark-haired woman who was in a humiliating way busy with a man in his mid-forties who looked to have money (and money meant he had his own multiroom house, adequate ventilation, enough fresh water, a well-stocked kitchen!) no doubt in the hope that he would turn into a prince right out of a fairy-tale book and take her into his castle.

Now that I have obtained free treatment because of my professional qualifications, Meinhard thought, I have a three-year guarantee and cost-free aftertreatment for half a dozen susceptible organs, but suddenly I am not satisfied with all that anymore.

He was surprised at his own thoughts. What had made him think like that all of a sudden? The run-in with that arrogant individual whose cultivated background you noticed fifty meters away? He shrugged. Had the arrogance of this "It belongs to me as an important member of society and if you don't like it, you can get out" character actually made him feel insecure in such a way that he could not be conscious of his luck?

Or had it been the morning encounter with that curious phantom? He had secretly left the site of the NEW Clinic when he had seen the crowd of people. The energy dome had drawn him like a magnet and hours later had set his thoughts in motion. What was it that the police officer had said after calmly berating him? "That man under the energy dome is dressed oddly, don't you think? Like someone out of the past. . . ."

What we now know about the past, Meinhard thought. Was it good or bad—or both? Maybe not good, but better. In any case it was different. It dawned on him that he really knew very little about it. How had people lived back then? They had laid the foundations of what reality was today. They had recklessly exploited the raw materials of the Earth even though they knew for sure that they would not last forever. How could it have happened? Had they done it intentionally without thinking about what would come next? Back then it must have been like today—Charity begins at home. You can look at it any way you want. The mistakes of the past have come home to roost today.

Meinhard thought: We have even painstakingly cast out our sins. Smoking, for example. Hardly anybody mentions the idea of smoking because not enough oxygen can be produced to breathe, but nobody *wants* to smoke anymore because smoking has been looked upon psychologically as a synonym for bad air, and we want to be reminded of it as little as possible since we have the good fortune to be able to stay in rooms with a tolerable percentage of oxygen.

Another example: gluttony. Gone is the variety of eatables that I once knew in my younger days—and most of all that I saw in old movies. No longer is there any wine and brandy because grapes no longer ripen; there is no more milk or cheese or butter; no fish, no spring peas, or asparagus and spinach. There is no more bratwurst, no steak, no schnitzel—only the same never-ending synthetic gruel in different-tasting courses that nonetheless smell strongly of chemicals. Alcohol is still drunk, but more than ever one becomes aware that life is being affected by it, a life that would be threatened from all sides without alcohol consumption. And there are only a few for whom everything is the same, whose chances for survival are so slim that it makes no difference what they die from. That alcohol consumption continues to exist is mainly a result of its mind-affecting influence and the flight from reality connected with it. What used to amuse people, auto travel, hiking, outdoor sports, mountain climbing, walking in the sand, sailing, swimming, is possible only by eliminating the hostile environment. Cut off, friendless, senses gone blank. Our life has become miserable. We have lost a lot and won nothing. And the little ball keeps rolling on. *Rien ne va plus.* No more bets. Every number loses.

He had left the subway train because he was quite suddenly overwhelmed by ravenous hunger. He still had some money, but the food in the high-priced restaurant he had patronized tasted no better than it did anyplace else. There was better food by far at the refuges of those who had long ago abandoned their private oases in the BDR, and had moved to South Sea islands where the air was clean and breathable.

"Be healthy." An old man was suddenly standing in front of him. He was incredibly old.

"Be . . . healthy," Meinhard stammered, startled from his thoughts.

"Is this place taken?" the old man asked.

"No, it's not. Say, aren't you. . . ?"

"I knew you were going to ask," the old man replied with

a smile. "I remind you of someone, a celebrity, a rarity, don't I? Yep, I'm the one. Methuselah, the man out of time, the oldest man on this weird world. My name used to be . . . oh, what does it matter?"

"Excuse me," Meinhard said. "I have no intention of bothering you."

"No problem." Methuselah's heavily wrinkled face changed into a friendly smile. "I'm used to being the center of attention. I thrive on it. Furthermore, you can take the filters out of your nose. You can tell the difference between a high-priced restaurant and a café. The air's better here."

"Actually, I'd forgotten. I'm a bit out of sorts, you see. I just came from the NEW Clinic. And this morning—" he stopped in mid-sentence.

"Aha, a lucky fellow." Methuselah thoughtfully stroked his chin. He was certainly old, but he seemed to have unbelievably robust health. Not once did his hands shake when he took the menu.

"All the same, I'm not happy," Meinhard went on with the conversation.

"Oh, problems?" Methuselah's water-blue eyes seemed to lock in on him.

"Not exactly," Meinhard said. "I have every reason to be happy. But I'm not in the right mood—in the middle of all this misery."

Methuselah seemed to be surprised. He let go of the menu and inched forward. "Are you by chance one of the ones that something has happened to? Have you noticed that carbonic acid stung less during the past year than it does today and that you have to put on more screen cream? Are you one of the ones looking for the reasons for it in order to stop it if possible?"

Meinhard shrugged. "Something like that."

"Welcome aboard, we're in the same boat. In order for the acidity to remain in the atmosphere, has it occurred to you that in the last three months the water level in the pedestrian preserves has been raised twice? The video press has published it in some hidden articles that went unnoticed in the confusion of small and business news items. And do you also know that the water levels are barely close to the absorbers?"

"Our world's dying, and we're dying with it," Meinhard responded sophistically. "This morning before I was discharged

. . . we were allowed to take a walk around the hospital grounds. I left without authorization. There was something . . . a man in a weird energy field. He was trying to tell us something. . . ."

Methuselah was all ears. A worn-out waiter the right side of whose face had been disfigured by a boil served them.

"A man in an energy field?"

Meinhard nodded. His eyes seemed to be looking off into space. "The squad leader told his men that the clothing on that weird guy reminded him of the clothing that *you* were wearing on your arrival—"

"What happened to that guy?" Methuselah pushed his dish aside and began excitedly to knead his wrinkled fingers.

"He disappeared. He suddenly disintegrated into thin air."

"A time traveler . . ." Methuselah mumbled faintly. "So they're still experimenting. . . ." Then he said aloud: "I've never been particularly interested in what was going on around me, in politics, I mean. Before, in my world. But here the realities have made me hard-nosed. This poverty, this senselessness and this depravity. . . ."

"What was it like in the world . . . back then?" Meinhard asked hesitantly. "Was it like in the old movies?"

Methuselah laughed sarcastically. Then he shook his head. "It was certainly nice. But it never was like in the movies. At least it was nicer than you have today. It had its wars, its poverty—as well as ruthless exploitation of nature and people—for the same reasons just like today. But you could still live a little better in it. Here and there you had a little *free space,* a corner where you could be all by yourself."

"And then they simply catapulted you here?"

"Yep, simple as that. Even today I don't know how they managed to do it. I'm a simple man. I didn't have any special training and I worked as a messenger for the Rand Corporation. The European branch of the biggest think tank on this continent. Rand was in direct control of US defense. That's where—as far as I could learn—new weapon systems were constantly being developed and tested. I went to bed one evening and woke up the next morning all beat up in a hospital in your time. At first I thought I was having a complicated dream, then I wondered if a miracle or divine action had brought me here. Some scientists have proven that an energy field has affected my organs, a special-type field—that's all I know about it. I took it for granted that they had used me as an unwilling guinea pig. Without my knowledge. Something went awry with the experiment. I'm stuck here. And with this realization I no longer believe it's a dream, a miracle, or heavenly intervention. Everything was so real and depressing, and hardly 'wondrous.' The puzzling pains that have up to now not left me for one second and that I can bear only with morphine, the frustrations and insults. I have been given the choice of paying for hospital costs with money—which I didn't have—or with my organs. I avoided surgical knives and the routine, matter-of-fact cruelty inflicted by those who wield them just because my fate became popular and I sold myself out as an evening-long story to one of the video companies. Now I work for a marketing enterprise, but one of these days I'll most assuredly find myself under the knife—or facing the Order of Butchers. What has actually saved you from them?"

"Nothing," Meinhard answered. "But the Order nevertheless offers the totally hepless cases a small chance."

"Sure, but at what price? I hate the butchers, and the butchers hate me because I spoke out against them publicly. Only too gladly would they see me as a candidate and torn apart in front of the public. One day it will surely happen, but I'm still too popular. Weren't you ever around when these perverse rites were held?"

The mere thought of it caused Meinhard to be sick to his stomach. He shook his head violently. "Nope, that was too repugnant for me."

"Many are fascinated by it, and that's what keeps the brothers in business. A minority, of course, but an influential one. It's a good deal besides because the video rights bring in a pretty penny. And it takes the minds of the spectators off their own problems. So it has always given something in return. For the Romans it was the circus where they fed Christians to the lions. Later on there was more blood, but for them it was so much more fanaticism. Car races where the drivers went up in flames in their cars after a certain length of time. *Rollerball*, made as a sensational movie, was a success and because of it there was a spate of deaths. And the faces of twenty candidates are ripped open by a butcher with a meat hook in front of millions of viewers so that the blood spurts with a vengeance. The candidates are always unusual in some way: extraordinarily handsome, extraordinarily ugly or some other exceptional features, otherwise they aren't taken first at all. Survivors of this butchery with their typically scarred faces are inducted into the brotherhood and receive a NEW treatment. But the Order's executioner sees to it that the number of survivors of these encounters remains under twenty percent."

Methuselah glanced at his watch.

"I see I must be getting along. The performance begins momentarily. The show must go on. Maybe we'll run into each other again sometime."

"OK," Meinhard said. "I'd like that."

"Come and visit me sometime. You know where you can find me."

"I'll do that. Be healthy!"

"Be healthy!"

The report that Gilla had undergone an abortion hit Meinhard hard. Sure, you had to be ready for anything in these times, but Gilla had had the best qualifications possible so that there had been hope that her unborn child would develop into a normal citizen of Earth.

She broke it to him as gently as possible with tears in her eyes and a slight tremor to her voice. He found that she was more upset over it than he was. He took her in his arms and stroked her gently.

"Something very weird happened this morning," he said, to take her mind off the subject. "Near the NEW Clinic a sphere-shaped energy dome materialized with a man crouching down inside it. I talked to Methuselah about it—remember him? He thought it was a time traveler."

Gilla did not respond. She took his arm away and stretched out on the couch. She was glad that Meinhard had taken the news so calmly. It was good when he had a subject he could talk about.

"Go on," she said.

"You couldn't understand anything he was saying." He explained the incident to her in terse but detailed language. He also repeated the conversation he had had with Methuselah practically verbatim. The old man's comments had penetrated his brain like acid.

He lay down next to Gilla, his fingers fumbling for the

knob that turned the stereo on. Exotic sounds flowed out of the loudspeakers.

We're living for the moment, Meinhard thought. Completely relaxed, a woman beside him, kissing her body, playing with her hair, soaking up the music. But even here reality made inroads. I won't be able to have a kid by this woman and maybe it has turned out all right because what kind of future does a kid have in this world? But it hurts, of course. You somehow felt shut off from eternity, felt that something has died.

"I love you," he said aloud.

"Hm?" Gilla mumbled sleepily.

"I love you."

"I love you, too, dear."

But life does not only consist of moments like this. On the contrary. Ninety-nine percent of it is made up of pain, oppression, frenzy, pointless, repetitive work, and boredom. And something tells you that it was not always like that and must not always be so. The old man had termed the force of self-realization *free space*. You had to recapture for yourself this free space always making it larger and for *all* people; a single free space has become liberation, a whole life.

As if from a long way off shouts reached his ears. The sound of running feet. The roar of engines. Shots. Meinhard jumped up and went to the window.

"What is it?" Gilla asked. She sat up halfway. The blanket slipped from her half-naked body and uncovered her breasts.

"Thousands of people," Meinhard said sticking his head out of the window. "They're running through the streets. Something must've happened. Maybe an accident. I'll get dressed right now." He hurriedly grabbed his clothes and slipped them on.

"Keep calm and remain in your own living units!" a loudspeaker boomed from up the street. An armored car formation was battling the running mob with water hoses. "Stay in your own living units!" the voice repeated. "You are subject to having your medical treatment completely taken away for ten years!"

"I'm going down," he said firmly, zipped up his plastic jacket, and grabbed his nose filters.

"Please stay," Gilla asked softly. "Let's not waste the time we have left so senselessly."

Meinhard cast her a brief glance. Wasn't she right? Did what was happening out there on the street have anything to do with him? Hadn't he just gotten a three-year guarantee on all important organs?

"An anarchistic group of insurgents is planning to throw the city into chaos!" the loudspeaker boomed. "Stay at home and don't interfere with the order-keeping forces in the performance of their duties!"

Machine-gun firing roared. Several screams alerted Meinhard to the fact that the shooting had slackened off.

"Stay here," Gilla said once again.

"It's time to take a stand," Meinhard replied. He inserted his nose filters and rushed out and down the hallway.

Down on the street indescribable chaos reigned. There were thousands of people desperately charging the armed tanks of the order-keeping forces. They were tearing up the street and trying to build barricades with the cars closest at hand. Some of the people were armed. They carried antiquated rifles and an occasional pistol.

Meinhard grabbed a man rushing past by the shoulder. He looked into a pale face in which only the eyes glowed with life.

"What's going on around here?"

The man looked him over in surprise. "Haven't you heard that the man's come back?"

"What man?"

"The man from this morning! The man in the energy dome!" The pale-faced man tried to shake Meinhard's hand away.

"No. Wait a minute! What does that man have to do with all the uproar here?"

"The man who came out of the past and went into the future this morning—this man's come back and stopped here again. This time he made himself understood. Reporters from the video stations who were immediately on the scene broadcast his words over every channel. His most important sentence was that the Earth will be dead in fifty years. Understand? Dead, poisoned. A lifeless cesspool. Then he turned transparent again and vanished."

Meinhard flinched as if stung by a scorpion. Methuselah had been right.

A jet of water suddenly struck him in the chest and knocked him to the ground. When he had regained his senses, the man he had been talking to was gone. Meinhard saw him later on. A bloody abrasion ran the length of his face, but the man seemed nevertheless optimistic.

He ran into Methuselah on a side street. The old man was wearing a white armband like the ones he had already seen on a few men and women. When their looks met, he smiled and grabbed something behind him.

"Here, take this," he said and handed Meinhard a pistol. "You might need it sometime. Show no more consideration for human life. The Rhineland's overpopulated. An opportune occasion to decimate the population."

"How did it all come about, Methuselah?" Meinhard asked bewildered. "The city's gone out of control."

"It might be a lie if I were to say this was a spontaneous uprising," the old man replied. "It was of course staged. The point in time merely was not fixed. The time traveler's words were the catalyst. The masses stormed into the streets and threw rocks and stones at chemical company high-rises. The most advanced forces were organized in the inner city. They wanted to prevent total chaos from developing and at the same time lead the uprising against the oppressors."

Somewhere off in the distance sirens were howling. The revolutionaries had seized some armored cars and were pushing their way down an alley.

"The SWAT teams have surrendered for the most part!" yelled a helmeted man from a turret hatch. "Most people realize that we're fighting for them!"

"We change the future by changing the present," Methuselah said. "Are you in on the act?"

"That I am," Meinhard said. He gazed at the pistol. It took him some effort to realize that he would have to use it. "That I am."

Rogier walked right into the riot when he left his hotel room to pick up some video newspapers in a store across the street. All of a sudden the streets were filled with people.

At first he thought that something must have happened in the area, a traffic accident or the like. But he soon came to the realization that he had deluded himself. Hordes of people were screaming. They were yelling slogans in unison that

made him suddenly aware that something was up that could
turn out ugly for him. He left the papers where they were
and left the store as fast as he could. But it was a bold venture to cross the street safely when crowds of people seemed
to be flocking there from all directions.

It was a never-ending stream. Rogier saw that some of
them were armed. Many were wearing crash helmets and
waterproof clothing, others carried clubs, and still others were
toting rifles and pistols. On their belts hung oxygen masks,
which could mean that they were planning on continuing
with their rioting at least up until the evening.

Chaos was waiting for him in the hotel lobby. The manager, his lips bloody and face chalk-white, was leaning
against the desk and mumbling unintelligible words. The
waiters had disappeared, several white aprons lay on the floor
here and there.

"What's going on around here?" Rogier asked. He had to
control himself to keep from grabbing the weeping coward by
the collar. "What's the meaning of this riot? Speak up, man!"

"De're storming de chemical companies," the manager
stammered. Rogier noticed that all his teeth were missing.
Obviously one of his employees had been using him to practice upper cuts. "De've knocked my teed out!" The man
wiped a blood-soaked handkerchief across his mouth and escaped to his office.

The chemical companies? He pulled the video phone
around and punched up MDC's number.

Right after it had rung the third time, he discovered his
hands shaking. He was surprised to get Corcoran directly on
the screen.

"Lock up the place and distribute firearms to the security
guards," he said. "Mobs are running wild in the streets!
They'll tear everything to pieces."

Right then he saw that Corcoran's face was inscribed with
a bloody gash.

"Maybe you want to tell me how I should do it," he yelled.
"They overran the few men who stood in their way without a
bit of trouble! The security guards have mutinied, Rogier.
They're in here taking over the place!"

"The police!" Rogier fumed. Now the time had come for
him to lose his otherwise well-pronounced self-control. "Get
the cops! Why aren't they there guarding our property?"

From somewhere a violent explosion resounded. Plaster crashed down from the ceiling and smashed the video phone, that went up in a flash of flame. In a fit of tremendous rage Rogier flung aside a chair standing in his way and rushed up to his room.

Corcoran, that miserable failure! He should have fired him right after he got there. With an automatic rapid-fire pistol in hand he hurried back, took the elevator from the ground floor to the underground garage, and got in the first good unlocked car.

If he did not want to have the stockholders all over him like a pack of wolves, he now had to bet everything on one move. He had to take the matter into his own hands.

Meinhard had joined up with the group storming the MDC building. The security guards had confronted them with only a few men who in addition had been completely cut off from the news in their quarters, so they had no idea what was going on.

With hastily drawn weapons, the security guards tried to prevent the mob from forcing its way into the work area, but behind their backs in the work rooms word had already gotten around about what was happening. Hordes of workers shed their uniforms and explained the state of affairs to them. Most security guards acted dumbfounded when it was explained to them that criminal elements had ganged up (supposedly paid by the competition) to try to disrupt MDC's production schedule, which meant loss of wages for workers and employees. Within a few minutes the mood of the security guards made an about-face. The vision of a dying Earth hit them with full force and engendered horror in them.

Everywhere Meinhard saw men and women with white armbands who were trying to maintain order and keep down excesses.

"Save the technical equipment and the means of production!" shouted a red-haired man whose face had a constantly twitching muscle. "We won't get anywhere with useless destruction! All we want is to suspend production!"

Methuselah turned up in the crowd and struggled his way over to Meinhard. His face was scratched up from doing battle with a night stick. But he was smiling.

"As far as I can assess the situation, the revolt against the

chemical company dictatorship is proceeding quite blood-
lessly—if you disregard a scratch here and there," he said.
He pulled Meinhard aside. A jeep, driven by a man wearing
an armband, suddenly appeared and pulled up right in front
of Methuselah. The old man seemed to hold an important
position in this organization.

"Any news?" Methuselah asked.

"MDC's in our hands," the driver nodded. "We've taken
the chairman of the board of directors, a guy by the name of
Corcoran, into custody. He denies any responsibility in the
matter and claims he's just an employee in the firm."

Methuselah grinned. Meinhard noticed a feeling of serenity
spreading inside him. They got in the jeep together. The
driver took them to the main building.

A big car broke through the line of sentries that was
posted around the MDC building at full speed. The two men
guarding the main gate stood in the path of the vehicle and
gave the driver to understand that he could not enter, but he
seemed not to understand the hand signals or did not want
to. One of the guards—a young lab assistant—was struck by
the car and hurled aside. He was instantly dead. His partner,
who was armed and had never in his whole life shot another
person, was too dumbfounded to get off a single round. The
men and women who were gathered in front of the MDC
main building scattered in alarm when the car approached at
a frantic pace. There were over five hundred there, but nobody wanted to get flattened by a metal monster.

The car stopped and Rogier jumped out with pistol in
hand. He had only one thought in mind. He had to defend
the three hundred stockholding families, under whose man-
date he managed MDC, against the mob. Corcoran had
turned out to be incompetent. And Rogier knew exactly how
to deal with street mobs, namely coldly and brutally. They
only understood the language of force, otherwise there was
no way to handle them. He would search out the ringleaders
and kill them. Deprived of their leaders, the masses would re-
vert to their usual indifferent lethargy and give up the fight.

"Who's in charge of this bunch of hoodlums?" he bellowed,
beside himself. He brandished the gun and aimed at the
stomach of the man standing nearest him. He was wearing an

MDC security guard's uniform, so he must have been a turncoat.

Some of the bystanders were armed, but none made a move to aim at him.

"You and your ilk have made a cesspool out of the Earth," said a rather fat young woman with braided pigtails. Her face was white as a sheet, her teeth crooked, and she had a lisp. "And how dare you call us a bunch of hoodlums."

"The time when a few led and the masses followed is over with," said another man and shoved the shaky security guard out of Rogier's field of fire. "We've taken the freedom to determine our own future. And we're not the only ones."

The crowd held its breath. Rogier stepped a pace forward and looked over the faces glaring at him. He perceived them as ugly, repulsive, and disgusting. Pale or wrinkled. A mob of emaciated starving wretches, the majority of whom was suffering from some disease. A source of infection.

He quickly backtracked a few meters. The entrance to the main building was open. He reached the stairs in a few quick steps and made his way into the lobby. It was empty. The reception desk was unoccupied. Had they all turned against him?

From somewhere or other voices found their way into his consciousness. Rogier followed the sound.

". . . not responsible for anything," suddenly issued from a nearby office. "I'm not responsible for anything. Grab the stockholders, the ones I get my instructions from! Or Rogier—he's the company's trustee, the hatchet man, the worst one of the whole lot!"

It was Corcoran delivering eloquent testimony about his incompetence. Rogier nervously licked his lips. They were putting that pitiful coward through the wringer.

An armed man stood in front of the door to the office that the voices were coming out of. He looked coarse and unkempt. And he seemed to be incredibly exhausted. He had probably joined up with the insurgents after getting off the night shift; he used to be on the MDC staff, as Rogier saw by his clothing.

"You're a flunkey, Corcoran," another voice said. "You're nothing but a man who once long ago understood that you get further personally by making a deal with the overlords and kissing their ass. You make me puke."

The other man's voice was unfamiliar to Rogier, but the man was speaking with a discernible German accent.

"But I in no way want you to lay the blame on everybody, Corcoran. You're actually just a small cog in the workings of a well-thought-out system that the people in my day already considered finished in the not-too-distant future. A wise man once said existence determines consciousness. What does that mean to you?"

"Nothin'," Corcoran whined. "Lemme go. Lemme live."

"Oh, go to hell."

Corcoran seemed to interpret these words as a sign of dismissal. Two seconds later he left the office. Walking at a fast pace, he ran smack into Rogier.

Rogier blew him away without further ado. Corcoran fell to the floor, a peculiar, almost surprised look in his eyes. He squirmed around twice in a circle, and the hole in his forehead went past Rogier like a bloody moon crater.

He also hit the man standing guard in front of the office. He doubled up and yelled a warning. Seconds later a submachine gun was spraying smoke and flames into the hallway, but Rogier had wisely hidden himself on the floor behind a staircase.

"Come on out here!" he yelled in a rage. "Cops and robbers is over!"

He heard a noise behind him. Startled, he made out the figures of more men watching from the main entrance. The mob was really on the loose. . . .

He shot once, twice. A scream told him that he had not missed. But they had taken cover by now. The barrel of a rifle snaked its way around the corner of the main entrance. A shower of bullets rained down the hallway. Rogier began moving in the opposite direction. The only open door within reach was the one Corcoran had come out of. There had to be at least one man—the one who had been interrogating Corcoran—holed up in there. If he could catch him by surprise. . . .

He reached the room and immediately hit the deck, firing wildly. Ricocheting bullets zinged, somewhere a table fell over. Before Rogier's face lay the labored-breathing form of an incredibly old man.

"Lay down your weapon!"

It soon painfully dawned on Rogier that he had struck out

twice. The old man had not been by himself in the office! He saw a pair of legs rising up right in front of his eyes and the muzzle of a pistol aimed at his head. The voice talking to him sounded strangely forced and somehow seemed familiar to him.

"Haven't we met before?"

Rogier glanced up. His gun dropped out of his hands and fell on the floor. With eyes bulging out of their sockets he was staring into the face of the man that he had recently run off by warning that their paths had better not cross again. The man—Rogier now remembered that his name was Meinhard—had made a faint, intimidating impression on him. He had backed off because he realized that Rogier was more than a match for him.

He must have been mistaken. At the same instant that he saw the determination in the face of the man opposite him, it became clear to him that not only he, but also the whole system through which he and his masters had wielded power for centuries, had to step down.

MEET THE AUTHORS

THOMAS ZIEGLER (Pen name for Rainer Zubeil)

Born in 1956, he is part of the new wave of young German science fiction writers. He has already had published more than thirty short stories and novelettes as well as a dozen short novels. His first long novel (in collaboration with Uwe Anton), *Die Zeit der Stasis,* was published in 1979. This novel is clearly political in nature. Thomas Ziegler is also the translator of some American science fiction novels, namely those by Cordwainer Smith and J. Haldeman. Never having had a submission rejected up to now, Thomas Ziegler plans on becoming a professional writer.

RONALD M. HAHN & JÜRGEN ANDREAS (Pen name for Hans-Joachim Alpers)

Ronald Hahn was born in 1948. His first published work (a short novel) came out in 1971. After that, he published some thirty other short novels (science fiction and horror), some short stories, and a great number of articles in political journals and magazines. He has also worked for Radio Germany. Today he professionally combines his activities as literary agent, translator, anthologist, and writer. Two of his novels are to be published in paperback.

Jürgen Andreas (Hans-Joachim Alpers) was born in

1943, and he is also a writer, an anthologist, and a professional literary agent. In addition, he is a recognized literary critic. He has had published a dozen short novels, plus twelve novels (science fiction and detective) in collaboration with Ronald Hahn. He has been working with Werner Fuchs and Wolfgang Jeschke, two writers who are publishing an international science fiction encyclopedia, *Lexicon der Science Fiction Literatur*. The first anthology of German science fiction in West Germany, *Science Fiction aus Deutschland* (1974), was the result of work done by Ronald Hahn and Jürgen Andreas.

RICHARD D. NOLANE (Pen name for Olivier Raynaud)

Born in 1955, he collaborated, as a critic, on specialized magazines since 1973 before becoming one of the editors on the staff of the magazine *Spirale* until 1976. His short stories started to appear in print that year. Some have been translated. Before the present anthology, he did one devoted to Australian science fiction for a Hungarian publisher. He is also a specialist in English-language fantasy and in 1979 he compiled the best short stories of J. Ramsey Campbell into an anthology entitled *L'Homme du souterrain* for a paperback publisher. He furnished the French section of *Lexicon der Science Fiction Literatur* to be published in West Germany. He has just finished his first novel and has several others in progress. He hopes to become a professional writer and anthologist in the near future by trying to work full time for the foreign market. Published in West Germany, Sweden, and Italy, his short story "Where Neuroses Thrive" has yet to see print in French.

GIANNI MONTANARI

Born in 1949, he had his first science fiction short story published in 1968. Gianni Montanari has since had published three novels, *Nel nome dell'uomo* (1971), *La sepoltura* (1973), and *Daimon* (1978). He writes few short stories and is considered one of the best contemporary writers in Italy. In 1977 he published an essay on British science fiction, *Ieri, il futuro*, comprising five monographs on John Wyndam, E.F. Russell, A.C. Clarke, Fred Hoyle, and J.G. Ballard. In addition, he is in charge of research and has been working with Wanda Ballin on updating Pierre Versins's huge *Ency-*

clopédie de l'utopie et de la science fiction for publication in
Italy.

LINO ALDANI

Lino Aldani was born the same time as *Amazing Stories*
(1926). . . . In 1963 he was editor for the magazine *Futuro*.
He is the author of numerous short stories, some of which
have been compiled in *Quarta Dimensione*, and some novels,
among them *Più in alto delle stelle* (1960), and *Quando les
racini* (1977). These works have made him an author appreciated throughout Europe and most likely the best-known
Italian writer outside his own country.

KATHINKA LANNOY

Born in 1917, Kathinka Lannoy had first written some
mainstream novels. Then she turned to fantasy and science
fiction. Her first anthology in the genre dates from 1959, *Tus-
sen elf en een*. She stands out in Dutch fantasy and science
fiction for her somewhat old-fashioned, somewhat delightful
style, which has invited comparisons to Belcampo or Henri-
ette Van Eyck.

PAUL VAN HERCK

He is the number-one humorist in Belgian science fiction
circles. His first book, an anthology entitled *De Cirkels*, was
published in 1966. He is also the author of two particularly
screwball novels, *Sam* (1968), translated and published in the
U.S.A. by DAW Books (*Where Were You Last Pluterday?*),
and *Caroline, Oh Caroline!* He has been published several
times in fanzines and professional magazines. Each piece he
writes is a kind of happening for devotees of the absurd and
impossible, comical situations. A grand master of laughter. . . .

BERTIL MÅRTENSSON

Also an author of detective novels, Bertil Mårtensson
was born in 1945 in Malmö, Sweden. He is one of the most
appreciated authors in the younger generation of Swedish
writers. In addition to his numerous science fiction short stories, he has written at least four novels in the genre, *Detta är
verkligheten* (1968), which was awarded a prize in Trieste

in 1970, *Skeppet in Kambrium* (1974), *Samarkand 5617* (1976), and *Jungfrulig Planet* (1977).

SAM J. LUNDWALL

Here is the one-man band of Swedish science fiction since he is an author, translator, editor, anthologist, singer, radio and TV producer and still more things all rolled up into one. He is also editor of the magazine *Jules Verne Magasinet*, which may be the most international science fiction magazine in the world. In addition Sam Lundwall is without a doubt the first-rate European author who has been translated into English most often. Among his most important books are two novels, *2018 AD or the King Kong Blues* (1974) and *Alice's World* (1971), and two studies on science fiction, *Science Fiction: What It's All About* (1971) and *The Illustrated History of Science Fiction* (1978). Finally, Sam Lundwall is one of those responsible for the enormous five-volume *Survey of Science Fiction Literature* published by Salem Press in 1979.

MICHEL JEURY

Born in 1934, Michel Jeury is perhaps the best French science fiction author at the present time. He made his debut in March, 1960, under the name Albert Higon with two good space operas, *Aux étoiles du destin* and *La machine du pouvoir*. Then thirteen years of silence before coming back in force in 1973 with *Le temps incertain*, a novel influenced by Dick and published under his real name. (In France it is fashionable to write under a pen name.) Intrigued by time, Jeury then went on to have several top-flight novels like *Les singes du temps* (1974), *Soleil chaud poisson des profondeurs* (1976), and *Le territoire human* (1979) published. Some children's books and adventure novels have also appeared under the name of Albert Higon. Michel Jeury has in addition written a large number of short stories for almost every French magazine. One last thing. Be sure to note that *Le temps incertain* will be published in translation in the US.

PHILIP GOY

This author, a true rara avis, was born in 1941 and can be considered the only French author of hard science. He has only two novels, *Le père éternel* (1974) and *Le livre-*

machine (1975) to his credit. The latter novel is noteworthy because of its originality which put writing and typography to the test. Goy has also written some short stories, the majority of which are found in the anthology *Vers la révolution* (1977). Philip Goy is a physicist working for the *Centre National de la Recherche Scientifique* (CNRS), which fact explains the scant time he (unfortunately) has to devote to writing.

GABRIEL BERMUDEZ CASTILLO

Born in 1934, he today lives in Saragossa where he is a legal adviser. His first novel, *Amor en una isla verde*, dates from 1972 and won an award in Trieste. This was followed by *Viage a un planeta wu-wei* (1977), *La piel del infinito* (1977), and *El Señor de la rueda* (1979). Also a short story writer, he is considered one of the brightest hopes on the Spanish science fiction horizon.

INGAR KNUDTSEN, JR.

One of the most gifted on the Norwegian science fiction short story scene, Ingar Knudtsen, Jr., was born in 1944. He is an autodidact. He has done a little of all kinds of work and hopes to become a professional writer. He has had published three short story collections, one of which is *Lasersongen* (1977), from which the short story translated here is taken, and three short novels, two of which are *Jernringen* (1976) and *Tova* (1979).

ERWIN NEUTSZKY-WULFF

Born in 1949. He is quite a prolific author whose works often deal with philosophical problems, frequently with a certain humor. He has written some science fiction short stories, some plots for fantasy and science fiction comic strips, some "fantasy-occult" novels (his *Adam Hart* tetralogy), and some science fiction novels like *Anno Domini* (1975) *Gud* (1976), *Den 33. Marts* (1977), and *Havet* (1978). His short story "Aruna" is the only one in this entire anthology to come out of a fanzine (*Proxima*).

DAW·sf
BOOKS

Presenting JACK VANCE in DAW editions:

The "Demon Princes" Novels

The "Tschai" Novels

The "Alastor" Trilogy

Others

If you wish to order these titles,

please see the coupon in

the back of this book.

Outstanding science fiction and fantasy

To order these titles,

use coupon on the

last page of this book.

DAW presents TANITH LEE

"A brilliant supernova in the firmament of SF"—Progressef

Presenting C. J. CHERRYH